S0-ARL-279

Bryan Smith

The
Killing
Kind

LEISURE BOOKS NEW YORK CITY

This one is for my brother,
John Eric Smith,
The Rockin' Kind.

A LEISURE BOOK®

July 2010

Published by

Dorchester Publishing Co., Inc.
200 Madison Avenue
New York, NY 10016

ISBN 10: 0-8439-6356-5
ISBN 13: 978-0-8439-6356-4
E-ISBN: 978-1-4285-0893-4

The name "Leisure Books" and the stylized "L" with design are trademarks of Dorchester Publishing Co., Inc.

Printed in the United States of America.

10 9 8 7 6 5 4 3 2 1

Visit us online at www.dorchesterpub.com.

JUST FOR FUN

Roxie was standing next to the Neon. The gun was still pressed to her thigh. She leaned down and rapped the knuckles of her left hand against the passenger-side window. The punk girl turned toward her and rolled the window down. Rob opened his mouth to scream a warning, but it was already too late. Roxie's gun hand was like a striking cobra. One moment it was still against her leg, the next nanosecond the barrel of the gun was pressed against the punk girl's forehead. Rob heard the report of the gun and knew for sure Roxie had actually shot the poor girl in the face. There were screams from the Neon now. . . .

ACKNOWLEDGMENTS

As always, thanks to my wife, Rachael, for all the usual reasons, and extra special bonus points for making last year's Hypericon party a smash success despite being very sick. Thanks to my brothers, Jeff and Eric, who rock hard. Thanks to my longtime friends, Shannon Turbeville and Keith Ashley, who also rock. Hmm, rocking seems to be the theme this time around. Anyway . . . thanks to my family, especially my mom, Cherie Smith, for all the love and support, and my grandmother, Dorothy C. May, as well as Jay and Helene Wise, my in-laws. Thanks to all the following for various reasons: Brian Keene, everybody at the Keenedom, Don D'Auria, Tod Clark, Kent Gowran, Mark Hickerson, Joe Howe, Derek Tatum, Paul Legerski, Paul Synuria, Ben and Tracey Eller (www.worldofstrange.com), Mark Sylva, Brittany Crass, Blake Conley, John Everson, Rhonda Wilson, John Barcus, Shane Ryan Staley, Elizabeth Rowell, Kim Myers, David Wilbanks, Fred and Stephania Grimm, whoever it was who invented beer way back in the long, long ago, and all the people who bought *Soultaker* and *Depraved* last year. It should go without saying that you all rock harder than a drunken 80's metal band with its amps perpetually on 11—but I'm saying it anyway.

THE
KILLING
KIND

PROLOGUE

Diary of a Mixed-up Girl blog entry, dated March 27

Holy shit, this geezer looks so funny with his ear cut the fuck OFF.
OH MY GOD.

2 comments
lord_ruthven: Where are you? You need to call your folks ASAP. Everybody's worried sick about you (and nobody believes this ear-mutilation bullshit, okay?)

darkest_rogue: LOL. Yeah. Love ya, but SOMEBODY'S just wanting attention.

CHAPTER ONE

March 22

The girl looked like one of those goth rocker chicks he was always getting friend requests from on MySpace. They all had sort of the same look. Pale, clear skin. At least one visible tattoo. Hair always that same alluring shade of raven black, usually cut in a style at least vaguely reminiscent of Bettie Page. Interests always included body modification, metal, rockabilly, burlesque, and horror movies. The overall look—hot groupie backstage at a Marilyn Manson concert. Pinup models for a dark new age.

Sexy?

Fuck, yeah.

And this one was rocking that gothic-slut look as well as any chick on MySpace. Black pumps, thigh-high black-and-white-striped socks, very brief (and tight) black skirt, black Misfits skull shirt, plump lips a shade of scarlet so vivid it was almost blinding, the requisite black-as-night hair framing a pretty, pale face, subtly applied makeup accentuating intense blue eyes, thin silver necklace draped about her slender throat, from which dangled what, holy shit, looked like a pentagram pendant. She was fucking gorgeous. Satanic eye candy. Slender, but not so skinny that she looked like one of those starving Hollywood bimbos, with some nice but not too dramatic curves that stretched those socks and that tight little skirt in some very interesting ways. And that tantalizing glimpse of creamy thigh visible between the tops of those socks and the hem of that skirt . . . Man.

Rob Scott always approved those friend requests. His page was full of horror graphics and his interests all skewed in the same direction—dark. He listed Asia Argento as the person he'd most like to meet. He knew the girls only added him as part of a relentless drive to pump up their friend counts, but he didn't care. He was their natural audience. As he leaned against his car with his right hand squeezing the handle of the gas pump, he idly wondered whether this chick had a MySpace page. Probably. Hell, she might even be on his list. Wouldn't surprise him, from the looks of her. Or maybe not. Even among the many dozens of girls on his list with the same basic look, this one would stand out.

He was so entranced by her he at first failed to notice that she was looking right at him. She was on the opposite side of the street from the Kwik Mart, standing at the edge of a little strip mall's parking lot. Rob's heart fluttered a bit when he became aware of her scrutiny. But then he decided she was merely looking in his direction, not at him specifically, though it was hard to tell from this distance.

Then the traffic cleared and she started across the street.

Toward the Kwik Mart.

Toward *him*.

No.

That was just stupid wishful thinking. As soon as she was on this side of the street, she would almost certainly veer into the store, where she would buy . . . hell, whatever chicks like that buy at shitty little convenience stores. Cigarettes? Gum? A can of Red Bull?

Who knew? And did it fucking matter?

No.

She reached the Kwik Mart's parking lot and continued in a straight line toward him.

Rob gulped.

There could be no doubt now. Her eyes were locked on him. The subtlest hint of a smile twitched the corners of those bloodred lips. His breath quickened. He had to force his hand to relax its grip on the gas pump, which had already clicked off anyway. She was close now, ten yards away, too close by far for a more analytical part of his mind to wonder why on earth one of the most mind-numbingly attractive women he'd ever seen was so focused on him. But the sexy, subtle sway of her hips turned his brain to mush. Too bad. Because if he'd been thinking at all, he might have detected a hint of something predatory in her.

But then she was standing in front of him, those startling blue eyes still locked on his. He figured he should say something, so he opened his mouth. But no words came out. He didn't have the first clue what to say. As it turned out, it didn't really matter.

A canvas tote bag was slung over her right shoulder. Her eyes never left his as she reached into it and removed something.

She stepped closer to him.

Close enough to touch.

Rob swallowed hard, struggled to breathe for a moment as he felt his face turn hot.

Then he felt it.

The thing pressed hard against his belly.

He frowned.

That can't be . . .

He glanced down and excitement gave way to confusion and terror. The barrel of a revolver—a .38?—was pressed into his midsection, the sight digging painfully into his navel. Rob didn't know much about guns, but he knew enough to understand this was no toy.

Holy shit, he thought, *I'm being mugged by a fucking hot chick.*

It was crazy.

She could have just asked him for his money and he would have given it to her. Every cent.

"Look at me."

Rob looked at her. "What . . . I . . . I don't . . . what . . ."

"Shut up."

Rob closed his mouth.

The girl twisted the gun barrel harder into his stomach, eliciting a small whimper. "I need a ride. I like your car."

"You can have it."

She smiled. "No shit. You're coming with me."

"But . . . why?"

She leaned closer, her voice dropping to a whisper as her lips grazed his own. "Simple choice, boy. Come with me or"—she laughed softly—"bang bang."

Rob made himself swallow and cleared his throat. "I guess . . . I could go for a ride."

That soft laughter again—seductive, but insidious. "That's what I thought. Let's go."

The wheels started spinning in Rob's head. He had to think of a way out of this. He couldn't let this girl carjack him. Hot or not, she had a gun. She was threatening him with it. She was a fucking criminal. The crazy bitch might even kill him once she was able to get him somewhere isolated and quiet.

He had an idea. It wasn't much, but it was all he could think of with this much stress bearing down on him, so he seized on it. He gestured at the convenience store with a slight tilt of his chin. "I have to go inside to pay for the gas."

That little laugh again, her breath warm on his face. "I don't think so, asshole."

"Fine. Whatever. We'll just drive off without paying." Rob couldn't believe how calm his voice sounded to his own ears. Not even a hint of a quaver. Of course, his heart was racing and his guts felt like they were trying to rearrange themselves into new and deeply uncomfortable configurations, but at least he didn't *sound* rattled. It might not count for much, but maybe, just maybe, it'd render the fib he was telling a touch more believable. "Hell, I think it's a great idea. The cops'll be on our ass fast and I'll be rescued from your psycho clutches, so let's go."

The girl pressed the gun even harder into his stomach, which he wouldn't have thought possible. If she had a knife in her hands instead, she'd be disemboweling him right now. "I saw you swipe your card at the pump from across the street, you lying fuck."

Rob's heart sank. *Fuck.*

The girl's expression hardened, but strangely, this only enhanced her prettiness, emphasizing her cheekbones and the elegant curve of her jaw line. "You know what I hate?"

Rob looked at her lips. God, he hadn't known Revlon or whothefuckever made a shade of lipstick that bright, that *red.* And the *way* the lips looked, so plump and moist . . . holy hell . . . he ached to kiss her. Which was about six thousand shades of fucked-up, given the circumstances. He made himself swallow again and said, "What do you . . . hate?"

There it was. That quaver he'd expected to hear before.

"Liars."

Rob's brow furrowed as he squinted at her. "What?"

"Liars. I fucking hate liars."

Rob couldn't help it—he laughed. "Hold on. You have no problem with threatening to kill a guy and steal his car, but you hate liars?"

"That's right."

Rob grunted. "Huh. Well . . . shit, I don't really know what to say to that."

"You don't need to say a goddamn thing. Your approval isn't something I require, liar boy."

"You're not very nice."

She almost smiled. It was very quick and he nearly missed it—just the slightest and most fleeting twitch at the edges of her mouth. There and gone in the space of a nanosecond. "No shit. What was your first clue? The gat in your gut or my sweet disposition?"

"Did you just say 'gat'?"

"Yeah. Problem?"

"It makes you sound like a gangster moll in some old movie."

"So?"

Rob thought, *This conversation is insane*.

He shrugged. "Whatever. Just an observation."

Rob's head turned slightly at the sound of an approaching motor. A silver Hyundai was pulling up on the opposite side of the pump. The girl saw the Hyundai and pressed herself against him. Her lips were soft against his ear. "Put your arms around me."

"What?"

She made an almost inaudible sound that nonetheless managed to convey deep exasperation. "Hold me, you fucking idiot. You've got about five seconds to make these people think I'm your girlfriend. Unless you want me to shoot you now and blow them away, too?"

Rob didn't bother commenting on the craziness inherent in this question, but only because there was no time. The Hyundai's doors were opening. He put his arms around the girl and drew her close. She pressed against him. He suppressed a whimper as the gun sight dug harder into his navel. A middle-aged man stepped between gas pumps en route to the Kwik Mart and shot an approving half smile–half smirk at Rob. The guy was a bit on the heavy side and probably envied Rob more than a little right then. An even heavier middle-aged woman with sagging breasts appeared and followed him toward the convenience store. She glanced at Rob and his "girlfriend" and scowled, which did nothing to enhance an already sour expression. Probably knew her man had been ogling the superhot chick in his arms. Rob figured any jealousy either of them felt would vanish if they could see the gun.

Rob watched the portly couple enter the Kwik Mart and sighed. "They're gone."

The girl didn't say anything for a long second. Her lips were pressed against his ear, and he felt her draw in a slow breath. "Okay." Another second or two passed. "Let go and ease back."

Rob did as ordered, removing his arms from her waist and shuffling backward a step. He glanced at the gun and then looked her in the eye again. "So what now?"

The girl turned her head to stare at the strip mall across the street. Rob sensed she was searching for something specific. He followed her gaze, but couldn't identify whatever it was. There were a lot of cars over there and a number of random people strolling through the parking lot. Hard to tell what she was looking for, but in another moment he detected a new sense of urgency from her. It was evident in her suddenly rigid posture and a slight quickening of breath. She stepped back and slipped the gun back inside the tote bag, but held the bag in a way that made it clear the gun was still pointed right at him.

"What happens now is you finish up here and open the passenger door for me, just as if I really am your girlfriend. Then you go around to the other side and get in behind the wheel. You do all this smooth as shit or I will really fucking kill you, man, no joke."

Rob studied her steely expression.

She definitely was not joking.

He removed the gas nozzle from the rear of the Galaxie 500 and docked the handle on the pump cradle. The pump's digital display asked him if he wanted a receipt. He pushed the button marked N and turned back to the car. The girl was already waiting for him on the convertible's passenger side. He circled the car and pulled the door open for her.

The car's top was down. So were the windows. Of course. It was a nice, sunny day. Only a jackass would cruise around in a cool old car like this with the top up on a day like this. But now Rob wished it had been raining. With the top and the windows down, there would be no blind spots for the psycho chick as he circled back around the car, and she would have a clear shot at him the whole time.

Her smile told him she knew exactly what he was thinking. "Close the door after me like a gentleman and get in. And be cool about it. I feel like anything hinky is happening, I'll start blazing."

"Hinky?"

The girl gave him a quick peck on the cheek—presumably for the benefit of any casual observers, a continuation of the boyfriend-girlfriend charade—and smoothly eased herself into the Galaxie's passenger seat. Rob wiped lipstick from his cheek and stared for a second at the bright smear of red on his thumb. It looked like blood.

Fuck, he thought. *This is really happening.*

Run. For fuck's sake, run.

The girl was looking up at him, her expression hard again. And her right hand was in the tote bag again. "This," she said.

"What?"

"This thing you're doing. Standing there." The girl's hand moved inside the tote bag. "It's *hinky*. You should do something to ease my mind right about now."

Rob started moving. He was shaking. The hard asphalt beneath his feet felt like it was on the verge of turning into quicksand. That would be great, actually. Super. Let the world open up and swallow him whole. It couldn't be any worse than having some crazy chick with a gun take him for a ride down the highway to hell, which was sure to be a dead end.

Emphasis on *dead*.

Somehow, though, he managed to reach the Galaxie's

other side without falling over or otherwise freaking out. A miracle. He opened the driver-side door and slid in behind the car's big red steering wheel.

He pulled the door shut and started shaking again. "Oh, Christ. Fuck. Oh, fuck."

The girl stared at him. "Scared?"

"Shitless."

"Good. You'll be fine as long as you're too scared to try anything stupid."

"Okay."

"Start the car."

Rob stared at his right hand and made himself concentrate until it stopped shaking. The key was already in the ignition. He twisted it and the old V-8 engine roared to life.

He leaned back against the seat and looked at the girl again. "What now?"

"Hold on."

She set the gun on the dash and began to root around in the tote bag. He heard a lot of things clanking around. He looked at her. The whole of her attention seemed focused on the task of locating something inside the bag. He looked at the gun.

He reached for it.

Her fist came out of nowhere, drilling hard into the side of his nose. Pain snapped through him and he rocked backward in his seat. A trickle of blood leaked from one nostril and dribbled past his lips into his mouth. His eyes went wide as he stared at her. The gun was still on the dash. But any thought of reaching for it again withered and died. Rob's mind reeled. The world was spinning off its axis. The things happening to him were so completely alien and beyond the realm of his experience. He'd seen his share of schoolyard scraps like anyone else, but no one in his adult life had ever punched him. The violence was beyond shocking.

And it didn't matter one bit that she was a girl. Or that he was bigger and probably stronger. She possessed the savage quickness of a feral thing. And she would never hesitate to wound or inflict pain. These things were every bit as obvious as her beauty. He had never felt so intimidated in his life and was terrified at the thought of doing anything else at all to anger her.

She set the tote bag on the floorboard.

The sun glinted off something shiny in her hands.

Rob frowned. "Handcuffs?"

She reached across him and grabbed his left wrist. She slapped one of the bracelets around it and snapped it shut. Then she snapped the other one around the steering wheel. Rob gaped at the sight of his cuffed hand.

He looked at her. "Is that really necessary?"

"I've found the judicious use of restraints an effective way to keep morons like you in line."

"Seems a bit overkill to me. And I'm not a moron."

"I don't care what you think. So shut up and drive, idiot."

Rob put the Galaxie in gear and tapped the gas pedal. The car rolled away from the pump.

"Stop."

Rob stepped on the brake pedal and looked at her. She was staring at the strip-mall parking lot again. The Galaxie was stopped at the edge of the Kwik Mart's lot. The street between the strip mall and the convenience store was temporarily clear of traffic.

He coughed. "Um . . . should I just drive over there?"

"No. Wait."

They waited.

Several minutes passed.

A van pulled out of the strip mall's parking lot and turned right onto the street.

The girl punched his shoulder. "Follow that fucking van."

Rob stared after the van for a moment before obeying the command. The road between the strip mall and the Kwik

Mart was a narrow two-lane deal. He'd gotten a good glimpse at the people inside the van as they'd pulled onto the street. It was filled with several young people roughly the same age as his abductor. They were all maybe three or four years his junior. College age. But they didn't look like this girl at all. They looked . . . well . . . normal.

His hesitation was brief, but long enough to be noticeable.

He tried to think of a nonsinister reason why she would want to follow the kids in the van.

Nothing came to mind.

The gun was in her hand again. She pressed it against a spot on his thigh. "This is where your femoral artery is. I shoot you here, you bleed out fast."

Rob stepped on the Galaxie's gas pedal.

There was a blare of horns as the old car shot out into the street. Rob ignored the subsequent angry gestures. He cranked the wheel hard to the right and hurried to catch up to the receding van.

CHAPTER TWO

March 22

She could no longer stand the sound of his voice. Seriously. This is how fucked-up things had gotten between Zoe Martin and Chuck Kirby, her boyfriend since the summer between their junior and senior years at Smyrna High School. Her head started hurting every time he opened his mouth. It set her teeth on edge. It didn't matter what he was saying. Or what the tone of it was. He could be happy and laughing, cracking jokes. Or angry and lashing out at her (though that was pretty rare). He could say something sweet, the kind of thing that should melt a girl's heart, and it would only make her want to throw up.

Thing was, they'd just been together too long.

More than three and a half years now, coming up hard on four full years. Spring break was here, which meant summer was just around the corner. The prospect of yet another anniversary as Chuck's girl stirred feelings of desperation and dread. Sometimes she could feel her youth melting away, disappearing in slow but relentless drips down a cosmic drain. Every passing day was another lost chance at something new. It made her so fucking sad. And maybe that made her immature, a notion she'd lost some sleep over in recent months, but she'd come to accept her feelings as genuine. She didn't care if it meant she was shallow. She was young, still a few months shy of legal drinking age, so she was allowed. The time had come to embrace immaturity while she was still in a stage of her life where that was acceptable. In two short months her junior year at Vanderbilt University would be history. As would her relationship with Chuck. She wanted to be truly carefree again, to revel in her youth and experience a level of emotional freedom that hadn't been hers since high school. There would be a time for a forever relationship somewhere else down the line.

Somewhere *way* down the line, preferably.

And with someone other than Chuck.

She'd made the decision weeks ago.

She'd kept it to herself so far, whispering nary a word of it to anyone, not even her closest friends. This goddamn excursion to Myrtle Beach was the main reason she hadn't made it official yet. The trip had been in the planning stages since the end of the previous summer. Chuck's father, a big-shot developer, was paying for everything, the ostentatious beach house and the van rental being the primary expenses. The big Chevrolet Express guzzled enough gas to give your average environmentalist a coronary, but Conrad Kirby's platinum-card largesse rendered even the rising fuel prices meaningless. *Everything* was covered, down to the incidentals.

But it wasn't just the money holding her back.

There were her friends to consider.

Annalisa Collins and Emily Sinclair. Not just her friends, but her best friends, a connection extending back into childhood, long before Chuck had come into the picture. So Conrad's undeniably generous invitation had been extended to them, as well. Zoe just didn't have the heart to ruin it for them. So she'd decided it'd be easier to just delay the big breakup drama a little longer. She wouldn't do it right after they returned either. Too tacky, that, not to mention a touch too obvious. After a lot of thought, she'd come to the conclusion it would be best to wait until just before the end of the spring semester. That way she'd get free just ahead of the dreaded summer anniversary. Sure, Chuck would be upset for a while, but he'd get over it.

It was something to look forward to.

In the meantime . . .

"You shouldn't have been so mean to that girl."

Emily was talking to Chuck again, giving him more shit about the run-in with the goth chick back at the strip mall. Unlike Zoe, she was not at all reluctant to confront Chuck or call him out on his bullshit. Zoe generally thought Chuck was all right. A touch too arrogant, sure, but some of that was to be expected, given his privileged upbringing. But underneath all that he was a decent, caring guy.

Still . . . Emily was right.

He *had* been pretty mean.

Chuck and Joe Walker, *his* best friend, were up front, with Chuck planted behind the wheel and Joe slouched down in the shotgun seat, an open tallboy can of Bud held between his legs. Chuck grunted. "Ooh, Little Miss Bleeding Heart's all offended and shit."

Joe laughed and knocked back a swig of beer. "Yeah. Em's all about cultural diversity and respectin' our mutual fuckin' differences and shit." He twisted in his seat and poked his head through the gap, a grin lighting up the part of his handsome face visible beneath the black shades perched atop his nose. "Good thing she's such a good lay."

Emily's tone turned frosty. "Hmm . . . Want to guess who won't be getting any for a while?"

There was a snort from the back, and Annalisa's exuberant voice rang out. "Yeah, right! You're like this one." She nudged her boyfriend, Sean Hewitt, who was back there with her. "Too horny to go without more than a day. I've heard the stories. He'll come begging for it, you'll mess with him a little, and then you'll both wind up making enough noise to scare the neighbors half to death. Go on, tell me I'm wrong."

Zoe glanced up from the copy of *Entertainment Weekly*

open in her lap and saw Emily struggling to hold back a smile. She gave up and shook her head, hiding the smile by twisting it into a smirk. "Whatever. He *will* have to beg for it, though, I guarantee that."

Joe shrugged and laughed again. "I'll beg all you want, baby. Hell, you can tie me up and spank me for being such a bad boy, too."

Emily's smirk deepened. "Yeah. And maybe even make you wear a dress again."

"Again!" Chuck looked like he wanted to puke. "Oh, man. My best friend's a fucking cross-dressing perv. *Gross*, dude."

Emily chuckled. "Perfectly harmless fetish."

Joe knocked back some more beer and laughed. "Dude, you'd do it too if it meant you got to hook up with that every night." He jerked a thumb in the direction of his girlfriend. "No shit, man, and I'm not just saying this because I'm already half-buzzed and it's barely noon, but Em is the greatest fuck of all fucking time. I'd shoot a man in Reno for just one taste of her sweet, sweet pussy."

Zoe made a face. "You're disgusting."

Joe grinned. "Disgusting, but adorable."

Emily rolled her eyes and heaved the sigh of the long-suffering. "Joe, because you worship the ground I walk on, I can cut you some slack for the stupid things that come out of your mouth. But your friend up there is a fucking douche bag."

Zoe slapped the magazine shut and gaped at her. "Emily!"

Chuck laughed. "Oh, you're gonna get it now. My girl won't take that kind of talk about her man. Will ya, honey?"

Sean Hewitt chimed in from the back. "Catfight! Hot lesbian catfight!"

The comment elicited a boisterous round of laughter and hooting. Joe started looking for his camera and making comments about putting up a video on YouTube.

Emily looked at Zoe. She was still smiling, and there was a disquieting knowing quality in the cast of her features. Zoe stared back at her and, as always, was struck by her friend's classic, elegant beauty. She looked like a film star of the 1940s. Refined, assured, oozing intelligence and sexuality, with a slender neck, kissable lips, and the cheekbones of a silver-screen goddess. The kissable part Zoe could attest to, having made out with Emily a time or two. That radiant face was framed by dark hair cut in a choppy style. Looking at her now, Zoe realized her friend bore a passing resemblance to the goth girl Chuck and Sean had treated with such obnoxious derision. The resemblance was pretty close, actually, with Emily as a less garish and more sophisticated version of the younger girl. And maybe that was a little part of why Emily was so pissed at Chuck.

The larger part being that she simply hated his guts.

Emily's eyes flicked toward Chuck. "Oh, please. She's no more your girl than I am. And I'd rather be flayed alive and fed to rabid weasels than touch you."

The van's interior went deathly silent. Zoe's heart began to race. Emily couldn't know about her plans to break up with Chuck. Right? Or had she gotten too drunk one night and told Emily something she couldn't remember? It was vaguely possible, but she hadn't done a lot in the way of excessive drinking since making her decision. Nonetheless, paranoia took root inside her and made her want to scream.

It was too soon for this.

And pretty much the worst possible time for it.

Chuck glanced at the rearview mirror. "You're full of shit, Emily."

An amused grin played at the corners of Emily's mouth. She looked at Zoe again. "Am I, Zoe?"

Zoe seethed inwardly. There was only one way to defuse the situation and prevent the vacation from turning into a total disaster before it was barely under way. *Shit*. "I'm your girl, Chuck. Em's just fucking with you, but she does have a point. You shouldn't have been such a dick to that girl."

Chuck slapped a palm against the steering wheel. "But she was a freak! Christ, you saw her!" His voice took on the thick, warbly tone Zoe thought of as his Retard Voice. "Oooh, look at me, I'm all fucking alternative. I'm all goth as *fuck*. Look how *different* I am. Look at all my piercings and tattoos and my freaky fucking clothes. Oh, I'm just *so* much cooler and with it than all you square preppy fags. Oooohhh . . ." He cleared his throat again and shifted back to his normal tone. "And fuck it, I'm not apologizing for anything. I hate that shit. People like that are the biggest posers of all. Maybe she learned herself a good fucking lesson today."

Joe barked laughter. "The one and only Chuck Kirby, ladies and gentlemen. The man, the myth, the legend . . ."

"The fucking asshole," Emily added, but this time she was ignored.

Joe opened another beer and slurped foam from the top of the can as it burbled out of the opening. He wiped his lips and leaned between the seats to show Emily a foamy grin. "Can't let any go to waste. That'd be alcohol abuse."

Emily sighed again and glanced at Zoe. "Boys. How I hate them."

Zoe shrugged, a what-can-you-do? gesture. "Yeah."

Joe gasped. "How dare you! We're not 'boys.' We're men. We're . . . we're . . ."

"Barbarians?" Chuck suggested.

"Yeah!" Joe swigged more beer. At this rate he'd be passing out later in the afternoon. "We're barbarians! We're fucking *cavemen!*"

He held his hand up for a high five and Chuck obliged him.

Zoe listened to them trade beery inanities back and forth and felt the beginnings of a fresh headache. Every stupid thing out of Chuck's mouth just made it worse. She snared some Tylenol from her purse and washed the pills down with a gulp of Coke.

She picked up her magazine and again tried to concentrate on it.

But it wasn't easy.

She could feel Emily staring at her. It made her anxious and paranoid. She had the uneasy sense that her friend could see her every thought. Eventually she turned away from Emily and closed her eyes, pretending to fall asleep.

But the feeling didn't go away.

CHAPTER THREE

March 15

The days were getting warmer, but it wasn't quite full spring yet, and the nights in Tennessee still possessed enough of a chill to set teeth to chattering, especially this close to the border with Kentucky. The breeze didn't slice through your flesh quite the way it did up north when the weather was cold. But any sane person would find the conditions nippy enough to at least wear a light jacket or sweatshirt.

However, the man sitting cross-legged in a grassy field adjacent to a stretch of I-40 was not sane. At all. The earth beneath him was still slightly damp from last week's rains. With his eyes closed and his head tilted upward, he appeared to be in a meditative trance. He sat perfectly still and outwardly looked as peaceful as a Buddhist monk.

However.

He wore only a ragged and dirty piece of clothing that had once been—in its former life as a young woman's halter top—as brilliantly white as a mound of uncut cocaine. The bit of flimsy fabric was tied in a knot around his waist and the little flaps in front and back just managed to cover his genitals and ass cheeks.

The doctors who had cared for this man up until a month earlier would not have referred to him as "insane" in any official documentation. That word long ago fell out of vogue in the medical community, mostly because it has come to be seen as too limiting a term, or too inflammatory or insensitive, a relic of a less enlightened time. The man's doctors instead said that he exhibited a number of symptoms typical of various abnormal brain syndromes. Schizophrenia, bipolar syndrome, psychosis, etc. His chart back at the facility, where he'd spent the bulk of the last fifteen years, contained reams of notes detailing what was described as hallucinations and an elaborate but clearly delusional belief system, including reports of his frequent consultations with a "spirit guide" he called Lulu.

The man knew the details of his chart well. He'd snagged it on his way out of the loony bin and carried it with him in his bag. It made for very interesting reading when he wasn't raping or eviscerating someone. Although he'd not been labeled insane anywhere within those pages, he knew what his doctors really thought. For instance, there'd been the time Dr. Freeman had referred to him as a "fucking psycho" when instructing a team of orderlies to remove him from his office.

Well.

Their opinions of him no longer mattered.

They were all dead. Zebulon Elias Geddy had slaughtered them in the process of escaping the facility and he'd done so without regret. Lulu said they deserved to die, and that was good enough for him.

Telling him who should die was just one of the many ways in which Lulu was useful. She would often also tell him how he should go about killing the people she identified as wicked. Tonight, for example. She had specified that a particular target deserved to suffer an especially prolonged and agonizing death. Zeb always did his best to do what he was told, although there were times when Lulu would fall silent in the middle of a killing and he would be forced to improvise.

"Wooooo-eeeeeeee!"

Zeb's eyes fluttered open.

A man was dancing in the tall grass some twenty feet

straight ahead of where Zeb sat. The dancing man was wiry, his slender, rawboned body a whirling mass of flesh that looked translucent in the moonlight, legs spinning him about in a drunken stagger, arms upraised and stretched out to his sides in imitation of a helicopter's rotors—in this case, apparently, the rotors of a badly damaged helicopter on the verge of a flaming spinout toward the ground below. The man made chugging sounds between crazed whoops, noises meant to mimic the sound of failing rotors. Here in the dark, you could squint and almost imagine he was a child on a playground, engaged in a bit of innocent, rambunctious fun. A few things made it impossible to buy into the illusion completely. The haggard, gaunt features. The livid knife scar down his left cheek. The explosion of bushy, scraggly hair atop his head, which might have resembled a cut-rate clown's bedraggled fright wig had it not been so irretrievably, disgustingly *foul*, quite likely not washed in years. But all of this only served to make him look like a career hobo. Unpleasant, yes, but hardly remarkable.

The man's name—supposedly—was Clyde Weatherbottom.

Two other things distinguished Clyde from your garden-variety psycho vagrant: (1) He was completely nude. (2) Wound in the fingers of his right hand were many long strands of formerly lush (and now sticky with coagulating blood) blonde hair. The hair was attached to the severed head of an attractive young woman.

Formerly attractive, Zeb thought, and smiled.

The rest of her body was staked to the ground on a patch of pushed-down grass directly in front of Zeb. She'd been stripped of her clothes at the outset of the evening's festivities. And though she'd endured a lot, her body remained a work of natural art—from the proud jut of her large breasts to the sweet swell of her hips and the tender slope of her flat but soft belly, and down to the sculpted length of her long, elegant legs. Zeb supposed the ragged and bloody neck stump would've robbed her of any inherent eroticism for most people. But he was not most people. For Zeb, it was just another means of ingress.

In other words, he'd fucked it.

This was not normal, of course. Even he knew that. It was the kind of thing crazy people did. He was crazy. Hence, stump-fucking. Fuck that politically correct BS the docs were forced to spew. Some had attempted to link his "erratic" behavior with the onset of puberty, and hormones gone haywire. Others had looked for a root cause in the ferocious abuse he'd endured at the hands of his father. All a crock, far as Zeb was concerned. He'd been stone-cold cuckoo from the beginning. He could recall watching Mr. Rogers on PBS as a toddler and thinking how he'd like to pull the man's eyes out and eat them raw.

So, yeah, Zeb knew the truth. He was crazy, like the regular folks said, and had probably had been born that way. When you looked at it that way, you could almost see all these killings as being the work of the Lord. Kind of. But not really.

God was the creator, and He had made him this way.

Crazy.

But God didn't make him kill.

That was all on Lulu.

And Lulu had always been there, whispering naughty things to him during his childhood. Things that had disturbed and excited him at the same time. Ideas about interesting things to do with knives and bricks. He would sit in a classroom and smile at a cute girl, who would maybe smile back, never imagining his thoughts. She would think he had a crush on her, but instead he would be thinking about smashing her head in with a rock. The things Lulu suggested had ignited an obsession so feverish, it was inevitable he would follow the typical path of the young serial-killer-to-be and experiment on animals. It taught him some valuable things, like how hard living things will fight against you to avoid pain or death. By the time he was ready to move on to his first human victim—shortly after his sixteenth birthday—he knew to always be sure to have the upper hand in any situation. Mostly that meant selecting weaker victims. Like that first one, the fourteen-year-old neighbor girl he'd lured into the woods.

Priscilla.

So pretty.

My, what a mess he'd made of her.

Later, as he grew taller and stronger, the field of potential victims widened to include just about anyone. He could go toe-to-toe against any man out there, even the kind of muscle-bound behemoths you'd see in a wrestling ring or shoring up an NFL team's offensive line. And he would come out the victor every time. But he preferred female victims. He enjoyed them on an aesthetic level, that simple appreciation of beauty, but he loved to defile beauty even more. For Zeb, there were few joys in life equal to carving up a bit of lovely flesh with a sharp knife. He loved how the flesh parted so easily, the fresh wound spilling forth that sweet torrent of precious life blood.

Mmm . . . He liked to drink their blood.

It was wrong that he'd gone so long without knowing that pleasure. The memory of those long years of confinement still made him throb with anger. But now he was free again. And crazier than ever.

With a head full of new ideas he was eager to road test.

Clyde ceased his impression of a doomed whirlybird and staggered toward Zeb. He came to a woozy stop several feet short of his seated friend and flashed a fiendish grin. Though there were some gaps, his teeth were still mostly there. This Zeb attributed to good genes. Hell, even crazy hobos could spring from otherwise-sturdy stock. And Zeb's friend was proof that even the sturdiest of family trees can sometimes sprout a diseased limb.

All of Clyde's worldly possessions were contained in a canvas knapsack he carried everywhere. Zeb had poked through its contents a time or two. There were three dog-eared paperback westerns, decades old. There was a lot of assorted junk. Lighters with no fluid in them. A jar filled with dirt. Sets of keys he'd saved as souvenirs from various murders. But most revealing was a stack of old photographs bound together with several thick rubber bands. The pictures showed various members of an obviously healthy and prosperous family over a period of maybe ten years. Some were vacation photos, shots of men in khakis and sunglasses relaxing with drinks, and attractive women in string bikinis stretched out on beach blankets. Others images were from birthday and graduation ceremonies. Clyde was in many of the photos, but the Clyde from that vanished time bore little resemblance to the man Zeb knew today. Somewhere along the way, obviously, something had gone very wrong for him. Clyde Weatherbottom wasn't even his real name. Various clues from the photos made this clear.

Not that Zeb cared, really.

Clyde wasn't that person anymore. Hadn't been for many years.

Clyde held the severed head close to his face and pressed his chapped lips to the dead girl's blood-caked mouth. Zeb watched him push his tongue between the dead lips and felt another little twitch at his groin. He glanced at the headless corpse and thought about spreading her legs for another go. But the exaggerated slurping, smacking sounds Clyde was making distracted him.

"Come on, baby. Gimme some lovin'." Clyde kissed the dead lips again, made the same absurdly exaggerated smacking sounds. He glanced at Zeb and grinned, turning the head's slack features toward him. "Ain't she the sexiest bitch you ever seen, Zebbo? I think I'm gonna marry her. What do you think?"

"You have my blessings."

"Superb! You'll be my best man."

Clyde did a wobbly half spin away from Zeb and cupped his free hand around his mouth. "Hey, asshole. I'm engaged to your bitch now. What do you think about that?"

A longish moment passed.

The only sounds were the sigh of the wind and the hiss of tires on the nearby interstate, which was obscured by a stand of tall trees.

Then a muffled whimper drifted across the field.

Zeb grinned.

Clyde whooped and waved the head again. "Yeah! I knew you were faking being unconscious, motherfucker! Check out the blushing bride!"

Another wild wave of the head.

Another hopeless whimper.

"She's mine now, ya fuckin' punk! *All miiiiiiiiiiiinnnne!*"

The whimpering briefly gave way to an outburst of impotent bravado. "I'll kill you! Both of you. What you did . . . both of you . . ."

The voice cracked again and the whimpering resumed.

Zeb snorted. "Typical."

Clyde shot him a wild, gleeful grin. "Well, shit, I guess we're gonna have to take some reasonable steps to defend ourselves, Zebbo. I do think I heard that boy threaten to kill us. Did I hear right?"

"You heard right."

Zeb got to his feet and started across the field, stepping on the dead girl's stomach en route to where her handsome boyfriend hung upside down from the sturdiest low-hanging branch of a tall tree. When Zeb and Clyde reached the tree, they could see the headlights of cars zipping by on the interstate.

Zeb held out a hand. "Your knife."

The Buck knife was embedded in one of the dead girl's ears. Clyde extracted it and passed it to his friend. Zeb approached the dangling boyfriend, savoring the fear evident in the way he thrashed and screamed. The thick branch creaked, but showed no signs of breaking.

Zeb stared down at him. "I spent a lot of years in a nuthouse, boy. I got out. Obviously."

Clyde snickered.

"One time I heard an orderly talking. He was saying how there's different kinds of crazy. There's your regular, everyday crazy. Folks take pills for it and they're mostly okay. Mostly they're only dangerous to themselves. Then there's a middle-ground kind of crazy. People who are mostly just a threat to themselves but might snap one day and hurt somebody else. But this would just be an isolated incident. These people can still be treated, and maybe there's even some hope for them. And then this orderly talked about me. According to him that day, I'm the worst kind of crazy. The hopeless kind. The killing kind. You see, I don't struggle with my feelings or any of that shit. I like to hurt people. You might say it's my main interest in life. My calling."

Clyde said, "Your raison d'être."

The boyfriend looked up at Zeb and sniffled. "Fuck you, man."

Zeb's expression didn't change, nor did his tone. "That orderly was right. And I told him that right before I slit his belly open. Which, by the way, is what I'm about to do to you."

Clyde laughed. "Gut him!"

Zeb plunged the knife into the man's flesh at a spot just below the waistline and drew it downward in a single vicious slash. He tossed the knife aside and gripped the edges of the wound with both hands, tugging at the gash and ripping it open as far as he could. Blood and loops of viscera spilled through the opening. The man wasn't dead yet. He thrashed some more, but Zeb easily held him in place, pinning him against the tree. Then he pushed a hand all the way through the gash, groped around until he found a soft, squishy organ . . . and squeezed.

The man screamed one last time.

Clyde kept laughing.

Later, as they sat around their campfire roasting bits of human flesh on sticks, Clyde took a swig from a flask filled with cheap whiskey and sighed. "Beautiful night."

Zeb pulled the stick away from the fire and eased the bit of flesh off the end. He popped it into his mouth and chewed, savoring the taste for several moments before the delightful morsel slid slowly down his gullet. He smiled. "Indeed."

Clyde cleared his throat. "You, uh . . . you talk to Lulu lately?"

Zeb affixed another piece of meat to the stick and held it over the fire. "Indeed."

"She tell you where we should go next?"

"Yes."

A long moment passed. A big semi's horn blatted out on the interstate. "Well, don't keep a man in suspense, Zebbo. Where we headed?"

Zeb was still smiling. "Myrtle Beach."

CHAPTER FOUR

March 22

"You can back off now."

Rob flinched. "Huh?"

It was the first time she'd spoken since they'd merged with the interstate traffic. Some twenty minutes of tense silence. The girl had spent most of that time sitting forward in her seat, her eyes intent on the back of the rental van. Rob knew it was a rental from the Enterprise sticker on the rear bumper. There were all sorts of questions he wanted to ask her. For instance, who were the people in the van and why was it necessary to abduct a stranger to follow them? What did she intend to do once she caught up with them? But he kept his mouth shut. Her generally hostile demeanor made it clear this was for the best. She scared the hell out of him, so much so it was almost possible to ignore how hot she was.

Almost.

She sat back in her seat now, folded her hands almost primly in her lap. "I said you can back off. Are you fucking deaf?"

They were maybe two car lengths behind the van. Rob eased off the gas and the distance quickly increased to three car lengths, then four. A blue Dodge Neon with flaking paint and stickers all over the back window changed lanes, moving into the space between the van and the Galaxie. Rob hit the clicker and started to change lanes.

"Don't."

Rob turned the clicker off and looked at her. "What's the deal here? I thought you didn't want me to lose them."

She shrugged. "Doesn't matter. I know where they're going."

Rob couldn't help it—he laughed. "Oh, yeah? That's funny. Because for a while there I thought it was critically important that I stay right on their fucking ass and not lose sight of them if I wanted to live."

The girl kicked off her shoes and scooted farther down in her seat. She raised her legs and propped her feet on the dashboard. She set the gun in her lap and examined the fingernails of her right hand. The black nail polish was chipping away in places. "It was. But I've calmed down some. I'll kill them later, after they get where they're going."

Rob looked at her feet. The socks were the kind with toes. She wiggled the toes as he stared at them. It sent a strange little tingle through him. He glanced at the road. The blue Neon was still between them and the van. "Well, thanks for not killing me. Or them. Yet." He jerked his left hand, rattling the handcuff bracelets. "So tell me something. Say we get pulled over for some reason. Obviously any cop with more than one or two functioning brain cells would want to know why I'm cuffed to the wheel. What's your explanation?"

She smirked. "That's easy. It's a sex thing."

"Say what?"

Her smirk deepened. "A sex thing. Bondage. The cop will accept it because cops are worldly people and they know people are into all kinds of kinky shit. And you'll play along because your only other alternative is a fucking bullet in the brain."

Fuck, he thought.

She was right. He'd been thinking he might try a bit of subtle erratic driving to hopefully draw the attention of the police. It wouldn't have been too difficult. During their brief

time on the highway, he'd already spied several cop cruisers.
A part of him had even become cautiously optimistic as he'd
thought about it, but now he regretfully scratched the idea
from his too-short list of potentially ass-saving schemes.

Fuck!

He sighed. "So . . . uh . . . what now?"

"We stay on the road until dark. Then we find a little
motel somewhere and get a room with your credit card."

Rob thought about that. It seemed to indicate she had no
intention of killing him for at least the next several hours.
Still, hot babe or not, the notion of being alone in a motel
room with this girl scared the shit out of him. Christ, she'd
come up to him with a gun in a public place in broad daylight. What might a girl crazy enough to do that do with
him with a little bit of privacy and some time to kill? Rob
tightened his grip around the steering wheel to quell the
sudden tremors in his fingers, which had been triggered by
the sudden conviction that he wouldn't leave that room alive.

She looked at him. Her eyes were cold, pitiless. "You need
to stop being such a nervous bitch."

Rob grunted. "Oh. Right. Okay. I'll work on that, but I
can't guarantee anything. I mean, go figure, right? Some crazy
chick with a gun kidnaps and threatens me. Why should I be
nervous?"

The girl stared at him for a long moment, her features
fixed, expressionless. Rob couldn't bear the scrutiny and decided to stare at the road instead.

"Look at me."

It was a tone that would brook no disobedience. Icy, and
carrying an unspoken promise of pain if ignored. He looked
at her. "Okay. I'm looking at you. Now what?"

The girl smiled. Just a little one, a slight dimpling of the
corners of her mouth. But her eyes stayed cold. "I haven't
decided about killing you yet. That's gonna depend on a lot
of things. There are some things you can do to better your

odds. One of them is to do everything I tell you without question or hesitation. It'll make things a lot easier for both of us."

Rob nodded. "Right. Because there's no reason a friendly little kidnapping-slash-carjacking should be anything other than a thoroughly pleasant experience for all involved."

"The other thing you can do, the main thing at this point, is to cut the sarcasm. It's making me want to shoot you right now and be done with it."

Rob frowned. "You'd shoot me right now? Seriously? Doing seventy-five on the interstate, with me behind the wheel?"

The girl's gaze didn't waver. "That's right."

"You're crazy. Fuck, you are really fucking crazy."

"Maybe." Her smile deepened a little. "But you should take what I'm telling you seriously."

Rob shrugged. "Okay. Whatever."

They continued in silence for another several minutes. The Neon stayed in front of them, but Rob soon realized he'd lost sight of the van. The girl was sitting up straight and staring straight ahead now. She had to have noticed, too. Rob briefly considered shifting lanes again and putting the pedal down in an effort to catch up to their quarry, but the girl didn't seem concerned about this development, so he did nothing.

Unable to bear the silence any longer, he glanced at her and asked, "So where are they going?"

"Myrtle Beach. Same place we're going."

"Okay. Well . . ." Rob had turned his attention back to the road, but now he looked fully at her, astonishment evident in the twist of his features. "Myrtle Beach? That's . . ."

He trailed off and glanced at the road again. The Neon swerved and nearly struck a pickup truck in the far left lane. A horn blared and the Neon jerked back into its proper lane. Then it swerved slightly again. Rob began to suspect the driver was impaired in some way. He eased off the gas pedal a bit more and put another car length between the Galaxie and the Neon.

He looked at the girl. "So if I behave, I'll live to see Myrtle Beach? Is that what you're saying? Because we won't be there by sundown."

She shrugged. "Maybe. Maybe not. One way or another, you'll find out."

Rob didn't press the issue any further, deciding he had no choice but to accept the answer he'd been given, which was at least vaguely hopeful. But he had some other questions. "So I guess you know these people?"

"No."

Rob's brow creased. "Huh. But you know where they're going?"

"That's right."

"How?"

"Heard them talking about it at Starbucks. Heard everything I needed to know, down to the street address for the beach house one of their rich daddies rented for them."

Rob hit the brake pedal as the Neon abruptly slowed down and swerved again. He slapped the palm of his uncuffed hand against the steering wheel. "Fucker!"

"Calm down."

Rob looked at her and laughed. Once again, he just couldn't help it. "*You're* telling *me* to calm down? That's rich. The crazy chick who impulsively decides to follow some rich kids several hundred miles for no apparent reason thinks I need to calm down." He shook his head and laughed again. "That is awesome. That is fucking awesome."

Her voice dropped to a near whisper. "There's a reason."

"Great. I'd like to hear it."

Her voice remained almost inaudible as she said, "They were mean to me."

Rob looked at her.

Her eyes were narrow slits and her lips were pooched out.

The childlike pout was a forceful reminder of how very young she was. She couldn't be any older than twenty. He felt an unexpected twinge of sympathy for her. "Look . . . whatever they did, and I don't doubt they were assholes to you, but . . . it can't be worth the trouble you're going to here."

A corner of her mouth twitched. Her hands curled into fists. "You don't know what you're talking about."

"Maybe not." He saw the way her clenched fists were shaking and almost kept his mouth shut. He didn't want to piss her off. But he thought he had a chance of reaching her. She was a tough chick, no question, but maybe there was a softness behind the hard-core exterior. "Seriously. Please think this through. Nothing really bad has happened yet. I know you're mad. You're right to be mad. But maybe there's some better way to vent that anger. Right here and now, you're still okay. It's not too late to head off some possibly life-ruining choices."

That corner of her mouth twitched again. "You *really* don't know what you're talking about."

"So help me understand." He snapped the fingers of his free hand. "Oh! And what about your family and friends? Won't they worry once they realize you're missing?"

She laughed and didn't say anything.

He shook his head. "What's funny?"

"You are. This whole understanding-big-brother bullshit. If you knew anything about me, you'd know how stupid you're being."

"So tell me about yourself. Help me understand. Maybe start by telling me your name."

"It's Roxie. That's R-O-X-I-E."

"Huh. Sounds like a stripper's name."

"Yeah. That's why it's cool."

Rob nodded. "So . . . Roxie . . . why is my attempt to reason with you stupid?"

She reached between her legs and pulled the tote bag into her lap, then talked as she rummaged through it. "Everything you think you know about me, all of your fucking little guesses, are all wrong as shit. I don't live locally. There's no one here to miss me. There's no one anywhere to miss me. Not anymore." Her hands came out of the tote bag with a pack of American Spirit cigarettes and a Zippo lighter. She lit up a cig and exhaled a cloud of smoke. "I'm not a regular girl under the surface, like you think. And I *know* that's what you think. When someone hurts me, I don't run home and write a fucking blog about it. I'm a bad bitch. A really, really bad bitch. There's no hidden heart of gold here." She blew out another stream of smoke, this one right at Rob. "As the stoners in that shitty Neon are about to find out."

"Say what?"

Rob coughed and waved away smoke. He'd ignored the Neon while listening to Roxie talk, but now he focused on it again and saw that its driver's impairment appeared to be worsening. The little car swerved yet again as Rob stared at the profusion of faded stickers advertising the owner's politics and taste in music. Left-leaning and into punk. Though there were also Grateful Dead and Phish stickers, which seemed kind of strange. In Rob's experience, punks and stoners rarely intermingled.

"Ugh." Roxie made a sound of disgust. "Check that shit out. A fucking 'Coexist' sticker. That shit makes me wanna puke."

Rob nodded. "Yeah. I actually agree with you on something. It's a fucking miracle."

Roxie grunted. "Get in the left lane. Pull up beside these fuckers."

Rob put the blinker on and glanced at her. "What are you—?"

"Just shut up and do what I say, you fuck."

Her face was hard again, the blue eyes projecting enough malice to stop a suicide bomber in his tracks. The transformation was alarming. For a few moments there, while she was talking about herself, she'd seemed almost like a normal person. Like a person he could even like, despite the extreme circumstances of their meeting. But the psycho part of her personality had reasserted itself. By now he knew better than to defy her when she was like this.

He pulled into the left lane and drew up alongside the Neon.

Roxie leaned out the Galaxie's open passenger-side window and made a cranking motion with her hand. Rob craned his head to look past her and saw that there were four people in the car. All youngish, maybe midtwenties. The driver had long blond hair and a bushy beard. The girl in the passenger seat looked like a young punk. Skinny. Tattoos. The two in the back—another guy and gal—were harder to peg. They almost looked sort of straitlaced. But as Rob watched them, he saw that a fat bomber joint was being passed among the car's passengers.

The Neon's driver grinned goofily and cranked his window down. He stuck his head out the window and tried to say something, but the words were lost in the rushing of the wind.

Roxie leaned farther out her own window and gestured frantically at the back of the Neon. Then she cupped her hands around her mouth and put the full force of her lungs into her next words: "YOU NEED TO PULL OVER!"

The Neon's driver frowned and glanced at the punk girl in the passenger seat. The girl shrugged. The driver nodded and looked at Roxie again, giving her a thumbs-up gesture even as he began to guide the Neon across multiple lanes of traffic, toward the road's shoulder on the right.

Roxie looked at Rob. The hard mask was gone. She was smiling. "Pull up behind them."

Rob put the blinker on again and did as instructed, easing the Galaxie to a slow, crawling stop behind the Neon. He stared at the back of the other car for a moment. Then he shot a confused look at Roxie. "Is there really something wrong with their car?"

Roxie reached across him and turned the key backward in the ignition. The Galaxie's engine ground to a rumbling halt as she pulled the key from the ignition slot. "So you don't go anywhere. Hang tight while I take care of these fucks."

She opened the passenger-side door and began to get out.

Rob's heart began to beat faster.

The gun was in her hand again.

She was out of the car now and walking toward the parked Neon. The Neon's passengers were oblivious to the danger approaching them. And why wouldn't they be? A glance in their mirrors would show a very pretty girl approaching them. And who would ever consider that a thing to fear? Of course, things might be different if any of them were sober. They might notice the gun pressed flat against her right thigh. She was almost to the car now, and Rob was close to hyperventilating. He felt he should warn them somehow. Maybe lean on the horn and jerk them out of their dope stupor for a few lifesaving moments. It might work. They might even get away.

But he'd still be stuck right here.

With a very pissed off Roxie to face—Roxie and her gun.

He placed the palm of his left hand flat against the horn pad.

It was the right thing to do.

He *knew* that.

And yet . . . there was the fear of that gun pointed at him instead.

So he hesitated.

Roxie was standing next to the Neon now. The gun was still pressed to her thigh. She leaned down and rapped the knuckles of her left hand against the passenger-side window. The punk girl turned toward her and rolled the window down. Rob opened his mouth to scream a warning, but it was already too late. Roxie's gun hand was like a striking cobra. One moment it was still against her leg, the next nanosecond the barrel of the gun was pressed against the punk girl's forehead. Rob heard the report of the gun and knew for sure Roxie had actually shot the poor girl in the face. There were screams from the Neon now. Then another shot. The driver slumped over. Roxie pushed the punk girl's corpse aside and leaned farther into the car, twisting her body so that she could point the gun into the backseat. Rob heard more screams, only barely distinguishable from his own cries. The rear door on the driver's side started to open as one of the backseat occupants tried to escape. Another bullet ended the attempt. Roxie's body twisted again and she aimed her gun at the Neon's last living passenger. There was a brief hesitation, almost as if she was savoring these last moments before the final kill.

There was one more scream. Another bullet cut it off. Rob saw an explosion of red against the Neon's back window and felt bile rise into his throat. His gut churned. He was shaking and hot tears were spilling down his face. Any illusions he might have harbored about Roxie's supposed vulnerability had been vanquished forever within the space of a few moments of extreme violence. She'd been right.

She wasn't a regular girl.

She was pure fury.

And now, finally, he understood just how much trouble he was really in.

Roxie extracted herself from the Neon and strolled calmly back to the Galaxie. Rob stared at her. He couldn't believe how cool and unconcerned she seemed. She was still holding the gun by her side but was making no real attempt to hide it. Cars were zipping by on the interstate. Lots of them.

There were still several hours of broad daylight left. How could she be so fucking nonchalant?

Back inside the Galaxie, she reached across Rob and slid the key back into the ignition. She turned the key and the engine came to life.

Then she pressed the gun's hot barrel against his crotch and said, "Drive."

Just the one word.

It was enough.

Rob put the car in gear and eased back into the traffic.

Picking up speed, he glanced at the rearview mirror for one last look at the Neon. From this perspective and distance, it looked like just another stalled car. No big deal.

Roxie was laughing. "Now what was that you were saying about it not being too late or some shit? Something about choices?"

More insane laughter.

Rob's hands tightened around the steering wheel again.

He was holding on for dear life.

Whatever little was left of it.

CHAPTER FIVE

March 16

She was still asleep when he came naked out of the bathroom. She was lying on her side in the bed with her mouth hanging open. A thin stream of drool leaked from a corner of her mouth to dampen the pillow beneath her head. Loose tufts of frizzy blonde hair obscured some of her face. Tucked away there beneath the covers, she could almost be any anonymous woman. Some truck-stop floozy or roadside whore. A last-call bar pickup. Or better yet, that hot little jailbait babysitter from down the street, the one with the platinum Paris Hilton hair. Sixteen going on ninety-nine-to-life, as his buddy Franklin had said once, adding that he'd almost be willing to do a stint in jail for one night of fun with the hot little tease.

John was inclined to agree. Screw morality.

He pictured Julie Cosgrove, the babysitter, asleep there in his bed. Imagined her throwing back the covers to reveal her lovely, nude body. He could almost see her big tits, how ripe they would look. How inviting. And there would be a dazzling smile on her face as she held her arms out to him. He would go to her. Hell, yes. There would be no pause to consider the right or wrong of the situation, nor even the slightest impulse to resist temptation. Fuck, he'd embrace the wrongness of it. *Revel* in it. Just dive into that silky soft mound of succulent, tender girl flesh and put a fucking on her that would make her head spin for days. Thinking of it made his cock stir. God, what he'd give to have sweet little Julie for real.

But no such luck.

This was no mystery woman, no stranger to his bed. This was his wife of twenty years. A woman he'd once lusted after intensely. But now he could hardly stand to look at her. It'd been ten years since he'd fucked another woman and he'd almost forgotten what it was like to caress unfamiliar flesh. For a while that had been okay. It was the way of things. You get older and settle down, leave the tomcatting around to the younger guys. John had accepted this as his lot for some time, but lately, ever since his recent fortieth birthday, he'd begun to feel restless. He couldn't shake the gnawing feeling that he was wasting what was left of his . . . well, not youth, obviously, more like that last dwindling slice of time when he might still possess some virility or fading attractiveness to the opposite sex. No, not youth, more like the last fading echoes of youth, and he didn't—

Christ.

He reflected on his last thoughts and felt disgust. He was a *man.* And real men didn't wallow in self-pity. He was self-aware enough to know he was on the verge of a stereotypical midlife crisis. Most men in his position would seek the help of a therapist, or perhaps slake that renewed thirst for strange flesh by blowing a wad in some cheap hooker's mouth. But he needed something better than that.

A dramatic change.

A *forever* change.

And the time for that change had arrived at last. He stepped closer to the bed, curling his fingers tighter around the blade of the carving knife as he searched Karen's face for any signs of impending wakefulness. He'd stashed the knife in the bathroom closet several hours earlier, while Karen had been so immersed in that night's episode of *Survivor* that she'd been oblivious to anything he was doing. Which included the twenty-plus minutes he'd spent locked in the bathroom, slowly masturbating to pictures of Julie stored on his cell phone. Mostly these were pictures taken on the sly, when she wasn't looking or didn't know he was around. But the one that got to him the most was the one she *did* know about. A candid shot snapped at his daughter's tenth birthday party last week. He'd made some lame joke and she'd laughed and stuck her tongue out at him. He stared at that picture for minutes, at that wedge of glistening tongue protruding between glossy, pink-painted lips. That was the image that got him over the edge, making him come harder than he ever did with Karen these days.

He circled the bed and then stood staring down at his wife, knife held at shoulder level, hand shaking, his soul burning with the need to bury the blade in the sleeping woman's body. A latex glove was on his right hand. When she was dead—and after he'd inflicted a few superficial wounds on his own body—the glove would go down the toilet. Then he'd call the cops with his practiced sob story about a masked assailant. He was sure he would be convincing enough in his fake grief to make them buy the story.

But he wondered about his daughter. Nancy was asleep in her own room at the far end of the hall. She *should* be asleep. It was well past her strict bedtime. Still, it bore thinking about. The cops would question her, maybe ask her if she'd heard anything. John debated the idea of killing his daughter before dealing with Karen. On the upside, dead girls tell no tales. Downside, he'd leave telltale signs of blood and possibly other evidence, traipsing back and forth between her room and here. No, he'd just have to take his chances. Odds were she was stone asleep, and if not, he'd figure a way to deal with it.

Meanwhile, it was time to stop fucking around and do this thing. His lips curled into a sneer as he raised the knife higher and psyched himself up to bring it down. He imagined how it would feel to slam the heavy blade into living flesh and felt his cock twitch. The sneer became a smile. It would be a *fucking rush*, that's what it would be. He pictured himself pulling the blade out and ramming it in over and over, butchering her the way a genuine random psycho would. It was too bad he couldn't rape her, too. But that would leave DNA evidence and . . . well, what if he wore a condom?

Scratch that.

No condoms in the house.

Just do it, an inner voice berated him.

John sucked in a big breath and raised the knife still higher. Then, in that last moment before he would have brought the knife down . . . he heard something.

A rustling out in the hallway.

John turned away from the bed to stare at the closed bedroom door. He held his breath and waited, counting off seconds. Ten. Twenty. Half a minute. He began to let his breath out, sure now that he'd heard nothing. Or maybe just rodents scurrying through the walls. He'd been meaning to set out mousetraps for weeks. Yeah, that could be it.

Then he heard it again.

That rustling, closer now.

He moved a step closer to the door. The sound came again. Quieter, this time. A shuffling rather than a rustling. An attempt at stealth, feet gliding softly over hallway carpet. John clenched his teeth and swallowed hard as genuine fear leaped into his heart. In his mind, he saw himself as he must look and almost laughed. A naked man, intent on murder and possible sexual assault only moments earlier but now paralyzed with fear. Predator turned prey? No. Ridiculous.

Someone was in the hallway, no doubt.

But the interloper's identity was obvious.

Nancy.

She was restless, was maybe trying to sneak downstairs for

a cookie or some other late-night snack. John grinned. Sudden impulse hurried him to the door. This was too perfect an opportunity to miss. He would take her in the hallway, do it so fast she'd never know what was happening, then return quickly to the bedroom to do Karen. The cops would see that the intruder had stumbled upon Nancy en route to his primary prey. The little snot wouldn't be around to raise suspicions or cramp his style as he swaggered into a glorious new phase of his life.

He yanked the door open and charged into the hallway—and collided with a big man in a fringe jacket. The man had long, scraggly gray hair and eyes that conveyed insanity even in the gloom of the hallway. His grin was wide and displayed yellow, crooked teeth. And holy Jesus, but he fucking *stank*, a stench like something from a backed-up sewer drain. It made John's eyes water. A blinding terror gripped him before he remembered the knife in his hand.

He raised it again.

And was shoved backward into the room, *hard*, causing him to stumble over his feet and crash into the nightstand next to Karen's side of the bed. A lamp tumbled off the nightstand and Karen's stack of paperback romance novels went flying. Struggling for balance, John lurched away from the nightstand. He turned and raised the knife as the big man in the buckskin jacket came into the room, followed by another man. The second man was less stout than the first, wiry, and also had long, filthy hair, but not straight and fine like the other man's. It was big and bushy. If anything, he stank even worse than his partner.

Karen awoke with a gasp and sat up straight in bed. "John! What's going on?" Then she got a glimpse of the intruders and unleashed a shrill scream. "OHMYGOD! HELLLLLLLLLP!"

She rolled to the other side of the bed, tried to get up, and got her feet tangled in the twisted bedsheets. She took a tumble off the bed and hit the floor hard, crying out in terror and pain.

The big man chuckled. "Don't let her get nowhere, Clyde."

"On it."

Clyde swaggered past his partner and leered at John. The lean man faked a lunge in his direction and cackled at the girlish shriek this elicited. Then he continued around the bed and scooped Karen up off the floor. She screamed again and flailed against him, battering the sides of his head with her tiny fists. If the blows had any effect on him, it didn't show. He just grinned and let her hammer away a few seconds longer before cracking her across the face with the back of his hand. The sound was loud. And there was a crunch as the cartilage in her nose snapped. Intense pain made her cry out again. Another punishing blow stifled any additional screams. She mewled and blubbered, pleading for mercy, sounding to John like Nancy sometimes did when he put a good spanking on her for misbehaving.

The sounds of her distress affected him in ways that were ironic given what he'd been about to do to her. Some primal part of him felt anger and an instinct to protect. He made a move toward Clyde, but the bigger man intercepted him, grabbing him by the wrist and twisting the knife out of his hand. Then, before John could even begin to consider defensive tactics, the man stuck the knife in his belly.

And now John screamed, a sound even shriller and louder than what had come out of Karen. His attacker just stood there, grinning, those madman's eyes conveying an avid fascination. He was studying John, tasting the quality of his pain and terror. John glanced down and saw that only the tip of the blade had penetrated his flesh. No more than an inch of steel was inside him, but it was more than enough to send shock waves of agony cascading through his body. Blood streamed down his belly and soaked his pubic thatch. The man gave the blade a little twist and John screamed again, but the blade penetrated no farther. The sick son of a bitch was toying with him.

John tried to twist the knife out of his hand, but he wasn't as skilled at the maneuver as the intruder. The man swatted his hand away and delivered a closed-fisted blow that hurt like hell and sent him sprawling backward across the bed. He hit the plush mattress and bounced. His head went up and down a time or two, and a fresh stab of agony at the center of his face told him his nose had been broken.

Karen saw the wound to his belly and cried out in anguish. "John! Don't hurt him, please!"

The lean one cackled and leaned close to Karen, teasing one of her earlobes with his tongue. "Oh, we're gonna hurt him, baby, you can count on that. Gonna hurt you, too, you want to know the truth."

Karen cringed away from him, but he held her close, holding her by the back of the neck as he rubbed his crotch against her bare bottom. His other hand roamed over the front of her body, cupping her breasts and squeezing the big pink nipples. Primitive instinct spurred John to action again as he rolled over and prepared to leap at the man attacking his wife. He was on his hands and knees, readying to launch himself at the filthy bum, when the other man stabbed him between the shoulder blades. John screamed and arched his back, hands clawing at the blade as it sank deeper into his flesh. He felt it scrape bone and screamed again. The big man rode him down to the bed, straddling him and pulling his head back by the hair. He felt the knife against his throat and knew he had only moments to live.

He looked up at Karen through eyes misty with tears and felt something he hadn't experienced in a long time—shame.

What he'd been about to do . . . well, it was an abomination.

Unforgivable.

The least he could do was tell her he loved her one last time before he died. It wouldn't be a total lie, either. He really had loved her once upon a time. With his whole heart and every fiber of his being. He guessed maybe there was some of that feeling left somewhere inside him, after all. Recognizing this deepened his shame and broke his heart. He just wanted this over now. Nothing could be worse than this feeling. Not even death.

Then he heard it.

They *all* heard it.

That small sound drifting in from the hallway.

"Daddy?" The delicate, fragile voice was thick with tears. "What's . . . happening?"

The wiry man cackled yet again. The pressure of the blade against John's throat ceased as the big man climbed off him and started toward the open bedroom door and the tiny figure just barely visible in the darkness beyond.

John lived a while longer.

Hours, maybe.

And during that time, he learned beyond all dispute that there absolutely are things infinitely worse than death. Worse even than the emotional and spiritual betrayal of his wife. Things that blackened his soul. When death finally came, he greeted it like the embrace of a long-lost love.

CHAPTER SIX

March 22

The girls were sitting at a picnic table at a rest area, talking while they watched the guys toss a football around. Zoe and Emily sat next to each other on the edge of the table, their feet planted on the bench beneath them, while Annalisa sat on the bench on the opposite side and jabbered into her cell phone.

Chuck cocked his arm and flung it forward, sending the football in a high, wobbly semispiral in Joe's general direction. Joe took off down the gently sloping hill, head up as he tracked the ball's progress across the bright blue sky. He held his hand up against the glare of the sun and it was obvious to Zoe that he'd lost track of the thing.

Emily sighed. "Shit. Joe fall down, go boom."

Joe twisted his body and scanned the sky again, but the ball was already coming to the ground some twenty yards ahead of him. He saw it an instant before he got his feet tangled and crashed to the ground with a startled yelp.

Emily shook her head. "Stupid boy. Asshole. That's what he gets for getting so sloshed this early in the day."

Zoe laughed. "Your guy takes a fall and you call him an asshole. It must be true love."

Emily snorted. "I do sort of love him. I guess. But he *is* an asshole, especially when he drinks so much."

Zoe sipped from a fresh can of Coke. "Yeah. But he seems like a good guy, deep down. At least when he's sober."

"Too bad I can't say the same for Chuck."

Zoe tensed, her fingers dimpling the moisture-slick can as she squeezed it harder. "Emily . . ."

Emily nudged her with an elbow. "Fucking relax. They can't hear us. Admit the truth to your best friend. You're about to break up with the prick, aren't you?"

Zoe's grip on the can eased some. She sighed. "Yeah." Then she tensed again as a wave of anxiety surged through her. "But don't tell Joe! God, he'd blab it to Chuck right away."

"Right. If I tell him not to do something, he'll damn well not do it." She smiled, watching as Joe awkwardly picked himself up and dusted off before limping away to retrieve the fallen ball. "But yeah, I'll keep my mouth shut. Although . . ." She looked at Zoe now, mouth curling in a strange expression that was almost a leer. "It could open the door to some interesting possibilities."

"What do you mean?"

Emily leaned close to Zoe and whispered in her ear. "Joe's always hinting around about how he'd like a threesome with me and another girl." She laughed. "Typical guy. But I'm thinking maybe it'd be fun if you were the other girl."

Zoe's face reddened. "Um . . . I, uh . . ."

Emily's breath was warm against her ear as she laughed softly again. "Just think about it. No pressure." She patted Zoe's knee. "If nothing else, you and I could get together at some point over the week."

Zoe's blush deepened as she stared at Emily's hand, which hadn't moved from her knee. This was pretty weird. She and Emily made out now and then. But it was usually when they were high, and Zoe just thought of it as harmless playing around. Still, given that history, this blatant proposition shouldn't come as such a shock.

Yet it did.

She made herself swallow and said, "Yeah . . . I'll . . . think about it."

Emily patted her knee again. "You do that. It'd be fucking fun as hell." She climbed off the table and stretched. Then she put on her dark sunglasses and smiled at Zoe. "You're gonna be so much better off without that piece of shit in your life."

Zoe started to say something, but Emily turned away from her and started back up the hill toward the van.

Annalisa snapped her phone shut and made a shrill sound of frustration. "Motherfucker! Can you believe that fucking motherfucker!"

Zoe turned to face Annalisa. "I can't believe it. The nerve of that fucker. Um . . . what are you talking about?"

Annalisa rolled her eyes. "Sean's fucking mother."

"Sean's mother is a motherfucker?"

"Yeah!"

"Okay."

Annalisa shook her head. "Nothing's ever good enough for that cunt, I swear. I mean, I'm hot, right?"

"Absolutely."

"And smart, right?"

"Your GPA is four-point-oh. You're the smartest foul-mouthed bitch on the planet."

Annalisa nodded. "No shit, right? So what mother in her right fucking mind wouldn't want her son dating a girl who looks like me and has a brilliant fucking future ahead of her?"

Zoe squinted at her. "She's . . . I don't know . . . *jealous?*"

"Of course she is!" She unleashed a shrill screech of frustration and exhaled heavily. "Okay, change of fucking subject. I saw Emily whispering in your ear. What was that about?"

"Um . . . it was sort of . . . private."

Annalisa lifted an eyebrow. "Oh yeah? Too private to tell your best friend?"

"Um . . ."

Annalisa reached into her purse for a pack of Marlboros and lit one up. "Oh, that's right. I'm only your second-best friend. Emily is your *actual* best friend. The one you tell the really important shit. I see how it is."

Zoe frowned. She hated the idea of Annalisa seeing things that way. But what really sharpened the sting was recognizing that she'd only spoken the truth. "We were talking about me and Chuck."

"Yeah?"

Zoe nodded. "I'm breaking up with him after this trip is over."

"Good."

Zoe laughed. "Good?"

"Yeah. Chuck sucks. Fuck him."

"Christ, does *everybody* hate my boyfriend?"

"Everybody with half a brain. Personally, I'd like to throw him off a fucking cliff."

Zoe laughed again. "I don't want to kill him. I just want him out of my life."

"Well, it's the smartest move you've made in a long time. But I think you're lying to me. Or half-lying. That's not all you and Emily were talking about. Was it?"

"Christ, you are so suspicious." Zoe climbed off the table. "I'm gonna hit the bathroom again. And I'm not fucking lying to you."

She turned and started toward the rest area's main building.

Annalisa called after her in a singsong voice. "Liar, liar, pants on fire . . ."

Zoe quickened her pace as her face turned red again.

CHAPTER SEVEN

Diary of a Mixed-up Girl blog entry, dated March 10

There's this one guy. Talked about his lame ass before. Asshole makes me want to vomit every time I think of him. Swear to fucking God, he needs a lobotomy so bad. I'd love to stick a needle in that frontal lobe of his and give it a good twirl. This guy, though, most people would never know he'd been lobotomized because he's kind of a drooling vegetable already.
Fucking MORON.
I think about killing him sometimes Seriously. I think about getting him somewhere nice and private. Someplace where he could scream and scream and nobody would ever hear him. Then I'd get him drunk enough to pass the fuck out. He's a lightweight, so that'd be pretty damn easy. Next I'd restrain him. Tie him to a bed or something. Then the *real* fun would start. I actually think about this a fuck of a lot because this dude seriously needs to fucking die, and there's this one funny image I keep thinking of that I'm desperate to make real. This guy tied to a bed. Body spread-eagled. His dick cut off. Not the balls. Just the dick. Every time I think of that, just those useless balls sitting there without a dick attached, I crack the fuck up. I'm cracking the fuck up RIGHT NOW. HAHAHAHA.

Seriously, he's a douche bag and I want to make him dead.

But I sort of want to fuck him first.

LOL. If I were a guy, it wouldn't matter what order I did it in. I could kill him and then fuck his corpse with my big, throbbing dick.

OH SHIT! Look at the time! Homework!

3 comments

lord_ruthven: The only way I know you're not talking about me is the constant references to this guy's stupidity. But you are one twisted bitch.

Mixedupgirl: Aw . . . that's sweet. But I do want to kill you. I want to stick red-hot needles in your eyes and watch them liquefy. I want to cut off your head and FedEx it to your parents. LOL. I totally don't get why anybody would call me "twisted." Oh, and thanks for the flowers. Kisses.

darkest_rogue: I'm pretty sure I'm in love with you. You are awesome. But you probably know that already.

CHAPTER EIGHT

March 22

Rob kept glancing at the Galaxie's slightly askew rearview mirror with the expectation of seeing a column of police cruisers with blue lights flashing bearing down on them. They were some forty miles down the road from the scene of the roadside massacre by now, and he couldn't understand how it was they'd driven away from something as spectacularly horrible as that with, thus far, no repercussions or complications and no hint of pursuit by law enforcement.

Okay, that bit about no repercussions was sort of bullshit. His psyche had been dealt a serious blow. If through some miracle he managed to survive this ordeal and was able to resume his normal life, he was certain he would have to deal with some level of posttraumatic stress the rest of his days. He foresaw years and years of costly therapy just to be able to function.

"Pull off at the next exit."

Roxie pointed at a blue road sign coming up on their right. It was the kind with icons indicating local motels, restaurants, and gas stations. A green road sign a little farther down the road indicated the exit was one mile away.

Rob frowned as he glanced at the Galaxie's gas gauge, which showed its tank as still more than three-quarters full. "Um . . . why?"

She stared at him in silence for a moment, her eyes unreadable behind dark sunglasses. "Because I said so, that's why."

Rob nodded. "Right."

It had been stupid to even ask. He'd already learned the uselessness of arguing with her. She was unpredictable. Unstable. These were understatements of epic proportion. She was dangerously deranged. He had to be careful. A person like Roxie, anything could set her off. A wrong word. A wrong look. Or something he had no control over, some quirk of her fucked-up brain chemistry causing her to lash out for no reason. Rob realized there was no way he—or anyone, for that matter—could successfully navigate this crazy chick's moods for long.

The exit came up fast. He put the Galaxie's blinker on and applied steady pressure to the brake pedal as they neared the ramp.

"I'm sort of horny."

The out-of-nowhere comment startled Rob. He didn't know what to say, but knew she'd expect some sort of response. "Um . . . yeah?"

"Ever fuck a murderer?"

"Well . . . no."

She laughed. "Ever fuck anybody at all?"

"I'm not a virgin, if that's what you're asking."

"Good. Turn left."

They'd reached the end of the exit ramp, which intersected with a stretch of faded two-lane blacktop. To the right, maybe a quarter mile distant, lay an array of fast-food joints, gas stations, and a motel. To the left was a stretch of open road curling into a thickening expanse of wilderness. The only business establishment in that direction was a Shell station. It looked kind of grubby compared to the gleaming, gigantic convenience stores to the right, with their dozens of pumps and huge, brightly lit signs. The station to the left had just two double-sided pumps, and the towering old Shell sign in a corner of its nearly vacant parking lot looked like it had been there maybe half a century—and probably had been.

Rob cranked the wheel to the left and started in that direction.

"Pull in at the gas station."

Rob turned in at the Shell's lot, angling the Galaxie toward one of the pumps.

Roxie slugged his shoulder. "Not here. Side of the building, toward the rear."

Rob steered the car away from the pumps and parked where Roxie indicated, in the last slot on the side toward the rear of the building. A metal door marked MEN stood opposite the front of the car. Roxie took the keys from the ignition and the Galaxie's engine ground to a rumbling halt. She dropped the keys in her tote bag, pulled the bag up on her lap, and began searching through its contents. She'd slid her sunglasses up over her forehead and her face had a pinched look of concentration. She made little noises of frustration. Whatever she was looking for, she was having a hard time finding it.

The sound of an approaching engine drew Rob's attention back the way they'd come. An old lime green Fiat turned into the Shell's parking lot and pulled up alongside the pump closest to the front of the store. An overweight guy of about forty heaved himself out of the car, took out his wallet, and inserted a debit or credit card in the pump's card slot. He punched in some numbers. His PIN, probably. So, a debit card. He stood there watching the digital display until the sale was approved. He then removed the pump handle from its cradle and inserted the nozzle in the Fiat's gas tank. He held the pump handle as he watched the digital numbers tick by.

"Not worth robbing."

Rob looked at Roxie, face drawing down into a frown.

"Do we really need to rob anybody? I mean . . . I've got money. A couple hundred in my wallet. A few thousand more in my bank account. You don't even have to shoot anybody to get it."

"Oh, I'll be taking all that. Count on it. I'm just saying, this fucking schmuck wouldn't be worth the bother anyway."

Despite himself, Rob was curious. "Yeah? Why?"

Roxie nodded in his direction. "Look at him. The way he's holding the pump handle and watching the numbers. This is a guy with overdraft concerns. A sad sack of shit just scraping by on a daily basis. Only reason I'd shoot that poor bastard would be to put him out of his misery."

Rob looked at the guy again, noting saggy, grime-encrusted jeans and a faded, raggedy T-shirt that looked like something retrieved from the reject bin at a Goodwill outlet. His face was unshaven and doughy. There was a wide, shiny bald circle at the crown of his skull, but the hair he did have was long and scraggly.

"Huh."

She was right. He wouldn't be worth robbing. He tucked this fact away in his mental file of Information I'll Fucking Never Need. Still, it was sort of interesting. She had a sharp eye for things an experienced criminal would know at a glance. Which made sense, what with her being exactly that.

"Aha!"

The exclamation drew his attention away from Mr. Downward Spiral. His brow knitted as he studied the slim, silver object pinched between the thumb and forefinger of her right hand. "Is that what I think it is?"

"Yes."

She unlocked the cuff attached to the steering wheel.

"You're letting me go?"

"Don't be an idiot."

"Right. That was stupid. What *is* happening?"

She nodded at the bathroom door. "We're going in there." She hoisted the tote bag. "I have to change into regular girl clothes. I can't very well go around dressed like this when I'm off on a spree, now can I?"

Rob shrugged. "I don't have a lot of experience in that area. I am not a 'spree' person. But that sounds . . . smart?"

"You don't sound sure."

Another shrug. "Like I said . . ."

"Yeah, yeah, lack of experience, et cetera. Look. Here's what's happening. Obviously I can't leave you out here while I'm changing. You're gonna get out. Do it nice and easy. Calmly. Like any regular dude getting out of his car to take a piss. Keep the open cuff tucked in your palm and don't look at the fat fuck at the pump. Walk straight to the bathroom with me. Got it?"

She was pointing the gun at him again.

Yeah, he got it.

He nodded.

"Good. Let's go."

She got out and stood at the side of the car, waiting for him, the gun tucked away in the tote bag, which she held in front of her. Rob got out and carefully kept his head turned away from the gas pumps as he followed her toward the bathroom. And though he was aware of how obscenely inappropriate it was in light of the monstrous thing she'd done not even an hour earlier, the prurient part of him couldn't help noting that she looked just as good from behind. The backs of her thighs and calves were shapely and toned, and her high-rise ass looked amazing framed by that little black skirt. Her walk was the effortless, seductive strut of a born sex kitten. The swivel of her hips made him think about things he had no business thinking of in light of the horrible thing she had done. When they reached the bathroom door, she glanced at him, a corner of her mouth quirking in a way that made it clear she knew exactly where his attention had been and exactly what he had been thinking. That smug surety made him at once angry and ashamed. This was an awful woman. A heartless killer. The knowledge of that alone should kill any flicker of lust looking at her might inspire.

But it didn't. Not quite.

And knowing that deepened the shame.

She opened the door and pushed him into a dark space. She followed him inside and flicked a switch, summoning light to swallow the darkness. Rob heard her push the door shut behind him and turn the lock. It hit him. He was alone in a closed space with a murderer. No one could see them. She could kill him now and no one could stop her. Hell, it would be the perfect time to do it. He heard something hit the floor and realized she'd dropped the tote bag.

Leaving just the gun in her hand.

He tensed, expecting to feel the press of a gun barrel against the back of his head any moment. He tried not to whimper. Tried to be brave.

He closed his eyes and waited for the end.

Then he felt something small and hard hammer the small of his back. He cried out and pitched forward, his knees painfully smacking the hard and filthy floor tiles. His eyes came open a moment before something—her open palm, he realized an instant later—struck the side of his head and drove him the rest of the way to the floor.

"Get under the sink."

Rob rolled onto his side and stared up at her through eyes misted with tears. "Jesus. You didn't have to hit me."

She kicked him in the shin and he cried out again.

"Do what I fucking told you before I lose my patience."

Rob got to his hands and knees and stared at the small porcelain sink. It was mounted against the wall to the left. A rust-corroded pipe protruded from the bottom of the sink and fed through a hole in the wall. Roxie kicked him again, in the ass this time, and he yelped. He hurriedly crawled under the sink and stared up at her again as she knelt in front of him. The dark sunglasses were up over her forehead, nestled in the raven black hair. She looked sexier than ever, down there on her haunches, so close to him now, the thrust of her breasts against the tight T-shirt more evident than ever. He stared into her eyes and felt the shame come back. This beautiful face . . . at this angle . . . It was probably exactly the way those poor fucks in the Neon had seen her in the final, unsuspecting moments of their lives. In his mind he saw the bright splash of red against the Neon's rear window. He started shaking again.

She smiled. "Scared?"

He swallowed. "Yeah."

She stared at him silently a moment, head at an angle, lips pursed as she studied him. Then she smiled again and said, "Good. I like that." She grabbed the open cuff and snapped it shut around the pipe. "You just hang out there while I get changed." She laughed. "Though I guess you don't have much choice, huh?"

Rob just stared at her.

Still smiling, she grabbed the tote bag and stood up. She turned away from him and leaned against the sink as she rummaged through the bag again. Rob stared at the backs of her legs and again tried not to think of . . . things. She hummed a tune as she dug through the bag, a jaunty melody he couldn't place. It sounded wrong coming from the likes of her.

The bathroom was small. There was a single stall without a door and a single urinal next to it. Mounted on the wall next to the door was a coin-operated condom dispenser, mostly the novelty type that were no good for actual contraception. He'd purchased some once as a gag gift for his ex-girlfriend. God. Charlene. What an amazing girl she'd been. That radiant smile. Her enthusiasm. What he'd give to see her now. Breaking up with her had been such a dick move.

And for what? To sow some wild oats? How stupid was that? He'd already had the perfect girl. So what if Lindsey—his best friend and roommate—loathed her?

If I ever get out of here—

The tote bag dropped to the floor again and Roxie moved away from the sink. She stood in the center of the room and began the process of shimmying out of her goth-slut outfit. First the T-shirt came off over her head. Charlene's image was vanquished in an instant. The black, frilly bra juxtaposed against the pale, smooth skin was a compelling sight to behold. The skirt came off next and she tossed it into the tote bag. She kicked her shoes off and leaned against the stall. She lifted one leg and began to peel off a striped sock. Slowly. Rob's gaze went to her face. She was looking right at him. And it hit him. She was doing this as much for effect as necessity. She rolled the sock up and tossed it in the bag. Then she repeated the same slow process with the other sock. Rob kept staring at her. He knew he should look away and not allow her to manipulate him this way, at least muster some small show of respect for the people she'd killed.

But he just couldn't do it.

She tossed the other sock in the bag. "See anything you like?"

She laughed.

And Rob yelped as something struck the other side of the bathroom door three times. A muffled voice called out: "Hurry up in there! I gotta piss like a Russian racehorse."

Roxie looked Rob in the eye. She didn't need to say anything, her intense expression communicating a command as clear as any verbal directive. "Just gimme a sec to finish up in here. I'm going as fast as I can. I'm having . . . uh . . . feminine issues."

A snort from the other side of the door. "Feminine issues, my ass. Fucking whore. I saw you go in there with that guy. It's against the law to have sex in public bathrooms, did you know that? Now get out of there and let me take a piss or I call the cops."

Roxie went to the door and drew it partially open. "Look, I'm taking care of some business in here. This guy's paying me good money to go off on his ass with some kinky shit." She opened the door wider, and a man Rob remembered as the dumpy dude from the gas pumps peeked in at him.

The man grinned and looked at Roxie. "No shit?"

Roxie smiled some more and posed seductively. "No shit. You'd be surprised at some of the twisted shit these bondage freaks are into. He's even paying me to verbally abuse him." Roxie glanced at Rob. "Isn't that right, you miserable piece of shit?"

Rob swallowed thickly and managed a weak nod.

The man laughed and licked his lips. "Takes all kinds, I guess. Look, I don't care what you people are up to, but I really do need to take a piss. Like, right now."

Roxie leaned forward slightly, thrusting her breasts at him. He looked, of course. "So come in and take a fucking piss." She laughed softly. "Maybe you'd like to join in."

The guy stared at her tits. He stroked his chin. You could see he really wanted a piece of this action. "I . . . well, that sounds fucking awesome, but . . . I'm kind of . . . cash poor at the moment."

"Oh, that's okay."

Roxie grabbed him by a wrist and tugged him into the bathroom. She closed the door and locked it again. She wrapped her arms around the man's neck and writhed against him, eliciting a tortured moan. "Baby, you're so fucking sexy. I feel like giving you a freebie."

The man's face turned red. "Holy shit. Are you for real?"

She giggled. "You've never met anybody more real than me, baby."

She broke the embrace and pushed him into the stall, maneuvering him into a sitting position on the toilet. Rob's heart began to pound. He didn't know what Roxie had in mind, but it couldn't be anything good. And he was pretty certain she wasn't about to fuck this guy. Curiosity made him push away from the wall and scoot out as far as his cuffed hand would allow. He was able to get a pretty good view of Roxie standing over the guy.

The man stared up at her in rapt amazement and adoration, apparently having forgotten that he needed to piss like a Russian racehorse. Whatever that meant. Roxie leaned over him, bracing her hands on the toilet tank lid as she dangled her breasts in his face. She giggled again. "Close your eyes, baby, and I'll give you a big surprise."

The man's whole body shuddered. "Holy shit. It's my lucky day."

Rob grimaced.

No, dude, it really isn't.

The man closed his eyes.

And Rob saw Roxie's fingers curl tight around the edges of the tank lid. She lifted the lid off the tank and held it high over her head. The man's eyes came open and he stared up at her in confused astonishment. A guttural, animal sound ripped out of Roxie's throat as she slammed the lid down on top of the man's head. The heavy wedge of white porcelain went up again and came down again. Over and over. Until Rob heard a sound that reminded him of an eggshell cracking. But it didn't end then. She kept hitting him with the thing. He had no concept of how long it went on. He vomited on the floor, heaving violently for several minutes before retreating to his previous position under the sink. He closed his eyes and tried to will the world away. He felt clammy and sick. Some time passed and he became aware that the sounds of violence had ended.

He opened his eyes and saw Roxie staring down at him, face impassive. She was dressed in tight jeans, white sneakers, and a plain blue T-shirt.

"It's time to go."

Rob sniffled. "O-o-o-o—"

"Shut up."

Rob closed his mouth.

Roxie uncuffed him and they departed the scene of yet another murder. Within moments they were back on the interstate. The road unfurled endlessly toward the hazy horizon. But Rob no longer saw the open road as a place of charm and limitless possibilities. The path ahead of him was a devil's highway to nothing but doom and damnation.

CHAPTER NINE

March 17

A car loaded with teenage boys drove by Julie Cosgrove as she walked down the narrow residential road. One boy leaned out a rear window and made a rude comment. Julie's thumbs moved rapidly over the buttons of her cell phone as she entered a response to a text from Alicia, her best friend. She heard laughter from the boys in the car, but barely perceived it. They weren't worth her attention. She didn't bother flipping them off either, as that would only reward their obnoxious behavior. Balding tires screeched on asphalt and the car zipped away.

Julie rolled her eyes.

Boys.

They were so stupid. Oh, she liked them on a physical level, but she couldn't stand how immature most boys her age were. These losers, for instance, with this half-assed drive-by come-on. Too chickenshit to get any closer or deal with her on a face-to-face level. She smirked, knowing how they would blush and mumble if forced to spend more than two consecutive seconds in her presence.

She hit a button to send the text and snapped her phone shut. Seeing she was only a block away from the house owned by John and Karen Lee, she picked up her pace. It was a little after three in the afternoon. Karen usually didn't get home from her bank job until around four. But John was a CPA and often worked from home. She saw his car in the driveway, a black BMW. She felt a little flutter in her stomach at the sight of it. She knew John had a thing for her. He was always trying to look at her when he thought she wasn't watching. It was cute how innocent he tried to act when she caught him in the act.

She'd been thinking of him a lot just recently. A man his age would know how to treat a woman right. He wouldn't always be making crude cracks or laughing like an idiot at his own jokes, like most of the boys she knew. And John was pretty fucking hot for an old guy. Julie sometimes wondered what it might be like to kiss him. The thought made her feel naughty. It was "inappropriate," as her mother would say. But the hell with her. Julie smiled. Truth was, she had all kinds of naughty ideas about all kinds of things running through her head all the time. Things that would absolutely horrify her mother. It was a good thing the woman barely knew how to turn on or operate a computer. Her laptop was full of things that would cause a snooping parent to freak the fuck out.

She couldn't wait to see his eyes get big when he got a look at her sexy body in very short denim cutoffs and tiny halter top. He would struggle not to look at her tits and fail. The only guys who could avoid checking out her tits for long were the gay ones. And sometimes even they stared. She would ask for last week's babysitting money and he would invite her inside, maybe offer her a cool drink while he counted the cash from his wallet. And he would joke with her, flirt with her in that goofy old-guy way, like he had at little Nancy's birthday party the week before. Only this time Julie thought she might respond with some suggestive comments of her own, and, well . . .

She smiled.

We'll just see how things go from there.

But the smile dropped from her face as she spied the blue

Mini Cooper parked on the other side of the BMW. Karen's car. So the bitch was home early from her stupid job. Julie had a quick fantasy of punching the older woman in the face.

Her phone vibrated and she flipped it open to see a new text from Alicia. *U cant be serious, he's like a thousand yrs older than u.*

Julie sent a quick text back. *I know. Shut up.*

She turned the phone off and flipped it shut again.

She crossed the Lees' immaculately tended lawn and climbed the front porch steps to ring the doorbell. A little chime sounded inside and she heard a male voice say something indistinct. That had to be John. She hoped he would come to the door instead of Karen. She badly wanted to see that lustful look in his eyes. That would be enough to sustain her until her next shot at having some time alone with him. While she waited, she pondered again the question of how far she might let John go when that finally happened. She wanted to kiss him. God, yes. But would he be satisfied with that? He might think she was just a tease.

But maybe—

The doorknob started to turn and she quickly summoned her brightest smile, hoping to really dazzle him. Her first hint something was wrong was the stink that assailed her nostrils as the door began to open. When it was fully open, her face paled at the grinning nightmare standing before her.

A man with wild, filthy hair sticking out in all directions stood naked before her. His eyes looked wild, too, like the eyes of a feral animal. He was so scrawny, like a flesh and blood stick figure, but there were hard muscles under the stretched-taut skin. A substance that might have been dried blood was matted in his chest hair. And as Julie watched, his limp penis started to rise.

Instinct drove her back a step, but he seized her by a wrist and yanked her inside the house. He slammed the door shut and dragged her screaming into the living room.

He snarled at her. "Shut up, bitch!"

He backhanded her and she went stumbling backward. Her feet got tangled and she fell. The glass top of a coffee table shattered beneath her as she landed on it. Shards of glass cut her and drew blood. She screamed as her assailant seized her slender throat with one strong hand and lifted her up again. She felt his penis leap against her and tried to scream again, but the hand clamped to her throat limited her to a barely audible gurgle. The man laughed and licked her face with a tongue that felt dry as sandpaper. The feel of it on her flesh made her insides curdle.

He sucked on her lower lip and breathed into her mouth. His stink made her eyes water. Bile rose into her throat and she wondered if she would choke on it—the man's iron grip allowed only a very thin air passage. He pressed himself against her and said, "Gonna fuck ya now, sweet thing."

The tip of his engorged penis poked through a rip in her torn halter. The feel of it sliding over her flesh repulsed her. But even through her terror, Julie saw how she might have a slim shot at extracting herself from this nightmare. He was so intent on sampling various parts of her anatomy—his free hand ripping the halter to pieces to paw at her breasts—that he had neglected to fully restrain her. Or maybe it wasn't neglect. Maybe he didn't consider her a threat. Or thought she'd be too terrified to fight back.

Think again, you freak.

Her right hand came up and long fingernails jabbed into an eyeball. He howled in agony and let go of her. Julie staggered backward and struggled to catch her breath as she watched the man flail about with a hand pressed over the wounded orb. Blood streamed between his fingers. He stopped thrashing long enough to look at her with his one good eye and screamed at her, "YOU'RE GONNA DIE FOR THAT, BITCH!"

He started to come at her again, but screeched as a piece of broken glass pierced the bottom of his foot. Julie took a quick look around while the crazy man hopped about and mewled like a baby. The living room was outfitted in the standard way. Large entertainment center. A long sofa and a couple of recliners. And a large liquor cabinet with an impressive array of bartending tools arranged in a rack above it.

Yes!

Julie grabbed a corkscrew, flexed the handles to extend the screw to its full length, and charged her attacker. The man was sitting on the edge of a recliner as he worked to pull glass shards from his bleeding foot. He looked up and saw her coming, but not in time to retreat or ward off the attack. The fear evident in his remaining eye as it widened was gratifying. The corkscrew slammed into his temple and his body began to convulse. Julie yanked the screw out and plunged it into his other eye. Now the eyes sort of matched again—pierced and bleeding. The thought made her giggle inappropriately even as a new wave of sickness rose up inside her. She pulled the corkscrew out of his eye. She stared at his throat, watched the slowing pulse ticking beneath the flesh.

There, she thought. *That's where the carotid is.*

The corkscrew slammed into the man's throat and there was another leap of blood. Julie was covered in it now. Her own and that of the man who'd tried to rape her. She giggled again. *We're all the same on the inside.*

Julie stabbed him with the corkscrew several more times. She kept doing it even after she knew he was dead. There was a strange sort of fascination to watching the instrument puncture flesh. It was sort of the way she felt when pulling the petals off a flower, ruining it a little bit at a time. And the *really* weird thing was how little any of this bothered her now that he was no longer a threat. It was actually sort of fun, the way she'd always imagined it might be. But she did finally tire of stabbing the corpse and climbed off it.

She stood panting in the center of the living room, wondering what she should do next. Call 911. Obviously. But something made her hesitate. The man she'd killed was clearly an uninvited guest here. The thought made her laugh. Like, no shit, right? Like John and Karen would have this freak over for dinner or whatever. No, he was an intruder. He'd probably killed the whole family. And their bodies were somewhere else in the house. It was this thought that kept her hand from going to the cell phone in her pocket.

She wanted to *see*.

Yeah, it kind of sucked that John was probably dead. She could never kiss him now. Or fuck him. She could admit it now. That would have been the ultimate goal. But now she was just as hot to see his corpse. She had a vast collection of crime-scene and autopsy photos stored on her laptop. And here fate had dumped her into a situation where she had an opportunity to make a prolonged inspection of the real thing. It was a chance she simply couldn't pass up. And hell, the cops would never know she'd lingered over the scene a while.

She crept out of the living room and into a long hallway she knew led to the bedrooms. There was probably no real reason for stealth at this point, but she couldn't be certain everyone in the house was actually dead yet, so she moved forward with caution. About halfway down the hallway, she began to hear a sound she identified at once as the squeak of bedsprings, that rhythmic motion associated with intercourse. The sound was coming from the master bedroom at the end of the hall. She moved a little closer and was able to hear a series of muted grunts. The bedroom door was partly open. She could see a corner of the bed. She pressed her back against the wall to her right and edged carefully down the remaining length of hallway. After reaching the bedroom, she peered around the doorjamb and reeled at the horrific scene.

John's head was on the floor. His headless body sat slumped in a chair against the far wall. His legs were spread and she could see a gaping, bloody hole where his genitals had been. Nancy was on the floor. She had been gutted. Her abdomen was a bloody, ragged mess. A length of intestine was coiled about her slender neck. There were several large, dark splotches on the beige carpet that could only be blood.

Karen was on the bed, legs spread wide as the big man on top of her continued to grind away and make those grunting noises. Karen's legs were long and sleek. Julie noted with some surprise a pretty butterfly tattoo on her right foot. But the muscles in those shapely legs looked strangely slack for someone having sex. Then awareness of what was actually happening on the bed seeped in and Julie reached into her pocket to pull out her cell phone. She flipped it open and stared at a black screen.

Fuck.

She'd forgotten about turning it off after responding to the text from Alicia. If she turned it on now, that stupid chiming tone it made would alert the powerfully built necrophiliac to her presence. And then he'd kill her, of course. She had no illusions of handling this man as easily as she'd handled the other one. He'd just take the corkscrew from her and jam it up her ass. Or some other orifice. Her stomach knotted at the thought. The smart thing here would be to scoot back down the hallway and get the hell out of the house. But she desperately wanted a picture of the atrocity occurring on the bed. It would be the crown jewel of her morbid photo collection. She could maybe hurry down to the kitchen, turn the phone on there, and hurry back. But no, judging by the increasingly frenzied nature of the man's grunts, it would all be over by then.

She thought, *This is the single stupidest thing I have ever done or ever will do, the end, no doubt about it at fucking all.*

She pressed the phone's power button. Then she clasped both hands tightly around the phone and pressed it to her chest. The hope was to muffle the electronic chimes enough that the man wouldn't hear them. But of course, the sound came through clear as a bell.

The man paused in midthrust and looked over his shoulder at Julie, who stood framed and vulnerable in the open doorway. His hair was long and white, and fine, like the hair of a hermit in a fairy tale. Only this hermit was built like a lumberjack on steroids. His nostrils flared and his lips curled in a snarl. His pitiless eyes conveyed a promise of pain and savagery. He climbed off the corpse and Julie saw Karen's head lolling on the pillow, mouth slack, eyes still and staring at nothing.

The man grinned.

Then he charged her.

Julie screamed and bolted back down the hallway. She flew through the living room and made it as far as the foyer before the big man caught up to her. He grabbed her by the hair and jerked her to a stop, eliciting another scream. Then he slammed her to the floor and fell atop her. He pressed a powerful forearm against her throat and pawed at the remains of her shredded halter with his free hand. She couldn't move. Couldn't get her hands free to jab at his eyes. She felt his erection swell against her and knew there'd be no stopping the rape this time. She cursed her stupidity. She'd been dumb not to get out when she had the chance. Obviously. And she cursed her morbid nature. The two things seemed inextricably tied at the moment.

The man abruptly stopped groping her. The pressure on

her throat eased and Julie coughed and spluttered. The man's face was turned away from her. Shock etched itself across his features, deepening the age lines and making his face resemble a Halloween ghoul mask.

He looked down at her again. "You killed my friend."

Julie coughed again and cleared her throat. "I didn't have a choice. Look, you don't have to force me to do anything. I'll do whatever you want. I'm sorry about your friend."

The man's teeth were clenched tight. His whole body shook with rage. He closed a hand around her throat and began to squeeze. "You fucking whore. Fucking little slut. *You killed my only friend!*"

A detached part of Julie's mind marveled over the absurdity of a man as depraved as this stone psycho feeling grief for the loss of anyone. But the emotion did appear genuine. His eyes watered. A thin stream of moisture began to move down one cheek. The pressure on her throat increased and Julie's vision began to blur. Realizing she was likely in her last moments of life, she thought maybe she ought to ask God for forgiveness. She had allowed a number of evil and wicked thoughts and ideas to live and breathe inside her brain. Surely God would frown on that. But before she could begin to consciously form her plea, the pressure on her throat eased up again. She blinked moisture from her eyes and stared up at the curious sight of a man listening to something only he could hear.

His head was tilted to one side and his brow was furrowed. He stared up at the ceiling. He shook his head and said, "No. It's not right."

Julie frowned.

What the fuck?

The man shook his head again. "No. She killed Clyde." His mouth twisted in a scowl. "I know. I always listen to you, Lulu. But this cunt has to die."

Lulu?

Julie almost laughed. This deranged, sick fuck was hearing voices. Voices telling him not to kill her.

Hooray for mental illness!

The man's shoulders sagged. "All right. Yes. Okay."

Julie summoned a smile. "It really is okay. You'll see. I'll—"

She didn't get to finish the thought.

The man cocked a fist and slammed it into the side of her head, turning out the lights for a while.

CHAPTER TEN

March 22

Chuck needed some time away from Zoe. She was giving off a weird, standoffish vibe. That coldness was nothing new. It'd been going on for months, but had become worse recently. She didn't always refuse his advances, but getting her to shed her clothes took a lot more work than it once had. And it was getting to be pretty goddamn frustrating. It didn't take a genius to see where things were going. They were almost over. It bummed him out. They had been together a long time. It wasn't the end of the world, he guessed. He was young and good-looking. There would be other girls. Hotter girls, even. The idea of exploring all that fresh meat once he and Zoe were finally, really through had its appeal.

Still.

Here they were. Probably on their last vacation together. They should be having one last good fling, along with a lot of wild vacation sex. He couldn't help thinking of Christmas break at his parents' house. Zoe had been insatiable that week. The frequency. All those different positions. The crazy experimenting. Hard to believe that was only a few short months back. Now he was lucky if she let him fuck her once a week. He'd probably been stupid to hope she would knock off the frigid routine for vacation.

He knocked on the bathroom door. "Hey, babe. I need some fresh air. I'll be back in a bit."

A muffled voice answered from the other side. "All right."

The monotone reply made him linger at the door a moment longer before departing. He wondered how she would have sounded if he'd said, "Hey, babe, I'm going outside to step in front of a bus."

Would he hear that same dead voice say "all right" to that as well?

He thought he would.

Fuck.

This was crazy. The situation was starting to get to him. He felt like he was on the verge of a genuine depressive episode, which was way unlike him. His eyes misted a bit. He knew he had to get out of there before he had some kind of embarrassing breakdown. He left the motel room without another word, barely resisting the impulse to slam the door on the way out.

Damn her, anyway.

He wanted to be all macho about this. All blustery and don't-give-a-shit, the way he was with everything else. But that was turning out to be harder than he'd imagined.

His thoughts turned back to earlier in the day and that incident with the goth chick. He'd given her a hard time for no good reason. Oh, he sort of half-believed the bullshit explanation he'd spewed earlier, but the real truth was more pathetic. The girl was just a victim of his frustrations. He was upset about the way things were going with Zoe and so he'd vented some of his anger on a stranger. The girl had just been unlucky enough to line up in his sights at exactly the wrong time. Thinking about it now, he felt bad.

Sorry, whoever you were.

He lit a cigarette and leaned against the second-floor-balcony railing. The rental van was parked directly below. A neon VACANCY light blinked and fizzed at the other end of the motel's half-full parking lot. The original plan had been to make the trip to Myrtle Beach in one long day of driving. But there'd been too much fucking around and drinking going on for that to happen. The numerous lengthy pit stops to drain overinflated bladders hadn't helped matters. Chuck was a little bummed about not being able to wake up in Myrtle Beach the next morning, but in truth he was grateful for the opportunity to get off the road. He was looking forward to a good night's rest. Hell, who knew? Maybe a fresh sunrise would wash away all the bad feelings of the day and allow for a fresh start. Probably not, but a guy could hope.

He stubbed the cigarette out and flicked the butt over the side. Just as he was turning away from the railing to go back inside, a door to his left opened and Emily Sinclair stepped outside. She saw him and smiled. That was a little odd. She didn't spare a smile for him too often. Never, in fact. She left the door to her room partly open and joined him at the railing.

She tapped the cigarette pack in his hand with a glossy nail. "Give me one of those."

Chuck laughed. "Well, as long as you're asking nicely . . ."

He passed the pack to her. She tapped a cigarette out and placed it between her plump lips.

She stared at him.

Chuck laughed again and lit her cigarette. She turned her head slightly and blew a stream of smoke just past his face. She smiled again. "Thanks."

"No problem."

Chuck leaned against the railing again. No point going back inside now. Zoe was probably still in the bathroom, hiding away from him. And Emily was actually being sort of friendly toward him, an extremely rare thing. As long as she didn't mind his company, he would stay out here.

Emily leaned over the railing and stared in the direction of the malfunctioning neon sign. "So . . . Chuck?"

He glanced at her. "Yeah?"

She exhaled more smoke and still didn't look at him. "Wanna fuck me?"

Chuck's jaw dropped open. He turned fully toward her and stared at her in astonished silence for several moments. If she'd suggested he join her in a conspiracy to assassinate the president, he would not have felt this flabbergasted. After a while, he managed a nervous laugh. "You're fucking with me. Right?"

She smiled, but still didn't look at him. "Nope."

He frowned. "But . . . you're Zoe's best friend."

"That's right."

His frown deepened. "What kind of friend comes on to her best friend's boyfriend?"

Emily dropped the half-smoked cigarette and extinguished it with the tip of a high-heeled shoe. "The horny kind, Chuck."

"This is crazy. What about Joe?"

Emily indicated the partly open door behind her with a jerk of her head. "Take a look in there. But be quiet about it."

Still frowning, Chuck stepped past her and peered through the small opening. Joe was on the bed. He was naked. His wrists were tied to the brass headboard. He was blindfolded. A pair of red panties had been stuffed into his mouth as a gag. Loud snoring indicated unconsciousness, which wasn't surprising given the amount of beer the guy had consumed. Chuck's pulse ticked upward and his face reddened. Seeing his best friend like this was embarrassing as hell. He became aware of a presence behind him and gasped when Emily pressed herself against him and reached around to grab his crotch. The erection was immediate and painful. She squeezed it through his jeans and gave it a hard twist, eliciting another gasp.

Her breath was hot against his ear as she whispered, "Get your keys and meet me down at the van."

Then she was gone. Chuck turned away from the door and stared after her retreating form. She cut an amazing figure in that tight black dress, with curves much more pronounced than Zoe's. She started down the stairs to the first floor, disappearing from view within seconds.

Chuck stared at the empty space where she'd been a moment longer.

I shouldn't do this. It's not right.

But then he thought about Zoe and how cold she had become. It'd been more than a week now since they'd last had sex. Hell, wasn't it possible they'd already fucked for the last time?

He thought about Emily.

That killer figure.

Those long, long legs . . .

He went back into his room and retrieved his keys from the nightstand. Zoe was still locked away in the bathroom. If she'd been waiting for him in bed, his ultimate decision might have been different. He loved Zoe. He wanted to fix things between them. But he knew it wasn't happening.

So he went downstairs.

Emily was leaning against the van. She looked up and smiled as he approached. "When you're inside me, think about how much it'd hurt Zoe to know about this."

Chuck grabbed her and kissed her. She hooked a leg around him and they writhed against the van for several moments. She felt so good. So alive. So *hot*. He whimpered as she reached into his jeans and seized his erection. At last they broke the embrace and Chuck fumbled with the keys. The electronic lock beeped and he threw the side door open. Emily climbed into the van's dark interior and shoved the seat back to make room. Chuck followed her inside. Emily was already tugging his pants down as he slid the door shut. He peeled his shirt off and fell atop her. The clingy black dress came off after she rolled him over and straddled him. She wasn't wearing panties. Of course not.

Then he was inside her and groaning.

And he did what she said.

He thought of Zoe.

The experience was agony and ecstasy intermingled and overlapping, and it ended with Chuck crying as Emily held him and laughed softly.

CHAPTER ELEVEN

March 22

They stopped for the night shortly after crossing the state line into North Carolina. Rob was pretty sick of driving by then, but the relief he felt at the prospect of being off the road was tempered by a deep anxiety over what she had in mind for him now that this leg of the journey was done. He had watched her kill five people. He had no illusions. He was nothing to her. Just one more corpse-in-waiting. Roxie was remorseless and ruthless. A monster hiding in a pretty girl's skin.

After leaving the interstate, they stopped at an ATM first to drain some money from Rob's checking account. Roxie pocketed the thick wad of twenties and directed Rob to a motel a mile down the road from the ATM.

They pulled up at the curb outside the lobby. The Weaver Inn was a dump. Rob didn't need to see inside the rooms to know that. The poorly tended grounds were evidence enough, as was the building's grubby exterior. The nearly empty parking lot was another strong indicator. The place was *seedy*.

Roxie took the key from the ignition. "Sit tight and keep your mouth shut. I'll have an eye on you the whole time. Anybody tries to talk to you, you don't respond. Let them think you're a rude asshole. You listening to me, Robin?"

That again.

The bratty little insult. The intent was to emasculate

him. That was a joke. Hadn't she already thoroughly un-manned him? Now she was just being a bitch and rubbing it in. He felt a little flare of anger, but it fizzled quickly. He was no match for her on any level. Taking the bait would only get him in a world of hurt.

He forced a nod. "I'm listening."

"Good. Hey, Robin?"

"Yeah?"

"Fucking up isn't an option. Draw attention to yourself, try anything dumb, and I start killing every motherfucker in sight. And that definitely includes you. Okay?"

What else could he say? He shrugged. "Okay."

Roxie got out of the Galaxie and kicked the door shut. The male desk clerk's gaze was riveted to her from the moment she stepped out of the car. He was a young guy. Barely more than a teenager. Like Roxie. His mouth hung open as he watched her push one of the glass lobby doors open and strut right up to the desk. Even though she'd traded her goth goddess outfit for more subdued garb, she was still sexy as hell. But it was a dangerous kind of sexy. The swivel of her hips in those tight jeans. The way the equally tight, low-scooped T-shirt emphasized her jutting breasts. It was a lethal package, the kind that renders most guys instantly helpless, rendering them vulnerable to just about any level of temptation. The kind that made happily married men break wedding vows without a second thought. The kind that would make some men willing to die for her. Or even kill for her.

But not me, Rob thought. *I'm a more or less normal guy caught up in something I can't control. I'm many things, but I am not a killer. There's a limit to what I'll endure or do for this girl.*

Roxie leaned precariously over the desk, presenting her breasts in a way that ensured the clerk's attention was on nothing else. She laughed at something he said and her breasts jiggled. The poor desk clerk looked like he might faint. The kid wiped sweat from his brow and gave Roxie something to sign. Roxie signed and peeled some twenties from the wad of Rob's money. The kid took the money but didn't bother to count it—he was too entranced by the sight of Roxie's round behind as she strutted back out of the lobby.

"You made that kid's day with your sex-kitten routine," Rob said when she was back in the car.

Roxie pulled the door shut. "I know. We're in room one nineteen, down at the end."

She put the key in the ignition and gave it a twist. The engine came vibrantly to life, filling the lonely patch of rural night with its throaty roar. Rob put the car in gear and drove down to the far end of the lot, pulling into a space directly in front of room 119. Roxie took the key from the ignition again and dropped it in her bag. She then dug another key out of a pocket and unlocked the handcuffs. The handcuffs also went in the bag. Rob groaned and rubbed his aching right wrist.

Roxie smiled. "Oh . . . was that too tight? Did I hurt you, Robin?"

Rob didn't say anything. He stopped rubbing his wrist and stared at the door to 119. They'd be inside the room within moments. He took a look around, checking out the withered shrubs lining the sidewalk, the sliver of moon visible in the clear night sky above him, and the wavy outlines of dark trees in the distance. It was possible these things constituted his last glimpse of the natural world. The motel room's interior could well be the last thing he ever saw. Not a terribly inspiring possible final vision. He didn't want to get out of the car.

Roxie said, "Get out of the car. Now."

His hand went to the door handle ahead of any conscious thought. Then he thought of something. "Oh, wait."

He pushed a button inset in the dash just below the steering wheel, triggering a grinding, ratcheting sound that made Roxie gasp in surprise. But she relaxed when she saw the car's top unfold from the back and stretch out above them. The top thunked down. Rob pulled it into place and secured the corner on his side with a latch. They got out of the car after Roxie fastened the latch on her side.

Rob took one last wistful look around and followed Roxie across the sidewalk. She unlocked the door to room 119 with an old-fashioned metal key, the Weaver Inn apparently being too poor to invest in electronic-card lock technology. Rob followed her into a cramped space furnished with a single queen-size bed, a recliner, a small table, and two rickety chairs.

Roxie closed and locked the door. She set her bag on the table and looked at Rob. "Get on the bed. Lie flat on your back."

Rob's breathing quickened. "Wh-what . . . ? I don't—"

She came at him fast, too fast to react, slamming a fist into his solar plexus. It was a devastatingly hard blow, her strength and fury stunning him again. In the instant before he toppled backward, he saw her eyes and got a look at that same wild expression he'd glimpsed as she'd bludgeoned that guy to death in the gas station bathroom.

This is it. I'm about to die.

Then his back hit the mattress and he bounced. The bed squeaked and the brass headboard thumped against the wall. Roxie moved to the side of the bed and stared down at him. "What have I told you about not doing what I say?"

Rob grimaced as another knot of pain formed in his gut. He groaned and writhed slightly. "Oh, God. That fucking hurts. I learned my lesson. Swear to fucking God."

She smirked. "Good."

She grabbed one of the chairs from the table and set it on

the floor next to the bed. She straddled the chair and wrapped her arms around the back of it. "We've got some things to talk about."

Rob groaned again and looked at her. "Yeah?"

Roxie smiled. "I'm gonna ask you some questions. I expect absolute truthfulness. Remember what I told you earlier. I hate liars. Here's a fact. I can tell when people are lying. I am never fucking wrong. I'll hurt you every time you lie to me. Lie enough and I'll fucking kill you. Clear?"

Rob let out a big breath. The pain in his gut was beginning to recede. "Crystal. I'm all out of fight, I promise."

She laughed. "Really? Oh, by fight, do you mean that tendency to run your mouth you had before I put you in your place?"

"Yeah. That."

Another laugh, *very* amused this time. "Okay. First question. You've been gone all day. Who's gonna miss you first? Look me in the eye when you answer."

Rob looked at her. He cleared his throat and spoke in a calm, measured tone. "My roommate. Lindsey."

Roxie arched a brow. "Your roommate's a girl?"

"Yeah."

"And she's just a roommate. Not your girlfriend?"

Rob shook his head. "No."

"You've never fucked her? Not even once?"

Another shake of his head. "No."

Roxie frowned. "Why not? Is she ugly?"

"No. She's very cute."

"Are you fucking gay?"

"No."

"Then what's the deal? Something doesn't add up."

Rob shrugged. "I just . . . well, we've known each other forever. Since we were kids. We've just always been great friends. I like being friends with her. I'd hate to ruin it by . . . well, you know."

Roxie made a face. "Does she have a boyfriend?"

"No."

"You're an idiot."

Rob didn't say anything.

Roxie's look of disgust deepened. "Jesus. You fucking moron. Anyway. I'm gonna need you to call her. Think you can come up with a good cover story for your absence?"

"Probably."

"Good. We'll take care of that in a few minutes. Next question. I assume you have a job. Did I cause you to miss going in, or were you off today?"

Rob opened his mouth to reply, but hesitated a beat. Roxie noticed it. Her eyes sharpened. He saw her muscles tense and knew she was on the brink of another violent explosion. He quickly decided against the lie he'd briefly considered telling. "I was off today. I work tomorrow. It's my uncle's company. If I don't call him with some excuse, he'll worry. He's the closest thing I've got to a parent these days. So he's pretty lax with me, far as the job goes. I could tell him I decided to take off for a bit and he'd probably buy it."

Roxie unclasped her hands and drummed her fingers lightly against the back of the chair. "Hmm. Okay. So you'll call him, too. Tell him something believable. Something to buy us enough time to change cars and get farther down the road."

Change cars?

Rob was bewildered.

His car was the whole reason he was on the road with her in the first place. He could see her wanting to ditch the Galaxie. It was too conspicuous. But wouldn't that mean his usefulness to her was over? Maybe not. Because it sounded like she meant to keep him around a while. He couldn't figure it out. To what end?

Or maybe, he thought, *she just put it that way to put my mind at ease while she figures out her next move.*

She opened her mouth to ask another question, but a

tentative knock at the door caused her head to snap around. "Who is it?"

There was the muffled sound of a throat clearing. "Uh . . . it's, um . . . me."

Rob didn't recognize the voice. He frowned. "Come on, you're not really expecting anyone out here in the middle of nowhere, are you?"

"Shut up."

Roxie got up and went to the door. She peered through the peephole and grinned. She glanced back at Rob. "It's party time."

She opened the door and Rob saw the awkward, lanky desk clerk standing there. Roxie seized him by a wrist and pulled him inside. She threw the door shut and pushed the boy toward the bed.

"Hey, honey . . ."

Rob guessed he was "honey."

So fucking weird.

What's going on?

"This is Billy. He works here. I told him he could party with us tonight. You don't mind, do you?"

Rob had no idea what to say. Not a clue what her expectations were. "Um . . . yeah. Whatever. I guess."

Billy wasn't paying any attention to him. He was too busy ogling Roxie's tits. "Yeah . . . uh, I called this guy, Earl. He works here, too. Days. He came in to cover my shift. But I didn't mention you, like you said. Told him my brother was in the hospital." He forced himself to look at her face. "So I'm now free to, uh . . . party."

Roxie beamed at him. "That's so awesome!"

Billy grinned back. "Hell, yeah."

His gaze went helplessly back to her tits.

So of course he never saw it coming.

Roxie punched him in the throat and he crumpled to the floor, gagging as he curled into a ball.

Rob sat up. "Jesus, not again. Don't kill him!"

Roxie glanced at him. "Sit back like a good little bitch and watch the show. Unless you want this to be you." Her smile was broad, a gleaming display of perfectly aligned white teeth with only the faintest hint of nicotine staining. "Is that what you want?"

The boy on the floor was crying softly.

Rob looked at him.

Then looked at Roxie—and saw the deadly eagerness in her eyes.

His shoulders sagged.

Roxie laughed. "That's what I thought."

She went to the table and took something from her bag. Rob saw what it was and squeezed his eyes shut. He did not want to see this. Not one bit of it. He'd seen enough terrible things today.

"Watch."

A command. Disobedience was not an option.

He opened his eyes.

Watched.

And felt another indelible stain form on his soul.

CHAPTER TWELVE

March 17

The first thing she was aware of as she returned to consciousness was pain. Her head hurt and her jaw throbbed. One of her teeth felt loose. She probed it with her tongue and whimpered at the fresh jolt of agony this triggered. Her eyelids fluttered and she saw the hazy form of a man looming in front of her. She squeezed her eyes shut, opened them again, and the image crystallized.

It was *him*.

Her mouth opened wide.

"Scream and the lights go out again." He cocked a fist and moved a step closer. "Maybe forever."

Julie closed her mouth.

And in the next moment she became aware of several other things. It had all really happened. John, Karen, and Nancy Lee were all dead. She had killed a man, this psycho's partner. And now here she was. Naked. Tied to a chair. She flexed her wrists, testing the bonds. Electrical cords or cables, felt like. He'd cinched them painfully tight, making the flesh bulge at her wrists and ankles.

She scowled at him. "Why am I naked?"

"I wanted to look at you."

"Perv. Did you rape me?"

The big man smirked. "You'd know if I had."

Julie's face crinkled in disgust. "Gross. So you didn't . . . right?"

The man shook his head. "I wanted to, but Lulu forbade it."

"Who the fuck is Lulu?"

"You wouldn't understand." His smile was bitter, devoid of humor. "But she's the reason I haven't shoved a knife up your cunt."

Julie gulped.

Yay, Lulu.

"Where is she? I want to talk to her."

The man stared at her and didn't say anything. He was still naked. His body was covered in dried blood. He was well into middle age, a fact betrayed by the gray hair and the deep lines in his face, but his physique was impressive. Thick musculature just about everywhere, but with a small bit of flab through the middle. She studied his face and decided it might have been sort of handsome twenty years ago, with that square jaw and those piercing eyes. But now he was old. He was one of those hard-living scumbags who looked old before his time. He had a destined-to-die-on-skid-row-in-a-puddle-of-piss kind of vibe. And he was a fucking pervert. He was licking his chapped lips and looking her up and down, his cock stiffening as he scrutinized her.

"You want me to suck that for you?"

Please say yes, you fucking freak. I'll bite that nasty thing clean off.

His nostrils flared. "You know I do. But Lulu won't allow it"

"Yeah. And speaking of her . . . you didn't answer my question. Where is she?"

"Ya can't see her."

Julie stared at his swollen cock. The guy was jerking it right in front of her. She didn't want to stare, but it sort of compelled the eye. It was huge. "Why not?"

"You just can't, that's all!"

Julie sighed. "Okay. Fine. Whatever. You're in charge here." She smiled and looked him in the eye. "Look, you can tell her I said it was okay. I wanna do it. Or if she's not around, we just won't tell her. It'll be our little secret. What do you think?"

He grunted. "Hold on. Can't think straight. Be right back."

He trotted out of the living room, disappearing down the hallway that led to the bedrooms. Soon she heard the faint squeak of bedsprings again and her stomach fluttered. He was giving Karen's corpse another bounce.

What a sick fuck!

Of course, she was the one who'd wanted to snap a picture of him performing this very act, so who was the sick one here?

He returned some ten minutes later. This time he was no longer completely nude, wearing a clean pair of briefs probably swiped from John's dresser. No way this piece of human garbage owned anything remotely clean. It was almost sort of funny. He was too much a prisoner of his twisted sexual appetites to think clearly. So he'd banged one out and put something on to take his dick out of the equation.

"So why doesn't Lulu want you to do anything to me?"

"She says you're . . ." His lips curled in his hesitation, making his distaste for the next word clear. ". . . special."

Julie stifled a laugh. This guy was insane. That was a given. Clearly this "Lulu" existed only in his head. But the asshole just as clearly believed she was real. Which was good. Because Lulu was on her side. God knows why. But maybe it was something she could exploit.

Julie smiled. "She's right. You should listen to her."

"I always listen to her. That's why you're not dead, bitch."

Julie's expression sharpened. "Don't call me that. You think Lulu would like that? She said I'm special. Well, treat me like I am."

The man frowned. "I . . ." His jaw clenched and his hands curled into fists. Deep lines formed on his brow. He looked frustrated. Probably wasn't used to getting this kind of attitude from a girl. Women were supposed to tremble in his presence. Or cringe away in disgust if he happened to pass them on the street. He didn't have the first clue what to do with her. Well, here was another thing she could exploit.

"Hey, asshole. You forget how to talk? You look like you're having a fucking seizure. And Christ, but you stink. You smell like you've been submerged in shit the last ten years. Please go take a fucking shower." She smiled. "A nice, *long* one."

His whole body was shaking. "Don't. Talk. To. Me. Like. *That!*"

Julie's smile never wavered. "Relax, baby. I'm just playing." She giggled. "Did Lulu tell you why I'm special?"

The man let out a long breath. His hands slowly unclenched. "She said you're like me on the inside."

Julie's smile drooped a little. She thought of her collection of crime-scene photos. Recalled with only a small echo of shame her first impulse upon spying this crazy fuck's defilement of Karen's body. Only a few very close friends knew about her secret obsessions and fantasies. And yet . . . no. She was reading too much into this. Lulu wasn't real. And this guy wasn't psychic. Psycho, yeah, no shit, but not psychic.

Still . . .

Play along.

"She's right. I'm just like you."

The man's expression was somber. "Yes. And that's why you're coming with me when I leave."

Julie shook her head. "What? No . . . I . . ."

The man began to smile. "Yes. Lulu says it's your destiny."

Julie kept shaking her head. "No."

The man laughed.

Then he went out of the room, disappearing down the

hallway again. He came back a few minutes later with another item pilfered from the Lees' belongings—a bottle of sleeping pills. He forced a few down her throat and slapped a strip of duct tape over her mouth. She cried and struggled against her bonds a while longer as he puttered about the house gathering things to take with him.

The crash came fast. Her head felt thick. She stopped struggling and closed her eyes. When she woke up again, briefly, she was in the trunk of a car. The space was cramped, more than it should be. She moved around a little, enough to determine she had company in the tight space. The man she had killed was her companion in darkness. She couldn't see him, but the god-awful stench was proof enough. She began to cry. Mercifully, the swish of tires on pavement soon lulled her mind back into that hazy, gray drugged space, and she fell asleep again.

CHAPTER THIRTEEN

Diary of a Mixed-up Girl blog entry, dated
September 10, the previous year

Sometimes I think I really don't feel human at all. I
mean, I KNOW I'm a member of the fucking species.
What I really mean is I feel disconnected from hu-
manity. Like I don't understand the inner workings
of a healthy human being's brain. I guess I'm mostly
thinking about emotions. Most people seem to feel
things really deeply. Like the love they supposedly
feel for the people they care about. That's something
I just don't get at all. Seriously, I don't think I could
ever love anybody for real, in a romantic way, like
you see on TV and the movies. That fairy-tale shit.
There's this guy I just met, right? Really cute. Like
cute verging on hot. So I talk to him. I see how he looks
at me. He's into me already. I bet I could make him
love me. And it'd be cool 'cause I'd definitely like to
fuck him. And maybe when he says he loves me, I'll
say it back, because he'll want to hear it.
But it won't be real.
People like to think humans are some kind of ele-
vated creature. Yeah, we're capable of things beyond
the abilities of any other species. We have the ability
to reason and figure shit out. But humans also do a
lot of ugly things. Read a fucking history book and

you'll see. Genocide. War. Slavery. And it goes deeper than the bigger things like that. Every day, somewhere out there, some crazy fuck is killing somebody else just for kicks. Rape. Murder. Abuse. A fucking pandemic of violence. It doesn't ever stop and CAN'T ever stop. So when you get right down to it, we're not really any better than dogs, cats, apes, llamas, lions, wolves, or fucking aardvarks. We're savage animals, and all this shit about love and whatnot is just that—SHIT. It's something we're taught to believe in so the world doesn't fall apart. Me? I think the world could use a good dose of anarchy. Some fucking chaos. YEAH. I want to run wild in the streets!

I want to break something. Scream and shout. I want to get in my car and go run somebody down. Last night I had a dream I shot my mom in the face.

I don't love any of you.

Later, bitches. Cold Case Files is on.

4 comments

lord_ruthven: You make me sad.

Mixedupgirl: It's pathetic how hard you want me.

lord_ruthven: About as hard as I want a chainsaw enema.

Mixedupgirl: That can be arranged. God, you're boring. Stick your head in an oven or suck on a shotgun, okay?

CHAPTER FOURTEEN

March 22

Chuck was still gone when Zoe came out of the bathroom, and that was fine with her. She hoped he would be gone a while yet. With any luck she'd be asleep by the time he returned. It would be one less night of fending off awkward advances.

Her hair was wet from the shower and she had a fresh white towel wrapped around her torso. The towel was there to hide the temptation of her body from Chuck. Because he just wouldn't be able to help himself. He simply couldn't keep his hands off her when she was sans clothes. But with Chuck still missing in action, the towel could go. She tugged it loose and let it fall to the floor.

Someone knocked on the door.

Chuck.

"Shit."

The idiot had probably forgotten the key card. She snatched the towel up from the floor and hurriedly wrapped it around her body again as she strode quickly to the door. She'd planned to knock herself out with some Ambien and be asleep by the time he returned. So much for that. *Goddammit.* She yanked the door open and an epithet froze at the tip of her tongue as she saw who was actually there.

"Emily?"

Her friend smirked. "You look pissed off."

Zoe sighed. "Sorry. I thought you were Chuck."

Emily laughed. "That explains the pissed-off part. Can I come in?"

"I was just about to go to bed."

"Come on. Just for a few minutes. I'm bored."

Zoe shrugged. "Okay. But just for a few minutes. I really want to get to sleep soon."

Emily walked into the room and sat at the edge of the bed. Zoe closed the door and tugged the towel a notch higher over her breasts before sitting in a chair next to the bed. She crossed her legs, clasping her hands over a knee. "You didn't happen to see Mr. Wonderful out there, did you?"

Emily made a face. "Yeah. I ran into him."

"Something wrong? He say something obnoxious again?"

Emily shook her head. "No. Not really. Just talking to him is awkward for me. He knows I fucking hate him."

"Yeah. I guess he does. What was he doing?"

"I think he was going to a bar across the street. At least that's what he said. Sounded like he's gonna be gone a while."

Zoe smiled. She wouldn't need the Ambien to get to sleep now. Just knowing she wouldn't have to deal with the stress of fending off Chuck relaxed her in ways no drug could. "Well . . . good. Maybe he'll get drunk and hook up with somebody there."

Emily laughed. "Maybe *you* should get drunk and hook up."

"Maybe. But I'm too tired for that tonight."

Emily stared at Zoe without speaking for a long moment, biting her lower lip as she looked her friend up and down. Zoe frowned and fought the impulse to squirm in her chair. She remembered Emily's whispered proposition during their stop at the rest area earlier and began to feel uncomfortable again.

Emily chuckled. "Are you okay?"

"I'm fine. Why do you ask?"

Another chuckle. "You seem . . . uptight."

"I'm not."

Emily shrugged. "Whatever. Look. I know you said you're tired, but I kind of want to party a little."

"What do you mean?"

Another shrug. "I have a little coke. We could do a bump and go to my room."

"Um . . ." Zoe's face reddened. "Emily . . . you know I love you. We've been friends forever. But . . . I don't know."

Emily laughed. "What do you think I'm suggesting?"

Zoe's blush deepened. "Well . . . there's that thing you talked about earlier. No offense, but I'm not really into the idea."

Emily cocked an eyebrow. "Oh? And how do you know until you give it a whirl?"

Zoe was starting to feel frustrated with the conversation. She just wanted Emily to stop talking about this weirdness and leave so she could go to bed. "I don't know, okay? It's just not my thing. I'm sorry."

Emily stood and brushed her hands over her thighs, smoothing the hem of her clingy dress. "That's cool. I just wanted to put the idea out there. It's an open-ended invitation, so if you ever change your mind . . ."

"I won't."

Emily shook her head and looked Zoe over one more time. "A shame. It would be the perfect night to play around a little. What with Chuck being gone and all. I've got Joe naked and tied to the bed next door."

Zoe's blush returned. "Um . . ."

Emily smiled. "Too much information?"

"Yeah . . . you could say that."

Emily kept smiling. "Still, think of the fun we could have. He's blindfolded, too. You could climb on top of him and pretend you're me. Wouldn't that be a trip?"

Zoe thought about it.

Like Chuck, Joe was a very well-built young man. She had
no doubt Emily was telling the truth about his current situation. And admittedly it was kind of a hot image . . .

No. Don't even think it.

"You're thinking about it."

"No. I'm not."

"Are, too."

"Jesus, Emily."

Emily rolled her eyes and went to the door. She stood
there with her hand on the knob and looked at Zoe one
more time. "You keep on thinking about it. We'll be up for a
while yet."

Then she opened the door and was gone.

Zoe sat in the chair and stared at the closed door for some
time, too stunned to move. She hadn't expected Emily to
repeat the proposition again so soon, or to be so pushy about
it. It stirred discomforting doubts about the true depth of
their friendship. Would a real friend put her in this kind
of position? It wasn't something that could just be ignored or
forgotten. It was out there now. There was no taking it back.
Emily was smart. She knew what she had done. It made Zoe
feel lonely. Here was this big issue to confront, and the person she discussed hard things with was the one person she
couldn't talk to about it.

Unless . . .

She gave her head a hard shake. "No. Absolutely not."

But she kept thinking about it, the images in her head
growing more vivid the longer she sat there. She squirmed
in the chair again, but this time it was not from discomfort.
She closed her eyes. Pictured Joe tied to a bed. She drew in a
sharp breath and her nipples stiffened. She uncrossed her
legs and slipped a hand under the towel.

Christ, I can't believe I'm doing this. Stop it!

But she couldn't stop. The fantasy had gone too far and
she was too aroused. An impulse made her stand up and tug

the towel off. She grabbed her duffel bag from the floor and set it on the bed. She sorted through the clothes, pulled out shorts and a T-shirt, and donned them.

She left the room and stood for a moment on the balcony, searching the motel's parking lot for any sign of Chuck. He didn't seem to be around. She saw the bar Emily had mentioned on the other side of the street. Dimly audible music wafted from that direction. If he had really gone there, he wouldn't be back anytime soon. Chuck wasn't the type to quit after one drink.

Good. Drink yourself into a coma for all I fucking care.

She turned away from the parking lot and approached the door to Emily's room. She raised a hand to knock, but hesitated a moment longer. She took a deep breath. Her heart was racing. She could hear it.

This is crazy. It's not too late to stop. Just go back to bed.

She took another deep breath.

Then she knocked.

The door came open and Emily stood there smiling at her. "Changed your mind?"

Zoe forced a smile. "Yeah."

Emily stepped aside and Zoe walked into the room. She felt a wild thrill of excitement when she saw Joe on the bed, just as Emily had described.

Jesus Christ. Holy shit. I can't believe I'm doing this.

Joe stirred on the bed. "Who's there, baby?" He sounded groggy.

"Don't talk!" Emily snapped.

Joe opened his mouth again—then closed it, saying nothing.

Emily took Zoe by the hand and guided her over to a little table by the window. "Coke first, then fucking."

Zoe sat and accepted the clipped straw Emily handed her. She gaped at the chopped lines of powder arranged on a tray. "I thought you said a *little* coke."

Emily shrugged. "I lied. So what?"

"Whatever." Zoe inserted the straw in a nostril and bent her head to the table, snorting up most of a line in one go. "Oh. Wow. Fuck."

"Good, huh?"

Zoe grinned. "Hell, yeah."

Emily stood and peeled the black dress off over her head. She went to the bed and climbed in next to Joe, curling one long, shapely leg over his groin. She flashed Zoe a naughty smile and reached over Joe to pat the other side of the bed. "Join us."

Zoe finished the line of coke with a final snort. Feeling deliciously, wickedly debauched, she stood up and undressed.

Then she went to the bed and climbed in.

She didn't see Chuck until the next morning.

CHAPTER FIFTEEN

March 22

The first one went down easy, the next one even easier. Tonight that normally harsh tequila burn tasted sweet. He welcomed the sting. Savored it. Reveled in it. He wasn't normally the sort to wallow in pain or misery, but tonight felt like a good night for it. A good time to open up hidden recesses in his psyche and see what dark things lurked there.

Chuck rapped the empty shot glass on the bar and the bartender filled it again. He threw the shot back, screwing his eyes shut and wincing as the strong booze hit the back of his throat. It was cheap tequila. House brand. The place was too much of a dump to stock anything good.

Who cares? It'll do the job.

The bottom of the glass hit the bar again and the burly barkeep—who hadn't moved, and stood ready with the bottle—filled it to the rim again. The man had a bushy mustache, a receding hairline, and a ponytail. Faded jailhouse tattoos festooned his muscular forearms. A livid scar under one eye hinted at a violent past.

Chuck picked up the glass. "What's with the scar? You get that in jail?"

"None of your business."

Chuck laughed. "Yeah. You're right." He raised the glass again, but didn't throw the shot back right away this time.

He swiveled side to side on the stool, swaying, his head already buzzing pleasantly from the booze. "It always this fucking dead in here?"

The barkeep shrugged. "Sometimes. Sometimes not. Gets busy on the weekends."

"Huh. Lots of weekend-warrior rednecks, right?"

"Yeah. You got something against rednecks?"

"No, man, not really. You know, other than just how fucking dumb they are. You know what I'm saying, right? Most of them don't have more than two working brain cells to rub together." He knocked the tequila back in one go again, whooped, and slammed the glass down. "Hit me again, Pedro."

The big barkeep squinted at him. "My name's not Pedro."

No shit. Guy didn't look even vaguely Hispanic. Where the hell had that come from? "Sorry about that, Hoss."

"Name ain't Hoss, either. It's Joe Bob."

It started as a snort. A helpless, reflexive expression of mirth. Then he thought about it again. *Joe Bob!* Another snort, followed by an almost girlish giggle. *Fucking Joe Bob!* It perfectly fit any number of country stereotypes, the kind of name that just screamed "lobotomized sack of backwoods monkey spunk."

The barkeep didn't look amused. "Something funny?"

The laughter boomed out of him then, making his whole body quake as the stool rattled beneath him. He laid his head on the bar and kept laughing until at last the fit began to release him, winding down to a last few quiet giggles and snorts. Then he raised his head and saw the murderous glare the barkeep was leveling at him.

"I think you're done, son."

Chuck reached into his pocket and pulled out a wad of cash. He peeled off a hundred in twenties, placed the bills on the bar, and pushed them across. "I'm sorry, man. Seriously.

I can behave. I've just had a rough night. That there's a bonus on top of whatever booze I might buy from you tonight. Yours to keep. What do you say?"

The barkeep picked up the bills, leafed through them, and looked at Chuck again. His expression was a little less malevolent now. "One more."

"Just for spite, right?"

A corner of the man's mouth twitched, a near smile. "Yeah."

Chuck pulled out the wad again and peeled off two more twenties. "You drive a hard bargain, man, but I'm willing to pay top dollar for the privilege of drinking myself blind in this fine establishment."

He dropped the extra bills on the bar and the barkeep snatched them up. He filled the shot glass again and set the bottle in front of Chuck. "That one's yours."

Chuck grinned. "Appreciate it. Could you get me a pitcher of Bud, too? And maybe a plate of those nachos? But don't spit in my food, bro."

The barkeep shook his head. "You're gonna feel like warmed-over shit in the morning, kid. And it won't be 'cause of any spit in your nachos."

Yet another shot of tequila hit the back of his throat and sizzled. "That's sort of the idea, man. Wanna hurt so hard I can't think."

The barkeep chuckled. "Well . . . you're on the right path, then. I may have to take your keys, though."

Chuck squinted at him through bleary eyes. "Not necessary, bro." He jerked a thumb over his shoulder. "I'm at the joint across the street. I'm a fucking pedestrian."

The barkeep shrugged and served up the pitcher of draft Bud and a frosty pint glass. A plate of nachos showed up soon after. Chuck sat there and drank and ate the gloriously unhealthy food, which consisted of warm tortilla chips piled high with melted cheese and hot peppers. Time ticked by.

He got woozier and woozier. He was aware of people coming into the bar and leaving again. He glanced at the clock on the wall now and again. It progressed from eleven P.M. to a shade beyond two A.M. in seemingly the blink of an eye.

He thought about Zoe a lot during that time. Thought about their years together and the impending end of their relationship. More than once tears welled in his eyes, but he never let them spill. Couldn't let these redneck fucks see him as weak. But keeping the mask in place wasn't easy. His feelings for Zoe were deeper and more complicated than he'd ever suspected. He didn't want to lose her. Not even in light of the impromptu tryst with Emily.

And holy fucking Jesus, how fucked-up was *that*? The bitch was supposed to be Zoe's best friend. He couldn't figure her out at all. Until tonight she'd never shown anything but total contempt for him. Then all of a sudden, she's practically raping him. Yeah, nothing that happened was against his will, but she was *so* aggressive, and so blatantly taking advantage of his vulnerable state. Thinking about it made him angry, but he had a hard time seeing how it could have turned out any other way. He'd been in need of comfort and there she was. And it'd been good. Very, very good. Still, he couldn't stop thinking of the way she'd laughed as he cried in her arms.

That was just . . . sick.

Evil.

The world went blurry. His head felt thick, almost like he was underwater. He was slumped over the bar, his face inches from the wood, close enough to make out the swirls in the grain. He shook his head and sat up straight. The clock on the wall behind the bar now read 3:17 A.M. More than a quarter hour after last call. Chuck swiveled on the stool and took a look around.

Holy shit . . .

He was the only person in the bar. The neon OPEN sign in

the main window had been turned off. Chairs were upside down on the tables. The overhead lights had been dimmed.

He frowned. "Where did everybody—?"

The words were cut off when someone behind him slapped something around his neck and cinched it tight. It felt like a strap of leather. A belt, maybe. Chuck gagged and clawed at the belt with fingers rendered sloppy by drink. His assailant yanked him off the stool, drawing the loop around his throat even tighter. His face flushed and his temples throbbed. His eyes felt like they would pop out of their sockets as he was dragged backward. He dropped to his knees in an effort to halt the journey to wherever his attacker was taking him, but the guy was just too strong and kept pulling him backward. Chuck craned his head back and saw the leering face of the barkeep. The scar beneath his eye looked bright red in the dim light.

Pure terror and adrenaline cut through the booze haze.

Oh, shit! I'm about to die.

Part of him knew it was his fault for being so careless. *Shouldn't have flashed all that green around.*

Also shouldn't have been such a dick.

These things he knew to be true. He also was pretty damn sure he'd never have a chance to benefit from these valuable life lessons.

I'm about to die! OH FUCK!

The barkeep dragged him through a door into a back room. The lighting here was brighter. He saw stacks of beer and liquor cases. He saw kegs and other bar supplies. There were two other people in the room. One was a sleazy-looking bottle blonde in a miniskirt and a black halter. And there was another burly guy cut from the same redneck cloth as Pedro or whatever his fucking name was.

He was dragged into the center of the room. The barkeep removed the belt from Chuck's neck and tossed it aside. He had only a second to suck air into his lungs before Joe Bob slammed a powerful fist into his gut, sending him to the floor in an awkward heap. He rolled onto his back and stared up at the trio of ugly faces leering down at him.

He found his breath and uttered a helpless whimper. "Please . . . I've got money. Lots of money. You . . . you can . . . have it . . . all of it."

Joe Bob grinned. "That's mighty generous of you, *Hoss*. And we'll be taking your money. But you ain't getting off that easy."

The other man grinned, too. "Hear you need a lesson in manners, boy."

The woman placed the sole of a high-heeled shoe on his throat and pressed down hard. There was hate in her eyes. He sort of knew why Joe Bob was pissed at him, but what had he done to these other people?

He tried to think back over the night.

The long hours of drinking at the bar. Drinking and occasionally making snide comments to anyone who tried to strike up conversation. A blur of venom and negativity.

Fuck.

The woman sneered. "Gonna fuck you up, pretty boy."

The men laughed.

"Got that right," said Joe Bob. "And you ain't gonna tell a soul how it happened, unless you want some of my biker buddies to kill your whole fuckin' family. You want that, motherfucker?"

Chuck gulped. He didn't doubt the threat. "No."

After that, Chuck didn't care.

They weren't going to kill him, and that was all he needed to know.

They were true to their word, though.

They fucked him up.

But they were wrong about the other thing. A time would come when he would tell the truth about this night.

CHAPTER SIXTEEN

March 22

"What's your fucking problem?"

Roxie had stripped down to T-shirt and black thong panties. Rob could see a tattoo of some sort on an inner thigh. There was another tattoo on her right foot. Words in Latin. He didn't ask for a translation. He'd seen her bend over a time or two and knew there was yet another tattoo on her lower back. The T-shirt hid other illustrations he'd glimpsed in that gas-station bathroom. She was sitting cross-legged on the floor now, with the overstuffed tote bag in her lap, staring up at him with an expression betraying irritation and impatience.

Rob sat on the edge of the bed. He hadn't moved from the position in well over an hour, ever since . . .

Oh, God . . .

A blood-stained vision filled his head and he felt sick all over again. At least she'd hauled the body into the bathroom. He hoped he wouldn't have to see it again. Looking at what she'd done to the poor fuck made him want to tear his eyes out.

"Goddammit." Roxie set the tote bag aside and came out of the cross-legged position to lean toward him on her knees. "I asked you a question. Answer me right now or . . ."

Rob frowned. He waited a beat. Then he said, "Or . . . what?"

Her expression went blank. "Or I'll cut your face off, too."

Rob nodded. "Yeah. That's it, I think. My fucking problem, as you put it, has a lot to do with you cutting that kid's face off. What kind of sick bitch are you?"

Roxie continued to stare at him blankly for several moments, that dead expression unsettling him nearly as much as any of the atrocities he'd witnessed today. Then her eyes opened a bit wider, a reflected glint of light from the overhead bulb hinting at a twisted playfulness. "You know what's really interesting, Robin?"

"I really don't want to know."

She laughed. "What's *really* interesting is the way you sat right where you are now the whole time I was in the bathroom. That was, what . . . at least fifteen minutes? Yeah. At *least* fifteen, between dragging that dead boy in there and showering off. And you just sat here. Didn't budge an inch, far as I can tell. You're not cuffed or tied up. You could have slipped out and gotten away, no problem. Now why is that, Robin? Why did you stay?"

Oh, shit. She's right . . .

Rob groaned. "I was . . . I don't know . . . numb. Out of it. In shock. Scared to death. I didn't know what was happening. I just . . . I . . ."

Roxie leaned closer to him and crossed her forearms over his knees. The playful, twisted gleam in her eyes sparkled brighter as she stared up at him. "Bullshit. You stayed because you *wanted* to. Because this is the most exciting thing that's happened to you in your whole life. Because *I'm* the most exciting thing that's happened to you." The small smile that curved the corners of her mouth stirred a maddening desire to kiss her. "Admit it, you're enjoying the ride. You don't want it to end."

Rob shook his head. "Bullshit. You're crazy. This . . ." He looked helplessly around the room, eyes darting about, taking in the large, sticky stain behind Roxie, the bloody scalpel propped atop the glass ashtray on the table, and the hideous thing stretched tight over the cover of the Gideon Bible on the dresser. The face mask. He looked Roxie in the eye again. That playful quality hadn't diminished an iota, had only amped up as she watched him mentally cataloging the horrors. "This is insanity. Pure insanity. I don't want to be here. I don't think I was . . . conscious of being left alone or I wouldn't be here now. You're evil. Pure fucking evil."

A shuddery sigh escaped trembling lips.

His eyes began to water.

Roxie tossed her head back and laughed with gusto. "Oh, Robin . . . and you wonder why I call you that? You're such a scared little girl." More laughter. "But no, that's not right. A girl would be smarter. A girl would've run. I think a better word for you would be . . . let's see . . ." She rolled her eyes around a bit, pursed her lips, and tapped her chin with a forefinger. "Got it!" She snapped her fingers. "The word for you is . . . *pansy.*"

She giggled. "Robin the sissy-wissy pansy."

The words stung. Mostly because her accusation seemed to be sort of true. Never in his life had he felt so physically cowed by another human being. No schoolyard bully could ever have done this to him, nor any badass biker or street thug. The helplessness he felt in the presence of this girl made him feel like a piece of shit. Weak. Useless. Pathetic.

In other words . . . not like a real man.

He realized he was shaking again and this only intensified the self-loathing.

Robin, he thought. *She's right. It fits.*

Roxie uncrossed her arms and ran a hand up his thigh. "You need to calm down. I think I know a way I can help you relax."

Rob pushed her hand away from his crotch. "No."

Her smile slipped some. "What?"

"You heard me."

Roxie's expression turned smoldering, just shy of murderous. "Bitch, you don't get to say no to anything I want." Her hand slid up his thigh again and roughly cupped his crotch. "You really think this is gonna stay limp when I start working on it?"

The answer to that was already obvious. Rob tried to twist away from Roxie, but she pressed a hand against his chest and shoved him backward. She climbed onto the bed and straddled him, writhed against him, rubbing her pubis against the hard bulge straining the fabric of his jeans with raw, unbridled enthusiasm. She braced her hands on the mattress and leaned close to him, sneering as she continued to grind her pelvis. "What about it, Rob? You want me to stop that?"

Rob's helpless whimper was the only answer necessary. She kept at it for a while, driving him mad with the need for physical release. A cascade of emotions swirled through his head. Hate, lust, shame, and anger. Then she climbed off him and left Rob panting there as she picked up her tote bag and took a seat at the little table by the window. He stared up at the ceiling through a mist of fresh tears. Some time passed and a little of the unfulfilled need began to dissipate, a greater swelling of fresh shame rushing in to take its place.

What the fuck is wrong with me? How did that happen?

It hardly mattered how it had happened, really. She had proven a point and there was no way to refute it. He wanted her. Even now, after bearing witness to the awful things she'd done, the most primitive part of him looked at Roxie and responded first with consuming lust. But the feelings her near-perfect body stirred didn't negate the horror of her heinous acts. That lust was totally apart from everything else he felt about her. And one way or another, he swore, he would not allow himself to become a prisoner to those baser feelings.

I'm still me, he thought. *I'm not the monster.*

A fucking pansy, maybe, but nope, not a monster.

The thought triggered a helpless laugh.

"What's funny?"

Rob stifled another laugh. "Nothing."

"I don't like not being in on the joke. Maybe I should come over there and be mean to you. And I mean *really* mean, Robin. Not like a few minutes ago."

Rob knew she meant it. So he told her.

"That's not funny."

Rob sat up and shrugged. "I'm sorry. It just made me laugh."

Roxie grunted and her attention went back to a magazine spread open on the table. She had one leg crossed over the other, foot jiggling as she slowly turned the pages. Her toenails were painted black, like her fingernails. The polish was beginning to fleck away. The sole of her foot looked soft and free of calluses. She had the kind of slender ankles that always looked good in high heels.

Roxie chuckled.

Rob flinched and lifted his eyes. "Huh? What?"

Another chuckle. "Foot fetish, Rob?"

He felt heat in his cheeks. "I guess I was staring."

"Yeah. I don't mind. I do have nice feet." She laughed. "The rest of me ain't bad, either."

Rob swallowed a lump. "Yeah . . ."

Roxie turned another page, appeared to read a few paragraphs, and then directed a cool, level gaze at him. "So . . . this sex thing. It's gonna happen."

Rob lowered his eyes. "Yeah. I guess so."

"Look at me."

He looked at her. Waited.

She turned yet another page of the magazine, but this time didn't even glance at it. "Ain't no guessing involved. Rob." She smiled. "Question is, we go for it right now or draw out the anticipation a little longer?"

"I don't know, Roxie. It's whatever you say, obviously."

"No shit."

"But before it happens . . . I have a question or two for you . . . if that's okay."

Roxie shrugged. She flipped the magazine shut, the bright and garish cover drawing Rob's attention for a moment. It was an old issue of *Rue Morgue*, the one with Lux Interior on the cover. She laced her fingers over her knees and leaned back in her chair. "Ask away."

"You've killed six people today."

She smiled. "Impressive. Little Robbie can count."

"Is this . . . a normal day for you? Because I don't see how you could still be walking around . . ."

She shook her head. "No, Rob. Duh." She put special emphasis on the last word and rolled her eyes. "I'd be, like, the most prolific serial killer fucking ever if I were doing that."

"So . . . what's the deal?"

She shrugged again. "I don't kill people all the time. Hell, I go months without doing it sometimes. Then something happens, some kind of trigger, like this morning, and I go off on a fucking spree. It's just something I have to get out of my system and then I'm back to normal for a while. Well . . . normal for me."

"How many times have you done this? How many people have you killed?"

She made her head swivel around on her slender neck, pulled her features into an expression of exasperation. "Christ, Rob, I don't know." She unlaced her fingers, moved the digits up and down and silently mouthed numbers as she pretended to count. "Let's see . . . first time I killed a dude I was sixteen. That was my dad."

"Jesus."

Roxie ignored the comment and went on. "I'm twenty

now. I've had a bit more than a half dozen of these . . . explosions. And in between I've offed a few random fucks when it was convenient for me. Needed money, a car, or something. Shit, I don't know. I'd say I'm up to at least thirty, maybe forty."

"Holy fucking shit."

Rob felt dizzy. He gripped the edge of the mattress to keep from pitching over. The enormity of the number rocked him, forcefully reminded him this wasn't just some cute girl he was having a flirty conversation with in a bar. Based on all he'd seen today, he had no reason to doubt her or suspect exaggeration. If anything, the number she'd come up with was probably a conservative estimate.

"You look sick."

"I feel sick."

"We should probably fuck now. It'd get your mind off it."

Rob massaged his eyes with the heels of his hands, blinked hard, and stared at her. "You like killing, don't you? Jesus, you actually enjoy it."

"No shit, Rob. Any other observations, Captain Obvious?"

"Another question."

She sighed. "One more. That's all."

Rob hesitated. This was the big one. The one he was most afraid to ask. He had to force the words out. "Why am I still alive? Why lure that boy here instead of just killing me?"

"You are so fucking dense."

"What do you mean?"

Another sigh. "Thing is . . . I think I like you."

"What?"

"I like you."

He stared at her and his mouth worked for a time with no words coming out. Then he closed his mouth and thought for a minute before at last managing to squeeze out two simple words: "Like . . . how?"

"As in *like* like, stupid."

"But . . . you don't even know me."

"I know you enough. I can't really explain it. Being next to you all day just sort of felt . . . right? You know?"

Rob shook his head. "No. I don't know."

"I think you do. You do, and you're just trying to hide from it."

"No."

"Yes. It's that simple human-chemistry thing. That special heat you feel only once in a while, with someone really special. I felt it almost from the beginning." She slid out of the chair and came across the floor to him on her hands and knees, moving right through the big, wet stain where the boy had bled out on the floor. She crossed her arms over his knees again and smiled up at him. "Yeah, I've been a fucking cunt to you. But that's just how I am."

Her hands were moving up his thighs again, pressing firmly as they reached for his crotch.

Rob gulped. "Oh, God . . ."

She slithered up his body and pushed him backward onto the bed. She straddled him again and leaned close, her soft lips less than an inch from his. His hands went to her knees, brushed flakes of drying blood, and almost jerked away again. Almost. "You want to stay alive, Rob? Here's my advice to you." Her tongue flicked his lower lip, eliciting a shudder. "Stay interesting. Let me know you feel it, too."

Rob's hands moved from her knees, up silken thighs, over her delectably round ass, and settled at the small of her back. She let the full weight of her body settle against him and they writhed slowly against each other, maintaining eye contact, still not kissing.

Then his hands went to her shoulders and he rolled her over.

She laughed.

A sound he silenced with his mouth.

It was hungry, fierce, desperate.

Electric.

And Rob screamed at the end.

CHAPTER SEVENTEEN

March 18

The hours passed in a haze of half-remembered horrors and confusion. The stench of the corpse filled the tight, hot space, covering her like a suffocating blanket. The smell of her own vomit beneath the death smell, steadily tickling her gag reflex, a slow torture that never seemed to end, though there was some small measure of relief after she at last managed to work the strip of duct tape off her mouth. The car's tires hummed over interstate asphalt. She heard the roar and buzz of countless other cars and big trucks, along with the occasional blare of horns or blast of passing sirens. So many people so close to her, all of them passing her by, totally oblivious to her plight. She drifted in and out of sleep. Once she woke up and knew they had stopped. She heard voices from the car. A man talking. The crazy man. And a woman. The woman laughed. And just as Julie was summoning the strength to scream, the mystery woman screamed. The sound was pure fear at first, but then it changed, became more shrill, and went on and on, an awful evocation of blinding, desperate agony.

Until it abruptly stopped.

Then they were on the road again. Julie heard country-and-western music, the old, really twangy stuff, coming from the car's stereo. She cried some more and eventually fell asleep with the music in her ears. Then she woke up and knew at once they had stopped again.

The trunk came open and blinding daylight made her blink fast. The first thing she saw was the dead man, her dried vomit in his wild, matted hair. Next she saw the trunk lid standing tall above her. Then hands, reaching for her. She was yanked from the trunk and thrown roughly to the ground.

She cried out as her knees hit the ground first. She kept tumbling, pitching forward and then onto her side, rolling twice before coming to a stop on her back. The man loomed over her. He was bare chested, his muscled torso gleaming in the sun. He wore very tight jeans and white sneakers. More of John's pilfered belongings, she guessed. The too-tight jeans were far cleaner than the filthy pants he'd been wearing. His body was cleaner than she remembered, too. But his attitude toward her hadn't changed a bit. She saw it in his hard eyes and the way his upper lip kept twitching.

He was holding a shovel. "You've got work to do, cunt."

He threw the shovel at her. The blade struck her hip and made her cry out again. "Ow!" She sat up and took a look around. They were in a field somewhere, parked next to an expanse of wilderness. She looked at the crazy man. "Where are we?"

His lip twitched again. "Ain't any concern of yours, bitch. You got a hole to dig. Get to it."

"I thought I told you not to talk to me like that."

His hands curled into shaking fists. "Shut up. Shut the hell up. You do what I told you or I'll thrash you."

"I don't think so."

There was murder in his eyes now, a palpable need to kill. "Don't test me, little bitch. You'll be sorry, I swear."

Julie brought her knees up to her chest and crossed her arms over them. "Lulu will be pissed off if you do anything to me. You know that. I'm special, remember?"

"I remember."

There was an undertone of bitter resentment in the words. Hearing it made Julie uneasy. The man's Lulu delusion was keeping her alive for now. But the man's drive to rape and kill was strong. Logic told her those urges would override the delusion at some point. And then she'd be fucked. Fucked and very, very fucking dead. And someday crime-scene photos of her defiled and decaying corpse would be saved on some other morbid kid's computer. She needed to buy time somehow, and the only obvious way was to go along with whatever he wanted, all the while keeping an eye out for an opening, some way out.

"I'll dig the hole, okay? Just try to be a little nicer to me, that's all I'm saying."

"Dig. The fucking hole. Right now."

Julie picked up the shovel and used it to steady herself as she stood up. She wiped grass and bits of dirt from her bare body and looked at him. "I don't wanna do this naked, dude. You got any clothes for me?"

He smirked. "Got some of that woman's things in a bag. You can dress after you dig the hole."

Julie shook her head. "No. Now."

"After."

Julie scowled. "It's because you're a fucking pervert, right? You just want to stare at me."

He almost smiled. "Like to do a lot more than stare."

"But Lulu won't let you."

He wiped moisture from his mouth with the back of a hand. "Right. For now. She's changed her mind on things before."

Julie rolled her eyes.

I'll bet.

"Whatever, man. If you get wood and wanna spank it, please do it in the car, okay? I don't need to see that shit. That too much to ask?"

The man just laughed.

Julie thought about whacking him upside the head with the shovel. It was a good, sturdy tool, with a clean, sharp blade. Probably taken from John's garage. A solid blow to the head from this thing would put most guys down for the count, at least long enough to do some more damage before he could get up again. But this guy was no normal dude. He was big and crazy. He would probably see it coming. He'd just take the shovel from her and spank her with it.

"So. This hole. Where should I dig it?"

"Anywhere. Right where you're standing is fine."

"Uh-huh. And how big should it be?"

"Big. It's a grave."

Julie gulped. "Um . . ."

"Not for you."

Julie glanced at the body in the trunk. "Oh, right."

"You killed Clyde. My only friend. It's only right you should do the work. And when you're done digging the hole, you'll put him in the ground and bury him."

Julie's nose crinkled. "This is gonna take a while. Hours, maybe."

He smiled. "We've got all the time in the world."

Julie glanced down at her bare feet. "I should at least have shoes for this. Or sandals. You can still have your sexy show and my feet won't get all fucked-up."

The man shrugged and went to the car. He opened the passenger side door and leaned inside. In a moment he came back and tossed her a pair of white sneakers with pink trim. Julie dropped the shovel and put the shoes on. They were about a size too big, but comfortable enough.

She picked up the shovel again and started digging. It was hard, sweaty work. The day was unseasonably warm for early spring. A sheen of sweat covered her entire body within minutes of beginning the task. The crazy man watched her intently the whole time. She glanced at him once and saw him licking his lips and rubbing his hairy chest, his palm flat against the flesh, moving in slow circles. And, of course, the crotch of those too-tight jeans was disturbingly swollen. She tried not to look at him too often. It was too easy to imagine what was in his head. Same thing most guys would be thinking about—putting his dick inside her. So she concentrated on the work, pausing only to wipe sweat from her brow and take a brief rest. Her pleas for water were ignored. By the time the hole was big enough to accommodate a man's body, she felt like she would die of thirst. She climbed out of the hole and fell to her knees, tears spilling down her cheeks as she begged again for something to drink.

"Your work ain't done yet."

She sniffled. "Please. I'm so thirsty. P-please . . ."

"Get Clyde in the ground and you'll get your drink."

She looked up at him through gleaming eyes. "You promise?"

He sneered. "Yeah. I promise. Now quit your bawlin' and get this shit done."

Julie sniffled again and managed a shaky nod. "Okay. Thank you."

She got to her feet and wobbled over to the BMW's open trunk. Her features twisted in disgust as she reached inside and gripped the dead man under the armpits. She lifted him and hauled him out, grunting loudly from the exertion several times. She dragged him over to the hole and rolled him into it. Then she got to work filling the space with the pile of freshly turned earth. There was an odd kind of satisfaction to watching the man she'd killed disappear beneath the soil. She stared at his dead flesh and thought of how it'd felt to stab him with the corkscrew. She wanted to experience that sensation at least one more time. She imagined the still-living one at her mercy. A knife in her hand. The blade penetrating his flesh. Ruining it. Cutting through muscle and sinew. Oh, how she'd love to cut him. Over and over. And fucking over. Until he was still and the breath was gone from his body.

Soon the task was complete, the hole filled in a tiny fraction of the time it had taken to dig it. Julie threw the shovel down and took a staggering step in the man's direction. "Water . . ."

He screwed the cap off a metal flask and passed it to her. She brought it to her lips and tasted cheap whiskey. She gagged and spat the first swallow out. Then she whimpered and drank a little more. It was better than nothing. At least her mouth didn't feel so parched.

The man took the flask from her, screwed the cap back on, and shoved it into a rear pocket of the jeans. Then he seized her by an arm and started dragging her toward the woods.

Julie's eyes went wide. "Hold on. Stop. What are you doing?"

"Got another job for you."

"Are you fucking kidding me?"

"No."

She whimpered. "Jesus. I can't. I swear. I'm about to pass out."

He laughed. "This one's gonna be easy. It's all set up for you already. Just one little thing you have to do."

Julie didn't have the first clue what he was talking about and figured asking him to elaborate would be useless. Whatever he had in store for her was bound to be something horrible, and knowing what it was in advance wouldn't do her any good anyway.

The man pulled her roughly through the woods, keeping a steady grip on her arm the whole time and jerking her upright every time she stumbled, which was often. Low-hanging branches and bit of bramble poked and scratched her bare flesh. The forced march through wilderness went on for at least ten minutes, maybe longer. She began to think the other "job" had just been a ruse to get her deep into the woods, far enough out to kill her and leave her body without worrying about having to dig another hole. And maybe those baser instincts had already trumped the Lulu delusion.

Oh, God, I'm about to die.

She started crying again.

No . . . wait.

That wasn't her.

The sound was coming from somewhere directly ahead. Someone else was out here. She saw some bushes and some very leafy trees. The man dragged her through the bushes, inflicting numerous new scratches on her body. They emerged into a very small clearing. A nude woman leaned against the thick trunk of a very tall tree. Her hands were stretched high over her head, the wrists bound with rope and tied to a low branch. Her ankles were tied with another length of rope. Several layers of duct tape were wound around her mouth and the back of her head. The woman saw them coming and began to mewl.

The man planted a hand at the small of Julie's back and gave her a hard shove. She stumbled deeper into the clearing and dropped to her hands and knees in front of the bound woman. She looked up and saw the desperate terror in the woman's shiny eyes. The eyes went wide, silently begged her for help. The man stepped past Julie and removed a big hunting knife he'd left embedded in the trunk of the tree.

Then he yanked Julie to her feet again, eliciting a startled screech as he pressed the knife into one of her shaking hands. "Kill her."

Julie gaped at him. "What!"

"You heard me."

"No. I can't. I won't."

The man's face went hard again. "You have to kill her. It's what Lulu wants."

"What? Why?"

His grip on her arm tightened to a painful degree. "This is a test. You have to show you're worthy. Prove you're like us." His upper lip twitched. "Kill her."

He released her arm and shoved her forward again. Julie looked at the woman. She was pretty. Slender but curvy. She was maybe thirty. Her brown hair was long and curly. She wore a necklace with a little heart pendant, the kind of thing a boyfriend might give her. Then she saw the ring. Strike that. Not a boyfriend. Her husband. A man who loved this woman was out there somewhere, maybe scared and wondering where she was. That man was never going to see her again. Not alive, anyway.

She threw the knife to the ground and moved away from him. "I'm not killing her. Fuck that."

The bound woman made that mewling sound again.

The man smirked. "So you admit you're not like me? Lulu was wrong?"

"No."

He frowned. "But—"

"I won't kill a woman. Bring me a man. Any man. I don't care. I'll do any nasty thing you want to him. Slit his throat and drink his blood. Open his gut and pull his intestines out. Cut his dick off and feed it to him. Whatever. But this . . ." She gestured at the woman. "No fucking way."

He stared at her for a long time.

Then he started talking to Lulu.

Which was really weird, watching the crazy fuck talk to the voice in his head. Arguing heatedly with himself, basically. After a while he appeared to surrender. He sighed. "Lulu says we'll do it. I'll put you back in the trunk and go find you a man to kill."

Julie shook her head. "No."

"No?"

"No." She shook her head again. "I'm done with the trunk. I get to ride up front with you." He started to protest, but she pressed on. "And the reason for that is I'm not letting you pick who I get to kill. That's my call. I meant what I said. We'll grab some fucker and I'll fuck him the fuck up. But you don't get to tell me who it's gonna be. Got it?"

She expected him to argue the point, but he just shrugged and said, "Okay."

Then he picked up the hunting knife.

Julie shook her head vigorously. "Don't."

He laughed.

Then he rammed the big blade into the bound woman's flat belly up to the hilt and jerked it back out. A thick gout of blood spilled from the wound and the woman bucked against her bonds. Her eyes got even wider and instinct made her try to suck in breath through her mouth, dimpling the thickly layered duct tape beneath her nose.

Julie staggered backward, tripped on a rock, and fell hard on her ass. She sat there and watched the crazy man do some more things to the doomed woman with his big knife. Then she rolled onto her stomach and squeezed her eyes shut.

Help me, she thought. *Somebody please help me . . .*

CHAPTER EIGHTEEN

**Diary of a Mixed-up Girl blog entry, dated
October 31, the previous year**

You would not believe the fucked-up day I've had so
far. And on my favorite day of the fucking year. Of all
fucking days. I'm so fucking furious. I'm shaking. Like
seriously shaking like one of those hard-core alcohol-
ics locked in a detox cell. I keep backing up and starting every sentence over because even though I'm
so goddamn angry I can't get past my anal hatred of
typos. Christ, my life is ridiculous.

It's true. I'm a ridiculous person. Like I'm the boiled-
down cliché essence of every tortured fucking goth
kid ever. I hate being a TYPE. A fucking category. But I
am. I fucking AM, man. The only thing distinguishing
me from the rest of Team Gloom is my look. I've got
that All-American Girl thing happening. I was sort of
proud of that. Thought it set me apart. It was the
best disguise fucking EVER. No one could ever guess
the truth about me or see the darkness inside.

WRONG.

I for sure thought I was fooling the fuck out of my
parents. Especially my mother. I always thought she
was fucking stupid and clueless, what with that
bland, pleasant way of talking, sounding like a fifties

housewife. Barely a working brain cell in her bubble head, I thought. Until today. Because it turns out the joke was on me.

This is a lot of beating around the bush. The thought of actually writing it down makes me start shaking again. But fuck it, I'll just spit it out. Came home from school and right away knew something fucked was happening. First clue was the extra cars parked outside. Came inside and saw all these serious-looking old fucks. I thought somebody had died. A grandparent, maybe. I got a little nervous and started psyching myself up to fake some grief. But then Dad gets up and says some shit that went something like, "Honey, we don't want you to be mad, because we love you and this is all about how much we totally fucking love you, honey, and holy fuck, but we are so fucking worried and we just want to help you, okay?" And Mom starts bawling.

And suddenly I get what this is. This is one of those intervention things. So I start yelling at them, becoming a fucking profanity machine. But their bullshit goes on and on. Nobody's here to judge you, sweetie, they tell me. Could you please calm down, could you please fucking calm down? But I keep yelling. I'm fucking screaming. They're not here to JUDGE me!? Who are they fucking kidding!!!?

After a while some of them got all pissed off too and pretty soon everybody was screaming. The relatives. Some neighbors. Our family fucking doctor, for fuck's sake. I was surprised a priest wasn't there to conduct an exorcism. Seriously. That's how crazy this whole overblown thing is. The hysteria just kept building and building until Dad slapped the shit out of me.

No shit. I am not kidding. The bastard walloped me.

And I got sent to my room, just like a little kid. That's where I am now. Waiting. Fucking scared shitless how this is gonna work out. I can hear them all down there. Talking about me. Nobody's gone. Somebody's crying. Probably you're wondering what this is all about. It all goes back to that video I uploaded. Yeah, that one. The rabbit thing. Some parent got wind of it and sent Dad a link. He started putting this whole intervention debacle together as soon as he saw it. He asked around about me. Talked to my friends. Somebody out there spilled some more of my secrets.

I thought I could trust most of you. Thought making this a private journal would prevent shit like this. Guess I learned my lesson, huh? Somebody reading this has a big fucking mouth. I wish I knew who. Really. Because I'd fucking kill you. For real. Post a comment with your confession and I'll be out the window and on my way to slit your fucking throat faster than you can say, "I'm a miserable, worthless fucking snitch who should be gutted like a pig."

This is the last entry most of you will see. I'm deleting everybody I don't totally fucking trust tonight. FUCK YOU DIE!!!!!!!

Note: Above entry contained seventy-three responses before the journal owner locked it. A sampling follows below.

lord_ruthven: You do need help and you know it. This had to happen.

Mixedupgirl: Fuck. I knew it was you. YOU'RE DEAD.

lord_ruthven: Threats don't scare me, Julie. You should know that by now. And anyway, your snitch is somebody else. I'd tell you otherwise. You should know that, too.

Mixedupgirl: Yeah. I guess I do, at that. But I still fuck-ing hate you.

lord_ruthven: So delete me.

Mixedupgirl: No. I can't. And YOU should know that.

CHAPTER NINETEEN

March 23

The world was spinning as she began to emerge from the haze, consciousness returning in slow, painful degrees. She was in a bed. She wasn't alone. Someone was snoring. A warm body pressed up against her back. She pried her eyes open and saw that she was hanging over the side of the bed, one arm dangling toward the floor. A tall bottle of vodka sat on the carpeted floor, just out of arm's reach. It was empty. She turned her head and saw more empty bottles. Her head was pounding, a relentless throb that made her want to cry. She heard music. Lady GaGa gave way to the Ting Tings. Emily had plugged her iPod into a dock at some point and it was still playing. Zoe looked at the vodka bottle. She considered grabbing it and throwing it at the dock, but just thinking of the effort it would require made her stomach roll. Then the memories of the evening's debaucheries began to surface, and she groaned again.

Jesus, what a night . . .

She felt a hand on her hip. Long, manicured nails indented her skin. Bare breasts pressed against her back. Emily's breath was warm on her neck. The slow, regular sound of her breathing indicated she was still asleep. And that was good. Because Zoe wasn't quite ready to face her friend. Maybe would never be ready. Images from the night before taunted her. Riding Joe's erect cock while Emily groped her body. Emily penetrating her with a strap-on dildo

(Holy fuck, did that really happen?)

from behind. The rest of the evening was a blur of booze, cocaine, and more sex. She couldn't keep her hands off Joe. It'd been so long since she'd touched another guy and she just couldn't get enough. And Emily was only too happy to allow her to have her way with her man. They stayed up for hours and hours. The sun came up and they kept going. Eventually, though, the sheer quantity of booze consumed overwhelmed the coke. Zoe didn't remember passing out, but she knew it couldn't have been that long ago.

The digital clock on the nightstand near her head showed the time as 8:19 A.M. How long had she slept? An hour? *Maybe* two? *Jesus.* She thought of Chuck and felt a dim sense of alarm. She had been gone all night. He must have come home and wondered where she was. Had he come snooping around during the night? Things had been crazy, but she was sure they'd never been interrupted. And the blinds were shut tight. No one could know what was going on in here.

On the other hand . . .

She stared at the empty vodka bottle again for several long moments before shifting her focus to the array of brown and green beer bottles scattered all about. Someone had made a booze run during the night, but she had no idea who had done it. And if she couldn't remember that, what else might she be forgetting?

Oh fuck . . .

She started panicking. Maybe Chuck had come by during the night after all. He hadn't been happy with her last night, but he wouldn't just ignore her absence, not for this long. He would have worried. He would have come looking for her. She thought of him coming into the room and seeing her bouncing up and down on his best friend's dick. She cursed her stupidity. Yes, she'd been upset last night. Had been upset and anxious for a while. But that didn't excuse what had happened. Bottom line, this whole escapade was a colossal lapse in judgment. She had no business letting something like this happen—not, at least, until she was well and truly done with Chuck.

She swung her legs over the side of the bed and sat up slowly, groaning as the ache in her head flared brighter. She whimpered and scanned the floor for her clothes. The pain was bad, but the need to get dressed and out was more intense. It wasn't just the need to see Chuck and know the full extent of the damage done. That reluctance to face Emily after the things they'd done together was growing by the moment, verging on becoming something much more intense. *Fuck*. She might have to spend the remainder of the vacation avoiding all contact with her best friend. And that sucked, but she didn't see how she had a choice. Or . . . did she?

Nobody forced you to do any of those things.

This was undeniably true. She had come to this room of her own free will.

Guess what else? You fucking loved every second of it.

Also true. Acknowledging this only intensified her conflicted emotions. There were implications in last night's mad romp she wouldn't be ready to deal with for a long time.

So, yeah, she needed to be gone from this fucking den of iniquity, but where were her fucking clothes? She got to her feet and shakily wandered about the room. Her shorts and halter were in a pile of discarded clothes on the other side of the bed, mixed in with Emily's clingy black dress and Joe's jeans and underwear. She stooped to retrieve her things from the pile and let out a startled yelp as a fist thudded against the other side of the closed door. A voice called out her name. Female. Annalisa? The knock came again, louder, much more insistent. The voice became shrill as it called out her name again and then Emily's name.

Zoe groaned and managed to croak out a husky reply. "Hold on!"

She hopped into the shorts, the effort causing her to fall against the wall behind her. The insistent knock came yet again. Louder. Faster. Harder. Just like the relentless beat of the club music spewing from Emily's iPod. Zoe wanted to scream. It was all too much. She finished dressing, stabbed the iPod's pause button, and wobbled over to the door.

Emily stirred behind her. "Mmm . . ." She yawned sleepily. "What's going on?"

"Dunno."

Zoe opened the door and blinked against bright sunlight. She held a hand to her brow and squinted at Annalisa's livid expression. "Hey. What's up?"

Annalisa pushed past her into the room. Her friend looked like she was about to blow a gasket. She was shaking. Zoe was pretty sure she'd never seen her quite this angry. Watching her survey the room did nothing to still Zoe's fears. It was too easy to see it all through Annalisa's eyes. The naked bodies. The empty booze bottles. The tray on the table with still-lingering traces of white powder smudged across its surface. All that and the odor of sex still heavy in the air.

Annalisa turned to look at her. "So you've been here all night?"

Zoe grimaced at her tone and said, "Yeah."

"Having a little party, right?"

Zoe shrugged. "I guess."

Emily sat up in bed and stretched her arms high over her head as she yawned again. She was still nude and made no effort to cover herself. "Look, what's the big fucking deal? Seriously. Zoe's a grown-up. She can do what she wants. Who the fuck are you to judge?"

Emboldened by Emily's sharp tongue, Zoe felt a bit of her own defensiveness fade. Some of the shame seemed to vanish as well. "Yeah. So I had some fucking fun last night. So what? Nobody got hurt."

Annalisa did not look chastened by this reproach. "Well, that's where you're wrong, Zoe. Somebody did get hurt."

Zoe frowned. "What are you talking about?"

"You need to see Chuck." She clapped a hand around one of Zoe's wrists and began to drag her toward the door. "You need to see what happened last night while you were off playing with these creeps."

Emily raised a middle finger. "Fuck you too, bitch. I've never fucking liked you. Stupid whore."

Annalisa paused with her hand on the door and turned to face Emily. "I'm glad you said that, Emily. I always thought you were only pretending to like me for Zoe's sake. Now I know." She glanced at Zoe. "We all know."

Zoe's head was throbbing again. "Can we please just stop this?"

Emily sneered at Annalisa. "Boring cunt."

Zoe was pulled out into the bright sunlight. The door to her own room was standing open. She made Annalisa halt just outside the door, laying a hand on the other girl's shoulder and turning her toward her. "Look, I'm sorry Emily was so mean. She didn't mean any of that. I'll . . . talk to her about it."

Annalisa's expression softened some. "I appreciate the thought, but there's no need to play peacemaker, Zoe. Honestly, it's a relief. I'm so tired of the game. She's a user. The only sad thing is how totally fooled she has you."

"You're not being fair."

Annalisa shrugged. "Maybe, maybe not. But let's leave it for another time." She nodded at the open door. "This needs dealing with now."

Zoe frowned, feeling anxious again. "Is it . . . really that bad?"

Annalisa didn't say anything, but she didn't need to—the

grim look on her face said it all. Zoe's anxiety increased as she followed her inside. The bathroom door stood open at the far end of the room. She heard water running. And an intermittent splashing sound. She brushed past Annalisa, stopped at the door, and put a hand to her mouth to stifle a gasp.

Chuck was in there, attired only in his jeans. He was leaning over the sink and splashing cold water on his face. He looked at her and tried to smile, an effort rendered grotesque by his swollen lips. His face was bruised and abraded in several places. There was more swelling around both eyes. His bare torso bore similar signs of abuse. Someone had kicked the living shit out of him.

Zoe's eyes watered. "God. Chuck . . . what happened?"

He shrugged and stood up straight, gingerly patting his face dry with a white washcloth. "Got jumped outside a bar across the street at three in the morning. Couple guys in ski masks. It looks worse than it is."

Zoe wiped tears from her cheeks with the back of a hand. She stepped into the bathroom and cautiously touched one of the welts on his face, eliciting a small wince. "Jesus, Chuck. You poor thing. I'm sorry."

More tears came then, followed by a sob, then still more sobs. She was shaking. Chuck pulled her into his arms, allowing her to press her damp face against his warm neck. He stroked her hair and patted her back, whispered words of reassurance. She'd already felt pretty damn guilty, but hearing and feeling his sincerity only made it worse. She thought of what she must have been doing while Chuck was being assaulted and felt like pure shit. He'd only gone to that bar because of his frustrations with her. This was all her fault. The sobs intensified and pretty soon she was wailing like a baby. Chuck just held her and rocked her very gently, cooing in her ear until she began to calm down.

She moved back a step, but stayed in his arms as she

looked up at him and blinked away more tears. "What did the police say?"

Chuck's expression turned stony. "Police?"

"You did call the cops?"

Chuck shook his head. "No cops."

"Are you shitting me? You can't be serious."

Annalisa snorted behind her. "Oh, he's serious. We've spent the last hour going round and round on this. Got fed up and said I'd call them myself. Would've done it, too, except Chuckles here threatened to smash my BlackBerry into a million little pieces. Can't have that."

"Why on earth wouldn't you call the cops? They might have killed you, Chuck." Zoe started trembling again as she said this. Because it was absolutely true. Chuck could easily have died while she was off screwing and snorting half of Colombia up her nose. The thought brought the enormity of it all home again, causing fresh tears to spill. "Oh, Chuck."

He cupped her face in his hands. "Hey, look at me. Listen to me, okay? I'm fine. I'm not dead. Sure, I look a mess, but it's nothing permanent. They got my credit cards and all the cash I had, but I've already canceled the cards, and Dad's wiring some money." He forced a laugh. "How old-school is that? We'll have to go to a Western Union. It's kind of funny when you think about it."

The crease in Zoe's brow deepened. "No, it's not. It's not funny at all. I want you to call the cops, Chuck."

"No."

"Goddammit. Why not?"

"I'm trying to tell you. The money's covered. And we're on fucking vacation. I'm not about to let anything ruin that. The way things stand, we can still get to Myrtle Beach today and get on with having a good time. We can put this bullshit behind us and have a great vacation. Or"—a smirk indented a corner of his mouth—"I can call the cops and it'll become this huge stinking deal." He shook his head. "Fuck that. Me?

I'm ready to hit the road." He ruffled her hair. "Looks like you had a rough night, too. Take a shower. We'll grab some breakfast and get moving again. What do you say?"

Zoe stared at him without speaking for a long while. It was clear a part of him really believed in what he was saying. But something still didn't feel right. He was putting a lot of effort into making this thing go away. It was odd. This was no mere petty theft he'd endured. He'd been violently assaulted.

Still . . .

Chuck had always been good at talking people into doing things his way, a talent handed down to him from his bigshot father. She had been sure she'd developed an immunity to his manipulations, but now she wasn't so sure. She wasn't sure about a lot of things. She stared at his wounds and her heart ached for him. Some remaining ember of the passion she'd once felt for him began to flare back to life. It was stupid, but she couldn't help it. She looked at his beaten face and wanted to help him heal.

Make him whole again.

She sighed and summoned a smile. "Okay. You win. No cops."

He grinned, then winced in pain. "Awesome. You won't regret this, Zoe. I promise."

He pulled her into his arms again and she hugged him back with all her might. She looked over his shoulder and saw Annalisa's reflection in the bathroom mirror. There was a look of intense disapproval on her face. Regardless of the sympathy she obviously felt for Chuck today, she just as obviously still didn't like him. It'd take more than one savage beating at the hands of masked strangers to change that.

Zoe tilted her head and stared at the ceiling.

There was no judgment there.

None she could see, at least.

CHAPTER TWENTY

March 23

He knew what he should do. It was what any sane person would do. He slowed slightly as a side road came up on the right, eyeing the potential path to freedom with a mixture of longing and trepidation. The old Tercel was some twenty yards ahead of him and had already passed the side road. He eased off the gas some more, hanging back a little as he thought about it. He still had time. A few precious seconds. He could whip the Galaxie in that direction, put the pedal down, and be on his way out of this madness. It was a tantalizing thought. He imagined Lindsey, Charlene, and his uncle Bill seeing this situation through his eyes, watching it like a scene in a suspense movie, sitting on the edge of their seats and loudly urging him to take the turn.

The Galaxie rolled past the side road. He spared it one last yearning look and returned his attention to the road ahead. The Tercel had slowed some, too. Roxie was probably watching him in the rearview mirror, waiting to see what he would do. What would she have done if he'd tried to flee? Probably execute a wide, gravel-and-dust-spewing turn and come after him at high speed. She couldn't just let him go. Could she? He was a witness to several brutal murders. He could testify against her. Put her on death row. Why in hell would she risk that? It made no sense. He thought about it some more as he pushed the gas pedal down and narrowed the gap between the two cars.

He decided he was wrong. What Roxie was doing made no sense from the perspective of a normal, rational person. But she wasn't normal. Or rational. She was the most reckless person he'd ever met. So in a way, what she was doing made perfect sense. It was part of a larger pattern of wild unpredictability. Also, she seemed utterly fearless and confident. She wasn't worried about the possibility of Rob calling the law down on her because she was absolutely certain he wouldn't do that. Didn't doubt it for even a second.

And the hell of it was . . . she was right.

He might yet flee. He was still alone behind the wheel of the Galaxie. He wasn't out of escape opportunities just yet. But even if he ran, he would do nothing more than return to his old life, covering his absence with a story about a wild bender to mollify his friends and loved ones. He would never tell the cops about Roxie or any of the things she'd done. Sure, she deserved to face some kind of justice for those things. And maybe one day that would happen. Hell, it was probably inevitable. She couldn't run from that long trail of dead bodies forever. But it didn't matter. Not right here and now. All Rob knew for sure was he would not be the reason it happened.

Not after last night.

Memories of the long evening of carnal indulgence made him shiver with renewed desire. *Holy shit. Seriously, holy . . . fucking . . . shit.* He had been with seven other women prior to Roxie, had no real bedroom complaints about all but one of them (the exception being weird Miss Carmichael, his sophomore English teacher). But nothing in his past matched the sheer erotic intensity of sex with Roxie. She was beyond wild, like a frenzied animal at times, and yet not out of control. She knew what she was doing and was able to manipulate him to the brink and back again over and over. She bruised and wounded his body, leaving scratches and bite marks all over his torso. He got hard again as he thought about what it had been like to penetrate her as she writhed and growled beneath him, her eyes alight with a fierce and intimidating hunger.

Holy ever-loving goddamn . . .

The Tercel started slowing down.

Rob gave his head a hard shake to clear the erotic memories and tried to focus on the task at hand. They were on a narrow and winding rural back road, a route Roxie had selected after careful consultation of an atlas. The road was very lightly traveled. They had passed only one other vehicle for the last three miles, a lumbering old pickup driven by a hunched-over elderly man. The road wasn't just off the beaten path, it was the highway to the middle of fucking nowhere. At least it seemed that way. Considering what she had in mind, Roxie had chosen wisely. Of course, what she had in mind was more violent madness and he wasn't too thrilled about that, but he couldn't say he didn't know what he was in for by this point. Nope, he was going into this with his eyes wide open, with the full knowledge that something horrible would be happening very shortly.

The Tercel continued to slow down. Rob craned his neck and saw another narrow side road coming up on the left. Roxie put on the Tercel's blinker and slowed almost to a full stop. Rob laughed, the blinker being sort of unnecessary. She turned left down the little road and Rob followed her lead, leaving the gravel rural route for a rutted dirt passage that was more like a path through the woods than an actual road. The road was rough on the Galaxie's old frame, and Rob winced at every bump and jounce.

The dense line of trees to either side of the road seemed to grow taller the deeper they plunged into the woods, almost to the point of blotting out the sky. The path widened a little at one point, and Rob was unsurprised when Roxie chose to stop there. She parked the Tercel and Rob pulled in behind her. He turned the key backward in the ignition, silencing the rumbling engine. He got out and stretched, tired from the long hours of driving.

The Tercel's driver-side door popped open and Roxie stepped out. She was wearing the same tight T-shirt and jeans she'd worn the previous day. His breath caught in his throat as his eyes traced the luscious lines of her body. The memories stirred again. His hands flexed. Instinct. He could almost feel her soft flesh beneath his fingers. She saw him looking and smiled.

He smiled back.

Then he saw the gun tucked into the waistband of her jeans and the smile faded. He remembered why they were out here and a renewed sense of bleakness colored his perceptions, temporarily dampened his desire for her.

She came to him and put her arms around him, held him very close, let him feel the weight of the gun against his belly. She smiled. "You almost ran, didn't you?"

He shrugged. "No. Not really. Thought about it. It was never really gonna happen."

Her smile brightened. "Good."

He was getting hard again. Crazy. Even now, knowing what was about to happen, he wanted her. Wanted her bad. He cleared his throat. "Roxie . . ."

She laughed, touched a finger to his lips. "Time for fun later. Business first."

She let go of him and walked over to the Tercel's trunk, twirling a ring of keys on an upraised index finger. The keys belonged to the person locked inside the trunk. A man who was about to die. Roxie whistled a perky tune as she stood there with one hip cocked out and sorted through the keys. She found the right one and opened the trunk. The man lying in that dark space reached out to her with a shaky, pasty hand, which she knocked away. She tugged the gun out of her waistband, stepped back, and pointed it at him.

"Get out, fucker."

A sob emerged from the trunk.

Roxie's posture became more rigid and she thrust the gun toward the trunk. "GET THE FUCK OUT RIGHT FUCKING NOW, FUCKER!"

Rob cringed, his ears ringing.

More sobs came from the trunk, but now the man grasped the rubber-covered lip of the trunk and started to haul himself out. Rob's heart began to race, the harsh reality of what was happening hitting him again. A man was about to be murdered and he had no intention of doing anything to prevent it. His conscience jeered at him. *Still think you're not a monster, asshole?*

Rob felt like crying, but his eyes remained dry. Actual tears would only deepen his shame. The voice of his conscience was right. There was no way to absolve himself of his complicity in this heinous act. This was wrong. Flat-out fucking wrong. So that made him a bad guy. Okay, yeah, he wasn't the one pulling the trigger, but big deal. He was letting it happen, which made him just as bad as Roxie.

The man was out of the trunk now. He stood up straight and blinked against the bright sunlight. He was a pudgy guy in his thirties. He wore dirty jeans and a wrinkled old *Star Wars* T-shirt. The guy looked at the gun and whined. He was pathetic. The aging nerd had probably been getting his ass handed to him since grammar school. Why should the last day of his miserable life be any different?

He had been a ridiculously easy mark. An hour of cruising the tawdrier parts of Starkweather, North Carolina, had led them to an apartment complex called the Shire, a name that elicited predictable giggles from Roxie. The complex was not a hive of activity that early on a working day. Most of the parking spaces were empty. Just one car had been parked outside of building G, the beat-up old Tercel belonging to Mr. Lucky here. He'd come out of his apartment and approached his car at just the wrong time (for him). It was stunning how fast it happened. The fat moron just gaped stupidly at Roxie as she leaped out of the Galaxie and brandished the gun at him. She whipped the gun across his face, snapping teeth and drawing blood. Then she snatched his keys from his hand, got the Tercel's trunk open, and shoved him inside. It had all happened in just over a minute, and no one had seen a thing. No one inclined to do anything about it anyway. Roxie took the Tercel and Rob followed her to a nearby gas station, where Roxie purchased the atlas and outlined her plans. So now they had their new car.

And one last loose end to tie up.

Roxie waved the gun toward the line of trees on her right. "That way, fucker."

The man glanced at the woods, licked his lips, and looked at Roxie again. "You're about to kill me. Aren't you?"

Roxie snickered. "Fatty wins the prize."

"Then I'm not going anywhere. And the name's Greg, not Fatty."

Roxie glowered at him. "I care why?"

Greg sucked up his courage and sneered at her. "Don't you think you should know the name of the person you're killing? Maybe it makes it a little less impersonal, right? Like you're killing an actual human being instead of a thing." He shook his head. "I'm not a thing. You can't kill me with no more thought than you'd give to squashing a bug." His bottom lip began to tremble again. "It isn't right. So you can just shoot me here, bitch. I'm not doing a death march for you."

Roxie whipped the gun across his face, staggering him, then swung it back around for another blow. He fell back against the trunk and Roxie shoved the .38's barrel deep inside his open mouth. She leaned close to him, spraying his sweat-sheened face with spittle as she pushed out a string of tightly enunciated words: "You fuck. You fat fucking fuck. You're less than a bug. You're *nothing*. Think I can't make this hard, you fucking geek? Think I can't make you beg? Start walking or you'll find out just how low I can take you, bitch."

She stepped away from him and grabbed him by the neck, shoved him toward the woods. He staggered in that direction, cried out, glanced once over his shoulder, and kept walking. He was broken. It was painfully easy to see. He would do whatever Roxie said from this point on, despite knowing there was no way to alter the final outcome of his desperate plight.

Rob followed them into the woods. This patch of wilderness was thick with wildly growing vegetation. There were leafy vines, plants, and bushes everywhere. He was thankful for his jeans and long sleeves. He couldn't identify poison oak or ivy by sight, but there were enough prickly, strangely shaped leaves about to worry him. As always, Roxie just barged ahead, completely heedless of the potential dangers of nature. Rob hung back several feet, watching Roxie and the condemned man with a wary eye. He kept expecting Greg to bolt, maybe catch them by surprise and hope to get far enough away to seek cover in the woods. It was what Rob would do in his position. What other option was there? It would be futile, of course. The guy was fat and slow. Roxie was young and fit. She would pursue him, eventually take him down. Maybe she was hoping Greg would make a break for it. Hell, she would probably enjoy chasing her quarry through the woods, safe in the knowledge there was no way he could successfully elude her for long.

Roxie glanced over her shoulder at Rob. "Look at this fuck, Rob. All that fucking blubber. It's disgusting, right?"

"I . . . guess."

Roxie snorted and turned her attention back to Greg, whose already plodding pace was slowing by the minute. "Damn right it is. We should call Sea World, let them know one of their whales escaped. Hey, Greg. How did you get so far inland? You some kind of amphibian mutant humpback piece of shit?"

Greg didn't say anything, just kept shuffling forward.

Roxie laughed.

The mocking cruelty disturbed Rob, but it didn't surprise him. This was an absolutely unrepentant, cold-blooded killer. Cruelty was deeply ingrained in her nature. Greg was going to die. No doubt about it. Still, he should be allowed some small measure of dignity. Rob briefly considered voicing this opinion and immediately thought better of it. It wouldn't help Greg. And it might earn him a world of grief in the bargain. So he kept his mouth shut and kept walking, did his best to tune out her relentless barrage of belittling insults.

Sweat dampened the fabric of his shirt beneath the armpits. Rob wasn't sure how long they'd been out here or how far they'd come. Long enough to work up a sweat, anyway. A glance over his shoulder confirmed they'd come far enough to lose all sight of the road and the cars. They were surrounded by wilderness. It made him feel claustrophobic, which was an odd thing to feel in the "great outdoors." They kept trudging forward. Another sweat stain spread across the back of his shirt, causing the fabric to adhere to his flesh. Then, just when he thought he couldn't take it anymore, they arrived at a place where there was a bit more space between the tightly bunched trees, a sort of miniclearing.

"You can stop now, whale boy."

Greg was barely moving by this point. Coming to a halt required minimal effort. He stopped in his tracks and stared up at a tree directly ahead of him. Dim, unintelligible words emerged from his mouth.

Roxie giggled. "He's *praying.*"

Rob thought, *Who wouldn't?*

Roxie had been holding the gun down by her side. She

lifted it now and aimed it squarely at the man's back. Rob hoped she'd just pull the trigger and be done with it rather than draw it out any longer.

He should have known better.

"Turn around, fucker." Roxie wasn't giggling now. Her voice was hard and cold again. "Now, bitch! I don't mean later today or tomorrow. TURN THE FUCK AROUND RIGHT FUCKING NOW!"

Greg turned around and stared at the ground. His mouth was still moving, rapidly, as he hurried to share his last conscious thoughts with God.

"Knock that shit off and look at me, Greg."

The use of his actual name in place of an epithet apparently got his attention. Greg opened his eyes and stared right at her. His eyes were wet. A snot bubble swelled from one nostril and popped.

Roxie smiled. "Good boy. Now get on your knees."

There was no fight at all left in this man. He dropped slowly to his knees with a pained grunt and stared up at her.

Roxie stepped toward him and placed the barrel of the gun against his forehead. "Keep your eyes open, Greg. Do it or I'll make this worse, I promise. You believe me, don't you?"

Greg kept his eyes open and replied with a very slight nod.

Roxie smiled again. "Good. I've got a question for you, Greg. You don't really want to die today, do you?"

Confusion creased Greg's brow, but he managed a small shake of his head.

Roxie chuckled. "Didn't think so. I mean, whales are dumb animals, but even whales want to live, right?" Another chuckle. "Don't worry, I'm just fucking with you. Don't expect a real answer to that."

She stepped away from Greg and aimed the .38 at Rob's belly. "I want you on your knees too, Rob. Right next to the whale."

Rob's mouth came open. He just stared at her for a moment. Unable to speak. Unable even to form a single coherent thought. He searched her face for any hint of mirth, but there was nothing. He'd never seen a face so pretty look so hard. Her beauty was a mask. In that moment he could clearly see the ugliness lurking beneath. His eyes watered. Not so many hours ago he'd made love to this woman, had shared with her an experience more intense than he could ever hope to share with another human being. He couldn't fathom how the woman he'd shared that with now apparently intended to kill him. Which made him an even bigger idiot than he'd begun to suspect. He knew what she was. Had known all along.

So this shouldn't come as a surprise.

Shouldn't feel like a betrayal.

But it did. It *did*.

Oh God . . .

She thumbed back the .38's hammer. "I'm not asking again, Robin. On your knees next to the whale. Right now."

He sniffled and moved past her. She didn't back away to give him more room, her smirk telling him she knew he lacked the courage to make a lunge for the gun. He dropped to his knees next to Greg and stared up at her. "Why?"

She pressed the gun's barrel against his forehead. Her smug expression stung him. "Why do you think, Robin? To keep things interesting. I get bored easy. Besides, maybe you still have a chance."

Rob's heart beat a rapid, desperate rhythm against his chest wall. She was playing some kind of game here, indulging in another sadistic exercise, but he couldn't figure out what the point was. Probably there wasn't one. Not beyond drawing out the agony of anticipation anyway. He figured she'd meant to do this all along. Probably did this kind of thing all the time. Grabbed some guy and had a bit of fun with him. Maybe made him feel they had some kind of deeper connection, even in the face of so much insanity. And she would kill the poor fuck every time. He was just what he'd always been—the latest in a long line of marks and suckers.

She pushed the gun harder against his forehead. "Did you hear me, Robin? I said you still have a chance. What do you think of that?"

"I don't believe it. You're just fucking with me, like always."

She smiled. "That's where you're wrong, baby. I'm gonna play a quick little game. Loser gets to eat a bullet. Winner gets to walk away from here with me. Close your eyes, bitches."

Rob closed his eyes. He knew the other man had done the same. There was no defying Roxie and they both knew it. Had no choice but to accept it. Rob began his own recitation of prayers. But he kept his mouth shut, kept it internal. He didn't want Roxie to hear. He prayed for his uncle and other close relatives. He prayed for Lindsey and Charlene. Prayed for other close friends. But he didn't bother asking God for forgiveness. He knew he didn't deserve it.

The gun came away from his head.

What's she doing?

The need to know was almost overpowering, but his fear of her was even greater. He kept his eyes shut, finished his prayers, and strove to keep his mind blank. He wanted to enter a meditative state. A gray, formless place. Retreat mentally and just let it happen.

"Eeny."

He felt the gun barrel against his forehead again.

And Roxie giggled. "Meeny."

The gun moved away from him. "Miny."

It came back. "Moe."

Away again. "My."

Back. "Mother"

Away. "Told."

And on it went, back and forth, until the barrel grazed his forehead again on the last syllable. "It." Another giggle. "So, so sorry, Robin."

Greg heaved a big breath next to him. "Oh, thank God. Thank you, God."

Rob squeezed his eyes as tightly shut as he could get them and found he was willing to send out a last-ditch prayer or two after all. He tensed, waiting for the explosion that would blow his head apart and send blood and brain matter flying across the forest floor. He was shaking so hard he barely noticed when the gun barrel moved from his forehead.

But he did hear the boom of the gun.

He screamed and opened his eyes in time to see Greg's body toppling toward him. He screamed again and scrambled out of the way. Greg hit the ground and didn't move. He was dead, with a ragged hole in the center of his forehead and a much bigger one at the back of his head. Rob whined and scooted away from the body, twisting around to stare up at Roxie through eyes wide with terror. His heart felt close to bursting, it was beating so hard and fast. He tried to speak, but couldn't catch his breath.

Roxie was smirking and shaking her head. "Oh, come on, Rob. It was just a game. I was never really gonna shoot you. You lost, remember?"

Rob stayed there on his knees for several more moments, panting hard and struggling not to hyperventilate. By the time he at last found his voice, the terror was surging inside him again. "I wish you had killed me. Oh fuck. Fuck. Holy fuck. I can't take any more of this. I can't. I swear."

Roxie leaned toward him, holding out her free hand. "Oh, stop being such a pussy." She fixed him with a steely, unyielding glare. "I'm not gonna kill you, Rob. Not unless you put me in a position where I have to, and I don't think you're gonna do that. Are you?"

Rob took her hand and let her haul him to his feet. He looked her in the eye and said, "You're crazy. You are fucking crazy."

She opened his hand and pressed the gun into it, forced his fingers to wrap around the butt. She smiled and moved his hand so that the gun barrel was pressed against her belly. "There. Now you're the one with the power. You can kill me. Be done with me. Go on. What are you waiting for?"

Rob's hand started to shake.

Tears spilled from his eyes.

Roxie wiped some of the tears away with the ball of a thumb. "It's loaded, Rob. I'm not setting you up and this isn't another game. You can kill me if you want. You really can."

His shaking became more pronounced.

He let go of the gun and it hit the ground with a thud.

Roxie sighed. "It's funny. I should feel relieved, but a little part of me is disappointed. Isn't that funny?"

Rob swallowed thickly. "No. It's not funny at all."

"Sometimes I kind of want to die."

Rob's eyes filled with tears again. "Roxie . . ."

A small laugh. "Oh, relax. You're not getting rid of me anytime soon."

Rob kept shaking. This was all too much. He needed a tall bottle of liquor and a fistful of pills. He needed to make this all go away for a while. But he knew he was a long way from even that brand of empty solace.

Roxie retrieved the gun and tucked it in a rear pocket. "Come on, baby." She clasped hands with him and steered him back in the general direction of the road. "Time's a-wastin'."

Roxie had a few last things to attend to when they finally reached the road. She retrieved her overflowing tote bag from the Galaxie and stowed it in the Tercel. She switched out the Tercel's plates with plates stolen from yet another car. Those things accomplished, they got in the Tercel and drove away from there.

Roxie was driving and that was fine with Rob.

He'd done enough of it for a while.

He glanced at the rearview mirror and caught a last glimpse of the Galaxie's bright red finish before the road twisted and the deep woods swallowed the old car. He felt a pang at the loss of his grandfather's treasured antique, but it was a numb pain. Too much had happened. Maybe there would be time for sentimentality later. Time to grieve that lost link with his family's past.

He looked at Roxie.

Saw her watching him, face devoid of even a hint of a smile.

No.

Probably not.

He closed his eyes and tried—without much success—to make his mind blank. But he couldn't stop thinking. About all of it. The terror. The disconnection from his own life. All those dead bodies. So he opened his eyes again and watched the road ahead. Because he knew the truth.

There would never be any escaping the horror surrounding him.

It was too late to turn away.

Too late to run or make a different choice.

Too fucking late all around.

CHAPTER TWENTY-ONE

March 20

Zeb tied the girl to the motel-room bed and went into the bathroom. He shut the door, went over to the toilet, and flipped the seat up. Moments later he had his cock out and was pumping the engorged organ furiously with his fist. He closed his eyes and imagined it was the girl's mouth on him. The vivid image made him groan and inside of a minute he was shooting thick ropes of come into the toilet water. He stood there panting for a time and stared at the floating discharge. The ejaculate looked like strands of cheap pearls drifting in water. He groaned again and a feeling of intense relief flooded through him.

Never in his adult life had he experienced a level of frustration even close to what he had been dealing with the past few days, not even during his years in the institution, locked up for so long in that little room. That had been easy compared to the effort required to keep his hands off the girl.

He flipped the toilet seat down, letting it bang shut, and pushed the flush handle. A gurgle of rushing water carried his spilled seed away. He shuffled over to the sink and stared at his reflection in the mirror mounted above it. His long hair was gone. The girl had cut it for him last night, after they'd cut her hair into that bob style and dyed it an unnatural shade of bright red. He had been wary of trusting the task to her, but Lulu had insisted. The scissors were long and sharp, a potentially very effective weapon. He had felt vulnerable, another unfamiliar and unpleasant experience. But he wasn't in the habit of disobeying Lulu, and, as usual, she had been right. The girl did not attack him. And that was a hard thing to figure out. She could easily have inflicted a very severe wound, perhaps even killed him. So why hadn't she?

"I told you, Zeb. She's like you. Deep down, she knows it."

There was a new image in the mirror. Lulu had materialized and was standing a few feet directly behind him. He turned and faced her, folding his arms across his chest and leaning his butt against the edge of the sink. "Yeah, you keep saying that. But so far I haven't seen any proof."

Lulu smiled. "You will, soon enough."

This was another thing he was having some trouble accepting. Until yesterday, Lulu had always been a disembodied voice in his head. Completely real, he knew, but there had never been any hint of a physical component to her existence. Until she appeared out of thin air last night, after the girl had drifted off to sleep. That had spooked him. Zeb had never been genuinely scared of anything in his entire adult life, but that had done it. One moment he was sitting on the edge of the bed, smoking a cigarette and just thinking, and then—*poof!*—there she was.

Lulu was a dead ringer for Adrienne Barbeau, an actress he remembered from low-budget movies he'd seen on cable when he was young. She wore a tiny blue bikini and a necklace of withered human ears. The attire was bizarre, but it was her uncanny resemblance to the actress that initially made him think she was a hallucination. So, acting on the theory that no hallucination would have physical substance, he'd grabbed one of her large breasts. It had felt real enough—and pleasingly pliable—beneath his probing fingers. The subsequent stinging slap across his face had felt just as real.

She looked exactly the same as she had last night, except now she wore a red bikini instead of a blue one.

"You really think she wants to kill?"

"She killed Clyde, didn't she?"

Zeb's expression darkened. "Yeah. In self-defense. Ain't the same thing as what you're sayin'. I gave her a chance to prove herself and she couldn't do it."

Lulu made a clucking sound and shook her head. "It's because you picked the wrong kind of victim. Find her someone she'd like to kill and she'll do it. She'll do it and she'll love it. You'll see. And then you'll have a new partner, a better one."

Zeb frowned. "Wasn't nothin' wrong with Clyde. He was my friend."

"He was a nasty, disgusting piece of shit."

"So? Most folks would say the same about me."

Lulu laughed. "And they'd be right. You fuck corpses and eat human flesh. You are the very definition of disgusting, Zeb. But there's a difference. Clyde wasn't special. You are. And so is that girl."

"That's another thing you keep saying that I don't get. Special how?"

Lulu smiled again. "That's not for me to say yet. Some things you need to figure out on your own. It'll all become clear in time."

"I really want to fuck her."

Lulu's smile vanished. "You can't."

"Why not?"

She approached him and jabbed a finger against his chest, the long nail pricking his skin. "Shut up about this, Zebulon. The girl is special. That's all you need to know. You will not force yourself on her."

"What if I just can't help myself?"

Lulu reached up and clamped her hand around his throat. She forced him to his knees with astonishing ease and bent down close to him. Her hand was like a band of iron around his throat, and he struggled for breath as she spoke. "If you violate her, I will punish you. And then I'll leave you. You will never see me or hear my voice again. I'll be gone forever and you will never be the same."

She let go of his throat.

Zeb gagged and struggled to draw in breath. He got to his feet and managed to croak out an apology: "I'm . . . sorry."

Lulu's expression remained dark. "Not as sorry as you will be if you disobey me."

Then she was gone, the space where she'd been occupied only by air now. He thought about what she'd said and tried to imagine life without Lulu. The prospect terrified him.

So that was that. The girl was off-limits. Permanently.

Christ. He hoped like hell Lulu was telling the truth about her.

Hoped she was worth all this struggle and pain.

The crazy man was talking to himself again. Well, talking to Lulu. Which amounted to the same thing, as Lulu clearly originated from somewhere inside his fucked-up brain. She had almost gotten used to the strange one-sided conversations, but this time there was a new wrinkle. She was hearing both sides of the exchange. One part of it was in his usual gruff speaking voice, which normally was the only part she would hear, with Lulu's replies presumably only being audible inside his head. But now she was hearing the other side of the conversation too, a higher-pitched, almost squeaky voice. It was Zeb talking, but he was trying to make Lulu's contributions sound like they were actually being uttered by a woman. Upon hearing this, Julie had to suppress a giggle fit. It was so incredibly absurd. But then he said something that removed any trace of humor from the situation.

I really want to fuck her.

By which he meant rape. Fucking was something you did

with a willing partner. And while she might well be open to engaging in a lot of twisted activities, she knew for a fact she would never give herself to the creepy old necrophiliac willingly. The way he looked at her most of the time never failed to chill her. Those dead eyes made her feel like she had a million invisible bugs crawling all over her body. Especially when he'd undress her and stare at her for a while, as he'd done prior to going into the bathroom. It didn't take a lot of imagination to figure out what he'd been doing in there prior to Lulu's arrival.

The talk with Lulu got even stranger after a few minutes. It was hard to tell exactly what was going on in there, but she got the sense Lulu was administering some kind of physical punishment. Zeb made gurgling sounds and uttered a few strangled words, then spoke clearly as Lulu in that ridiculous faux-female voice. The latter sounded sort of like Mickey Mouse.

Julie couldn't help it—that impression *did* make her giggle.

The bathroom door banged open and Zeb staggered out into the room. He came over to the side of the bed and stared down at her. He braced a knee on the edge of the bed and leaned over her to undo her bonds. He licked his lips and stared at her breasts. "Can't decide whether I'd rather eat those or suckle on 'em."

Julie made herself stay very still. The physical proximity repulsed her, but she was afraid flinching away would agitate him. "Lulu says you can't do either."

He scowled and finished untying her. "It ain't nice to eavesdrop, bitch."

Julie scooped her clothes—denim shorts and a halter—up from the floor and began to get dressed. "Yeah. Real sorry about that, Zeb. But, you know, the fucking bathroom's only ten feet away. Don't want me to hear your talks with Lulu? Take it outside."

She finished dressing and grabbed the television remote

from the nightstand. The remote was on a cord, which was anchored to the nightstand. Which she thought was pretty fucking funny. Who the hell steals a remote?

Zeb frowned. "What are you doing?"

"*Gossip Girl* is on tonight. Let's see if this dump gets the CW." She thumbed the power button, the TV blinked on, and she began to scan through the limited array of channels. She squealed. "Yay! There it is. Wanna watch?"

Zeb turned and stared blankly at the TV for several moments. Then he looked over his shoulder at her. "You like this shit?"

"Yes."

He sighed. "I guess I'm too old for it. I don't under—"

Julie put a finger to her lips and shushed him. "Shut up! I'm trying to listen. Save it for the commercials."

She flopped onto her stomach, kicked her legs up, and propped her chin in her hands. Zeb sat on the floor. They watched the entire show. Zeb surprised her by keeping his comments and complaints to a minimum. She even had a bit of fun fielding his intermittent questions about the show and its characters. He really didn't get it at all, but he was struggling to grasp her interest. It was sort of what watching the show with her dad might have been like. That thought took her to a dark place briefly during one commercial break, but she shoved the bad thoughts away and lost herself in the show again when the break ended.

A touch of melancholy crept in with the end of the show. For that one hour things had seemed almost normal. But now it was over and she was again forced to deal with her new reality, which remained pretty fucking grim. She was being kept prisoner by a man who might snap and kill her at any moment. She couldn't stop thinking of what might happen. Every time she closed her eyes she saw him on top of her nude and very still body, face contorting in twisted agony as he penetrated her dead pussy. She was thinking of it again and this time it was worse, her morbid mind taking her down paths that repulsed her even as they stirred her curiosity. There was the question of lubrication, just for instance. Dead girls don't get wet for their postlife partners. Obviously. And the term *partner* was grossly inappropriate in this context, as it was another word implying consent, and dead people, duh, weren't capable of giving that. So . . . what did he use? His own spit? Some kind of lotion? Or . . . ugh . . . the victim's fresh blood?

Might as well come out and ask him. She doubted she could offend the kind of guy who did that sort of thing, so fuck it. "What do you use for lube when you bang a dead body?"

Zeb was still sitting on the floor. He turned toward her and propped a forearm on a corner of the bed. "Why you want to know?"

"Just curious."

He grunted. "Whatever's handy."

"Like?"

He told her. In detail. He used a variety of methods. Some obvious. Some . . . not.

"You are a sick piece of work, Zeb."

"Yeah. I suppose so."

"You fucking *suppose?*" She laughed. "Like maybe there's a little part of you that thinks you're normal or, I don't know, just *misunderstood?*"

He smiled. "I reckon."

The smile was a strange thing to see. It rendered the next string of sarcastic remarks she would've made DOA. It was genuine. Not his usual leer at all, but rather a reflection of simple amusement. It humanized the monster for a fleeting moment. But then she thought of the murder she'd witnessed in the woods. That terrified woman tied to that tree, strung up like some piece of wild game he'd captured. She had to keep reminding herself of things like that. His cruelty. His perversions. His willingness to kill and inflict extreme pain. It was strangely easy to lose sight of that in a moment like this. She had to keep her guard up, both physically and emotionally.

Zeb was still staring at her, a quizzical expression in place of the now-vanished smile. "What makes you special? What does Lulu see in you?"

"I don't know."

Julie sat up and scooted away from him. She picked up the remote and started clicking through the channels again. "There's got to be something else decent on. I wonder if these scrambled channels are porn. You know what I like? All girl. I'm not a lez or anything, but the guys in pornos are always so gross. The girls always have those fake tans and tits and tattoos, but they look hot anyway. I went through a phase for, like, a week of wanting to be a porn star. That would have killed my parents, which would be the main reason to do it, you know?"

Zeb smacked the remote out of her hand. "Enough of this shit."

Julie cringed away from him, whole body tensing as she awaited the long-delayed assault she was sure was imminent. "What the fuck, Zeb?"

He smiled again, but this time there was a definite leer in it. "It's high time you proved yourself, bitch. No more fucking around. You're gonna kill a man before the night's done. And if you don't do it, that's it for your ass, girl. Not even Lulu will—"

"Okay, I get it. Jesus." She rolled her eyes. "You don't have to go on and on. I have to kill a dude. Fine. Let's do it."

The conviction in her voice surprised Zeb. His brow creased as he squinted at her. The overall impression was of a man bearing witness to something utterly inexplicable.

A Bigfoot or flying-saucer sighting, maybe. He scratched the back of his head, his fingers sliding smoothly through the now much shorter locks. "I . . . really?"

She gave a single terse but emphatic nod. "Yes."

And she meant it. She didn't really want to kill anybody. But she didn't want to die, either. And there was just no other way around this. She couldn't manufacture any more delays or lame excuses.

The time to kill was at hand.

So let's get it the fuck over with.

"So how do we do this, Zeb?"

He grunted. "What do you mean? You stick a knife in the cocksucker. Or hit him over the head with something heavy." He shrugged expansively, making the muscles in his broad shoulders and neck ripple. "Don't really matter, so long as your victim gets dead."

"That's not what I mean. I mean . . ." She swept a hand around her. "Do we do it here? Or—"

"Not here."

"Okay. Where?"

"Someplace nice and private. Out in the woods is best."

"I want to use your knife. That big one."

A corner of his mouth curled up. "I like that knife." His nostrils flared and he did that weird chest-rubbing thing of his. "Wanna see you stick it in somebody."

Oh fuck, he's getting turned on by the idea. Fucking gross.

Julie covered a shiver by rolling off the bed and springing to her feet. "So let's make this happen. Fucking tired of hanging out here anyway."

Zeb opened his duffel bag and removed one of the several shirts he'd pinched from John's wardrobe. He pulled it on and grabbed the keys from the table. He was grinning as he took Julie by the arm and steered her out of the room.

Julie was somewhat less thrilled than Zeb.

But she was committed.

Tonight everything would change forever. No matter what happened after tonight, she would never be the same. And it wouldn't matter if she eventually escaped from Zeb. *Tonight*, she thought, *I become a cold-blooded murderer.*

A chill evening's wind touched her face.

It felt like the loving caress of Satan himself, welcoming a new acolyte to the fold.

CHAPTER TWENTY-TWO

March 23

After rounding everyone up, they hit the road again shortly after nine A.M., which was remarkable, given how little sleep most of them had managed during the night. Most of the credit for the amazing feat went to Chuck. He had gone into taskmaster mode after explaining his reasons for not calling the cops. Zoe retained some skepticism about that, but Chuck had been so adamant, and so earnest, that there had never been any real question of defying his wishes.

Besides . . .

I want to get to the fucking beach.

Okay, being honest, there had been an element of selfishness to her quick surrender. She hated knowing that the people who'd jumped Chuck were going to get away with it, but it was a price worth paying in order to be on their way free of any big hassle. Maybe she'd have felt different had Chuck suffered any kind of permanent damage, but he was alive and physically intact. The bruises and scratches would heal. Besides, she'd heard or read somewhere that most random robberies like that were never solved. Probably no one would ever be apprehended after the whole big ordeal with the cops, which would make the whole thing even more of a waste. And that, ladies and gentlemen, was as good a rationale for not doing it as any.

So here they were . . .

Chuck was at the wheel again, but Joe wasn't riding shot-gun this time. Zoe occupied that position now, and Joe was slumped next to Emily in the middle seat. His head was on her shoulder and he was snoring lightly. Zoe glanced at the rearview mirror and quickly directed her gaze back out the window on her side. Emily was still glaring at her. She was pissed at the way Zoe had snubbed her this morning. Zoe had stayed away from her when possible and ignored her re-peated attempts at initiating conversation.

Surely on some level Emily must have expected this. The things they'd done together during the night had been fun at the time, but in the light of day the memories were em-barrassing. Zoe was no prude. She enjoyed a bit of kink in the bedroom. But what she had done with Emily and Joe was more than that. It hadn't been any garden-variety three-some. She felt like a slut and a pervert, and she just couldn't deal with it right now, especially now that her dormant feel-ings for Chuck seemed to be stirring back to life. Which was confusing as all hell. It was tempting to write it off as a prod-uct of the guilt. But there was more to it than that. Maybe something potentially lasting, and maybe not. Either way, for now at least, she and Chuck were back on.

She saw the faint reflection of herself in the window. A small, private smile curved the corners of her mouth. She was thinking of those moments in the bathroom after An-nalisa departed, of how that concerned hug had shifted into something more passionate. She tugged at her shirt collar, feeling a little hot at the memory of Chuck penetrating her from behind as she braced her hands on the edge of the sink and watched him do her in the mirror.

She glanced at him and smiled.

"Zoe."

Shit.

Zoe sighed and looked out the window again.

"Zoe."

"What?"

"This cold-shoulder bullshit is fucking annoying. What's your damage?"

Zoe shrugged and shook her head. "Don't know what you're talking about."

"Like hell you don't."

Chuck shot her a puzzled glance.

Zoe shook her head again and rolled her eyes.

She turned in her seat and looked over her shoulder at Emily. "Look, stop the drama-queen crap. I'm just tired. Okay?" She forced a brittle smile for her friend. "Long night and not much sleep." She summoned an exaggerated yawn and groaned. "Christ, you should be as tired as me."

"I am wide fucking awake."

Zoe yawned again and this time there was nothing fake about it. She really was tired. And her head was hurting, an ache arguing with Emily wasn't helping any. She just wanted things to be quiet for a while. Was that too much to ask?

"Fuck you, Zoe."

Zoe flinched. "What?"

Emily was smiling now. "You heard me."

Annalisa sighed in the back. "Guys . . . come on . . . we're almost there."

Emily's tight smile remained in place. "Hey, I'm just kidding around. I'm just *so fucking tired.* You'll have to excuse me. I'm not in my right mind and shit."

Zoe didn't bother with a comeback to that. The situation was delicate enough. It was time for some damage control. "Emily, I'm sorry. I seriously am. It's been a weird and fucked-up morning, I think you'll agree, but I shouldn't have been such a bitch to you. Can you please forgive me?"

Emily stared at her a moment later, then looked away. "Whatever."

Zoe was satisfied. She wasn't exactly accepting the apology, but the edge had gone out of her voice. She was letting it go for now and that was good enough.

She turned away from Emily, scrunched down in her seat, and propped her bare feet on the dashboard. A while later a green road sign caught her eye: MYRTLE BEACH 51 MILES.

Almost there . . .

Feeling a lightening of spirit, she closed her eyes and started to drift toward sleep.

CHAPTER TWENTY-THREE

March 23

Rob sat slumped in the passenger seat, staring out the window at the passing scenery without really seeing it. They had been driving in silence on the interstate more than an hour. He could tell Roxie wanted to talk, but he hoped she'd keep her mouth shut a while longer. He was more afraid of her than ever and wouldn't know what to say. About anything. The incident in the woods had changed things between them. He sort of felt like he was coming back to his senses a little bit, but it was a classic case of a mixed blessing. He was seeing things more clearly, including how much of a fool he'd been. It'd been stupid in the extreme to let her manipulate him into sex. It'd complicated his feelings and made him vulnerable to being exploited even more, which had probably been her intent all along.

And he'd fallen for it.

Fucking idiot.

"Hey, asshole."

Rob winced. "What?"

"So you're admitting you're an asshole?"

"Yeah."

She laughed. "At least you admit it. It's okay. I'm an asshole, too."

"I know."

"I'm also a bitch and a right fucking cunt a lot of the time."

"Yeah."

She slugged him in the shoulder. Hard.

He looked at her, a frown on his face. "That hurt."

"Good."

Rob sat up straighter in his seat and turned toward her. "Good?"

"Yeah."

He shook his head. "Last night you said you liked me."

She smiled. "What about it?"

"Did you mean it?"

She glanced at him, her expression carefully blank. "Yeah."

"Okay. So ... if you mean that, if you're not lying ... why do you want to hurt me? If you fucking like me, Roxie, why would you for fuck's sake point a fucking gun at me and make me think you're about to kill me?"

She snorted laughter.

"It's not fucking funny."

She laughed some more and shook her head. "You should just see the expression on your face. So serious."

He glared at her. "Excuse the fuck out of me, but I think having a gun pointed at me is pretty goddamn serious. Maybe I'm just weird."

"You're definitely weird."

"Maybe. And you still haven't answered my question."

It was a strange thing. He'd spent much of the afternoon dreading and avoiding this conversation, but now that it had started he wanted answers. Direct, honest answers.

She looked at him. "I like to fuck with people."

"So that's what you were doing? Fucking with me?"

A small nod. "Yeah."

"Lovely. Nice."

"Stop being such a sensitive bitch."

Rob didn't reply to that.

She was still staring at him. "Admit it."

He frowned. "Huh? Admit what?"

"You'd like to fuck me right now."

Rob's expression then was meant to be withering, an "I can't believe you even went there, you fucking lunatic" look. An equally scathing and sarcastic comment should have accompanied it. But some primitive, below-the-surface part of him appraised her body even as he seethed with indignation. His eyes traced her curves and the swell of her breasts against that tight black T-shirt. He looked at that bright shade of lipstick and licked his lips. God, he wanted to kiss her.

He wanted to . . .

Shit.

She laughed. "You know what I'd like?"

He swallowed thickly. "What?"

"I'd like you to stick that gun in my pussy. Fully loaded. And fuck me with it."

"Jesus. You're crazy."

She smirked. "You're just figuring that out?"

"Jesus. Look. Seriously. I'm not sticking a gun . . . there." He shuddered visibly. "No. Just . . . no."

"Prude."

"If refusing to stick a firearm in your private parts makes me a prude, so be it. I can't get over how totally fucking insane you are. I mean . . . what kind of person thinks of things like that? There aren't words for how totally messed up you are."

Roxie's expression turned oddly thoughtful. "For me, sex and violence are closely related things, Rob. Think about it. Sex itself is a pretty aggressive, violent act. All that struggling and exertion. All that sweat and physicality. One person dominating the other a lot of the time. Most people don't let themselves see it that way. They wrap it up with all these phony ideas about romance and call it 'making love.' Pure bullshit. Sex is a brute thing. It's about asserting yourself and controlling the other person. It's about subjugation. And violence."

Rob scratched his head and squinted at her. "I don't know. Have you ever really been in love with someone, Roxie? Because I can tell you that sex with someone you really care about is more than what you're saying. It's . . . deeper."

Roxie made a dismissive sound. "Right. Whatever. I read about a woman on death row in Texas a while back. Maybe you'll remember this. She and some other people killed some people. She used a hatchet on one of them. She said she had an orgasm every time she swung the hatchet into the victim."

"Christ."

Roxie was smirking again. "That's what I'm talking about, see? Sex and violence, they're flip sides of the same coin. You can't have one without the other. That woman later repented and found God, the way they all do before they fry, but I guarantee she was never being more honest than when she said that thing about the hatchet."

"Is that what it's like for you, Roxie?" Rob couldn't bring himself to look at her as he asked this, fearing what he'd see in her expression. "Do you get off when you shoot people?"

"Not all the time. Not when things are happening too fast, which is how it usually goes down, right? But back there in the woods . . . a situation like that? Yeah. I got very excited when I was playing that little game."

Rob closed his eyes. "Jesus. God . . ."

She reached out and squeezed his knee, making his eyes snap open. "Hell, I've been thinking about it all day. I'm horny as shit." She laughed. "Shit, why do you think we're talking about this?"

He stared at her hand on his knee. He wanted to push it away, but he didn't want to upset her. She squeezed again, the fingers pressing more firmly into the denim-covered flesh. He looked at her. Her expression was serious and focused, her eyes blazing with seductive intensity. And as disturbed as he was by the turn of the conversation, a part of him shared that desire.

He coughed. "Um . . ."

Her hand slid away from his knee and moved higher up his thigh. "Next exit. We'll pull off and find a place. Okay?"

He nodded weakly. "Yeah . . . okay."

"This'll just be a quickie. But I have something special in mind for later tonight, after we stop for the day. Okay?"

Her hand moved up and down his thigh, stirring him to full arousal. He could barely concentrate now. He forced himself to shift his gaze from her caressing hand to her face. "What . . . do you have in mind?"

She smiled. "I want to tie you up. Do some things to you. Maybe make you come around to my way of thinking on some things. That feel good?"

He groaned. "Yeah. Jesus. Fuck, Roxie."

Rob felt helpless. And stupid. A few minutes ago he had been thinking how dumb it had been to let her manipulate him with sex. And here he was, letting it happen again. The truth was, he was powerless against her. Resistance was impossible, compliance a given. She began to really work at him, squeezing and stroking harder and harder. He groaned some more and writhed in the seat.

"You're about to go off."

Rob whimpered.

She let go of him and laughed. "You okay, Rob? You look sort of . . . frustrated."

He leaned back in his seat and listened to his racing heart. He shivered. "Jesus . . ."

She giggled. "You're addicted to me already. I'm your heroin. Admit it."

"There's a song about that."

"What song?"

"It's called 'She's Like Heroin To Me.' It's by the Gun Club."

"I know that name. Haven't heard them, though. Is it good?"

"Yeah."

"Cool. What other music do you like?"

Rob shrugged and shook his head to clear it. He didn't want to talk about music. He only wanted to feel her hand sliding up and down his leg again. "Um . . . rock. You know . . . hard rock. Metal. Punk. Psychobilly."

"Psychobilly? Like the Cramps?"

"Yeah."

"I love them. And Twathammer. Are you into horror?"

He nodded. "Yeah."

She smiled. "Me, too. Like, *massively*. You see, Rob? This shit was meant to be. You and I are so compatible it fucking *hurts*, man."

Rob didn't say anything at first. A lot about Roxie repelled and sickened him. She was a bad person. She did very bad things. But in truth, he did feel very in tune with her in some ways. "We sort of are, I guess," he said at last. "But I'm never sure whether you're telling me something you really believe or just fucking with my head again."

"That's part of the fun, Rob."

"No. It really isn't, Roxie."

Her eyes went wide and she sat up straighter behind the wheel. "Ooh! Let's pick up the hitchhiker!"

"What?"

Rob cranked his head to the right and scanned the road's shoulder. He saw a slim figure maybe a quarter mile distant. A man standing with his thumb out. He had that scraggly, weathered look of the long-term homeless. Rob was able to see deep lines on the man's face as they drew closer. He had hard, unfriendly eyes. Rob didn't like the look of the man at all.

"I don't think this is a good idea."

"Yeah, but I'm in charge and your opinion counts for shit."

Roxie slowed the Tercel and pulled over. She hit a button and the window on Rob's side slid down. The hitchhiker came up to the car and leaned down to peek inside. "Where y'all headed?"

Roxie grinned. "Wherever you're going. Hop on in. Back's unlocked."

The man moved away from the window and opened the back door. He tossed his backpack in and climbed inside, pulling the door shut. "Can't tell you folks how much I appreciate the kindness. Most folks these days can't be bothered to help a fella out."

Roxie twisted in her seat and stared at the guy through the gap between the seats. "Most folks should be ashamed of themselves. What's your name, stranger?"

"Carl McCoy."

Roxie reached a hand into the backseat. "Pleased to meet you, Carl. I'm Roxie. And my friend here is Rob."

Carl shook her hand and Roxie held onto it.

"Pleased to meet you both."

"Now, Carl, I hate to break it to you, but nobody rides for free, not in this car. I can see you don't have any money to speak of, but there is a way you can pay."

The man's voice became wary. "Yeah? What would that be?"

Roxie kept grinning. "Ass, gas, or grass, Carl. Ass, gas, or grass. In this case, ass." She nodded at Rob. "My friend here is feeling very frustrated right now. The price of your ride is a blow job."

Rob's mouth dropped open. "What the fuck, Roxie?"

Carl chuckled. "Ain't a problem. I suck a mean dick."

Roxie laughed. "I bet you do, Carl. I bet you do."

"Got real good at it in jail."

Rob shook his head. "No way, Roxie. Fuck this."

"It's that or the other thing. You know what I mean."

Carl was quickly becoming confused in the backseat. "What other thing? I don't know if I like the sound of that."

Rob hated being forced to make this choice. He would not let some foul-smelling, nearly toothless, butt-ugly homeless man put his mouth on his penis. There was no scenario in which he could ever imagine allowing that to happen. And yet the other option amounted to sentencing the man to death.

Carl coughed loudly in the backseat. "Uh . . . I think I'll be getting out now. If you'd just let go of my hand, young lady."

Roxie leg go of his hand, snagged the .38 from the tote bag, and pointed it at him. "You're not going anywhere, you fucking bum. Rob still has a choice to make."

Carl started crying. "Please. Don't. I'll do anything."

Roxie laughed. "Holy shit, really? Anything at all? Wow. You know what, I've never heard that before. People never, ever say that when they're about to die. Seriously."

Carl whimpered. He sniffled. "Please . . ."

"Shut up." Roxie glanced at Rob. "Gross old-guy mouth action or the other thing. Decide now."

Rob looked away from her and sighed. "Other thing."

She smiled. "Good choice. I approve."

Rob closed his eyes and cringed, waiting to hear the report of the gun, which would be painfully loud inside the car.

"Get out, Carl."

Rob heard the man's breath catch in his throat.

"Wh-what?"

"You heard me. It's your lucky day. Get out, bum."

Carl didn't need to be told twice. He hustled himself out of the car and slammed the door shut. Rob opened his eyes, glanced at the side-mounted mirror, and saw the man walking fast in the opposite direction.

Roxie laughed and slapped the steering wheel. "Fuck! That was *fun*."

Rob couldn't say anything. He just stared at her.

"You're probably wondering why I let him go." Roxie patted his knee. "You look like you just saw a ghost. Poor baby. Let me explain. I didn't want to kill that guy. And letting him go's no big deal. A guy like that's not going to the cops, so he's not a liability. The real payoff was you making that choice. Now I know you have it in you, too."

Rob squinted at her. "What?"

"Murder, Rob. You have murder in your heart. Just like me."

Rob opened his mouth to issue an automatic denial, but the words did not come. He stayed silent because the words would be a lie.

She was right.

He felt like crying.

Roxie was still laughing as she put the car in gear and pulled back into the stream of traffic.

CHAPTER TWENTY-FOUR

March 20

The guy seemed really nervous and she guessed she couldn't blame him. It was a pretty weird situation. Not to mention highly illegal, as he thought he'd been approached by a very young prostitute. So he was pretty fucking gullible, too. She was way prettier and fresher-looking than the usual crack-addicted, street-trawling whore.

They were in the parking lot outside the 21 Up Adult Video store. The man clutched a brown paper bag that appeared to contain several DVDs. He was fidgeting and kept glancing at the door to the smut shop. "You're sure you're not with the cops?"

Julie smiled and licked her lips seductively. "No, baby. I just want to make you feel good and make a little money."

He was staring at her breasts, which strained the fabric of the tiny halter she was wearing. "How much?"

"Fifty for a blow, hundred for a fuck."

"I've got the cash, but I don't have any rubbers on me."

Julie almost laughed.

I'm sure you don't, you ugly fuck.

"That's okay, baby. I've got you covered." She nodded at the BMW parked on the other side of the lot. "That's my old man's car over there. Get in the back with me and we'll set this up."

He frowned. "Your . . . old man?"

She smiled. "My pimp."

The man turned partially away from her and stared at the BMW. Zeb wasn't visible through the car's tinted windows. Good thing, too. Dude would be spooked for sure if he got a load of the crazy homeless man. And Julie didn't want him spooked. This guy was perfect. He was just the kind of slimy pervert the world would be better off without.

He faced her again. "I guess that's okay. That's a hell of a nice car. You and your . . . old man . . . must be doing well."

She smiled and kicked at a little rock with the toe of a sneaker. She kept her hands clasped in front of her and gave her hips a little swivel, really playing up the whole Lolita thing. "You could say that. We're picky, you know. We drive around and find people who look like they have a little class to 'em. Like you."

The man blushed. "Oh . . . thanks."

She started walking toward the BMW, glancing over her shoulder at the mark. He was staring at her ass now. "You coming?"

He hesitated just long enough to scan the parking lot again, probably still checking for cops, not quite trusting her denial. Then he took a deep breath and hurried after her. She opened the back door on the passenger side and stood aside for him to slide in. She climbed in after him and pulled the door shut. Zeb hit a button up front and the car's locks clicked shut.

The sleazy little fuck drew in a startled breath upon seeing Zeb.

Julie laughed. "Chill, baby. I know he's scary-looking. But a girl needs a tough guy around to survive in this business." Julie doubted any real-life whore said things like this, but the guy was clueless and horny, so it was probably okay. She put a hand on his leg and squeezed, eliciting a shudder from him. "Yeah. Feels good, huh?"

He gulped. "Y-yeah . . ."

"Let's get out of here, Zeb."

Zeb started the BMW and began to back out of the parking space.

The guy sat up straighter. "Wait! Where are we going?"

Julie scooted closer to him and draped an arm around his shoulders. "You shush, sweetie. We have a special place we go. You didn't really think we were gonna do business in the parking lot of a porn shop, did you?"

He clutched the brown paper bag in his lap with both hands, the paper crinkling as his fingers shook. Nervous? Shit. He was *terrified*. Julie figured he'd never been intimate with a girl on any level before. It didn't make her feel sorry for him. The sad sacks of the world only had themselves to blame for their problems. He wasn't fat. He could clean himself up. Maybe get some cream to clear up those zits. Pathetic. The guy was maybe in his midtwenties, but he still looked like some high-school loser. No one would miss this waste of space. It made her feel a little better about what she was about to do.

Zeb pulled into traffic and began to head for the spot they'd found earlier. The town wasn't tiny, but it wasn't terribly big either. It was one of those countless bland, midsized communities dotting the landscape between the larger cities. It took maybe ten minutes to return to the abandoned warehouse in the town's failing industrial area. The place was perfect. The empty lot behind the building wasn't fenced off and there was no evidence of any kind of security presence. Zeb parked the BMW at one of the empty loading bays at the back of the building. He turned the car off and pocketed the keys.

He got out of the car and threw the door shut without a word.

Julie grinned. "It's just you and me now, baby. You ready to have fun?"

She heard the paper bag crinkle again. A glance at his lap

showed that his hands were shaking harder than ever. She smiled and touched the bag. "Can I see your goodies?"

"Um . . . I don't . . ."

She kissed his cheek. "It's okay, honey. You don't have to be embarrassed about anything. I want to see."

Julie took the bag from him and pulled the DVDs out of it. There were four of them. The one on top featured a picture of a very young girl kneeling between the legs of another very young girl, who was sitting on the edge of a bed, with one leg dangling toward the floor and the other splayed along the edge of the mattress. The girl on the bed was squeezing her breasts and staring at the camera. The name of the DVD was *Teen Sluts 4: Lesbian Fantasies*. The rest of the discs were in the same vein. She sorted through them and made fake noises of arousal.

"Oh, wow. I wish we could watch these. I love shit like this. Makes me hot."

He was staring at her breasts again and wasn't shaking quite so much now. The edge had come off his nervousness as she'd sorted through the discs. She glanced at his crotch and saw how swollen it was. The physical intimacy was a big part of it. He probably knew it'd be a long time before he ever got this close to a girl as hot as she was again.

She set the discs aside and touched his leg again. "You ready?"

"Yes. God, yes."

Lips puckering, he leaned toward her, but she placed a hand flat against his chest and pushed him back. "Kissing is fifty extra bucks."

"I've got a hundred eighty in my wallet." He was breathing faster, the intensity of his desire overwhelming any other impulses. "You can have it all. Just let me kiss you a little before we . . . you know . . ."

She giggled. "Fuck?"

He gulped. "Yeah."

"Okay. We'll make out some. Just promise you won't tell Zeb. He doesn't like it when I cut customers a deal."

"I won't tell. I promise."

"Cool. Take your cock out while I get something from the front."

She disengaged herself from him and leaned forward, angling her lean body through the gap between the seats, positioning her ass so that it was pointing right at his face. With any luck at all he'd be distracted by its round lushness long enough to get this done. The big hunting knife was in the passenger seat. The fingers of her right hand curled around its heavy handle.

Something touched her ass. The mark's hand. The greasy little fucker was copping an unauthorized feel. Yet another mark against him in the grim reaper's ledger of doom, she figured.

She smiled and glanced over her shoulder at him. "Little impatient, are we?"

He squeezed her ass cheek. "Yeah. What are you doing up there?"

"You needed a rubber, remember?"

He nodded. "Oh, yeah. Right. I forgot. Hurry. Please."

"Okay, baby. Here I come."

She waited one beat longer.

This is it, she thought. *No going back from here.*

What surprised her most in that moment was her total lack of hesitation. *I want this. Holy shit, I really do.*

Keeping her back to him, she began to slither back into the rear of the car. She heard him groan in anticipation. Then she snarled and whipped around, jabbing the big blade at his throat. Instinct made him flinch to the side, his quick reaction time surprising her. But he wasn't quite fast enough. The serrated edge of the blade cut through his T-shirt and glanced off his collarbone, etching a deep, bloody groove in his flesh. He screamed and scooted away from her as she reared the knife back for another strike. He held his hands up and the blade jabbed into a palm, triggering another gusher of blood as it cut through muscle and hit bone. She yanked the blade out and pulled it back again. Blood leaped from the wound and struck her face. She felt some of it enter her mouth and realized she was grinning. It made her giggle, knowing how crazy she must look to him right now. He was pissing his pants, the little baby. He cried out and turned away from her, grasping for the door handle. His bloody hand curled around it and yanked, but the door stayed shut. Zeb had enabled the childproof locks on the back doors.

"You're trapped, motherfucker."

He looked at her and put his back against the door. "Why are you doing this?"

"Why not?"

She plunged the knife into his thigh, aiming for where she thought the femoral artery would be. He screamed and kicked out at her with his uninjured leg. The counterattack caught her off guard. His booted foot hit her stomach and drove her backward. She hit the door behind her and cried out. She stared at the man, panic blooming inside her. She didn't have the knife anymore. It was still buried in his thigh. He reached for it in the same instant she propelled herself away from the door in a screaming leap. She was faster. She drove the blade deeper into his leg, giving it a savage sideways twist. He screamed and bucked against the door on his side. Julie yanked the knife out of his leg and stuck it in his throat.

A jugular bull's-eye.

She pulled the blade out, releasing the biggest geyser of gore yet. She felt its warmth splash her chest and laughed. She leaned over him, got close as she could to his face, and taunted him in a singsong voice. "You're gonna die-eye, and there's nothing you can do about it."

He was still breathing, but his eyes were starting to glaze over.

Zeb opened the front driver-side door and leaned in to check out the carnage.

Julie beamed at him. "So what do you think? Did I do good? Did I pass Lulu's fucking test?"

Zeb smiled. "You did good."

"Yay. You know what?"

"What?"

"I want to do it again. Tonight."

Zeb just stared at her.

She rolled her eyes. "Yeah, I know. I'm a mess. I'm covered in fucking blood. But I'm not gonna be picky this time. We don't have to do it the same way. Let's just grab somebody. Anybody. A woman, if you want. I don't give a shit. Let's just do it. Okay?"

"You need to calm down."

"DON'T FUCKING TELL ME TO FUCKING CALM DOWN!" Julie took a deep breath and summoned a smile. "I want to kill somebody. Please?"

Zeb looked wary, but he nodded. "Okay."

He disengaged the childproof locks, pulled the body out of the car, and dragged it over to a Dumpster. Julie climbed up front and settled herself in the shotgun seat in time to watch Zeb heft the body and drop it in the container. Christ, but he was a strong bastard. He came back to the car, fired up the engine, and began to drive away from the warehouse.

Julie started laughing, was unable to stop for more than a minute.

Zeb glanced at her, frowning. "What?"

Her smile was playful. "Oh, nothing. Well . . . I was just thinking . . . wouldn't it be a kick if I turned out to be even more fucked-up than you?"

She laughed some more.

Zeb stayed glumly silent and stared at the road ahead.

CHAPTER TWENTY-FIVE

Diary of a Mixed-up Girl blog entry, dated March 14

Stayed up way late thinking about it again. That thing I'd like to do. What it would be like. I think it would be sort of like turning out the lights when you leave a room, except you could never turn them back on again. Unless you had super God-like powers or something. But there is no God and no magic. So . . . yeah. It's so trippy to think about. When someone decides to do this thing, that's real power.

I don't know if I'll ever have the guts to do it. I'd sure like to, though. I know I don't want the life my parents want for me. They want me to go to college, but I think what they hope happens in the end is I marry some upwardly mobile dude and raise a pack of brats in the suburbs. If it was good enough for Mommy dearest, then it's good enough for me, right?

They've got some disappointment coming their way, I can tell you that. MORE disappointment, I mean. LOL. Ha.

They think all my "troubles" are part of a normal rebellion phase.

They have no idea. NONE.

I hope to truly horrify them someday. To SHATTER them.

And I will. I promise.

I saw this squirrel in the road today. It'd been hit by a car or something, but it was still barely alive. The sound its skull made when I crushed it was awesome.

6 comments
lord_ruthven: Wtf? Awesome? Bullshit. I bet you were bawling your eyes out (if it even happened).

Mixedupgirl: No bullshit. I have pictures. I just mailed one to you.

lord_ruthven: I just saw it. I don't know what to say. You're one sick bitch.

Mixedupgirl: LOL. Yeah.

lord_ruthven: You make me so sad sometimes.

Mixedupgirl: Get over it. I'll probably never fuck you again.

CHAPTER TWENTY-SIX

March 24

Sean Hewitt picked up the heavy duffel bag and set it on the edge of the bed. He glanced out the big window above the bed and saw a maze of beach houses and narrow roads with sandy shoulders. The room he and Annalisa had taken overlooked the driveway and swimming pool out front. It would have been nice to have a room with a view of the beach and the ocean, but he wasn't about to complain. It'd been damn generous of Chuck's dad to foot the bill for everybody. The main thing was just being here. There had been some unpleasant delays. That whole weird thing with Chuck and whatever had happened to him. The even weirder tension between Zoe and her supposed best friend, Emily. But they were here now, with nearly a full week of sun and fun ahead of them.

He unzipped the bag and began to sort through its contents in search of the new swim trunks he'd purchased for the trip. Everyone else was down at the beach already and he was anxious to join them.

"There you are."

Sean turned around. "Uh . . . hi."

Emily Sinclair stood just inside the door to the room. She was wearing black pumps and a tiny white bikini. She looked sensational. The white fabric against her already pale flesh created an interesting effect. From a distance she would look naked. Hell, this close it almost looked that way. Her red lips curved into a smile beneath the dark sunglasses covering her eyes.

"Hey, Sean. I'm glad you're here."

He cleared his throat. "Uh . . . yeah. I thought you were down at the beach."

She was still smiling. "I was. But remembered something I needed to do."

"Huh."

Her smile gave way to a pensive look. "Yeah. I sort of need help with something in my room. Do you mind? It'll just take a minute."

Before he could answer, she turned and strutted out of the room, giving her hips an exaggerated sway. Sean stared after her. That ass was really something. He frowned. He wanted to get down to the beach with Annalisa. Oh, well. Whatever Emily needed help with couldn't possibly be that complicated or time-consuming. He'd just go help her out, then come back and change.

Emily was already waiting for him in her room. She stood near the foot of the king-size bed that dominated the room and waited for him to come inside. He hesitated a moment. Something was a little off here. He shook his head. That was silly. What could possibly be wrong? He smiled and came into the room.

Emily licked her lips. "Care to guess what I need help with, Sean?"

She hooked her thumbs inside the bottom piece of her bikini and wriggled her hips as she slid the tiny piece of fabric down over her thighs. Sean's mouth went dry as he got a look at her neatly trimmed patch of pubic hair. It looked like a porn star's snatch. Barely any hair at all, really. She sat on the edge of the bed and kicked the bikini bottom across the room. She braced her hands on the mattress and arched her back a little to emphasize the swell of her breasts.

His dumbstruck expression made her giggle. "I was getting all horny down at the beach. I can't help it. Sunshine and sand gets me all worked up. I was hoping you could go down on me for a few minutes. You know, just to take the edge off. What do you say, Sean? Can you help a girl out?"

He coughed. "Um . . . isn't this a job for Joe?"

"Joe could do it, sure." She smiled. "But you're cuter."

Sean watched in disbelief as she spread her legs and started fingering herself. What was wrong with this girl? "Look . . . you're hot and all, like seriously fucking hot, but I've got a girlfriend. And, shit . . . I love her. I'm sorry, I just . . . I can't do this. And what the hell is your problem? Isn't Annalisa your friend? This is some fucked-up shit. Do me a favor and stay away from me, okay?"

He turned away from her and started toward the door. Emily came off the bed with a snarl, grabbed him by a shoulder and spun him around. His feet tangled and he started to stagger backward. Emily slammed the heel of a hand against his chest and he stumbled backward into the wall.

"Jesus, Emily. What the fuck?"

Her hands curled into fists at her sides. He saw the muscles in her shoulders and arms tense. She looked ready to tear him apart. "Don't you fucking dare tell anyone about this."

He laughed—a nervous laugh. "Okay."

"I mean it."

Sean stared at her in silence for a few tense moments, and his own anger began to build. "You know what, Emily? I think I *will* tell Annalisa about this. She should know what kind of—"

"You won't say a word."

"I will. And you can't stop me."

Emily smiled again, but now there was something almost ugly in the expression. "Oh, but I can. Does Annalisa know about Melinda?"

Sean's heart almost stopped at the mention of the name. "Um . . . what?"

Emily's laughter was almost as ugly as that smug smile. "You heard me. Talked to the girl a couple weeks ago. She told me some very interesting things. Including a thing or two about you. Things you wouldn't want your *girlfriend* to know."

Sean's eyes filled with tears.

He watched her strut back to the bed. She sat on its edge and spread her legs again, beckoned him with a bent forefinger. He pushed away from the wall and started toward her.

Then stopped.

"No."

"What?"

He shrugged. "No. Seriously. Fuck this. Tell Annalisa about Melinda. I'll deal with it one way or another. I made a mistake. I've felt like shit about it ever since. It won't be happening again. And I sure as hell won't be pushed around by you."

He left the room without another word, pulling the door shut behind him. Something thumped against the door. She'd probably thrown one of her shoes. That sound and her accompanying cry of frustration were very gratifying things to hear.

Sean went back to his room and changed.

Then he went down to the beach and found comfort in the arms of his true love.

CHAPTER TWENTY-SEVEN

March 24

The low-slung canvas beach chair was a comfortable and peaceful place to be. The softly rippling ocean was so beautiful. It looked endless and eternal, so big it seemed nothing else could possibly exist somewhere beyond all that water. She imagined a world covered in water and populated by benevolent sea people. In her mind she pictured them as a weird cross between sea monkeys and mermaids and mermen. It was a silly, whimsical notion, but Zoe found it deeply appealing.

Most of her friends were wading in the ocean, either just standing there or splashing in the gently rolling tide. Chuck was farther out, floating on a rubber raft. Zoe was content to stay where she was for now. It was nice to just kick back from a slight distance, to just relax and observe. Zoe slipped her still mildly chilled Corona from the drink holder built into one of the chair arms and took a slow, refreshing pull from the bottle.

She heard footsteps approaching from behind—the distinctive slap of flip-flop soles on sand—and remembered there was one other of their number who had yet to dip her toes in the water.

She tensed.

Please don't let this be weird . . .

Emily flopped into the chair next to her. She seemed a little agitated. Not a good sign.

"I hate Sean Hewitt."

Zoe blinked. "What?"

"I hate Sean Hewitt."

"I heard you. I just don't understand what you're saying. Did he . . . do something?"

Emily grunted. "You could say that."

"Want to tell me about it?"

Even as she said it, Zoe regretted the words. She liked Sean well enough. He treated Annalisa well, from what she could tell, and he seemed a decent sort. Sure, he liked to joke around with the guys and make occasional rude comments. No big deal. It was what guys did when they drank beer and hung around together.

Emily huffed. "He grabbed my boob in the kitchen."

"What? Seriously?"

Emily took her dark sunglasses off and looked right at her. She looked pissed off, but there was another quality evident just below the surface of the anger. She looked . . . hurt. Zoe frowned. Maybe she was wrong about Sean.

"Seriously. Said maybe we should play around some while everybody else was down here."

"You're shitting me."

Emily sneered. "Nope. Had to pry his hand off my tit. The bastard."

"That son of a bitch."

"Yeah. You can't tell Annalisa, okay? Things are weird enough between us without throwing that in the mix."

Zoe was inclined to agree. There had been enough drama on this trip already. Enough for ten fucking vacations. She'd let it go for now and maybe bring it up at a later date.

She shrugged. "Okay."

Emily was staring at her. "Like the bikini. Baby blue suits you."

"Thanks."

"You look hot."

"Um . . ."

Emily laughed. "Don't worry. I won't go there again, I promise."

Zoe smiled. "Thanks."

"Are we cool then?"

Zoe shrugged again. "Sure. You're my best friend." A sudden welling of tears surprised her. "Shit."

Emily leaned toward her and patted the back of a hand. "Hey, it's okay."

Zoe clasped hands with her. "I'm sorry I was a bitch all yesterday."

Emily stroked Zoe's wrist with the ball of her thumb. "Don't worry about it. Seriously."

The words brought forth another gush of tears. She wiped them away and sniffled. "I guess I was suppressing this. God, I'm such an idiot. I'd hate to lose my best friend over one freaky night."

Emily smiled. "Honey, you're not about to lose me."

"Well . . . good."

Emily, as always, looked amazing. Stunning. Everything toned but shapely. Legs so long and lean. Hair so perfect. The face of an angel crossed with a 1940s femme fatale. She looked like a movie star, like a woman born for a life of glitz and glamor. Hell, she was young yet. Zoe suspected those things lurked somewhere in her friend's future.

Emily let go of her hand and reached into the tote bag she'd carried to the beach with her. She pulled out her cell phone, flipped it open, and punched in a number.

"Who are you calling?"

Emily smirked. "Remember Clayton Wilson?"

"That pitiful geek who had a crush on you last fall?"

"Yep."

"Why are you calling him?"

Emily's smile was evil. "To play with him a little."

Zoe laughed. "You're such a bad girl."

"You know it." Emily's face brightened, and when she spoke her tone was one of bubbly enthusiasm. "Hey, Clay!"

A tinny voice came from the cell phone's speaker.

Emily winked at Zoe. "Yeah, baby, I've missed you, too. Sooo much."

Zoe covered a giggle with a hand.

Emily touched her knee and mouthed the word *Stop!* She grinned and again spoke in that obnoxious bubbly tone. "I wish I could see you right now. I've been thinking about you every day for *weeks*."

That tinny voice emanated from the phone again.

Emily shook her head. "No, no, no. I *was* gonna go to Myrtle Beach, but I had a huge fight with stupid Joe right before we left and stayed behind." Her voice had turned pensive, and she nodded along as the voice from the other end spoke painfully earnest words of comfort and reassurance. "I know, I know. It's not fair at all. But I know what would make me feel better, baby. Do you think you could meet me up at the Villager Tavern tonight? Say around seven?"

Loud squeaking sounds emerged from the cell phone's speaker.

Sounds of joy.

Zoe covered another giggle, and Emily slapped her knee and waved an admonishing finger.

"Yeah, good. So glad to hear that, Clay. We'll just hang out and have fun. Maybe stroll around campus hand in hand." Now she sounded wistful, as if this would be the fulfillment of a fond wish. "Awesome. Excellent. Love you, too, sweetie. See ya at seven. We're gonna have so much fun. Ciao, baby."

She flipped the phone shut and giggled.

Zoe uncovered her mouth and laughed out loud. "That was fucking sick, Emily. That poor boy."

Emily smiled. "It was awesome. And you know it."

Zoe smiled back. "Yeah."

Emily laughed. "Can you just picture it? That little loser waiting and waiting, walking around, looking all over for me, staring at his cheap watch? Too bad all my friends are off campus this week, or I'd have somebody go over there and get some video footage, maybe put it up on YouTube."

Zoe thought of something and her smile withered. "Huh . . . don't you feel sort of hypocritical now?"

"Why would I?"

Zoe frowned. "Well . . . you were so hard on Chuck about how he treated that little goth girl. I was mad at him, too. I feel sort of bad now."

Emily rolled her eyes. "Oh, whatever. You know I just like to fuck with Chuck. I don't really give a damn about that stupid girl. Speaking of Chuck . . . are you two really back on? I thought the split was a done deal."

Zoe picked up her Corona bottle again and took a sip. "It's complicated. I guess we're back on. For now." Her mood shifted again, her eyes twinkling and her smile curving in a way that suggested naughty thoughts. "We've been having some wicked-hot sex."

Emily snorted. "Maybe he should get the shit beat out of him more often."

Zoe grinned. "Yeah. Maybe."

Emily stood up and stretched, purposely displaying the full glory of her gorgeous figure. "I think it's time I got wet."

Zoe stared at her. "Yeah."

Emily started walking toward the ocean. She turned and walked backward a few steps as she said, "Come on, Zoe. Come get wet with me."

Then she turned away again and sprinted toward the ocean. She waded out until the water was up over her hips, then she sucked in a breath and dove beneath the surface. She surfaced again some twenty yards farther out, bobbing above the water like the top half of the hottest mermaid ever.

She spotted Zoe and waved.

Zoe waved back.

She finished off her beer and stood up, began to walk toward the ocean. She smiled, her gaze alternating between the still-recumbent form of Chuck Kirby and the sleek, dazzling water acrobatics of the best friend she'd ever had.

She shivered with delight at the first sensation of water sliding over her feet.

Time to get wet.

CHAPTER TWENTY-EIGHT

March 24

The motel parking lot was jammed with the cars of spring breakers. The Tercel was wedged between a powder blue Mustang and a black BMW in a row of cars facing a long, two-story wing of the motel. Rob sat in the Tercel's driver's seat, drumming his thumbs along the upper curve of the steering wheel. Roxie sat scrunched down in the passenger seat, her feet propped on the dash. Rob kept glancing at her. Her new outfit was bugging him. She wore tan khaki shorts and a blue T-shirt with a picture of a surfboard on the front, both purchased from a nearby souvenir shop. The clothes looked good on her. That wasn't the problem. The girl would look good in anything. They just didn't look . . . right. If you ignored the several visible tattoos, she could pass for any preppie college kid out for a hot time in the sun and sand.

She looked at him. "For fuck's sake . . . *what?*"

"Those clothes don't look right on you."

She smiled. "I should be wearing something cool, right? Something tight and black, with a skull on it, maybe?"

"Well . . . yeah."

"This is a costume. We need to blend in. You, too."

Rob wore black jeans and a shiny button up black shirt with a bright red flame pattern across the front. The same duds he'd been wearing since she'd taken him.

"No. I . . . can't."

She smirked. "You'll do it if I say so, bitch."

Rob pulled a pained expression. "Please . . . don't. I couldn't bear it. I'm begging you. I'm allergic to khaki."

Roxie laughed. "I do like to hear a man beg, so whatever."

Rob gripped the steering wheel and started the thumb-drumming thing again. "Look. We've got money. Why don't we just check in?"

Roxie shook her head. "No. I don't want any motel clerk remembering us."

"You didn't seem worried about that before."

"Things were different then."

"How?"

"I wasn't in love with you yet."

Rob shifted in his seat, fidgeting a little as he became uncomfortable.

Okay, this is fucking crazy.

It was the third time she'd invoked the L-word today. He couldn't fathom it. He liked her. Liked her a *lot* when she wasn't killing somebody or doing something else completely insane. This was their third day together. Even leaving out all the craziness, wasn't it a little soon to be bandying that word around? He didn't know how he felt about her profession of love, assuming it was how she really felt. She could just be fucking with him again. But some deep-down instinct told him she wasn't playing with his head this time. She liked him. *Loved* him. Or at least thought she did. And if she truly believed it, for her there would be no difference between delusion and true love. Rob's feelings for her were complicated by so many things. The repugnant acts he'd seen her commit. His lingering feelings for both Charlene and Lindsey. But what truly troubled him was the sense this thing with Roxie was likely to be painfully brief. Her life-style was going to catch up to her sooner or later. One day she'd slip up and be caught or killed by the cops. There was no "happily ever after" waiting somewhere down the road

for them. Just a steep and rapid drop deep into the heart of
darkness.

"Snap out of it."

Rob blinked. "What?"

"Your head was off in the fucking clouds."

He sat up straighter in his seat. "Right. Sorry."

"I love you."

For fuck's sake . . .

"Right. You said that."

Roxie laughed. "You don't have to say it back yet. I know
you like me. You'll come around to the love thing sooner or
later. Probably sooner."

"Right."

"Anyway, as I was trying to tell you, going gaga over you
has sort of changed my perspective a little. Don't get me
wrong. I'll always be what I am. But I do mean to be more
careful." She pried one of his hands off the steering wheel
and laced fingers with him. "And that includes no interac-
tion with the staff here."

Rob grunted. "So . . . *instead* . . ."

He let the implied question hang.

She flexed her fingers slightly for a better grip on his
hand. "We watch for a likely target. Preferably someone vulnerable. Preferably alone."

"We catch them going in or out of their room."

"Right."

"Get them inside the room and tie them up."

"Wrong. Fucking waste of time. We kill them."

Rob groaned. "Is that really necessary? You haven't killed
anybody in over twenty-four hours. The bloodshed reduc-
tion was sort of refreshing."

"What's your favorite horror movie?"

Rob stared at her with his mouth hanging open for a long
moment. The abrupt conversational shift had caught him off
guard. "Um . . . I . . . wait. Seriously?"

"Seriously."

Rob shrugged. "I don't think I have a single favorite. I like so many. There's *The Texas Chainsaw Massacre* and *Dawn of the Dead*. Obviously."

"Originals or remakes?"

"Both."

She smiled. "Good answer. The *Dawn* remake is better than the original, though."

"Blasphemy. And what does any of this have to do with murdering innocent spring breakers?"

She laughed. "I didn't want to talk about that anymore, that's all. I'm killing them. End of story. Don't make me say it again."

Her hand tightened around his. A reminder.

This was a command, not a request.

He forced a smile. "Understood."

She relaxed her grip and smiled back. "Good."

Rob opened his mouth to say something, but the words died on the edge of his tongue, unspoken and forgotten. He stared at the black BMW parked to the right of the Tercel. Its doors had come open and two passengers climbed out. The very unlikely looking pair started walking toward the motel. It was a middle-aged man and a girl in her teens. The man looked like a powerfully built wino in ill-fitting clothes. The girl was cute as hell. But something about her haircut was off. It looked . . . unprofessional.

Roxie was staring at them, too. "Something's not right there."

"No shit. That car was there when we pulled in, which was"—he glanced at the dashboard clock—"an hour ago. So . . ."

Roxie nodded. "They hid behind those tinted windows the whole time, waiting for us to get out or go away."

"Because they didn't want to be seen together."

"Right. Or something like that."

"Weird."

The strange couple stopped at the door to a room on the first floor. The man opened the door with a key card and they slipped inside the room. The old bum tried not to be obvious about it, but he shot a quick look their way before shutting the door.

Roxie slipped on her sandals (also newly purchased) and retrieved the .38 from the glove compartment. "Change of plans."

She was out the door and moving toward the motel before Rob could protest.

He slapped the steering wheel.

"Shit!"

One day her impulsiveness really would get her killed. He glanced at the keys dangling from the ignition. For the first time in more than a day he gave serious consideration to the possibility of escape. He could drive away and leave Roxie to meet her inevitable doom on her own. He could go home. Make excuses. Maybe find a way to reconcile with Charlene. Then there was Lindsey. Sweet Lindsey. His best friend. Maybe Roxie was right about her. Maybe she really did want something more than friendship. Or maybe not. Bottom line, he had options. Possibilities. Normal, sane things he could do with his life. Somehow, it was all still just within his grasp.

He looked at Roxie.

She was already at the door to the room the strange couple had entered.

Rob sighed. "Shit."

He grabbed the keys from the ignition, hopped out of the car, and hurried after her.

CHAPTER TWENTY-NINE

March 24

"Are they just gonna sit there forever or what?"

Zeb didn't answer. He sat behind the BMW's steering wheel, his head cranked to his left as he watched the couple in the Tercel. They seemed permanently ensconced in the car. The girl, in particular, looked rooted to the spot, scrunched way down in her seat with her feet propped on the dash. She was pretty, but maybe just a little sleazy, with multiple visible tattoos.

"She looks like a Suicide Girl."

Now Zeb looked at her, a genuinely puzzled expression on his face. "A what?"

"A Suicide Girl. Alternative pinup models. They usually look sort of punk, with tats, piercings, and shit."

"Tats?"

"Tattoos."

Julie glanced at the rearview mirror. "I sort of look like that now. I need a tat, Zeb."

Zeb was staring at the couple in the Tercel again. "I want to kill these people."

Julie was still admiring her reflection. She fluffed her hair and blew herself a kiss. "Broad daylight, Zeb. Not a good idea. Look, they're obviously up to no good themselves. They're not gonna connect us to the guy in the room. And even if they did, they're not going to the cops. I mean . . . look at them."

Zeb nodded. His posture changed and the tensely coiled muscles in his back visibly relaxed. "Right. Enough of this bullshit. Let's go."

He opened the door and got out. Julie grabbed her new purse—a nice Gucci liberated from her third victim—and hurried after him. "Hey. Thought of something. What if they're cops? What if they're on a stakeout or something?"

"They're not detectives. Too young."

"Detectives? You mean like *Magnum, P.I.*? That old-ass TV shit? I'm talking about *cops*, man. Like *real* cops."

Zeb glared at her. He did that a lot when she was talking. It was sort of funny to wind him up. "I'm talking about *police* detectives, girl. Investigators. I had some experience with them when I was younger. They're the ones you'd see on a stakeout. These jackasses are not police detectives, I promise you."

"You hope."

"Shut up."

Julie giggled.

Zeb opened the door to room 109. Julie went in first and flipped on the light. She saw Zeb shoot a look at the Tercel before shutting the door. "Shouldn't have looked at them."

Zeb grimaced. "I know."

He rubbed his hands on his face, sighed, and sat on the edge of the king-size bed. He looked beat. Julie stared at him. Despite his size and imposing musculature, there were times when he just looked like a tired old man.

"Maybe you should take a nap."

Zeb yawned. "Maybe."

He scooted backward to the center of the bed, swung his body around, and stretched out, resting his head on the stacked-up pillows behind him. He closed his eyes and folded his hands over his chest.

"Hey, Zeb."

He opened one eye and looked at her.

"It okay if I play with this guy some?" She reached into her bag and pulled out the large hunting knife. "I'm bored."

He shrugged. "You can cut on him some. But don't kill him just yet."

Julie grinned. "Cool."

She turned away from Zeb and looked at the man tied to one of the room's two metal-framed chairs. A layer of silver tape was wound around the bottom part of his face. This was to keep the gag in his mouth. His eyes went wide and his nostrils flared when he saw the big knife. Tears leaked from his eyes and he began to shake. She couldn't blame him. She'd used the blade on him quite a bit during the night. He was nude from the waist up. His torso was a road map of red and pink lines. The red lines were the open, still-weeping wounds. The pink lines were places where she'd cut him and then applied a lighter flame.

She approached him and placed the tip of the blade to a fold of bruised and swollen flesh just beneath his left eye. "Hi, Ronald. I've missed you. Sorry we were gone so long."

Ronald whimpered.

"You've got a choice. Should I cut you? Or should I beat you with the phone book some more?"

Ronald looked up at her through eyes overflowing with tears. He looked like he wanted to be put out of his misery.

Not yet, Ronnie. So sorry.

She set the knife and Gucci bag on the table by the window and picked up the phone book. She liked the weight of it in her hands. She got a good, two-handed grip on it and positioned herself in front of Ronald again.

His bloodshot eyes seemed to beg her.

Have mercy. Please, please, have mercy . . .

She lifted the book over her head and swung it with all the force she could muster, smashing it across the man's face and snapping his head brutally in the other direction. The backswing blow that followed was just as devastating. The man choked and sobbed behind his gag. Tears spilled from his eyes in fat droplets, splashing his big belly. His whole body trembled nonstop. Julie watched him for a minute, savoring his misery. Then she raised the book again and smashed him across the face four more times in rapid succession.

She dropped the book and picked up the knife. "Wow, that was fun. A total fucking rush. But you know what? My arms are getting tired."

Ronald's eyes locked on the knife again.

Julie smiled. "Say hi to Mr. Pointy."

She poked the knife into the raw hole where his right ear had been. Ronald screamed behind his gag, but the gag and the tape effectively muffled the sound. Julie scraped the blade around the inside of the wound some more and laughed as he thrashed uselessly against his bonds.

This was too much fun.

"You need to stop. He'll die."

Julie took the knife out of the man's ear and turned to address Zeb. "Yeah? So? I *want* to kill him now. I haven't killed in two days."

Zeb chuckled. "You sound like a doper jonesing for a fix."

Julie laughed. "Yeah. You're right. I am definitely hooked on this shit." She began to pace the room, reluctantly backing off for now. "Four people, Zeb. Not counting Clyde. Four innocent motherfuckers I've fucking *ended*. And you know what? It's not nearly enough. I want more, more, more." She stopped pacing and stared at Zeb. "How many people have you killed?"

"Couldn't begin to guess, girl."

"More than ten?"

He just smiled.

"Right. Epic underestimation. More than . . . fifty?"

He kept smiling.

"Holy shit, Zeb. More than . . . a hundred?"

He shrugged. "Lost count a long time ago. But . . . probably."

She grinned. "That's awesome. I want—"

The blast made her yelp and drop the knife. She sucked in a startled breath and spun about as Zeb sat up quick. She saw the hole in the door right away. Another blast blew the lock mechanism off the door. Then the couple from the Tercel came barreling into the room. The one who looked like a Suicide Girl came in first. She had the gun. The man came in right on her heels and kicked the door shut.

Zeb snarled and leaped off the bed at the girl. Julie figured he'd take the gun from her and stick it down her throat. He was that lethally quick. She had seen more than enough proof of it. But somehow the girl was even faster. She got the gun up and aimed faster than seemed humanly possible. She squeezed the trigger three quick times and each slug hit home in the approximate center of Zeb's chest. He dropped hard, hitting the floor like a slab of granite, with a big, teeth-rattling boom.

Julie bent to pick up the knife.

The girl aimed the gun at her. "Don't."

Julie stood up straight. "Okay."

Reappraisal time. Zeb was out of the picture. You don't take three in the chest and get back up. Which sort of sucked. She wasn't exactly fond of him. And he remained creepy as all get out, what with the corpse-fucking and all. But she had grown sort of . . . *attached* to him in their week together. He'd allowed her to break through a barrier that otherwise might have taken her years to breach, if ever. She enjoyed killing and never wanted to give it up. Would rather be dead herself than have to give it up. But if these fuckers were cops, she wasn't going to have a choice. The man in the chair was still alive. He could testify against her, send her to prison for a very long time.

Hmm, prison . . .

The girl with the gun indicated the bound man with a jerk of her head. "You worried about him?"

Julie frowned. "Um . . . I . . . guess?"

The girl approached the bound man and pressed the barrel of the revolver against his forehead. She squeezed the trigger and a spray of blood and brain matter splashed the window blind behind him.

"Holy shit."

Okay. Re-reappraisal time.

Not cops. *Definitely* not cops.

"Who are you guys?"

The woman shook her head. "No time for that. Cops will be here soon. Grab that knife if you want it and come with us."

Julie didn't have to be told twice.

She scooped up the knife and followed the woman and her man—who looked sort of shell-shocked—out of the room.

They were gone by the time Zeb was able to push himself up on all fours and crawl over to the bed. He sat down, put his back against the side of the bed, and looked down at his chest.

"Fuck."

He heard a clucking sound. "You're a goner."

He looked up and saw Lulu standing over him. She was still the spitting image of Adrienne Barbeau, but she'd exchanged the bikini for a little black dress. Black for mourning, he supposed. Though it was far more revealing than any funeral dress he'd ever seen.

He coughed up blood. "Hurts. Hurts bad."

"I imagine."

"Can you help me?"

"Afraid not, Zeb. This is the end for you."

The tears that spilled down his cheeks surprised Zeb. He couldn't recall ever having cried as an adult. "Sucks. I don't want to die."

Lulu smiled. "Who does, Zeb?"

"Are you real?"

"I thought you'd never ask. Does it matter?"

Zeb's eyes fluttered and the world turned white for a second before snapping back into focus. More blood trickled out of his mouth. "I think you're real."

Lulu just smiled.

"You're real. I thought I was special and that was the reason I could hear you when nobody else could. But . . . I was wrong . . ."

Lulu shook her head. "It was always about the girl, Zeb. It was your job to get her here. To meet those people. That's done now. And now it's time for you to meet God." She laughed. "You ready to talk to God, Zeb?"

Zeb felt a sudden chill.

He thought of all the people he'd killed and their desperate pleas for mercy. He wasn't ready, not even close, but he had no say in the matter now. His breath hitched and he convulsed a little. When the convulsion passed, he heard the whine of approaching sirens.

Lulu lowered herself to the floor and straddled him. "Don't worry about them. You'll be gone before they get here. You've only got a few seconds, baby. Think about what you want to say to God. Be quick about it."

Zeb tried to think of something. Anything.

But all he could hear now was the echoes of his victims' screams.

Then he was gone.

Lulu watched him go.

She kissed him once on the mouth.

And then she was gone, too.

CHAPTER THIRTY

Diary of a Mixed-up Girl blog entry, dated March 25

Feels like I haven't updated in eons. But I guess it's only about a week or whatever. I'm sure most of you will be surprised as shit to even see this. Thought I was a goner, right? Well, guess again. I am alive and well and having a great fucking time. Hardly really have time for this, but I wanted you bitches to know I'm all right. Not sure why. I don't give a shit about any of you. LOL. Btw, I'm writing this on a new laptop that belonged to this guy who really won't be needing it anymore. It's nice. Bells and whistles out the fucking ass.

So I've made some new friends. This really hot chick and her boyfriend. Think I'm gonna be hanging with them for a while. The chick is fun. I've totally bonded with her. The boyfriend is okay. It's fun to mess with him. The chick's got this big thing planned and it is going to be a fucking BLAST. I can't wait.

Oh, I wanted to address some shit I've been reading online today. First off, what happened to the Lees was really sad. But seriously, me taking off is totally unrelated. Whatever psycho did that didn't abduct me. Yeah, I went to their house to collect my babysitting money, but nobody answered. End of story. Kind of creepy to think there were a bunch of dead people on the other side of that door, though. Anyway. So what DID happen to me? Simple. I hooked up with a guy passing through town and decided to take off with him. Total coincidence it happened the same day.

Bottom line, I'm fine. Better than fine, really. I'm finally free. I felt like a prisoner living with my parents and I'm never going back, so tell them to knock off this searching bullshit, okay?

So that's about it, I guess. I've wasted enough time talking to you losers.

OH! I got a tattoo yesterday. My first. Hurt a little, but totally worth it.

Laterz.

Note: Of the more than one hundred comments posted in response to the above entry, only the following received a reply from Julie Cosgrove.

lord_ruthven: I'm not sure what to believe, but it doesn't really matter. I'm glad you seem to be okay.

Mixedupgirl: You know what? You're the only person back home I don't want to drop down a black fucking hole. No bullshit. Still not gonna fuck you, though.

lord_ruthven: Thanks . . . I guess. What about Alicia?

Mixedupgirl: Fuck her. Seems she told the cops about my bullshit "crush" on John. Next time I see her I'm gonna chop her fucking head off.

lord_ruthven: Hah. Now I really know you're okay.

CHAPTER THIRTY-ONE

March 25

Three hours of lazing about on the beach and splashing in the ocean was more than enough for Chuck. He needed a break from the sun. He gathered up his towel and empty Corona bottles and told Zoe he was going back to the house to take a shower. Zoe smiled and told him she'd be up in a little bit. He leaned down for a kiss, felt her tongue slip into his mouth, and grinned.

"Sure you don't want to take that shower with me?"

She smiled. "Maybe later?"

He chuckled. "Sure. A guy can never get too clean."

He went up the beach toward the house, climbing first over a grassy dune and then traversing a short bridge to the fence that surrounded the swimming pool out back. He opened the gate and stepped inside, pausing long enough to blast sand from his feet with a hose. He entered the house through the bottom floor, padded on wet feet to the staircase, and began to climb toward the third floor. He stopped on the second-floor landing when he heard a feminine moan, very faint, emanating from one of the rooms down the short hallway. He turned and stared down the hallway. There were two rooms. Two doors. The one on the right was shut, the one on the left partly cracked. The sound came again. *Definitely* feminine. Chuck's penis twitched in his swim trunks.

God, I'm horny.

All that time spent baking in the sun and staring at the wide array of bare female flesh in the vicinity had him worked up. He suddenly wished he'd tried harder to lure Zoe back to the house. He wanted to have some of the same kind of fun someone in one of these rooms was having. He was pretty sure the sound was coming from the partially cracked door. A need to know who it was seized him. He was surprised. He wasn't normally given to voyeurism, but there was no denying the intensity of the desire. He glanced up the next set of stairs leading to the third floor. Empty. He then checked the stairs leading back to the first floor. Also clear. He took a deep breath and began to move as quietly as possible down the hallway.

This is crazy. What if somebody catches me peeking?

It was a good question. He had no business doing this. It was risky as hell. Yet the impulse was just too powerful to resist. He reached the partly open door and peered through the crack.

He stifled a gasp.

Annalisa and Emily were making out on the bed. They were prone on the mattress, with Annalisa on top. Chuck's erection pushed painfully against the fabric of his trunks as he watched the two women writhe and kiss. Annalisa didn't have a top on, just shorts, and Emily was in that tiny white bikini. There was nothing tender about what he was seeing. They were kissing with such hunger, almost as if they were trying to consume each other. Chuck couldn't believe it. The two were Zoe's best friends, but he had been pretty sure they loathed each other. But you could never underestimate Emily. He was sure she was the instigator here. Yet he couldn't begin to imagine how she'd seduced Annalisa.

Annalisa broke off the kiss and sat up, straddling Emily. "I wanna sit on your face."

She unbuttoned her shorts and twisted around to shimmy out of them. Chuck swallowed a lump in his throat and fought an urge to reach into his trunks. Voyeurism was one thing, but he'd be damned if he'd risk someone catching him in the act of jerking off in the hallway. A thought occurred to him, something that made him frown. Why was the door open? Talk about risky. But it was obvious, wasn't it? It had been done on purpose, probably by Emily. That'd be just like her. She *wanted* someone to see this.

He heard a voice from downstairs just as Annalisa began to position herself over Emily's face.

Joe.

Chuck moved away from the door and hurried up the stairs to the third floor. Heart slamming, he headed to the bar. He needed a drink and he needed it now. The shower could wait. He stepped behind the bar and scanned the rows of liquor bottles, again silently thanking his father for thinking of everything. His dad had a very open mind on the subject of underage drinking. Which made sense, as he'd been quite the tippler since his own teenage days. Chuck had been sharing drinks with his father for years. Some would label the behavior child abuse. Dad just saw it as continuing a tradition.

Chuck dumped ice in a rocks glass and filled it to the rim with Johnnie Walker Black. He had half of it down by the time Joe came thumping up the stairs into the living room. He spotted Chuck at the bar and grinned. His trunks were wet and his feet were coated with sand.

Chuck nodded at his feet. "You're tracking sand everywhere, asshole."

Joe shrugged and came over to the bar. "Ain't like we live here, man. Shit gets dirty, so what? The housekeepers can deal with it. Give me some of what you're having."

Chuck prepared another drink and passed it to Joe. "There. I should throw it in your fucking face, though."

Joe's grin faltered. "I do something, man? I didn't do it, whatever it is, I swear."

"So you and Emily didn't screw around with Zoe the night I got the shit beat out of me at that bar?"

"At the bar? I thought it happened outside."

"Never mind that. Answer the question."

"What do you mean, 'screw around'?"

"You know what I mean, motherfucker."

"Chuck . . . come on. We're friends. Don't be like this."

Chuck squeezed the rocks glass. Hard. Another ounce or so of pressure and it would shatter in his hand. He ached to release it and use his fist as a battering ram against Joe's face. The need to lash out was almost overwhelming. This wasn't new. A potential for violence had been simmering just below the surface ever since that night at the bar. He wanted revenge against the people who'd beaten him, but he couldn't have that. He was too afraid of them. They were genuine sociopaths. Hardened criminals. Just the thought of ever confronting them again paralyzed him with fear.

But Joe was another story. He wasn't afraid of him at all.

His grin felt ugly. Probably looked even worse. "When I came back that night, after nearly getting my ass fucking killed, I couldn't find Zoe. I came over to your room, but I didn't knock. I stood at your door and listened for a long time, Joe."

Joe's face began to turn pale. "Chuck—"

"Shut up. It was hard to tell what was going on in there at first. It was a lot of damn noise. A big fucking party, from the sound of it. I didn't leave until I heard something I'd recognize anywhere. Wanna guess what that was, *friend?*"

Chuck waited a beat. Joe didn't say anything.

"It was Zoe having an orgasm. She's a loud one, isn't she?"

Joe knocked back his drink and set the glass on the bar. "You know what, man? You can shove this high-and-mighty shit right up your fucking ass. Seriously, where do you get off? You think I don't know you fucked Emily the same night?"

"What?"

Joe's grin returned. "Yeah, she told me. Hell, she told me right after."

Chuck seethed inwardly. What Joe was saying astounded him, yet he had no reason to doubt it. And if she'd told Joe, why wouldn't she have told Zoe? Hell, maybe she had and Zoe had simply decided to let it go in light of the beating he'd taken.

"What the fuck is wrong with your girlfriend?"

Joe frowned. "What do you mean?"

"Why would she tell you about that?"

Joe laughed. "Man, she *always* tells me. We have an open relationship. It's a whole swinging-seventies thing."

"And you're okay with that?"

"Yeah. Why not? It goes both ways, you know." He grinned. "Sort of. She gets to fuck whoever she wants, and I get to fuck whoever she tells me to fuck. And she's such a freak that I wind up fucking a lot of people, man."

"Nice."

Joe laughed again. "No shit." He picked up his glass. "Now how's about a refill?"

"Get it yourself, douche bag."

Chuck left Joe standing alone at the bar as he walked through the living room and then down the hallway that led to the big master bedroom he shared with Zoe. He shut the door, stripped down, and went into the bathroom. He stepped into the shower stall and turned the water on, adjusting the temperature to a point just shy of scalding. The water felt good rushing over him. The steam felt good, too. He closed his eyes and tried not to think of all the things that were pissing him off, because there were just too many of them. As he began to relax, his mind drifted back to his brief glimpse of Annalisa squatting over Emily's face. A predictable physical result ensued.

His eyes snapped open when he heard the stall door open.

Emily peeked inside. She looked him up and down, smirking at the sight of his hand clenched around his erection. "Joe told me about your little spat. Said you could probably use some consoling. But, ah . . ." She laughed. "Here, let me help you with that."

She started to step into the shower stall.

Chuck stared at her.

She was naked.

And she looked as enticing as ever. More.

He knew he should tell her to go away. But desire overwhelmed his better judgment. He reached for her and pulled her into the stall. She laughed as his hands pawed at her. That mocking quality he recalled from the encounter in the van was there again. A wave of self-hatred assailed him. His erection began to wilt. He stopped kissing Emily and gripped her by the shoulders, prying her off of him.

Her expression was a mixture of confusion and anger. "What the fuck?"

"You're getting out."

He steered her back toward the open stall door, turned her around, and gave her a hard shove in the back. She cried out as she stumbled out of the stall and fell clumsily to the floor. Her knees smacked the plush bathroom rug and she cried out again. She got up and glared at Chuck. "You son of a bitch."

"Get out, Emily. Now."

She made no move to leave. "You could have hurt me. That was assault, Chuck. I could call the cops."

"I don't give a shit what you do. Just get out."

"You'll give a shit when I tell them you tried to rape me."

Chuck smirked. "You do that. And maybe they won't laugh in your face when they find out what a gigantic fucking slut you are."

Her glare turned murderous. She retrieved her bikini

from the towel rack and began to put it on. "Nothing good ever comes of pissing me off, Chuck. I'll put you in your place before long. You'll see."

She was gone before he could respond.

Chuck closed the stall door and stepped under the spray again, a smile stretching across his face as the hot water streamed down his body. He didn't doubt the sincerity of her vow to get back at him. She would try to exact revenge, somehow, some way. But for the moment it didn't matter. He felt like he'd won something. It was a little thing, really, but it felt important to him.

He'd made a stand.

And hadn't given in to temptation.

He felt a small flicker of some initially unidentifiable emotion. He needed a few moments to recognize it as something resembling pride. He felt good about something he'd done.

He smiled again.

It'd been a long time.

CHAPTER THIRTY-TWO

March 26

Rob was getting pretty sick of motel rooms. Roxie preferred to stay in the real sleaze pits to conserve cash and blend in with the other shady characters. The Starline Economy Inn, located on US 17 just outside of Myrtle Beach, was typical of the type. These dumps all looked basically the same, with some small variations in overall grime level to spice things up. He was missing the small but neat and comfortable apartment he shared with Lindsey a little more each day. He was weary of all the killing and drama, of course, but an even bigger factor in his deepening disenchantment with the situation was Julie Cosgrove.

He stared at her from his seat by the table. She sat crosslegged in the center of the bed, with the stolen notebook computer propped open in her lap. Her eyes were intent on the glowing screen as her fingers tapped rapidly on the keyboard. Every so often she'd start typing a little faster and a little harder, and when she did this, the tip of her tongue would emerge at a corner of her mouth and stay there until the typing pace slowed again. The girl was a fucking Internet junkie. Even Roxie, who generally treated her like a longlost little sister, was showing signs of annoyance with the girl's online obsessions.

She laughed at something on the screen and her fingers started flying over the keyboard again.

Rob shook his head and took a slow pull from a longneck Bud bottle.

He and Roxie had been sort of flying under the radar, but Julie's face was all over the cable news networks and the front pages of newspapers nationwide. She was a missing cute white girl and the media thrived on that shit. At least she'd done some things to alter her appearance. The hair was the most obvious thing. It made her look like Linnea Quigley in *Return of the Living Dead*. The shoulder tattoo and the eyebrow piercing helped some. Neither, obviously, were in any of the pictures circulating. Some subtle makeup tips from Roxie even seemed to change the shape of her face a little. But if you stared at her long and hard enough, it was still possible to discern the girl from the pictures. He was worried someone would guess who she was and bring the law down on them in a hurry.

Roxie came out of the bathroom wearing a black skull shirt and the short black skirt he liked. She scrubbed her wet hair with a towel and tossed the towel aside. She saw Rob staring at her and struck a pose, placing a hand on a thrust-out hip. "You like?"

Rob swallowed. "Yeah."

Roxie smiled. "Julie?"

"Yeah?"

"Take that thing in the bathroom."

"Huh?" Julie stopped typing. "Why should I . . . ? Oh. That skirt is hot."

Roxie didn't look at her. "Bathroom. Now."

Julie got up from the bed with a huff. "I don't see why I have to hide somewhere every time you guys fuck. Can't I stay out here and watch?"

"No."

"But—"

"No." Now Roxie did look at her. "That's final. Now go."

Julie huffed and stalked off to the bathroom, slamming

the door shut behind her. A few muffled curses emanated from the bathroom, but she soon fell silent and they again heard the dim sound of fingers tapping keys.

"We should take that fucking thing away from her. Sooner or later she'll say something online that'll give us away."

"I doubt it. She's smarter than you think."

"You're not worried at all?"

Roxie strutted over to him and leaned over him, bracing her hands on the arms of the chair. "Only thing I'm worried about right now is your failure to tear my slutty clothes off and ravish the fuck out of me."

Rob slid a hand up her leg and under her skirt. "No panties."

She giggled. "You like me, Rob?"

"Yeah."

"A lot."

"God, yes."

Another giggle. "So show me."

He showed her.

When it was over, Julie came out of the bathroom with the closed laptop tucked under her arm. She smirked at the sight of their curled-together nude bodies. "Guess what?"

Roxie raised her head off Rob's chest. "What?"

"Once you guys got started, I opened the door a crack and watched."

Rob groaned. "Jesus."

"It was a pretty good show. My favorite part was—"

Roxie threw a pillow at her. "Shut up."

Julie dodged the pillow and took a seat at the table, where she once again opened the laptop.

Roxie looked at Rob. "Maybe you're right about that thing."

"You're not taking my laptop. I'll crack your skulls open and eat your brains if you try."

"Eat our brains?"

"You heard me."

Roxie glanced at Rob and rolled her eyes. "Kids."

Julie snorted. "You're barely any older than me."

"Old enough to make a difference."

"What, three or four years? Yeah, big fucking difference."

Roxie rolled off the bed and gathered up her clothes. Rob followed her cue and did the same thing.

Roxie pulled on her T-shirt and stepped into the little skirt. "You are being careful, right? Not saying or doing anything that might lead the cops to our door?"

"Whatever. I heard your little discussion. More of that treating-me-like-a-child bullshit. Relax. I'm doing all my posting and shit behind a proxy server to disguise the IP address. And I'm not saying anything that'll give away our location." She looked up from the keyboard to glare at them. "Okay? Happy?"

Rob finished dressing and sat on the edge of the bed. "Listen . . . there's something we should all talk about."

Roxie and Julie traded puzzled glances.

Roxie folded her arms beneath her breasts. "Gosh, that sounds serious. Is this gonna piss me off, Rob?"

"It shouldn't."

"So spit it out."

"This thing with the spring breakers. We're doing it tomorrow, right?"

"Yeah."

"Okay. So . . . what comes after that?"

Roxie frowned. "What do you mean?"

Rob sighed. "I've been thinking . . . we can't maintain this lifestyle forever. It's a dead end."

"I guess you have some alternative in mind."

"I do. And it's totally workable. Look . . . I haven't even been gone a week yet. I can still go home and make excuses. I'll say I met you and took off on a wild, romantic adventure. And everyone will buy it, because you'll be there with me. When they get a look at you, they'll totally get why I did it."

Roxie chewed on a thumbnail. "I don't know about this. Where would we stay?"

"I already have an apartment. You'll move in with me. You'll just be my new girlfriend." He saw the doubt in her expression and pressed on. "You have to see how perfect this is. We can have a *normal* life together. Doesn't that appeal to you at all?"

She stared at the floor and toed a tear in the carpet. "What about Lindsey?"

"What about her?"

"This shit would piss her off. It wouldn't work."

"You don't even know her."

"She's a girl. She lives with you. She wants you. I can feel it."

"That's crazy. You sound fucking crazy right now. I *know* Lindsey. Trust me, she won't—"

"What about me?" Julie's voice, quieter than usual. "I notice you're not talking about me at all."

Rob looked at her and didn't say anything.

Julie scowled. "I don't fit into this big plan at all, do I? I guess I'm supposed to slink back home and make with the big apologies to Mom and Dad."

"I've heard worse ideas," Rob said.

"Fuck that and fuck you."

"Fuck me? Listen, girl—"

"*Shut up!*"

Roxie's strident tone silenced them. She sighed. "Rob. Baby. I love you. You know that. But I'm not gonna settle down into some nice fairy-tale life. I need to move around. Constantly. That'll never change. And Julie's welcome to stay with us as long as she likes. End of story."

"That's that, huh?"

"Yes. What I say goes. Thought we'd already established that."

Julie loudly cleared her throat. "A-hem. Besides, your plan isn't a realistic option anymore."

Rob looked at her. "What?"

Julie turned the laptop screen toward him. "Looks like you're about to become as famous as me."

Rob got up and walked over to the computer. The first thing he saw was a picture of the abandoned Galaxie. That was bad enough. It accompanied a story about his disappearance on a Nashville paper's website. As he began to read it, a sense of dread took root deep within him.

"Oh, shit. Fuck. I am so fucked."

"Okay, maybe not as famous as me, because I'm pretty fucking famous. I'm like a real deal movie star. You're more of a B-lister."

Julie grinned at him from the other side of the table. His life was falling apart and she was *amused* by it. Fucking snide little bitch.

"You think this is funny? Shut your face, you little cunt."

Julie's grin froze. "Don't talk to me like that."

Roxie hushed them again. "When was the last time you talked to Lindsey or your uncle?"

"Shit. Fucking shit. The day after you took me."

Roxie came over to stand next to him. "Looks like you were reported as a missing person the next day."

Rob scrolled down some more and groaned. "Goddamn. They found that guy you shot in the woods."

"I see that."

"They've connected me to that. I'm a fucking person of interest in a fucking murder, Roxie."

Roxie laughed. "That's wild."

He turned on her, his features twisting in disbelief. "*Wild?* That's all you've got to say? It's fucking *wild*? I can't believe this. What about this is fucking funny? Both of you are insane. Please tell me what it is about the end of my world that's so hilarious. I'd really like to know."

Roxie shrugged. "This is no big deal."

"How can you say that? There's nothing about you in this article. No hint of an accomplice at all. So maybe this isn't a big deal to you. Hell, maybe it just makes it easier to ditch me later. I mean, that's what you're planning anyway, right? After you're done having your fun with me?"

She shoved him against the table and got right up in his face, giving him a forceful reminder of how intimidating she could be. "It's not a big deal because I'm used to dealing with shit like this. I've been in the news before, too. For stuff I've actually done. I killed my whole rotten family. Butchered them. People freaked the fuck out and it was all over the news. But I didn't get caught and the press forgot about me after a while. Same thing's gonna happen with you. I've gotten real good at figuring how to stay free. When to lay low. When to move. How to look different. I can help you do the same. They'll never catch up to you as long as you're with me."

Her face was little more than an inch from his own. He trembled. He was in awe of her. It was like being within grabbing distance of the twitching, exposed end of a live electrical wire. He was afraid to touch her. He cleared his throat. "You promise?"

She smiled and placed a hand on his shoulder, giving it a reassuring squeeze. "I fucking *promise*." Then she squeezed harder, digging her fingers painfully into his flesh. "And if you ever accuse me of planning to ditch you again, I'll fuck your shit up but good. That's a promise, too. Understand?"

Rob nodded. "Jesus. Yeah. I understand."

Roxie relaxed the pressure on his shoulder and looked at Julie. "How do you think my man would look as a blond?"

Julie tilted her head and narrowed her eyes, studying him. "Could work, maybe. Do that really bright blond thing and cut his hair, make it spiky."

Rob shook his head. "No. No way."

Roxie laughed. "Sorry, Rob. What I say goes, remember?"

Julie clapped her hands and hopped up and down in her chair. "It's fugitive makeover time!"

An emotional numbness came over him as he listened to them talk excitedly about look possibilities, and he excused himself to go to the bathroom. Once he was inside, he closed the door and locked it. Then he sat on the toilet seat and covered his face with his hands.

How do I get out of this?

He sighed.

He didn't share Roxie's confidence in her abilities to keep him beyond the reach of the law indefinitely. That would be a far easier thing for one person traveling alone to manage.

Face it, he thought. *You're fucked.*

He was. He was sure of it.

And he had a sinking feeling they were just about at the end of the line.

CHAPTER THIRTY-THREE

March 26

The rhythms of the tide were even more soothing at night. The ocean was a mass of shifting darkness out there beyond the pale slice of beach. There was something more suggestive of the primordial about the dark waters at night, a feeling that instilled her with a level of peace that was elusive in her regular life.

The door behind her opened and Annalisa stepped out on the balcony with a drink in hand. She wore shorts and a purple halter. Her mop of strawberry blonde curls was still wet from the ocean and hung almost straight, the lustrous tips brushing her shoulders. "Mind if I join you?"

Zoe forced a smile. "Of course not."

She did mind. A little. The time alone had been nice. There had been precious little of it since their arrival in Myrtle Beach. And she felt a little weird around Annalisa in light of what Emily had told her about Sean. Still, Annalisa was her friend. She wasn't to blame for Sean's boorishness.

Annalisa sat in the rocking chair next to the one occupied by Zoe. "Nice out here."

Zoe's smile became genuine. "Mmm . . . yeah."

Annalisa cleared her throat. "I sort of had sex with Emily."

Zoe's eyes became perfectly round for a moment and she

twisted around in the chair to look fully at her friend. "What? Are you fucking serious?"

Annalisa winced. "Yeah."

Zoe gaped at her. "How do you 'sort of' have sex with somebody? Either you did or you didn't."

Annalisa raised the glass to her mouth and took a sip. She licked her lips and stared out at the ocean. "Right. Okay. I did. I had sex with her."

"I can't believe this. Jesus."

"Sorry. I know I've kind of blindsided you with this."

"What about Sean?"

Annalisa grunted. "What about him? This doesn't change anything. It was just a fun experiment."

"I thought you hated her."

"Still don't like her. I'm not dumb. I know she's just using me somehow, the way she does with everybody else." Annalisa stared at her lap and rolled the glass between her hands. "But, shit, Zoe, she's just so ridiculously hot. It's like I was helpless. I knew better, but couldn't stop myself."

Tell me about it, Zoe thought.

"That face. That body. So exquisite." She laughed and knocked back some more of her drink. "Plus . . . I was sort of sloshed. Had something like four or five margaritas before she cornered me."

"Funny how often alcohol's involved when you do things you wouldn't normally ever consider."

Annalisa laughed again. "I'm such a fucking cliché. Getting wasted and getting it on with a chick on spring break. Only thing missing was the *Girls Gone Wild* camera crew."

Zoe chuckled. "Yeah. I'm sorry, but you're right."

Annalisa groaned. "I know, I know." She shook the glass. "I need a refill." She started to rise. "Can I get you something?"

"No thanks."

Annalisa paused with her hand on the door's handle. "You don't seem to be partying very much. Something wrong?"

"No. I just don't feel like getting wasted. Maybe tomorrow night."

"Suit yourself, party pooper."

Annalisa opened the door and stepped back inside.

Zoe was happy to be alone again. The only person she wouldn't mind spending some time with was Chuck, but he was too busy slamming the drinks back with the guys. And there was a nasty edge in the ongoing banter between Chuck and Joe. She kept expecting them to come to blows. It hadn't happened yet, but it seemed like a real possibility. And it wasn't just those two. Something had happened to poison the atmosphere between all of them. No. Not something. Some*one*. She knew who was to blame. She wasn't completely blind. But it wasn't something she wanted to deal with right now. It raised too many hard questions.

A strong and sudden impulse to be away from it all got her up and moving. A staircase at the left side of the balcony led down to the swimming pool. She hurried down the stairs and padded across the cement deck to the gate at the back of the pool. She opened the gate and glanced back at the house. The second and third floor balconies were both empty.

Good.

No one to see. No one to know where I've gone.

She closed the gate and crossed the short bridge to the barrier dune. She paused at the far side of the bridge to remove her sandals. Then she was moving down the beach, relishing the gritty feel of the sand beneath her bare feet. The gritty texture gave way to a spongy feel as she neared the water. The tide was louder down here. More primal. It was like the roar of some great and ancient beast. She waded into the dark depths, kept going until the water

was nearly over her shoulders. She took a deep breath and
dove.

Darkness enveloped her.

It was like floating in an endless, sightless void.

She wished she could stay there forever.

CHAPTER THIRTY-FOUR

March 27

The twenty-four-hour Walgreens on South Kings Highway in Myrtle Beach wasn't exactly jumping at two in the morning. The three fugitives arguing in the hair-products aisle became the only customers in the store after an old lady with rollers in her pink hair hobbled out with her Geritol purchase.

"You're going blond and that's final."

"You know, you keep saying 'that's final' about things. You sound like a fucking dictator, Roxie."

"That's what I am."

"I just don't think blond is the way to go. It's too obvious."

Roxie snorted and rolled her eyes.

"I'm totally serious. My hair is very dark, almost black. A lighter shade of brown would be more subtle, less likely to draw a second look. You could even put in a bit of gel, I guess. How's that for a compromise?"

Roxie smacked his chest with a box of Clairol Born Blonde. "Fuck your compromise."

Rob stared aghast at the package pressed against his chest. "Come on, Roxie. This is for chicks. I'll look ridiculous."

Roxie seethed. "Rob. Pay attention. I'm starting to get pissed. Now think about that a minute. You really want me to lose it right here in the middle of this store?"

Rob groaned.

"AHHHHHHH!"

Julie couldn't take it anymore. The scream just came out. It was a full-volume blast of rage and exasperation. Probably not the brightest thing she'd ever done, given that they were supposedly trying to avoid attention. But the nearly identical shocked expressions on her companions' faces were totally worth it.

A lean black man in spectacles and a Walgreens vest poked his head in the aisle and said, "There a problem?"

Roxie summoned a high-wattage smile and batted her eyes at him. "No, sir. Just having a little disagreement. We'll keep the volume down, I promise."

His expression conveyed doubt, but after a pause he gave a terse nod. "If you need any help, let me know. My name's Tod and I'm the manager."

Roxie kept smiling. "Thanks *so* much."

Tod turned and left them without another word.

Roxie sneered. "*Gay.*"

Rob shook his head. "Let me guess. Any guy who doesn't fall down drooling at your feet is queer, right?"

"Obviously."

"What about the frat boy you're planning to—"

Roxie slapped a hand over his mouth. "Shut up. Fuck's sake, Rob, you know not to talk about that shit where people might hear."

Rob pushed her hand away. "And why should I care? Like it matters. Like there's any way this thing ends in anything other than total disaster."

Their voices had been rising again and Julie was unsurprised to see Tod the manager reappear at the end of the aisle. "Ladies. Sir. Please keep it down. You're disturbing the other customers. If it continues, I'll have to ask you to leave."

Roxie's brow creased. "What? Seriously? There *aren't* any other customers."

Tod's expression remained stern. "Nonetheless. This is my store. So, respectfully, please be quiet. I won't ask again."

He retreated again.

Roxie scowled. "That miserable little—"

"Fuck this shit."

Julie started walking away from them.

Roxie called after her. "Hey! Where are you going?"

Julie stalked quickly down the aisle and soon saw the automatic doors at the front of the store come into view. "Outside for some fresh fucking air. Problem with that?"

The door opened and she stepped out into the cool night air. The door whisked shut behind her, mercifully blocking the sounds of the ongoing feud. She moved a few yards down the sidewalk and dug into her purse for a pack of Marlboro menthols. The cop car pulled into the parking lot just as she was lighting up. The headlights hit her and she felt frozen to the spot.

Aw, shit. This just fucking figures.

She lit the cigarette and inhaled as the cruiser pulled smoothly into the spot directly facing her.

Well, this is it. Game over. Time to go home.

Or to jail.

Whatever.

The car idled there for more than a minute. Julie squinted against the headlight glare and was able to make out the shape of a big man behind the wheel. He didn't appear to be doing anything other than just staring at her. She smoked the cigarette down to the butt and thought about lighting another. But she was too spooked to reach into her purse again. Too afraid to move at all. Finally, after several minutes, the driver-side door opened and a big man in a uniform stepped out. He was really buff, filling out his striped trousers and crisply pressed shirt in interesting ways. He saw her looking and smiled, an expression that lit up a face that was just shy of handsome. His eyes were a little too close together and his lips were too thin, but he had a strong jawline. Given the rest of the package, the face was more than passable.

The cop slammed the cruiser's door shut and stepped up onto the sidewalk. The car's engine was still running, the key still in the ignition. How arrogant was that? *Fucking cops.*

"Evenin'."

Julie smiled. "Hey."

The cop stroked his chin with a thumb and forefinger as he walked in a slow circle around her, looking her up and down. "Mmm . . ."

Julie swiveled her head but didn't turn as he circled her again. "See anything you like?"

He moved in close behind her, leaned down some, and pushed his crotch against her ass, letting her feel his enormous erection. His hands gripped her by the waist. "*Feel* something I like." He chuckled, his breath warm and stinking of whiskey. "Like to break me off a piece."

Julie did a slow grind against his crotch. "Yeah. Maybe I'll let you. Mmm . . . but what about the surveillance equipment in your cruiser?"

He kissed the back of her head and slid rough fingers under the silky fabric of her halter. "The . . . what?"

"You know. The video camera. Like on *Cops?*"

"Um . . ."

"Isn't this the kind of thing you could get in trouble for?"

"I don't know. Is it?"

His hands moved to her breasts and gave them a none-too-gentle squeeze. She faked a groan of pleasure and said, "Yeah. Like that. I don't know. I guess I just thought soliciting a prostitute was still a crime in most places."

"That what you are, girl? A whore?"

Julie wiggled against him. "Maybe. Maybe not."

The cop laughed. "Yeah. Knew you were a pro. Can spot

'em a mile away. You're fresher meat than I usually see, though. You can't be any more than, what, seventeen?"

She giggled. "Almost."

He made a low sound deep in his throat. A *hungry* sound. "Don't worry about the, uh, surveillance equipment. I turned that shit off the second I saw you."

"Oh, good."

Julie had slipped a hand back inside her purse while he was preoccupied with the task of molesting her. She turned around as her hand came out of the purse and thrust herself against him, half-feigning lust again as she got her right hand up and ready to strike. Half-feigning, because she actually was sort of turned on. He did have a dynamite body. It was kind of a shame, really.

He grabbed her ass and pulled her tighter against him. "Gonna tear your pussy up, girl."

Julie slammed the big hunting knife into his side, jerked it out, and slammed it in again.

Then again.

And again.

The strikes were rapid, all happening within a few seconds, too fast for him to react efficiently. He shoved her away, causing her to stumble backward on the sidewalk and land hard on her ass. She bounced up and came back at him cobra fast, jamming the knife into his neck as he fumbled for his gun, his weakening fingers unable to get a good grip on the holstered weapon. She pulled the knife out and a gout of blood splashed her chest.

The cop wobbled a moment before crashing to the sidewalk, where he convulsed and spilled blood all over the white concrete. Julie wiped the blood-soaked knife on her shorts and put it back in her purse. The cop was clearly dying and no longer a threat. Julie got down on her hands and knees and rolled him off the sidewalk. She gripped him by his thick ankles and tugged him around so that he fit lengthwise inside the parking space to the immediate left of the cruiser, adjusting his feet so the toes didn't point straight up. She had to hide the body, at least temporarily, and there was only one way to do it. He was too damn big to drag off behind the building. Someone else would surely come along and see what was happening before she could manage that.

She reached for the handle on the driver-side door.

Mouth agape, she stopped and stared at the emblem on the door.

In the middle of a seal were two words in bold letters:

MALL SECURITY

Julie couldn't believe it. "Oh. My. Fucking. *God!*"

The guy she'd just killed wasn't a real cop at all. She suddenly felt very stupid. There had been some obvious subtleties that should have tipped her to the truth of the situation. The bit about the surveillance equipment seemed particularly telling. At some point the guy realized she'd mistaken him for a real cop and decided to take advantage of that.

Motherfucker!

She was angry as hell, but she knew she had to chill and start dealing with the situation before it got even more out of control. She got inside the still-idling car, found the gear-shift, and put it in reverse. She backed up and glanced in the rearview mirror. Some light traffic moved along South Kings Highway, but no one was approaching the drugstore. That wouldn't last. She backed the car up and began to move it into place. She felt the body catch on the undercarriage and slide forward some, but that part didn't go as badly as she'd feared. Turning the feet so they lay almost parallel to the ground likely had helped with that. She managed to get the cruiser parked nice and square in the space. Then she opened the door and got the hell out. Another car pulled into the lot just as she was slamming the door shut.

Her heart started trip-hammering again.

Shit! Not now!

The car was a very old and beat-up Oldsmobile. It moved slowly across the lot, almost painfully so, and eventually pulled into the handicapped space right outside the front door. Julie watched the car carefully and quickly became impatient. The driver was taking his or her sweet fucking time getting out. But a door finally creaked open and a stooped-over old lady emerged.

Julie wanted to scream. What was it with old women and their late-night trips to Walgreens?

Don't these bitches ever fucking sleep?

The old lady shut the car's door in slow motion and began to hobble toward the store. When the automatic door opened, Julie dropped flat on the pavement and reached under the cruiser. The rent-a-cop was dead as fuck. And was sort of all fucked-up after being run over and dragged a little bit with his own car.

She'd wanted the man's gun, but a closer look at his holster made her screech in frustration. He didn't have a gun. Of course not. He wasn't a real cop. He was just some minimum-wage douche bag out for a joyride on company time. The thing in the holster was some kind of electronic device. A Taser, maybe? Well, shit, it was better than nothing. She grabbed the device, got to her feet, and hurried back into the store.

Roxie and Rob were still arguing in the hair-products aisle.

Of course.

Roxie ceased berating Rob in midsentence and frowned. "Is that a gun?"

Julie sneered. "No, it's not a fucking gun. It's a fucking Taser."

"Where'd you get a fucking Taser?"

"From the fucking guy I killed in the parking lot just now."

Rob groaned. "Fuck. What is it with you two? Look, murder isn't the answer to *everything*. Just once—"

He broke off and stared at something behind Julie. She turned around and saw Tod the manager staring at them from the end of the aisle again. But his air of smug superiority was gone. He was shaking. He held up his hands and started backing away.

Roxie laughed. "Looks like somebody heard something they shouldn't have. I hate eavesdroppers. Don't you, Julie?"

"Yes."

She put her head down and charged the man. He back-pedaled faster a few steps before turning to run, but the soles of his loafers slid on the slick tiles and he fell awkwardly to the floor. His left hand hit the floor at a bad angle and snapped at the wrist. He howled in agony and rolled onto his back in time to see Julie leaning toward him. He opened his mouth to scream again, but by that time she'd already pressed the Taster to his chest. She pressed a button and thousands of volts of electricity poured into his body, making him froth and convulse. When he was done shaking, she zapped him again. And then again.

Someone grabbed her by a shoulder and pulled her away from him. "Stop that before you kill him."

She pushed the hand away and whirled around. "That's the point, asshole." She pressed the Taser against Rob's chest and savored the way his face paled. "You want some?"

Rob opened his mouth to speak, but no words came out.

Julie pressed the Taser harder against his chest. "I hate you. I'd be having so much more fun with just Roxie."

Roxie approached them, getting close enough to snag Julie's attention while still keeping a safe distance. "Julie. Don't. Okay? I know you're upset, just . . . please don't hurt him."

"Can't you see how weak he is? We'd be better off without him."

The poor bastard looked like he was about to crap his pants. She came very close to shocking him in that moment. The thing that stopped her was a sudden, jarring mental intrusion. It was the recognition of what her life had become, what it was in this very moment, on the edge of this act, versus what it had been a week and a half ago. Within that very short span of time she'd gone from slightly troubled teenager studying for exams to being a person on the verge of murdering her new best friend's lover.

It was somewhat disorienting.

She lowered the Taser and looked at Roxie. "Sorry. I know I get . . . out of control sometimes."

Rob let out a shuddery sound somewhere between a laugh and a terror-stricken moan. "Yeah. Yeah. That's right. You could say that."

Roxie stepped between them and steered Rob away from her. "Shut up, Rob. Let's get the fuck out of here."

The three of them started moving toward the exit.

A metallic click stopped them in their tracks. Julie turned around and saw the old lady from the beat-up Oldsmobile. She clutched a little revolver in her gnarled hands. The hammer was cocked and the barrel was aimed right at Julie's chest.

"Y'all ain't goin' nowhere."

Julie imagined a bullet ripping through her body, could almost *feel* the searing agony. It was too easy to imagine the messy aftermath. Those last dreadful moments as her life drained away. It was easy to imagine because she'd caused it to happen to several people now.

The old lady nodded. "Drop that zapper, you mean little bitch."

Julie forced her fingers to open and the Taser hit the floor with a clatter, just out of reach of the grasping fingers of Tod, who'd just begun to recover from the jolts he'd received. Right now he didn't have the strength to sit up and reach for it, but that wouldn't remain the case for long.

Holy shit, we are as fucked as fuck can be.

The old lady smiled. "Done called the cops. We'll just stand right here and wait for 'em, I reckon."

Then something came sailing past Julie's head, making her flinch. The object hit the old lady square in the center of her face and she staggered backward a few steps before letting go of her cane and crashing to the floor. Julie giggled when she saw the Clairol box hit the floor.

Robin to the rescue. It's a miracle!

Rob had been holding the package throughout their contentious exchange moments earlier. And now he dashed forward to scoop up the old lady's gun before she could recover it. Still giggling, she shoved Rob aside and kicked the woman as hard as she could in the stomach, eliciting a pained wheeze. "Take that, you ancient bag of fuck." She swung her leg back and brought it forward again, driving it hard into her chest. The woman was mewling now, holding her hands up and trying to beg. Julie kicked her a few more times.

Rob's hand on her shoulder. *Again.* "Maybe you could stop now."

She pried the gun out of his hand and shot the old woman in the face.

She smiled. "Okay. Done with her anyway."

She walked over to Tod, who had just gotten his fingers around the grip of the Taser. A bullet through the top of his head took him out of the game. She dropped the gun in her purse. "Ready to go whenever you guys are."

She strutted outside and stood in the cool air again. She smiled at the mental image of Roxie's shell-shocked expression. Roxie was one crazy bitch. When you had shocked the likes of her, you'd really done something noteworthy. Rob and Roxie followed her out of the store seconds later. They all got in the Tercel, with the usual seating arrangement— Rob and Roxie up front, Julie in the back.

Roxie started the car and drove away from the Walgreens at a fast clip. Julie was glad to see it recede and then disappear in the rearview mirror. As over-the-top as her behavior had been, she remained fearful of being caught by the authorities. The video from the Walgreens security cameras would soon be all over the network and cable news outlets. The chances of them eluding the cops much longer, already small, had just grown significantly dimmer. It was looking more and more like Rob was right. Going down in a blaze of glory was the best they could hope for at this point.

So why did she feel so good, with doom at hand?

"That was a hell of a throw, Rob."

Rob stared straight ahead, refusing to look back at her. "Yeah. I guess."

"You saved our asses. Were you a major-league pitcher or something in a former life?"

"I just didn't know what else to do."

"Well, it was mighty fucking brave of you."

He didn't reply to that.

They rode on in silence for several moments. Julie watched the headlights of passing traffic and thought about some things, including the likely imminent end of her life. "Roxie?"

"Yeah?"

"I haven't been laid in, like, forever."

More silence. Then Roxie said, "What about it?"

"Could you send Rob back here?"

An even longer silence. Roxie sighed. "Rob, get back there."

"But—"

Roxie's voice turned hard. *"Now."*

Rob climbed through the gap between the seats. Julie reached for him and pulled him down on top of her. She could feel how ready he already was.

It was hard to be surprised.

She got her mouth real close to his ear and made her voice as soft and quiet as she could. "It turns you on when you watch us kill."

He didn't say anything.

He didn't need to.

CHAPTER THIRTY-FIVE

March 27

The blare of a television roused Zoe as she emerged from the embrace of the soundest sleep she'd experienced in some time. She groaned and sat up, still feeling groggy as she rubbed her bleary eyes. She winced at the obnoxious, excited tones of the television-news announcer coming from the living room. Her door was shut, but the volume of the news report was such that the TV might as well have been right there in the room with her. Zoe started feeling a little pissed off. It had been nice to sleep so deeply, undisturbed by thoughts of having to get up at a certain time. It was one of the best things about being on vacation.

Someone was about to get a piece of her mind. And maybe even a swift kick in the ass. She rolled out of bed and scooped up a tank top. She pulled it on and stepped into the still-wet bottom piece of her bikini. Her eyes flicked to the clock on the nightstand to the left of the bed. The digital display showed the time as being after one P.M. Her anger cooled a little. It was hours later than she'd imagined. She was still upset, but the lateness of the hour meant she would come off as kind of psycho if she were to stomp out there and bitch about it. Okay. Fine. She could be more subtle about making her displeasure known. With the right combination of calm, measured tones and carefully chosen words of polite disdain, she could shame the offender just as thoroughly as she could with a loud diatribe.

She strode purposefully out of the bedroom and down the hallway to the living room. The sight that greeted her was so initially puzzling, the last of her anger was instantly forgotten and her complaint went unvoiced.

Her friends were all present. Chuck stood over by the bar in the entertainment area adjacent to the living room. He had a drink in his hand, naturally, but his eyes were focused on the television. He was completely transfixed by what he was seeing and hearing, as was everyone else.

Emily stood behind a sofa parked in front of the large flat-screen television. Annalisa and Sean sat at opposite ends of the sofa, each of them leaning forward and staring intently at the images on the screen. Joe stood away from them, closer to the television, shaking his head as if unable to believe what he was seeing.

Zoe got closer to the television and frowned. "What's going on?"

Emily's voice behind her: "A fucking bloodbath, that's what."

She looked at the report and saw a shot of a Walgreens parking lot cordoned off with yellow police tape. Within a few moments she knew the drugstore was the scene of a triple homicide. But she was still confused. Yeah, it was a terrible thing, but shit like this happened all the time. It sucked, but America could be a pretty fucking violent place. Why her friends should find this particular incident so mesmerizing was a mystery to her.

"I don't get it. What's the big deal?"

Joe glanced at her. "Give it a second. You'll see."

Zoe wanted to smack him for not directly answering her question. But her indignation was short-lived as the report soon made the reason clear.

"Oh . . . shit."

Joe laughed. "Yeah."

The crime had occurred in Myrtle Beach, not many miles from where they were now. An uneasy feeling settled over Zoe. The idea that something so horrible had happened so close to where she'd been sleeping at the time disturbed her. She might have crossed paths with the victims or even the perpetrators any number of times over the last few days.

"Does anybody back home know about this?"

Chuck came away from the bar to stand near her. "Zoe, this is CNN. It's national news. My dad already called, and your folks want you to call them."

Zoe gave him a puzzled look. "What? Why?"

"They're worried. Want to be sure you're all right." He shrugged and the half-empty drink sloshed in his hand. "Fair warning, though. They're freaked out and want you to come home early."

"What's your dad say?"

"You know my dad. Running home would make me a pussy in his eyes."

Emily snorted. "Right. Can't have *that* happening. God forbid."

Chuck stayed silent, refusing to take the bait. Zoe felt a surge of admiration and new respect for him. It was a down-right *mature* reaction. It stunned her to think he'd seemed as boorish as ever only days ago.

She reached for his free hand and laced her fingers with his. "I'm a grown-up and can make my own decisions. I'm staying. My parents will just have to deal with it. Besides, this shit?" She shrugged. "Happens all the time. Come on, you're all thinking the same thing. Sucks for the dead people, but this shit's just random. We're in no more danger than we were yesterday."

"Or maybe you're totally fucking wrong," Annalisa piped in. She nodded at the television. "Look."

Zoe focused on the report again. Three side-by-side photos

appeared on the screen, the images of two young women and a man. Names and ages appeared beneath the pictures.

   Rob Scott, 23
   Julie Cosgrove, 17
   Missy Wallace, 20

The three were being sought in connection to the Walgreens triple homicide. All were also suspects in other recent killings. One, the older girl, was suspected in a number of slayings going back at least four years.

She frowned. "That . . . sort of looks like . . ."

Chuck grunted. "Yeah. That goth chick."

Annalisa managed not to sound too smug as she said, "Maybe not so random."

"Oh, come on." Emily's voice dripped contempt. "Maybe that chick really is Chuck's little goth pal. So what? Ever hear of a thing called coincidence? You can't really think she followed us all the way from Nashville."

Annalisa's tone was just as sharp. "Why not? She's here."

"We traveled hundreds of miles. We would've noticed her trailing us somewhere along the way. She had no way of knowing exactly where we were going. So, yeah, it's a fucking coincidence. Pull your head out of your ass."

"Fuck you."

"Again, you mean?"

Sean Hewitt's voice: "Um . . . what? I think I, uh, misunderstood something."

Emily laughed.

Zoe moved to intercede before the exchange could take an irreversibly ugly turn. "SHUT UP!"

They all looked at her.

She sighed. "Emily's right. Think about it. There's no other explanation. It's coincidence. That chick winding up here is just God fucking with us. These"—Zoe waved a hand at the television—"crazy fuckers have been too busy with their wild fucking spree to properly follow anybody."

Annalisa stared at the screen again, but her expression now was less severe, more contemplative. A sliver of doubt had pierced her convictions. She shrugged. "Yeah. Okay. I guess I can see what you're saying. It makes sense. It's just . . ."

Emily laughed. "Fucked-up."

Chuck headed back to the bar. "Somebody turn that shit off and put on some tunes. And I can't be the only motherfucker in this house in dire need of a fucking drink. Who's with me?"

It was an offer none of them could refuse.

CHAPTER THIRTY-SIX

Diary of a Mixed-up Girl blog entry, dated March 27

Today is my birthday. I haven't told Roxie or the guy about it and I don't think I will. There's no real point to marking the day any other way than writing about it here. It's just such a strange thing to think about. No cake or candles to blow out for me this year. And I don't think I'll be alive when this day rolls around again. Not trying to be melodramatic. I really feel like I can feel the end coming. What's really sort of fucked-up is how okay I am with it. I think about it and it doesn't bother me at all. The not-caring thing disturbs me more than the idea of dying, but even that's just whatever.

I fucked the guy a little while ago. Straight up asked Roxie if I could. Half expected her to kick my ass. But she was okay with it. I guess it makes sense. She's so fucking cool. I could live a thousand years and never be half as cool as Roxie. I'd say I want to be just like her when I grow up, but I'm never gonna grow up, so that shit ain't happening. LOL.

So anyway, I guess that little backseat tumble with the guy was Roxie's b-day present to me. Only she doesn't know that's what it was. It was okay, I guess. Shit. People poking around outside. Gotta go.

Later. Maybe.

Note: This entry was closed to comments.

CHAPTER THIRTY-SEVEN

March 27

Chuck had a very pleasant buzz going by early evening. He felt pretty good overall. It was a pleasant change and it made him sad to realize how fleeting the feeling would likely be. He'd spent too much of the trip brooding over things. A man shouldn't be so filled with anger during what was supposed to be a relaxing time. But there had simply been too much crap happening. This bullshit with Emily, for instance, and the subsequent dissolution of his friendship with Joe. That shit alone would have weighed on any guy's mind. But the memory of the humiliation he'd endured at the hands of those redneck psychos kept coming back to taunt him. He'd suffered a deep wound to his pride that night, one he'd likely carry with him for years. It compounded all the other shit, like the thing with Emily, turning them into things that made him tremble on the edge of an explosion. At present, he could think of just two ways to cope with the emotional shit storm bearing down on him.

Go back to that bar some night and exact revenge.

Or drown all the bullshit in a sea of alcohol.

The glass in his hand was empty again. He tipped some more scotch into the glass from a nearly empty bottle. This time he had to grip the bottle's neck a little tighter to pour the booze without spilling any of it. As he brought the glass to his lips again, he realized his pleasant buzz was two, maybe three drinks from crossing the line into genuine drunkenness. Not that he cared. Getting drunk was the plan. He just didn't want to get too hammered too soon.

One of the balcony doors opened and Joe came wobbling into the house. The aroma of cooking meat wafted in with him. Sean Hewitt had some burgers going on the grill. The smell made Chuck's stomach grumble. He realized he hadn't eaten all day. Too distracted by drinking and watching the news, probably.

"Those burgers about ready?"

Joe turned a glassy gaze his way. "I always thought you were kind of a prick."

Chuck took a sip of scotch. "That doesn't really answer my question. I'm hungry and could seriously go for a tasty burger. Maybe two. Your opinion of me means jack shit."

"Fuck you, man."

Chuck smiled. "Tell me something, Joseph. What's it like?"

Joe swayed and almost fell. The empty bottle of Bud he'd been holding slipped from his fingers and shattered on the hardwood floor. He looked right on the edge of passing out, probably would've dropped right then and there, but something in him wouldn't let it happen. He swayed again and grabbed the back of a bar stool to stay upright. "What's what like, bitch?"

Chuck was still smiling. "You know what I mean." He mimed the flicking of a whip with his free hand. "What's it like being led around by the nose by that bitch? Do you ever still feel like a real man anymore?"

Joe's face reddened and the muscles in his jaw quivered as rage built inside him, restoring a semblance of near sobriety Chuck recognized as mostly illusion.

"I'm gonna kick your . . . your . . . ass . . ."

Chuck set his glass down and stepped out from behind the bar, spreading his hands in a bring-it-on gesture. "Give it a shot." He made a whip-cracking sound with his mouth. "Come on. Let's see who the *bitch* really is."

Joe let go of the bar stool and lunged at Chuck. He had a good head of steam, but his intoxicated state made him slow and clumsy. It was easy to get out of his way. Even easier to get a fist up and crash it across his former best friend's jaw. The blow was a hard, direct hit. It stung his knuckles and sent a shock of pain down his arm, but that was okay. The pain felt good. Hitting something felt good.

Joe pitched sideways and crashed into an end table. The table shot backward and the heavy brass lamp atop it hit the floor with a resounding clang. The noise and Joe's howl of agony as he hit the floor brought the others running in from the balcony.

"Joe!" Emily hurried over to Joe and knelt next to his prone body. Her head snapped up and she glared at Chuck. "You asshole! What the fuck is wrong with you!?"

Zoe had a wary look in her eyes, but she came up next to Chuck and touched his arm. "Chuck . . . what happened here?"

"Joe wanted a fight. I gave him one. He lost."

Emily sprang to her feet and got in his face. "Yeah, you're really fucking tough. Big, bad Chuck. Congratulations. You knocked out a guy too drunk to defend himself. You're a real piece of work, Chuck. And by that I mean real piece of fucking shit. You fucking dick."

"I may be a dick, but you're the biggest whore this side of the Mustang Ranch." He smiled. "Maybe we should talk about that some."

Her punch caught him off guard and was delivered with surprising strength, her fist slamming hard enough into his chest to drive him backward a few steps.

Zoe screamed and got between them. "Emily, stop!"

"Fuck you, Zoe."

Annalisa coughed loud enough to temporarily redirect

everyone's attention. "You children can start fighting again in a minute, but I need to say something. Sean and I are leaving in the morning. We'll take a cab to the airport."

Zoe turned a despairing look her way. "But . . . Annie . . . I need you here."

Annalisa's expression remained stern. "I'm sorry, Zoe, but we're going. I love you. I really do. But you need to make some changes in your life. And I do want to hear from you again if you can do what needs to be done. But Sean and I are leaving. We've had enough of this disaster."

Emily sneered. "Oh, right. You and Sean are so above the rest of us cretins. There's something you should know, Sean. Your—"

"I already know."

Emily frowned. "What?"

The look on Sean's face was almost serene. "Annalisa told me. And I've told her everything. You can't hurt us. I feel sorry for you, Emily. It must be damn lonely in that sick little head of yours."

Annalisa was nodding. "We're done with you. Play your head games with someone else." She smiled at Sean. "I'm still hungry, baby."

He smiled and steered her back toward the balcony. "Your burgers await, madam."

Emily was shaking. She looked ready to scream. "I hate them so much."

Joe groaned and slowly lifted himself off the floor. He wobbled again, started to fall, but this time was able to aim himself at the sofa. He landed on it lengthwise, an arm and a leg hanging over the edge, and immediately slipped back into unconsciousness. He began to snore.

Emily sighed. "Pathetic." She looked at Zoe. "We're still friends."

Zoe's brow furrowed. "I don't know, Em. I have to think about some things."

Emily nodded. "Right. Okay. Well, at least Annalisa came right out and said it. That puts her ahead of you in my book."

She stomped out of the room without another word. They heard her feet pounding the stairs to the second floor and then the distant slam of a door.

Zoe's eyes misted. "Shit."

Chuck touched her shoulder lightly and squeezed. "I'm sorry. I know it's hard to see right now, but this will wind up being for the best. You need her out of your life. We all do."

She turned toward him and buried her face in his chest. He held her and did the best he could to comfort her. He loved her. Truly loved her. He saw that more clearly than ever.

But the truth was, he wasn't sorry at all.

Not one bit.

Chapter Thirty-eight

March 27

Rob glanced at the Subaru's rearview mirror for maybe the hundredth time in the last half hour and again felt that strange delayed shock of self-recognition.

That's me. It doesn't look anything like me, but it's me.

The face was the same, of course, but his hair had been shaved down to the scalp. Roxie had done the job, using scissors and a razor from the old man's house. He ran a hand over the smooth dome of flesh and again felt a pang of loss. Women had always liked his thick, wavy hair. He felt naked without it. But though it pained him to admit it, the loss of his hair did make him look like someone else, at least at first glance. And right now that was pretty fucking important.

He squinted at the reflection. "I look like a fucking skinhead."

Roxie laughed and picked at her newly blonde, spiky locks. "Yeah. You do. Sorry, babe." She twisted in her seat and glanced at Julie in the back. "You, though . . . you make the bald thing look sort of hot."

Julie removed her Myrtle Beach souvenir ball cap and rubbed her own shorn scalp. "I guess I do, huh?"

Roxie nodded. "You ever read *Helter Skelter*?"

"Of course. I read all that kinda shit."

Rob thought, *Why doesn't that surprise me?*

"Remember the pictures of those cute little Manson

chicks gathered outside the courthouse? That's sort of how you look. Only hotter."

Julie giggled. "Maybe I should carve a swastika on my forehead. Or have you do it."

Roxie laughed. "I will if you want. It'd fit right in with Rob's white-power look."

"You totally should. We all should. Think of how freaky that'll be for those preppy fucks when they see us."

Both girls laughed at that.

Rob experienced that gut-squeezing feeling of encroaching doom again. His companions were completely insane. Earlier in this adventure, he'd derived some comfort in thinking he could ditch them anytime and run back to his old life. But that option was no longer on the table. He was a wanted man. Doom was on the horizon. He was sure he would either be dead or in handcuffs by the time the sun rose tomorrow.

Julie thrust an arm through the gap between the seats, pointing at something ahead in the road. "There it is!"

Rob leaned forward, squinting again because he couldn't make out what Julie was seeing. Apparently her night vision was much better than his own. They were on a winding seaside road. To their right, beyond the dunes, was a long stretch of beach and the vast ocean. To their left, acres of apparently empty land.

Except that—

Julie jabbed her finger forward again. "Right *there!*"

The road twisted, moved farther inland. Julie's finger was pointing to the right. Rob craned his neck as far as he could in that direction and the impression of emptiness was revealed as an illusion. Now he could discern the shapes of houses in the darkness, a big cluster of them along the beach. They were almost invisible beneath the dense cloud cover, through which only the faintest glow of moonlight penetrated. There was a scent of rain in the air, the promise of a storm approaching. He spotted an access road and began to slow the clunky old Subaru. The car's engine coughed and sputtered, almost died again. He cursed the poorly maintained junker and tried not to think of the corpse in the trunk.

Just a harmless old man, he'd been.

No threat at all.

There'd been no reason to kill him.

And yet they'd done it. The girls, that is. First they'd broken into his shabby home on the outskirts of town. That he understood. They needed a place to hide and lay low. The torture, though, had not been necessary. That had just been fun and games. Rob didn't want to think about it. It sickened him. Just as all the rest of it sickened him. And yet he was still with them.

Why?

He didn't know. And he'd like a real answer to that question. Not the crazy one Julie had proffered: *It turns you on when you watch us kill.*

It couldn't possibly be true.

Could it?

No. Hell, no.

He steered the car down the access road and came to a stop. A gate blocked the way into the beach-house community.

Julie swung her arm to the left. "Over there."

Rob saw it. He backed the Subaru up and pulled up alongside the electronic keypad, which was inset on a metal pole. He cranked the window down and looked at Roxie. She unfolded the sheet of paper she'd dug out of her tote bag earlier.

"The code is . . ."

Rob punched in the numbers as she read them. Then there was a click and the gate swung open. Rob put the car in gear, made a sound of frustration as the engine sputtered again, then slammed the gas pedal down as it finally caught. The old car shot through the opening an instant before the gate started to swing shut again. He tapped the brake pedal and slowed back down as they began to navigate their way through a web of very narrow sandy roads. Roxie kept glancing at the scrap of paper in her hand, reading off directions while he drove.

"Stop here."

Rob pulled to a stop at the side of the road. It was actually a bend in a road between two clusters of houses. He glanced past Roxie and saw the dark ocean. A cold breeze stirred the tall grass on the dune separating road and beach. He'd vacationed with his grandparents in places like this when he was younger. He longed to journey back to those days. Or to any saner phase of his life. He didn't want to die. Didn't like this feeling of being swept along by fate. And yet he was powerless to do anything about it.

Roxie flipped open the cell phone she'd taken from the Subaru's deceased owner. She punched in a number and a brief text message. A silent moment passed. The car's interior was thick with tension. It was almost choking them.

Don't answer, Rob thought.

Please, please don't answer.

Then the cell phone buzzed and Roxie flipped it open again. She read the message on the screen and smiled at Rob. "Let's go."

They got out of the car and set off down the road on foot. Rob's stomach twisted. He'd seen a lot of people die this last week. Many of them horribly. But this was personal and would be about a thousand times worse.

After a walk of some fifty yards, they arrived at the driveway of a three-story beach house. Roxie moved quickly down the driveway, not quite running but advancing with the long strides of someone anxious to get somewhere fast. Julie hurried to catch up to her. Though it pained him to do so, Rob picked up his own pace. That urge to turn and run was still there, a mental voice growing more frantic by the moment, but he knew he wouldn't heed it. It was too late.

They circled the house and then continued around a tall fence surrounding a swimming pool. They entered through an open gate. Rob moved carefully over the cement deck. It was dark out here and the last thing he wanted was to fall into the pool. Though the lights were off, he could make out the shapes of inflatable rafts and beach balls floating in the water, bobbing in the lazy currents like little corpses.

They stepped off the deck onto a wooden patio, where a set of sliding glass doors stood open. A beautiful woman who looked a little like Roxie before the bleach job stepped through the opening and stood on the patio with them.

Roxie smiled. "Hi, Emily."

The woman looked at Roxie. "Hello, Missy. So glad you could make it. You have no idea how ready I am for this."

Rob frowned.

Missy?

"Uh . . . Roxie? What did she just call you?"

"It's my real name."

Rob's frown deepened. "But . . . how did she know it? And . . ."

Roxie—Missy—laughed. "Why didn't I tell you?"

"Yeah."

She shrugged. "I call myself different things all the time. It's not real important. Let's get this party started."

She clasped hands with Emily and they went on into the house.

Julie started after them, but glanced back at Rob. "You coming?"

Rob felt dizzy. He felt like the whole world was coming undone around him. Roxie wasn't who she said she was. At least not completely. And if she'd lied to him about her name, what else had she lied about? He laughed. Did it really matter? None of it changed the essential core truth about her.

She was a killer.

She lived for it. Thrived on it.

Julie went on into the house, leaving him alone on the patio for a moment. And this was it. Finally. His very last chance to turn and run. To maybe turn himself in or summon the cops.

But that was another lie.

That chance was gone forever.

He drew in a deep breath and followed the rest of them inside.

CHAPTER THIRTY-NINE

March 22

Missy's breath came in quick, shuddery gasps. Her face felt hot. Sweat was beading on her brow. The thump of her heart seemed as loud as a drum. Her hands were shaking. Anger bloomed within her again as she watched the tremors. It had been so long since anyone had gotten to her like this. So long since anyone had made her feel so small. So stupid and insignificant.

Four years, to be exact.

Daddy used to make her feel like this. He'd call her stupid and ugly all the time. And though she knew she was neither, it felt true when her daddy called her those things. That feeling was worse even than the other things. The beatings. The bad touches. Those things were bad. Horrible. They made her want to kill her daddy. She didn't because a part of her clung to the need for her daddy's love and approval. He was a bad man. She didn't need anyone to tell her that. But she kept loving him anyway, hoping that somehow, just maybe, he would change and become the kind of daddy other girls had. But it never happened. He called her a "mistake," telling her how one of his biggest regrets was failing to raise the money to have her aborted. And he told her the reason she was so fucked in the head was a result of all the times he'd punched her mother in the stomach in an effort to make her miscarry.

"I scrambled your brains but good, kid," he liked to say.

She killed him the night she turned sixteen. He came into her room stinking of beer a little before midnight, stumbling around and cursing in the dark. Then he fell into her bed and reached for her, as usual. But this time she was ready for him and gave him a great big surprise.

The big carving knife penetrated his flabby belly with shocking ease.

He opened his mouth to scream and she slashed his throat, a deep gash that severed his vocal cords and brought forth a great geyser of arterial gore. Then she was on him and attacking him with a savagery worthy of the most ferocious and predatory segments of the animal kingdom. He struggled to no avail as she clung to him and slammed the knife into his body over and over. Dozens upon dozens of times. She kept stabbing him after he was dead. His whole torso was a sticky mass of coagulated blood and exposed organs. She would later guess she'd stabbed him as many as a hundred times, perhaps more. But she didn't stop there. Next she went to the room Daddy shared with Mom. Then she went to her brother's room. And then to the "guest" bedroom long inhabited by her deadbeat uncle. She killed them all. Brutally. Then she took a shower to wash away all the blood, gathered a few things, and burned that fucking house to the ground. She left her hometown that night feeling powerful for the first time in her life. She emerged from that nightmare a changed girl and since then not one single person had ever made her feel the way her daddy used to make her feel . . .

Until now.

She stared at her shaking hands and redoubled the mental effort to still the trembling. Her breathing became more regular. The trembling began to slow.

She reached into her bag and her hand dipped to the bottom, finding the grip of the gun by instinct. No. She was smarter than that. She couldn't walk into a coffee shop in broad daylight and blow a man's brains out.

She relaxed her grip on the gun's handle and groped around the bottom of the bag until her fingers closed around a cellophane-wrapped pack of cigarettes. She kept groping until she found a *lighter. A cigarette would help her think. They always did. She tapped a Marlboro menthol out of the pack, popped it in her mouth, and lit up. As she exhaled smoke, she began to feel more centered, more like herself. And as she grew calmer, she realized something. She could just let this go. Yeah, the guy had upset her, but she'd lived in a state of near normality for months. It was sort of nice. She rented a room on the other side of town and the city's bus system took her wherever she needed to go, like this funky little strip mall with its pseudo-bohemian vibe. It wasn't a glamorous life. Nor was it one she could likely maintain for long. But it was a nice break in the madness of life on the run, and she hoped she could hold on to it a little while longer.*

"Hello, Missy."

She jumped at the voice and whirled around. Her eyes got big and her breath caught in her throat. It was one of them. "Wh-what?"

The girl was roughly her age. She was gorgeous and looked like a model in her chic clothes and expensive haircut. Everything about her screamed money and privilege. She looked the way Missy often wished she could. Regal and poised. Above it all. As she stared at the goddess, Missy's feelings were a stormy mix of envy, hatred, and desire.

The girl smiled and looked her over. "You know, you're way cuter than you were at sixteen. You're a real stunner now, Missy."

Missy dropped her cigarette and ground it out beneath her heel. "That's not my name."

"Of course it is."

The girl's expression was very intent. Missy knew she should be afraid. Somehow this person knew who she was. But something in her demeanor set her at ease. It was crazy. She should be running. Should be on her way out of town right now. Recognition meant danger and an increased chance of apprehension by the law. And she didn't want to go to jail. She'd rather die. But she wasn't afraid. Not being afraid made no sense at all, but it was the truth.

"How did you know?"

The girl shrugged. "I saw your Cold Case Files episode."

"Oh. I . . . sort of forgot about that."

The girl extended her hand. "Too bad. It's one of my favorite episodes. I've seen it a bunch of times. My name's Emily, by the way."

Missy shook her hand. "Um . . . nice to meet you."

"What's it feel like to stab your father a hundred fucking times?"

Missy's face reddened. "Um . . ."

Emily laughed. "Never mind. We don't have time. Any second now my friends will finish their drinks and come outside. I've got a proposition for you."

Missy frowned. "Um . . ."

"It involves killing the fucking asshole who insulted you." She reached into her little handbag and pulled out a notepad and a ballpoint pen. She flipped the pad open and began to write. "You're probably wondering why I'd want you to kill him. I should clarify. It's not just him. I want you to kill them all."

Emily tore off the sheet of paper and gave it to her.

Missy frowned at the very neat handwriting. The note included a street address, some basic directions, a phone number, and another series of numbers. "I don't get it. Why would you want me to kill your friends?"

Emily smiled. "Friends. Well, I guess some of them think of me as a friend. But I don't have friends, Missy. Just people I spend time with because that's what people do. I want you to kill them all, preferably as violently as possible. When the story hits the media, it'll be big. Bigger than big. These are sons and daughters of important people. As the only survivor, I'll be in demand. I'll be fucking famous." Her smile broadened, becoming almost beatific as her eyes twinkled in the sunlight. "And, Missy, fame is what I want more than anything else."

Missy grunted. "That's fucking crazy."

"Maybe. But it's what I want."

"So, what . . . ? You recognized me in there and came up with this insane scheme on the spot?"

"Yes."

"Like I said . . . fucking crazy."

"Will you do it?"

Missy thought about it. Crazy though it was, the scheme did sort of appeal to her. She started to get excited. She hadn't killed anyone in months and she missed it. What was she doing in this town anyway? The idea that she could live a normal person's life, at least for a while, had been exposed as a delusion. She was an instigator of chaos, pain, and terror. She'd burned herself out on these things for a time, that's all.

She shrugged. "Yeah. I'll do it."

Emily grinned. "Thank you, Missy. You have no idea how much this means to me. Now get moving before my so-called friends see you talking to me. Take a good look at that big blue and white Chevy van on your way out. That's our ride."

Missy heard the coffee shop's glass door open. She turned away from Emily and set off at a brisk pace across the strip mall's parking lot. She scanned the lot, looking for something she hadn't needed in a while—wheels. She noted the Chevrolet Express and kept moving. She saw a few possibilities, but nothing very appealing.

Then she saw the Galaxie parked at a gas pump across the street.

She smiled.

And started moving that way, knowing these were the first steps in a great and wondrous journey.

CHAPTER FORTY

March 27

Joe was surfing gay porn sites on his laptop when he heard footsteps coming up the stairs from the first floor. He heard voices, too. Shushed whispers. Though he couldn't make out any words, the timbre of one of those voices was unmistakable. He took a hand out of his shorts, clicked away from the current site, cleared his browser history and cache, and flipped the laptop shut.

His heart was pounding when the door to the second-floor room he was sharing with Emily opened and she stumbled inside with tears in her eyes. "Joe . . . I'm sorry . . . they . . . j-jumped me . . ."

He was on his feet in an instant. "Honey, what's—?"

Then the others came in behind her.

Two chicks and a guy.

The barrel of a gun was thrust into his face. The bald girl holding it beamed like a prom queen posing for a yearbook photo. "Hi. Get on your fucking knees."

It was *them*.

Terror slammed into him and stole his breath.

He dropped to his knees and began to pray.

Annalisa sat cross-legged on the bed with her hands clasped around her iPhone. She smiled as she sent identical status updates to Facebook and Twitter:

Vacay a total wash. Drama drama drama. But I'm in love w/Sean & somehow happier than ever. :)

She heard the voices in the hallway as she finished sending the update. She recognized Emily's voice right away. No mistaking that sultry tone. It made her think of that afternoon and she felt a reflexive tingle of arousal. She felt bad about that. But she couldn't dwell on it. She had a great guy and a bright future ahead of her. The thing with Emily she could chalk up as just another of life's experiences.

She frowned.

The other voices were very soft. She sensed an obvious effort to be quiet. Despite the low volume, she was certain these were the voices of strangers. Her mind flashed instantly to the news reports of the Walgreens massacre.

She sighed.

Ridiculous. You're just being paranoid.

The door to the bathroom opened, making her gasp and jump. Sean came out wearing only khaki shorts and a grin. "Whoa. Nervous much?"

She laughed. "I—"

The bedroom door flew open and there they were.

Tears sprang to Annalisa's eyes.

She knew her bright future no longer existed.

Chuck had just gone back to the bar when he heard the footsteps coming up the stairs. There had been no sign of Annalisa and Sean for hours. It wasn't Zoe. She was down at the beach and always returned via the balcony staircase. The only other possibility was the one he dreaded most. He was still sort of baffled by how badly he'd misjudged Joe over the years. He knew the guy was wild and liked to have a good time. And that was fine. He was the same way. But there was a world of difference between that and being a total fucking sleazebag. Emily was even worse. She was the queen champion slut whore of all time, as well as a total user and manipulator. At this point it didn't even matter whether she'd corrupted Joe or vice versa. They were both beyond redemption, in his eyes.

Joe appeared at the top of the stairs.

He was weaving again and his face looked red.

Shit. Here we go again.

Chuck didn't care if the guy was still fucked-up. If he tried to start shit again, he was getting his ass handed to him.

Then he saw the red welt beneath one of his eyes and frowned.

What the hell?

Emily came up right behind him. She was also wobbling a little and there were tears in her eyes. Joe watched them and wanted to puke. So the drama had continued in private. More drama followed by fisticuffs, from the looks of it.

That theory gave way to reality an instant later.

Missy Wallace shoved Emily aside and strode into the living room with the malevolent confidence of an avenging angel. She had a gun in her hand. It was aimed at the floor, but it was rising. Chuck moved without thinking about it, instinct propelling him away from the bar toward the balcony door. She was here to kill him. He had to run, even if it meant a bullet in the back.

The gun boomed.

The big pane of glass in one of the French doors blew out and Chuck skidded to a halt. He stood shaking and breathing hard as he stared at the spray of glass. His mind calculated what the trajectory of the bullet must have been and he almost fell over. He'd just missed having his brains splattered against the door. She was still coming at him. He could feel her bearing down on him. Then he felt the gun against the back of his neck and screwed his eyes shut.

This is it, he thought.

This is how I die.

He had seconds left, probably. His heart raced. His head was filled with a whirlwind of clashing, confused thoughts and feelings. Regret, terror, loss, heartache, and a desperate hope for some kind of continued existence beyond this mortal plane. All the things anyone facing imminent death would feel. It was impossible to grab on to any one thing and focus on it.

Until he thought of Zoe again.

Shit.

She had been down at the beach for some time. More than an hour, easily. She could be on her way back right now. Could be moments away from walking in on this slaughter in the making. The odds were against her, but he figured she was the only one of them with any chance of surviving the night. She might yet live if Missy and her friends got down to business fast.

Chuck opened his eyes.

Several seconds had passed. The gun's barrel was still pressed to the back of his neck.

"What are you waiting for? Get it over with."

Missy laughed. "You'd like that, wouldn't you? A quick and merciful end."

Chuck swallowed with tremendous difficulty—it felt like he was trying to force a golf ball down his gullet. "Yes."

Another laugh, this one tinged with a merciless, taunting quality. "Sucks to be you, I guess."

The gun came away from his neck as she moved back some.

"Turn around, frat boy."

Chuck turned around.

They were all here now. All but Zoe. Emily and Joe. Annalisa and Sean. Missy and the other two wanted in connection with the Walgreens killings. The fugitives had all changed their looks. Missy had short and spiky blonde hair.

The guy and the younger chick were both bald. They looked like skinheads. The grin on the younger girl's face disturbed him as much as anything else. She looked like she was having the time of her life. The guy was lean and fit. He wore black jeans and a black button-up shirt with a flame pattern on the front. Chuck might have laughed at the duds under other circumstances. He looked like he shopped exclusively at Hot Topic. He also looked exactly like the sort of dude who'd get mixed up with the likes of Missy Wallace. But there was something off about him. Maybe it was just wishful thinking, but he had a feeling the guy wasn't as into this as Missy and the other chick. He looked nervous. Scared. Like he'd rather be anywhere but here. The insight gave him his first glimmer of hope. It was a small one, but it was better than nothing. He had to work on tweaking this guy's conscience, somehow nudge him into intervening before it was too late.

"Rob!"

The bald guy flinched when Missy barked his name. "Yeah?"

"Got a job for you."

Rob grimaced. "What do you want?"

Yeah. Definitely not into this at all. Yet here he is. Weak-willed little bastard.

"I need you to rearrange some furniture." Missy never looked away from Chuck as she issued her commands. Never stopped smiling. And never stopped aiming the gun right at his face. "Shove that goddamn sofa out of the way, up against the entertainment center. Then drag the chairs from that table and line 'em up in a row."

Rob set about his work with obvious reluctance. The listless way he moved made him look like a tired old man. He couldn't be more than a few years older than Chuck, but the haunted, faraway look in his eyes made him look like a combat veteran at the end of a tour of duty. He nonetheless got the job done within a few minutes. The sofa was up against the entertainment center and four metal-framed chairs were lined up in a row, facing the kitchen area.

Missy moved away from Chuck and pointed the gun at Joe. "You sit there."

She nodded at one of the chairs.

Joe staggered over to it and plopped down, tears leaking from his eyes. "Please. I don't wanna die. Please . . ."

"Shut up or I'll shoot you in the balls."

Joe stopped pleading, but his tears continued in a steady stream.

Missy ordered Sean and Annalisa into the two middle chairs and installed Chuck in the chair on the far-right end, the one closest to the balcony doors. Chuck glanced at the shattered door and tried to send a telepathic signal to Zoe to stay put. It was ridiculous, but what else could he do? He made himself stop looking at the door. He didn't want Missy developing any suspicions.

Missy knelt and set her big tote bag on the floor. She pulled out some clothes and tossed them aside. Then she reached into the bag and pulled out a plastic bag with a Walgreens logo. She opened the Walgreens bag and dumped its contents on the floor.

Rolls and rolls of gray duct tape. A dozen, maybe more.

Chuck groaned inwardly.

The situation was already seventy-seven shades of fucked-up, but the prospect of being restrained made it so much worse. He would be helpless, incapable of fighting or resisting. Maybe he should try one more desperate run to freedom while his hands and legs were still free.

Missy must have sensed his thoughts.

She got up and came over to him in two quick, long strides. The gun barrel was right in his face this time and he instinctively cringed away from it. "You're not going anywhere, fuck-o."

Chuck felt like crying, but somehow the tears wouldn't come.

He was becoming numb inside.

Rob and the girls scooped up rolls of duct tape and set about the task of taping the four of them to the chairs. Rob started with Chuck, pulling his wrists together behind the back of the chair and then winding more than a dozen layers of tape around them. The son of a bitch was very thorough. Chuck tested the tape. There was no give at all. Maybe he wasn't into this, but it was clear he would do whatever Missy wanted. Chuck felt that little flicker of hope snuff out as Rob used a full roll of tape to secure each of his legs to the chair legs.

Yes. Very, very thorough.

Just like a concentration-camp guard.

Chuck looked at Emily and frowned. They hadn't dealt with her yet. She didn't seem afraid anymore. In fact, she was smirking and her eyes gleamed with that same mad glee he'd seen in the younger girl's eyes.

"Emily—"

She came at him fast and whipped a hand across his face. It was a hard blow and it snapped his head hard to the right. A bright flash of pain set his cheek ablaze with pain, but that was a minor thing compared to what he felt when her arm swung back around and she backhanded him, her knuckles mashing a nose still tender from the beating he'd received earlier in the week. A spike of agony slammed through the center of his head. She slapped and backhanded him several more times. Through it all, he was dimly aware of the confused and startled voices of his friends. Even Joe wanted to know what the hell was wrong with her.

Emily stopped hitting him and seized a handful of his hair

to hold his head steady. His face throbbed and he stared at her through eyes bleary with tears. She spat in his face. "My hand hurts."

He coughed and blinked at her. "Wh-what?"

She was smirking again. "My hand hurts, you fucking asshole. But it's totally worth it. I can't wait to see what Missy does to you."

"You . . . know her?"

"Obviously. Now I have a question for you. Where's Zoe?"

Missy had been standing back, watching the scene with an expression of mild amusement. Now she frowned. "Who's Zoe?"

Emily let go of Chuck's hair and turned toward her. "She's Chuck's girlfriend. Remember the hot blonde with us at Starbuck's?"

"Yeah."

"That's Zoe."

Missy's frown deepened. "We need to find her."

The bald girl moved closer to Missy. "We've checked all the rooms. All empty."

Emily looked at Chuck and smiled. "She must be down at the beach. I'll go get her."

Chuck bucked against his bonds. "You bitch! You back-stabbing cunt!"

The bald girl offered Emily a big hunting knife crusted with flecks of what had to be dried blood. "Here, take this."

Emily smiled again and waved off the offer. "Won't need it." She shot another leering smile Chuck's way. "Zoe's not happy with me right now, but deep down, she loves me. She really does. And there's nothing I can't talk her into when I put my mind to it. She'll come back with me hand in hand, never guessing anything's wrong."

Missy nodded. "So go. But make it fast. I'm itching to get started."

Emily winked at Chuck and departed without another

word. Chuck's eyes tracked her across the room and out the shattered door, his soul seething with hatred unlike anything he'd ever experienced. He wanted to scream out a warning, but knew Zoe would never hear it over the wind and the sounds of the ocean. And he didn't want to exhaust his strength by exercising his lungs. He would need every ounce he could spare for the ordeal ahead.

He couldn't wrap his mind around what Emily was doing. She was a mean bitch, sure, but there were a lot of those in the world, just as there were a lot of mean, cold-hearted bastards. But there was a huge chasm between this and just being mean.

This was betrayal on a level beyond his comprehension.

It wasn't human.

It was . . . evil. Yes, evil. It was a strange thing to think, but it was true. There was a devil living in that girl's heart. She'd surrendered her soul to darkness.

He thought about the things she'd said about Zoe and wanted to weep.

Because he knew they were all true.

A dark figure came striding down the beach toward her as Zoe emerged dripping wet from the ocean. She wiped salt water from her eyes and smoothed her hair back, which fell in a thick, wet sheet across her shoulders. It was too dark to discern the figure's identity from this distance, but instinct told her it was Emily. A surge of anxiety swept through her as she slogged through the wet sand toward the row of canvas chairs where she'd left her things. She gathered up her beach towel and wrapped it around her waist like a sarong. She glanced up as she stuffed a hardback novel into her tote bag and was unsurprised to find her hunch verified.

Emily had closed to within ten yards.

She smiled as Zoe's eyes locked with her. "Hi."

Zoe didn't return the smile. She didn't want to talk to

Emily. Not right now. She didn't want to start bawling. But she couldn't just ignore her and walk on by. Well, she could, but it didn't feel right. "I was just about to go back inside."

Emily's smile faltered slightly. "You mind if I at least walk back with you?"

Zoe suppressed a groan. "I don't know, Emily."

Emily came closer, stopping just a few feet in front of her. "Look, I know this has been a rough week. Nobody's happy with me. Not even Joe, believe it or not. But you're the only one who matters, Zoe." Her voice became thick with emotion. She sounded on the verge of tears. It made Zoe feel bad. "You . . . you're my *best* friend. My only *real* friend. Please just let me walk with you and say a few things. We don't have to have a real talk until you're ready." A single tear traced a slow trail down one of her cheeks. "Would that be okay? Please?"

Zoe felt her heart begin to melt. And though it went against her better judgment in light of all that had happened, she found herself unable to deny Emily's request. She really was her best friend. Still. Even now. Accepting this frightened her because she had no idea how things would shake out in the end. There were her other friends to consider. They all hated Emily. It wasn't fair. She was an adult. Shouldn't she be able to choose her own friends? She sighed. "Okay. But—"

She gasped as Emily grabbed her and pulled her close. Emily kissed her. Her tongue slid between her lips and tangled with Zoe's tongue. Zoe braced her hands on Emily's shoulders and tried to push her away, but Emily tightened her embrace and kept kissing her. The towel came loose and slid to the ground. Zoe tried to wrench her head away, breaking the kiss for the slightest moment before Emily's mouth found hers again. This time she kissed back.

Jesus fuck, what am I doing?

She braced her hands on Emily's shoulders again and shoved with all her strength. This time the embrace was broken and Emily staggered back several steps. The strange thing was, she didn't look pissed. She was still smiling. She licked her lips. "You always taste so sweet."

Zoe scooped up her towel again, grabbed her tote bag, and gave Emily a wide berth as she started up the beach toward the house.

Emily hurried after her. She slowed a bit as she came up alongside Zoe, matching her stride for stride. "Remember that night in the hotel room?"

Zoe didn't say anything.

Emily laughed. "You sure didn't have any inhibitions that night. I guess the coke helped loosen you up. I've still got some, you know."

"I don't care."

"Liar."

The dune and the little bridge beyond were coming up fast. Anxious to be back inside and away from Emily's discomforting insinuations, she picked up her pace to trudge up the grassy dune.

Emily gave her a little sideways shove as they reached the bridge and moved into the narrow space ahead of her.

Zoe glared at her as she followed her onto the bridge. "Hey! What the fuck was that?"

Emily laughed and kept moving. She didn't respond.

Zoe's anger surged. "Seriously, that was really fucking rude. What's your problem?"

Even as she asked the question, Zoe figured she knew the answer. Emily wasn't used to having her advances spurned. She was very self-centered and couldn't abide rejection in any form. Some of Zoe's anger subsided as she realized it was at least partly her fault. A lot of her recent behavior had laid the groundwork for situations like this. If she'd always rejected Emily's amorous overtures, this wouldn't be happening now.

"I'm sorry."

Emily stopped at the far end of the bridge and turned to face her. She had moved fast and was some twenty yards ahead of where Zoe stood. Her figure was a dark outline in the dim moonlight. "Really?"

Zoe stopped five feet away from her. "Yeah."

Emily smiled. "Wanna go back down to the beach?"

"No."

Emily's smile vanished. "Whatever."

She turned away from her again and stepped off the bridge, but she moved slower as she continued down the dune to the gate at the back of the fence. Emily opened it and they stepped inside. Zoe paused inside the gate to wash the sand off her feet with the hose. Emily lingered, waiting for her. It struck her as passing strange. She sensed their conversation was over. There was no more to say on the subject of their endangered friendship until later. But Emily seemed to want to stick close anyway. Whatever. It didn't matter. She'd head back to her own room once they were back inside. No way she'd want to hang around upstairs with Chuck, not after this afternoon's debacle.

Zoe shut the hose off and started across the deck, angling toward the staircase leading up to the balcony.

Emily followed, hanging close, almost on her heels.

Zoe glanced over her shoulder at the other girl.

She frowned.

Emily was smiling, but her eyes looked hard, malevolent. *Weird.*

She started up the stairs and heard the slap of Emily's sandals on the stairs beneath her. The first little flutter of alarm hit her as she glanced down and again saw that same vaguely evil expression. But that was forgotten as they reached the balcony and Zoe saw the broken shards of glass sprayed across the wooden beams. An accident, she assumed. But why hadn't someone cleaned it up? This could be dangerous. She wasn't wearing shoes or sandals and would have to—

"ZOE! RUN!"

Zoe frowned again.

Chuck?

She heard pain in that voice. And terror. Something was horribly wrong here. She heard something else in the house. A whimper. A female sound. More evidence of something very bad happening. Then terrible, gleeful laughter. The laughter of a sadist. Followed by a scream.

Zoe moved back a step.

And she felt a hand at the small of her back.

The hand shoved her forward. She cried out as broken glass slashed at the soles of her bare feet. Emily grabbed her by an arm and wrenched her toward the space formerly occupied by a large pane of glass.

A glimpse of hell made her weak in the knees.

Emily shoved her again. Shards of glass still embedded in the door frame ripped at her flesh as she flew through the empty space and crashed to the hardwood floor. She rolled onto her side and stared straight up at Chuck. His face was streaked with tears. His mouth moved as he tried to speak, but he couldn't force the words out.

Oh, Chuck . . .

She felt a foot on her shoulder. It pressed down, forcing her to lie flat on her back again. She looked up and saw a familiar face above her. Familiar, but not the face of someone she knew. It was *her.* She looked different, but it was definitely her. The girl Chuck had picked on at the coffee shop.

The killer.

Missy Wallace grinned. "Glad you could join us, Zoe. Now we can finally get this party started."

CHAPTER FORTY-ONE

March 27

Julie held her hand a few inches over the burner. Heat warmed her palm as the metal coil began to glow a bright red. The kitchen was spacious and modern, with an island and lots of gleaming fixtures. To the left of the stove was a counter crowded with various snack foods. Bags of chips and boxes of cookies, among other things. She reached into an open bag of tortilla chips and plucked one out, popping it in her mouth and savoring the salty taste. She was tempted to gobble down the whole bag. There hadn't been a lot of opportunities to eat since yesterday. The pantry and fridge in that old guy's home had been pretty bare. She'd been kind of irritated about that and hadn't felt at all bad about sawing his ear off.

Her palm was hot now.

The big hunting knife was on the counter. She picked it up and placed the blade across the glowing burner coil. Someone screamed in the living room. A sound of unimaginable agony. Missy was probably doing something pretty interesting to one of the college kids. It wouldn't be Rob. He never participated. She turned away from the stove and saw him standing several feet away from the action.

He sure looked nervous.

Maybe she could calm him down.

Leaving the knife on the burner, she walked into the living room. "Hey, uh . . . Missy?"

Missy paused in the act of torturing the one called Joe with a pair of pliers and looked at her. "Yeah?"

"Can I borrow Rob for a few minutes?"

Rob stopped staring at the floor long enough to look up and frown.

Missy clamped the pliers around one of Joe's fingers again. "Sure."

Julie took Rob by the hand and began to drag him out of the living room and down the hallway toward the master bedroom. Once they were in the room, she removed her clothes and stretched her naked body across the luxuriant bed.

"Fuck me, Rob."

Rob glanced at the open door. Julie could see the backs of the people tied to the chairs from her vantage point. Rob wiped his mouth with a trembling hand and looked at her. "Shouldn't we close that?"

"No."

Rob sighed.

"I want to hear the screams clear as a bell. It'll make it hotter."

The look on Rob's face was priceless. She saw horror and disgust. And fear. He was afraid of her. But not *too* afraid, apparently.

He began to unbutton his shirt.

The orgasmic screams emerging from the master bedroom disturbed Annalisa almost as much as anything else that had happened so far. How could anyone sane pause in the midst of committing atrocities to screw?

The answer to that was obvious.

These people weren't sane. They were vicious and cruel.

They derived great pleasure from acts of sadism. Well, the two girls did. Their behavior bothered the guy, she could tell. But his presence made him equally complicit. And maybe he wasn't a sadist, but he was clearly twisted in his own way. He was screwing a young girl's brains out while listening to people out here scream and cry. He was just as sick as his female companions. The only real difference was his apparent cowardice.

These people meant to kill them all. She had no illusions about that. This was the last night of her life. It scared her. She didn't want to die. She didn't want to hurt like Joe was hurting now. Her only comfort now was her firm belief in an afterlife. She was smarter than the average person. Her grades and IQ scores confirmed that. A lot of smart people didn't believe there was anything beyond this life, but her faith in something bigger was strong and came from a place of calm, even in the face of all this horror. She would exist somewhere else in some form after her life here was over. She only hoped Sean would be there with her.

She looked at Emily.

Zoe was still lying flat on the floor, but now she was on her stomach. Emily sat on her back, pinning her there. She looked totally enthralled as she watched Missy torture Joe. All five fingers of Joe's right hand were mangled wrecks. The digits were twisted in different directions. In more than one place a bit of broken bone poked through torn flesh. Joe was shaking and sobbing in his chair. This was the man Emily supposedly loved. She hadn't actually loved him, of course. It was just another of her many deceptions. She didn't know or understand the connection between Emily and these psychos, but it didn't matter. Knowing wouldn't change anything.

She heard footsteps from the hallway and glanced that way to see the bald duo returning from their bedroom romp. The guy wouldn't look at them. He shuffled off out of view again while the girl went back into the kitchen. She returned to the living room a few seconds later, the big knife she'd threatened them with earlier in her hand again. Annalisa felt a pit open up in her stomach as the girl came right up to her.

"Look at me."

Annalisa raised her head and looked the girl in the eye.

The girl smiled. "You're pretty."

Then she grabbed a handful of Annalisa's hair and wound it in a tight knot to hold her head steady. Annalisa's eyes jittered in their sockets as she watched the girl's other hand slowly bring the big blade toward her face. She felt the heat of it as it closed to within inches of her flesh. She cried and started breathing faster.

Someone was saying, "Nononononono . . ."

She realized it was her own voice.

The girl placed the blade flat across one of her cheeks. Annalisa screamed as she felt her flesh blister and sizzle. The girl tightened her grip on her hair and managed to keep her head relatively still while continuing to press the blade into her flesh. Her cheek melted and a scent of cooked meat filled her nostrils. She sucked in a deep breath and unleashed another ear-shredding scream. Her lungs felt ragged, but she didn't care. She wasn't about to stop screaming. Maybe if they all screamed loud enough someone who could help would hear.

The girl at last relinquished her grip on Annalisa's hair. The hot blade came away from her face as she stepped back to admire her handiwork. She looked pleased. "There. Now you're not so pretty."

She giggled.

Annalisa's cheek throbbed and burned. It was near unbearable. She wished they would just kill her and be done with it, but she knew they were just getting started.

A crushing guilt assailed Chuck as he watched Missy go out to the balcony and return with another chair. This was all his fault. It was undeniable. This wouldn't be happening if he hadn't unleashed his inner asshole at the coffee shop that day. The truth was more complicated than that, another voice in his head argued. This was really all down to Emily. She had steered Missy Wallace here. And while that was true, it did nothing to lessen his guilt.

Missy set the chair in front of him and sat down.

She smiled. "Hello, Chuck."

He glared at her, didn't say anything.

She held out a hand and said, "I don't believe we've been properly introduced. My name is Missy Wallace. I'm a famous murderer." She glanced at her hand and lowered it, her smile becoming a smirk. "Oh, I'm sorry. You're hands are kind of tied at the moment."

The comment elicited a giggle from the bald girl.

Missy leaned toward him. "So . . . Chuck. What happened to you, man? You look like someone used you for a punching bag."

"They did."

"When did this happen?"

He sighed. "It doesn't matter."

She slapped him. "Tell me."

The slap wasn't a hard one, but he was still tender from the abuse Emily had dished out and it hurt like a bitch. "It happened in the early morning hours the day after . . . I insulted you. I . . . went off by myself. The others weren't there. I drank all night in a bar across the street from the motel where we were staying. A place called Big Sam's."

"Where was this?"

"Little town just inside the North Carolina border. I was there after closing time. Some people who worked at the bar dragged me into a back room and beat the shit out of me. Guy named Joe Bob, he was the bartender, and a couple of his friends. I was too busy getting stomped to get their names."

"What?" Zoe was looking up at him from the floor. "That's not what you told us at all."

"I know. This is the truth. What I told you was a lie."

"But . . . why?"

Missy twisted around in her chair and glared at Zoe. "Shut up! You don't have permission to speak. I hear your voice again, I'll cut your fucking tongue out."

She turned to face Chuck again. She flashed a smile of false sweetness. "So why did you lie to your friends, Chuck? Is it because you're a fucking dirtbag not fit to lick the shit off a bum's shoes?"

"They threatened me. I could've gone to the cops, but I was afraid of them."

Missy laughed. "So you're really a big fuckin' pussy?"

"I was that night, yeah."

Missy pursed her lips and looked away from him, staring at some vague middle point behind him. She was thinking seriously about something and that worried him. The situation was already awful and hopeless. But he didn't kid himself. This girl was a monster, but she was also smart and creative. She could—and probably would—devise ways to deepen and prolong their misery.

She focused on him again. Her smile this time was smaller and more mischievous. "That girl on the floor is your girlfriend?"

Chuck's eyes misted. "Yes. Don't hurt her. Please."

Missy's expression turned serious. "What if I told you I'll let her live if you help us torture and kill the rest of these fucks? Would you do that?"

"No."

He heard Zoe sniffle and he frowned. Would she want him to do that? He didn't believe the Zoe he knew would want her own life spared as part of some twisted bargain. But maybe he was wrong. You never really knew the ugliest truths residing in any person's soul until you placed them in a situation like this.

Zoe's sniffle gave way to a whimper. "Chuck . . . I don't wanna die."

Missy's nostrils flared as anger lit up her face. She stood up and kicked the chair aside. *"Didn't I tell you to keep your fucking mouth shut?"*

Zoe whimpered again.

It was barely audible over the moans of agony from Joe and Annalisa, but Chuck heard it and it tore at his heart.

Missy kicked Emily and sent her scurrying away across the floor. "Turn over, bitch."

Zoe whimpered and didn't move.

Missy kicked her.

Zoe cried out.

Missy kicked her again.

And again.

Zoe turned over with a great groan of exertion. Her whole face was wet from her tears. Missy took the hunting knife from the bald girl, then knelt and straddled Zoe. "This should be fun, if a little messy. I haven't cut out a tongue in a while."

She squeezed Zoe's mouth open and lowered the blade to her face.

"I'll do it."

The words surprised him as they came out of his mouth. The bargain remained a loathsome, sickening thing, but with the prospect of Zoe's mutilation and death right on the cusp of happening, it was suddenly much more palatable. And now he was seeing very clearly into the ugliest side of his own soul. Yes, he really could murder innocent people if it meant saving the life of the woman he loved. She wanted him to do it, after all.

She'd voiced the darkest wish imaginable.

And he was the only one who could grant it.

Missy let go of Zoe's jaw and stood up. Her smile as she approached him had a hideous knowing quality to it. She moved behind him and started slicing through the layers of duct tape binding his wrists. The blade was still warm and moved through the tape with ease. "Julie, get the gun and keep it on him. You're not gonna try to play hero are you, Chuck? Tell me you're not that stupid."

"I'm not. I'll do whatever you say."

She stood up and patted the top of his head. "Good boy."

Chuck brought his newly freed hands around to his lap and began the process of peeling the tape away from his wrists, wincing as the adhesive pulled out hairs.

Emily was on her feet again and she looked pissed. "What the fuck is up with this?" She looked like a spoiled child on the edge of a serious tantrum. Chuck expected her to start stamping her feet any moment. "You can't let her live. She knows I'm part of this and she'll fucking talk. You have to kill her."

Missy stepped back into view and approached Emily. "Really? That's interesting. Because I'm pretty sure I don't have to do anything I don't fucking wanna do."

Chuck saw it coming before it happened, but he guessed Emily never did. It was part of her bottomless arrogance. She saw herself as a real, integral part of Missy's little gang, but she was dead wrong.

Missy stabbed her in the stomach.

Then yanked the blade out and stuck it in again.

Emily gasped and her eyes widened in disbelief. She staggered backward and clasped her hands over stomach, blood jetting between her fingers and staining the front of her black dress. Missy stalked her as she continued to stumble backward, moving slowly, in no hurry at all to finish the job. Zoe sat up and watched. They were all watching. The bald girl, Julie, had turned away from him and was tracking their progress toward the kitchen.

"Yo, Missy."

"Yeah?"

"That burner's still on."

Missy laughed. "Cool."

Missy caught up to Emily, seized her by an arm, and dragged her into the kitchen. Chuck craned his head and caught a glimpse of the red-hot burner coil. His stomach twisted in anticipation of what was coming. Missy pushed the wounded girl up against the stove, turned her around, and took one of her hands by the wrist, guiding it toward the burner. Emily struggled, tried to twist her hand away even as blood from her wounds fell and patted on the kitchen tiles. Missy poked the tip of the knife into her side, making Emily scream and lose focus on the struggle with her hand. Missy seized the opportunity and pressed her hand to the burner.

Emily's wail of agony scorched Chuck's eardrums and he looked away.

Looked right at Zoe.

Who was free. And unwatched and unguarded. She had a chance. A very, very slim one, but she had to take it. He whispered her name and she looked at him. He nodded at the open balcony door. "Go."

She didn't need to be told twice. She got up and started running and was all the way to the door before the one called Rob shouted a warning. "She's getting away!"

Julie whirled around and saw her disappear through the door.

Missy screamed at her. "Get that bitch!"

Julie took off after Zoe, disappearing through the door seconds later.

Chuck heard footsteps pounding down the balcony staircase and prayed his girl could outrun the other one. But the other one had a gun. Zoe was pretty athletic, but she was wounded. And she couldn't outrun bullets.

Missy stabbed Emily again and let go of her to join the chase. She vanished through the balcony door as Emily moaned and crawled back into the living room, dripping a trail of blood across the hardwood floor. She came to within a few feet of Chuck and raised a shaking hand toward him. The underside of the hand was visible, and his stomach twisted at the sight of the ruined, blistered flesh. The reaction was purely physical reflex. He felt no real sympathy for her.

"Please . . . help . . . me . . ."

"No."

He balled his right hand into a fist and punched her dead-center in the face. He heard a very satisfying crack of bone as she pitched onto her side. She moaned softly and didn't move. Chuck started working at the layers of tape binding his legs to the chair. His heart was pounding. Maybe they all still had a chance after all. If Zoe could outrun the girls long enough, he could get loose and get to a phone, get the cops out here.

Footsteps, someone in motion.

Rob.

He went into the kitchen and started opening drawers. Chuck heard a clatter of silverware and his struggles with the tape became more frantic. He cursed. If only he could make his hands stop shaking. The fuckers had used so much tape. It was taking forever.

Rob came back into the living room.

He had a big carving knife in his right hand, the kind you'd use to slice up a Thanksgiving turkey. He waved it at Chuck. "Stop."

Chuck kept unwrapping the tape. He didn't have a choice. Maybe he could talk some sense into the guy before the girls came back. If he was ever going to exploit this dude's obvious conflicted feelings, now was the time. "I can't. I'm not gonna sit here and do nothing. Stab me if you want. I don't give a shit." Chuck continued unwinding the tape from his right leg. It was coming off faster and faster now. "You should help me. I'll tell the cops. And I'll tell them you didn't do any of the really bad shit. Maybe they'll go easy on you."

"It's too late for that."

Chuck screamed as the knife slashed across his face.

He didn't feel what the girls felt when he did it. He watched the blood pump from the guy's wound and felt no surge of adrenaline. He felt revulsion and a renewed sense of self-loathing. This wasn't for kicks. It never could be for him. He was just doing what needed to be done.

The girl with the burned face screamed at him, "*You son of a bitch! Why are you doing this?*"

Rob told the truth. "I don't know. Not really."

She called him a son of a bitch one more time and went back to sobbing.

A distant but sharp sound snapped Rob's gaze toward the balcony door. The sound came again and this time he recognized it for what it was—gunshots. Julie was out there blazing away on the beach. The beach was probably pretty empty this time of night, but someone from one of the neighboring beach houses might hear the shots and call the cops. Or maybe not, this late at night. Rob put the odds at maybe fifty-fifty. Strangely, his anxiety level stayed about the same.

"ZOE!"

Rob flinched.

The one he'd cut—Chuck—was also staring at the open balcony door. The guy was beyond agitated. Rob couldn't blame him. That was his girl dodging lead out there. He was a well-built guy. A workout addict. Every muscle in his body was bulging. It looked like a nest of snakes was trying to pop out of his skin. Blood poured down his face from the gash in his cheek, spilling past his lips and down his chin. He let loose a cry of rage at the sound of another distant pop. Then he kicked his right leg free of the remaining layer of tape, got his foot planted solidly on the floor, and drove himself headlong at Rob.

Rob shrieked and tried to backpedal, but the guy's rage-driven momentum made it impossible to get out of the way in time. The top of his head slammed into his gut, blasting the air from his lungs. They both hit the floor hard, Rob falling flat on his back and his attacker landing awkwardly with the chair still attached to his left leg. The rest of them were screaming and cheering Chuck on, urging him to kill the son of a bitch. It was a surreal moment for Rob. How had he arrived at this point in his existence? He knew how, of course, had been there for the whole ride, but it still didn't seem possible. He'd always thought of himself as basically a nice guy, yet now he'd become something others wanted to see dead.

It was fucked-up. Seriously.

Chuck had rolled onto his back and was working to remove the last of the tape from his left leg. Rob realized he'd somehow held onto the carving knife after taking the hit from the human missile.

And he realized something else.

He'd never stand a chance in a fair fight against this guy.

He sat up and jabbed the knife at Chuck.

Zoe fled down the beach in the dark, her long and toned runner's legs allowing her to put some distance between her and her pursuers. She was somewhat hampered by the sliced-up soles of her feet or it would have been no contest at all. She would simply have run until they could run no more. And then kept on running, until she was far, far away from that house and the horrors inside. But the places where the glass had chewed up her feet were sizzling slashes of white agony. Tears streamed down her face as she focused all her will on the task of keeping her legs pumping in spite of the pain. And it seemed to be working. She glanced over her shoulder and saw them falling farther back, becoming pale, dreamlike figures sliding through the gloom. She began to hope again. She was going to make it. She wouldn't die. Not tonight. A fierce, exultant joy rippled through her, overriding the pain, and she glanced backward again. She heard a pop and glimpsed a small spark in the darkness.

A gun!

They're shooting at me!

The knowledge triggered a rush of primal terror. She imagined a piece of flying lead penetrating her body at unbelievable velocity. They weren't likely to hit a moving target in the dark, especially from this distance, but they might get off a lucky shot.

But it wasn't a bullet that brought her down.

She hit the sand castle and let out a gasp as she went sprawling in the sand.

Get up! Get up! Get up!

Zoe obeyed the voice in her head. The fall had amped up the pain in her feet, but she ignored it and clawed her way to her feet again. The pale figures behind her had drawn a little closer, gotten a bit more distinct. She saw another spark in the darkness and got moving again. This time her right foot landed square on the metal arm of a folded-up beach chair. She screamed as the pain staggered her and made her fall again.

Get up! Get up! Get up!

She tried, but she just couldn't. She made it to her knees, but her right foot throbbed mercilessly, as if someone had poured battery acid inside the gashes. The pain was too much. She could go no farther.

And then they were on her.

The bald girl tackled her and drove her to the ground. She cried out in triumph and straddled Zoe, shoving the barrel of the gun into her open mouth. The gun's sight scraped the roof of her mouth and drew blood. The salty tang stung the back of her throat. The feeling reminded her of having strep as a child. She wished she could be a kid again, safe within the sheltering embrace of her family.

Mommy . . .

The bald girl, Julie, grinned and leaned close. "End of the line, bitch. I'm gonna watch your brains blow out the top of your head. That'll be fun. For me. Not so much for you." She giggled. "You just get to *die*."

Missy caught up to them then and stood panting near where the back of Zoe's head rested in the sand. "Don't . . . do . . . that."

Julie frowned and glanced up at her. "Why not?"

"Because you've damn near emptied that thing. Too much noise." Missy dropped to her knees and stared down at Zoe. The girl's smile was weirdly serene. "Boy, you sure fucked yourself there, girl. I was really gonna do it, you know. Let you live if Chuck helped me do the rest of them."

Zoe swallowed more blood as she struggled to talk around the gun in her mouth.. "I . . . couldn't let him do that."

Missy laughed. "Oh, sure."

Julie eased the gun's barrel out of her mouth. "Yeah. You're all noble and shit now. You were singing a different tune a few minutes ago."

Still smiling, Missy shook her head. "Doesn't matter now. I'm rescinding the offer. You're gonna die, just like the rest of them."

Zoe's eyes filled with tears as a bleak hopelessness overtook her. "Please . . ."

Missy leaned closer, her expression more intent now. "Say that again."

Zoe coughed. "Wh-what?"

"What you just said. Say it again."

Zoe couldn't think straight. Her fear was overriding everything. She couldn't remember what she'd said just a second ago. Then it came to her and she made her mouth form the word again. "Please."

"Again."

She whimpered. "Please."

"Please what?"

Another whimper. "Please don't kill me."

Missy made a sensual sound deep in her throat. It was the kind of sound you made when biting into something delicious. "I always dig the begging part."

Julie looked almost bored now. "So what do we do with her?"

Missy lifted her head and looked out at the ocean. The gentle roar of the incoming tide was louder at night. Zoe remembered how soothing the sound had seemed on previous nights. But now it just struck her as ominous.

Missy sat up, leaned back on her haunches. "I have an idea."

A corner of Julie's mouth tipped up. "Yeah?"

"I was just thinking . . . I don't think I've ever drowned anyone."

"NO!"

The word erupted from Zoe's sore throat, that one powerful syllable somehow invested with enough raw anguish and terror to express the entirety of the horror engulfing her. Desperation possessed her and she thrashed with all her might, nearly dislodging the younger girl until Missy got her hands around her throat and began to squeeze. Her hands were strong, surprisingly so, like a band of steel drawing tighter and tighter against her flesh. The pressure only let up when she stopped struggling.

Missy let go of her throat. "Let's do this."

They hauled Zoe to her feet again and began to drag her toward the ocean. She was weaker than before and let herself be dragged at first. She felt numb. Defeated. She was about to die horribly and there was nothing she could do about it. Then an inch or so of salt water tide rolled over her feet and reignited the agony in her wounds. She screamed and tried to tear out of the grip of her captors. But it was no good.

They held on and steered her deeper into the water. She stepped on a rock invisible beneath the water and screamed again. And she heard the most awful thing. Their laughter. Her misery amused them. Christ, they were barely fucking human. They continued to wade deeper into the water. She stepped on more rocks and shells. By the time they stopped, the water was up to their waists and Zoe had been reduced to a gibbering, insensible mess from all the pain. She couldn't scream anymore. Couldn't even plead anymore.

Missy laughed. "Big breath."

Julie's hands were at her waist and the small of her back. Missy had one hand at the back of her neck and the other wrapped firmly around a bicep. They were really going to do this. Drown her. How could anyone, no matter how cruel, do this to another human being?

She drew in a breath just before they plunged her into the water. She thrashed against them and tried to break free. If she could break free, she could swim way out there, a mile or more, whatever it took to make them give up. But they clung to her with a maddening tenacity, refusing to let go. They danced around her, shifting positions, pinning her under the water. She twisted her head and could just make out the shapes of their heads and the moonlight-limned clouds above. The surface was so tantalizingly close, but it may as well have been a million miles away. Missy's grip on her neck tightened and her head was pushed farther under the water. A minute passed. Longer. Her lungs burned with the need to breathe out and breathe back in. She knew it was time to start praying. She didn't believe the way Annalisa believed, but the possibility of something on the other side, no matter how slim, was the only hope left to her.

They held on to her. Never let up.

And the inevitable happened.

Her mouth opened and the salt water rushed down her

throat and into her lungs. Her struggles increased and became more frantic for a few seconds longer. She experienced a sensation like being crushed from within.

Then she stopped feeling anything.

They held on to her a while longer to be sure she was gone. Two or three minutes. Then they exchanged a look of mutual, silent assent and let go of her. They watched the body float beneath the currents.

Julie scratched the side of her head with the gun sight. "I thought they were supposed to float."

Missy shrugged. "Maybe the body has to get all bloated and gassy first."

"Huh. I guess. Anyway, that was fun."

"Yeah." Missy lifted her face as a pleasant breeze rolled over them. She stared out at the ocean. The endless expanse of inky blackness seemed to beckon to her. "Nice night. It's really beautiful out here."

"I guess."

"We should get back."

"Okay."

They slogged their way out of the water and began making their way back. The house they had invaded was some hundred yards or so distant. It was easy to distinguish because it was the only house with all its lights on. Missy had to give Zoe some credit. She'd given them a real run for their money. Had almost made it, in fact. Probably would have made it, if not for a little bit of dumb luck.

"Hey."

Missy glanced at Julie. "Yeah?"

Julie smiled. "I liked it when she went limp. That was my favorite part."

"Yeah."

"I mean, you just knew she was gone. You could feel the life going out of her. It was fucking awesome."

Missy smiled. "You'll have to describe that for Chuck."

Julie giggled. "I know! I can't wait to see the look on his face."

Missy's smile faded as they neared the dune separating the beach from the house. That was when she heard the screams coming from inside.

CHAPTER FORTY-TWO

March 27

The guy had stabbed him three or four times, at least. Twice in the arm, once in the side, and another time in the leg. The wounds all hurt like hell, but none of them were too deep. No mortal blow had been struck yet. Rob came at him with the knife again, a wild look on his face as he slashed down toward Chuck's chest. He looked almost as crazy as the girls now. Maybe he wasn't a killer by nature, but he was on the verge of becoming one by necessity. Chuck rolled again and got out of the way just before the knife came down and thunked into the floor. He heard a sound of exertion. Instinct made Chuck roll back over before Rob could pry the knife out of the floor. He launched a fist that landed with sledgehammer force on the guy's jaw and made him let go of the knife and go flying backward. Rob landed on his back and didn't move. Maybe he was out cold. He'd hit the motherfucker hard enough. Chuck grabbed the knife and yanked it out of the floor.

He heard footsteps pounding up the staircase outside.

Shit!

He sliced through the last of the tape binding his left leg to the chair and got to his feet just as Missy and Julie came sprinting through the balcony door, dripping water and trailing wet sand behind them. Missy saw Rob unconscious on the floor and screamed.

"No! Rob!"

Julie pointed the gun at him. "Drop it."

The adrenaline rush that had carried him this far began to ebb. He opened his hand and let the knife fall to the floor. He hated giving up his only weapon, but it was his only real option. Gun versus knife. No contest.

Missy dashed past him and dropped to her knees next to Rob.

Julie sneered. "Pick that chair up and sit the fuck down."

Chuck snatched the chair up and slammed it down on the floor. He dropped into it and crossed his arms, glaring at Julie, the insolent curl of his mouth feeling like a silent dare. *Go ahead, bitch, pull the trigger.*

Julie smirked. "Hey, Chuck?"

"Yeah?"

"Don't you wanna know where Zoe is?"

Chuck felt a cold weight settle inside him. He sat very still. A feeling of dread like nothing he'd ever known worked its way through his bones and turned his blood to ice. He didn't want to hear this. He knew the truth in his guts, but he didn't want to hear it. It made him feel hopeless. Like nothing at all mattered anymore.

"She's in the ocean, Chuck."

Julie watched the contortions of his facial muscles and laughed. Her grin conveyed pure joy. She was dripping. Her denim cutoffs and halter were soaked through. A fading sheen of water glimmered on her bare scalp.

"Yeah. She's in the ocean. And she's not out for a swim."

Chuck stared at her slender throat. She was so young. Still a child, really. But he ached to get his hands around her lovely neck and crush the life from her body. The muscles in his arms and legs were clenched to the point of pain. He was a bomb ready to go off and the girl saw that.

She was still smiling. "She's chum, Chuck. You know? Fish food?"

Chuck's breathing came faster and faster through his clenched teeth.

"We drowned her."

A sob surprised him. He was perched on the verge of an explosion of deadly violence, but his grief for Zoe was instantaneous and powerful. Another sob shuddered out of him, followed by another and another.

We drowned her.

He knew she wasn't lying to mess with his head. Her eager leer spoke the truth as plainly as her words. She and Missy had killed Zoe. Had held her under the water and laughed while she died. Chuck could only too clearly imagine the helpless, hopeless, awful horror of it from Zoe's perspective.

Tears spilled down his cheeks.

Julie giggled. "I've killed a bunch of people lately, but I think Zoe was the most fun. If I was a guy, I would've gotten my rocks off, big-time."

Annalisa had been whimpering quietly for the last several minutes, but the news of her friend's terrible death rallied her. "You evil cunt! You evil, twisted, sick piece of fucking filth! Zoe was better than all of you." Her voice grew thick with emotion, but stayed strong instead of turning shrill. Chuck feared for her, but he was proud of her, too. This took serious guts. "You're not fit to lick the shit off her shoes, you bald fucking skank."

A fast-moving cloud passed across Julie's face, a subtle darkening that was there and gone in the space of a second. Then she was smiling again. Keeping a wary eye on Chuck, she approached the line of chairs and placed the barrel of the gun against Sean Hewitt's forehead.

A low, cracking whine escaped Annalisa's throat.

"This one's your boyfriend, right?"

Annalisa shook her head. "No. No."

Chuck watched Julie's finger curl around the trigger and knew he had to do something. Sean's whole body was shaking. Bound up in all that tape, he looked like a convict strapped to an electric chair. His bottom lip trembled uncontrollably as he stared up at Julie's unforgiving face and struggled to voice a plea. Chuck decided he'd take a lunge at her. Enough of this shit. It had to stop. One more big breath to prime himself and—

Julie's slender finger squeezed the trigger.

The gun's bang caught Chuck off guard. He toppled sideways off his chair and saw a rain of blood and brains fly out the back of Sean Hewitt's head. Julie laughed and kicked the dead man's chair over as Annalisa screamed and screamed. Julie laughed some more, but when Annalisa kept screaming, the sound coming from her own throat shifted to mock the sound. She leaned down in front of Annalisa and screamed in her face. The ever-escalating volume of the crazy girl's screams easily eclipsed the noise Annalisa was making, and soon the bound woman's screams gave way to more subdued whimpers and sobs.

"Sean . . . Sean . . ."

Julie giggled.

Chuck hated that sound. She did it a lot and it made her sound like the brattiest little girl on the schoolyard.

She whipped the butt of the .38 across Annalisa's burned cheek, making her scream again.

Yet another of those perverse giggles. "Sean's dead, baby." Julie leaned close to Annalisa again, mouth almost up against her ear as her tone turned lilting and mocking. "Dead, dead, *dead*."

Chuck hadn't moved from the floor after landing there in the wake of Sean's murder. He was afraid to move. Not out of concern for his own life. That had stopped mattering the moment he knew Zoe was dead. But there was still the matter of revenge. These fuckers had to pay. And pay hard. But he wasn't in a good position to make a play. Julie was preoccupied with Annalisa at the moment, but he knew any sudden movement would make that gun swing his way. He needed a distraction of some kind, something to divert her attention long enough to get himself in position again. And the second it happened—if it happened—he was gonna come at her with everything he had.

He would not hesitate.

Not this time.

He'd fucked up before and Sean was dead as a result.

Movement beyond where Julie was standing caught his attention. Missy had managed to rouse Rob. He was sitting up and she was kneeling next to him, a soothing hand at the back of his head. His head wobbled. He looked woozy.

Julie looked at them. "He gonna be okay?"

Missy's attention stayed focused on Rob as she replied. "Yeah. I think so. He's lucky his jaw isn't broken."

Julie and Missy kept talking. Missy's enthusiasm for the evening's ghoulish festivities seemed to have waned. Her man was hurt. That confused Chuck. So they were both fucking him? Weird. A psycho threesome. Whatever. They could all rot together in the same putrid grave once he was done with them. Happily damned forever after. They were still chatting as Julie flipped open the .38's cylinder and knelt next to a big tote bag one of them had brought to the party. She reached into the bag and pulled out a white box. She opened the box and Chuck saw a glint of silver.

More bullets.

She picked up a few and slid one into an open chamber.

Now!

Chuck rolled almost soundlessly onto his stomach, braced his palms on the floor, pushed himself up, planted his feet, allowed his muscles the briefest of moments to coil, and launched himself at Julie's back. Rob saw him coming and raised a shaking finger in warning, but it was too late. He slammed into Julie's back, turning his head and drilling a shoulder between her shoulder blades. The gun flew from her hand and the handful of bullets went skittering across the hardwood floor. Someone screamed. Missy. Chuck drove Julie to the floor, pounding the wind from her as he landed on top of her with his full weight. He heard footsteps coming at him. Fast. Missy again. He surged upward, to his knees, and just managed to twist far enough to avoid a killing slash from the hunting knife. The blade scraped across his chest, raking his shirt open, and drawing a thin line of surface fire through his flesh. Blood streamed from the shallow wound as he cocked his fist back and unleashed another haymaker, this one connecting with the side of Missy's head. He felt her ear mash flat beneath his fist and then she was stumbling across the room. She tripped over Rob and crashed to the floor.

Chuck glanced down.

Julie was still pinned beneath him, but was trying to wriggle free.

We drowned her.

He grabbed her by the throat and jerked her upright. Her throat was so slender his big hand fit almost all the way around her neck. She clawed at his hand as he tightened his grip, her long nails piercing his flesh and drawing more blood. He was bleeding from so many places. It didn't matter. All he had to do was stay conscious just long enough to kill these people. He shifted position, turning her so that her back was to him. She gurgled and her clawing grew more frantic. He wrapped his free arm around her head, grasped the back of her head with his palm, and began to twist. The intent was to break her neck. Julie thrashed and tried to kick at him with her feet, but the effort was ineffectual. He continued to twist and apply pressure. He could feel how close the girl's neck was to giving way. Soon he'd hear the crack of snapping bone and she'd fall limp in his arms. He hated how much he looked forward to it. This was brutal and ugly, something no man should ever have to do. But it was also vengeance. Zoe was dead. This was her killer. She deserved to die.

Something hit his back and clung to him. He felt limbs wrapping around him and something tearing at one of his ears. Missy. Again. He'd made the mistake of turning his back to her. He'd thought she was out cold. Another mistake. He felt Missy's teeth clamp around his right earlobe and knew he wouldn't have the luxury of making additional mistakes. He let go of Julie in the same moment Missy's teeth pierced his flesh. She fell away from him, coughed, and spluttered. Missy gave her head a savage yank and his earlobe came off in her mouth. Chuck screamed and tried to shake her loose as blood poured down his neck. She spat his earlobe out and laughed, sounding like the world champion lunatic of all time.

Julie was on her hands and knees now and was scanning the floor for a weapon.

Rob was also making an effort to get up and join the fight. He managed to get to his feet, wobbled, and dropped to his knees again.

Chuck didn't have much time. Soon one of them would recover the gun or one of the knives and come at him. And then it would all be over. He would be dead and maybe on his way to some kind of ethereal reunion with Zoe.

And her killers would have gotten away with her murder.

He stopped trying to shake Missy loose. It was a losing battle, the equivalent of running out the clock in a football game. She just had to keep her hands on the ball long enough to help her teammates score the winning touchdown. Her teeth were on him again, digging into his neck. He propelled himself backward and they stumbled over Sean Hewitt's corpse and the tipped over chair it was strapped to. Then they were falling backward and Missy let go of him an instant before they crashed to the floor.

Chuck rolled onto his back.

Julie was coming at him, was almost upon him. Her face was twisted in a snarl and the hunting knife was in her upraised right hand. Instinct made him raise a hand in defense and the tip of the knife pierced his palm and scraped across bone. He screamed and yanked his hand away.

The knife came with it.

It was still embedded in his flesh.

Julie yelped and leaped at him.

Chuck screamed in pain as he pulled the knife out and tried to slash at her. The blade slid down the length of her upper arm and buried itself in the crook of her elbow. His grip on the knife wasn't good and it came out of his hand as she twisted away from him. She shook her arm and the knife went flying.

Missy was on her feet again.

Adrenaline and rage could only carry Chuck so far. He was wounded in too many places and was moving slower now. He could almost see that game clock counting down to 0:00. Missy moved far faster than he could and seized the knife.

He got to his feet.

His only option now was to run for it and hope to elude them long enough to get free.

Then Julie hit him from behind and he dropped to his knees.

Missy jabbed him in the stomach with the knife.

Game over.

He fell over and rolled onto his back. Julie was standing over him, a triumphant sneer on her face. She was holding the heavy brass lamp from the end table. She raised it again and slammed it into his face.

Lights out.

"We should finish him."

"No."

"Why, for fuck's sake?"

Missy had her gun again. She didn't like being without it. She finished filling the cylinder with fresh bullets and snapped it shut. "Because I want him to live."

Julie was beside herself with rage. Her whole body was shaking in the aftermath of the fight and her close call. "The motherfucker tried to break my fucking neck, Roxie!"

"Don't call me that anymore. You know my real name."

Julie gaped at her. "What the fuck!? I don't give a shit about your fucking name. I wanna kill this guy and I'm gonna do it."

Missy pointed the gun at her. "No. You're not."

Julie stared at the gun. "Are you seriously pointing that thing at me?" Her voice was quieter now, almost subdued. "I thought we were friends."

Missy laughed. "Yeah. I like you. It's been fun hanging with you these last few days. But there's something I never told you about myself."

Julie scowled. *"What?"*

"I don't like to share."

Missy squeezed the .38's trigger. A bullet ripped through Julie's shoulder and a spatter of blood arced through the air behind her. Julie hit the floor and squealed in agony. Missy approached her and stood over her, pointed the gun down at her. Julie looked up at her and blubbered, opened her mouth to plead for her life.

Missy shot her again.

She stopped moving.

"Holy shit. Why did you do that?"

Missy turned and saw that Rob was on his feet again and was at last managing to stay that way. She went to him and gingerly touched his swollen jaw, making him wince. "Does that hurt?"

"Yeah."

"Stupid question, huh?"

"Yeah. Now how about answering mine?"

Missy shrugged. "No big mystery. Like I told her, I don't like to share. She should have been satisfied with that one sympathy fuck, but that obviously wasn't happening. I'm sure you didn't mind having the little bitch rip your clothes off every few hours. That sort of pisses me off, you want to know the truth."

Rob's face reddened. "I . . . I'm sorry."

Missy touched his jaw again, this time not quite as gently. "I could make you *very* sorry."

He winced again but didn't look away from her as he said, "I know."

"You belong to me."

"I know."

"And no one else."

"I know."

She smiled. "I love you, Rob."

"I . . ." Tears welled in his eyes as he struggled to speak. "I . . . love you . . . Missy."

"I know you do, baby." She stood on her toes and kissed him lightly on the mouth. She took one of his hands and curled his fingers around the butt of the gun. "But it's time you proved yourself to me."

His brow furrowed. "What do you mean?"

She stepped away from him and nodded at the two vacationers still strapped to chairs. "Finish them."

Rob looked at them. His face twisted. "Oh God . . ."

Rob stared at the gun in his hand. It didn't look right there. It didn't fill him with the sick sense of power he imagined Roxie—Missy—derived from it. He knew what it could do, had witnessed its killing power too many times. It was a dangerous, despicable thing and holding it filled him with loathing. He couldn't imagine putting it to a human being's head and pulling the trigger. And yet it was what Missy wanted from him. There didn't seem to be a way out of it. Despite her profession of love, he suspected there was a strong chance she would kill him if he didn't do as she wished.

Her expression was hard, devoid of mercy. "No more hanging out on the sidelines letting me do all the work. No more illusions of being better than me just because you haven't gotten your hands dirty."

"I don't think I'm better than you."

"Prove it. Kill them."

Rob looked at the woman, grimacing at the sight of her burned face. One side of that face was still beautiful. The sickening contrast made his stomach twist. He was suddenly glad Julie was dead. No one capable of inflicting this level of cruelty deserved to live. But Missy was just as cruel. Didn't that mean she deserved to die, too?

He looked at the gun.

Then looked at the woman again. She watched him through bleary eyes, whimpering softly but otherwise waiting quietly for the end. He detected resignation in her expression. She was at peace with the idea of dying, would probably welcome it by now. So killing her could almost be seen as an act of mercy. But that was just a rationalization. Her wound looked awful, but it was hardly fatal. She could recover, maybe have plastic surgery, and go on with her life. It would be a life forever haunted by this night, but at least she would have a chance.

So he was at a crossroads. Again.

He could do what Missy wanted—kill this poor woman and the guy with the mangled hands.

Or he could do the right thing. Finally. For once.

He swallowed hard and pointed the gun at Missy. "I'm sorry."

She smiled and moved closer. "It's okay. It's sort of what I expected."

Her fist smashed across his bruised jaw.

Rob howled and staggered away from her, the gun falling from his hand. He stumbled and fell backward onto his ass. By the time he was able to sit up again, Missy had scooped up the gun and was standing over him. He tensed, waiting for her to point it at him and put a big fucking hole in his head.

Instead, she cracked the butt of the gun against the crown of his skull.

Rob wobbled and fell over.

His vision blurred as he lay on his side and watched her walk away from him. Everything went black for a moment. His eyes fluttered open again and he saw that Missy had set the chair formerly occupied by Chuck in front of the woman with the burned face.

His vision grew foggy again.

Blackness was descending.

But that was okay.

He didn't want to see this.

"He should have shot you. It would've been easier for you than this."

The woman met her gaze. She didn't seem afraid now. Missy didn't like that. Amazingly, the unburned side of her face almost seemed to smile. "It doesn't matter how I die. God will have mercy on my soul and the souls of my friends."

Missy snorted. "God? Really? How ridiculous. Religion is all meaningless bullshit, you know. I'm gonna stick this knife in you." She gestured with the hunting knife. The gun was back in the tote bag. She didn't think she'd need it again tonight. "Like, *way* up inside you. And it is going to hurt, let me tell you. A *lot*. At some point your heart will stop beating. Brain function will stop shortly after that. And that will be the end of you. Your essence won't continue in some other place. You'll be *over*."

The woman's hideous half smile didn't falter. "No. I won't.

I wish you could feel what I feel right now. The presence of the eternal. You'd be on your knees and praying with me."

"Feel *this*."

Missy pushed the knife in up under the woman's sternum. Just an inch at first, holding it there and letting her feel it. She wasn't smiling anymore. She started breathing faster and looked down at the knife. Her voice emerged as a whine. "It *hurts*."

Missy smiled. "I know. Didn't I tell you?"

She pushed the knife in another inch.

The woman cried louder and began to beg. "Please . . ."

Missy laughed. "I've been waiting for that. You'd like me to finish it fast, wouldn't you? That'd be nice, huh?"

The woman looked her in the eye. "Yes. Please . . ."

Missy made a tsk-tsk sound. "Wow, this just isn't your night." She twisted the knife a little, increasing the volume of the woman's whimpering. She laughed. "Nothing's working out the way you want."

She was able to keep it up another fifteen or so minutes, slowly sliding the knife in inch by agonizing inch, savoring the way the woman's eyes danced in their sockets as her pain and sense of desperation continued to increase.

Then she was gone.

She played the same game with the guy with the mangled fingers.

That just left Chuck.

He was still sprawled across the space where the sofa had been. She knelt next to him and watched the rise and fall of his chest. He was bleeding from a lot of places, but he'd been lucky. None of the wounds alone would kill him. Loss of blood, however, just might. She'd have to call 911 on her way out.

She wanted him to live for a couple of reasons. He'd fought hard to survive and had very nearly beat them. He was tough. She was impressed. But he was still the guy who'd insulted her. So living would be his punishment. For the rest of his life, he would feel the crushing weight of guilt.

She leaned down to kiss him on the mouth. "Good luck, Chuck. You'll need it."

She left him then and retrieved her tote bag. She cast a final, lingering glance around the room.

Another house full of dead.

A strong sense of déjà vu made her shiver.

She wouldn't be burning this house down, though.

Her gaze lingered on Rob's unconscious form a moment longer. A pang of regret flashed through her. She really did care about him. Him, and no one else. But he wasn't fit for life with her. At least not yet.

She turned away from him and walked out of the house.

EPILOGUE

Diary of a Mixed-up Girl blog entry, dated July 11

I can't believe the bitch fucking shot me. TWICE.
Like . . . how fucked-up is that? It HURT. I mean . . .
holy shit, I can't even tell you. Imagine a dentist doing drill work without happy gas or anesthetic. It's
like that. Times a million and ten. My advice? Don't
ever get fucking shot, because it fucking SUCKS.

Anyway . . . I guess the bitch got sloppy there at the
end because she didn't finish me off. But sometimes I
wonder . . . maybe she didn't want to kill me. That's
the only thing that keeps me from totally hating her.
That, and the fact she was kind of right about me
moving in on her territory. I guess I would've been
pretty pissed, too. But she could've just said something, you know? Like, "Hey, that's my man, bitch, so
BACK OFF." But no, she FUCKING SHOT ME.

But then she goes and leaves him behind too, so
WHAT THE FUCK!!!???

At least she didn't shoot me in the head. A kill shot
would have been easy. So maybe . . .

I guess I'm just lucky to be here. I could be in jail. My
bail was set at some ridiculous amount. We're talking
millions. So high I guess they figured I'd be behind
bars until my trial. But there's something I've never

told you guys. I know, you thought I spewed everything here, but not so. To me, this is more embarrassing than anything I've ever talked about. My father
is a CEO and is fucking LOADED. So I'm home. And I
am not having fun. You would not believe the tension. And I hate this monitoring thing I have to wear
around my ankle. But I have to stay focused on the
positive. Dad has hired the best fucking lawyers. You
wouldn't believe the schemes and machinations of
these guys. Turns out every bad fucking thing you've
ever heard about lawyers is totally fucking true, man.
They're sharks. Badass fucking SHARKS. At least the
ones my dad can afford are. I thought I was doomed
before I started talking to these guys, but now I'm
totally confident I'll never spend even one night in
jail. If you've been reading the news coverage—and I
know you have—you know it's all like "Patty Hearst,
Stockholm syndrome, blahblahblah." I had to Google
that shit. So there's that, and I guess they're gonna
play up the "crazy" angle, too.

I mean . . . I guess I am crazy. I don't know how else to
explain Lulu.

She's been giving me some pretty weird advice.
Things I might want to do after the trial's over and
I'm totally free again. Although "advice" isn't exactly
the right word. It's more like . . . instructions. It creeps
me out a little, but I'm starting to understand why
Zeb was so fucked-up. I guess I'm fucked-up, too.
Duh, right?

I am so hoping for a book or movie deal once this
thing is behind me. I don't think the victim's-rights
laws apply if you're exonerated, which I will be. Which
is the one big reason I hope Emily Sinclair is found
guilty and winds up on death fucking row. If she skates

and writes a book or something, all the big money people will go to her first. The TV fuckers can't get enough of her. Pisses me off. "The glamorous femme fatale, blahblahblah." Okay. I get it. She's gorgeous (too bad about the hand though, hahah). But I'm pretty fucking hot, too. Oh well. At least my hair's growing out. I'm looking less like Britney Spears during her meltdown phase, so that's good.

I guess I've said about all I have to say for now. All five of you still on my friends list should feel pretty up-to-date. LOL. Mommy dearest wanted to cut off my web access altogether after the cops seized my old laptop and found all those autopsy pictures and shit. But I whined to Dad and today he surprised me with a new laptop. Really must resist the urge to visit some favorite sites. Oh well. It'll be something else to look forward to once this thing is behind me. Ta-ta for now!

(P.S.: I really hope I see Missy again someday. I miss her. I know, I know. Crazy. No shit. We've covered that already.)

6 comments

lord_ruthven: You know I'll do anything for you or help any way I can.

Mixedupgirl: I know. And forget what I said about never fucking you again. I was just playing hard to get. I'm pretty horny. LOL. I haven't been laid since March.

darkest_rogue: I don't care what you did. You rule.

Mixedupgirl: I know. No shit.

Aliciaroxx: Can I come over tonight?

Mixedupgirl: Hey! I thought you were ignoring me. So

we're still friends? Yay! Yeah, if your parents let you, come over. And bring YOUR laptop!

The long table and the two chairs at its opposing ends were the only pieces of furniture in the white room. Rob sat at one end of the table. He and the guard posted at the door were the only people in the room. The guard wasn't talking. The correctional officer's cold, openly hostile glare made him uncomfortable. The man's right hand stayed on the collapsible baton clipped to his belt. Rob had the distinct feeling he'd like nothing better than some excuse to whip it out and beat him senseless with it. So Rob stayed quiet and barely moved. Not that he had much choice about the latter. The heavy leg irons and handcuffs made movement difficult. He wouldn't be any real threat without the restraints, of course, but he was considered "extremely dangerous." Which was really kind of funny. Here he was, basically rotting in jail, while the really dangerous ones were still out there in the world.

Funny, but not ha-ha funny.

It was pretty damn depressing, really.

The room's only door opened and another guard walked inside, followed by the person he'd been waiting to see.

Tears came to his eyes as he started to stand. "Lindsey . . ."

The guard who'd been watching him glared. "Sit down."

Rob sat but kept on smiling. "It's so good to see you."

Lindsey sat at the opposite end of the table. He'd never seen her looking more beautiful. She looked like a woman dressed for an evening at an expensive restaurant, wearing a pretty green dress with a hem that ended just above the knees. And high heels. That was amazing. She never wore high heels. She had on more makeup than usual and her hair had been done recently. It hung in thick, lustrous curls to her shoulders. She'd also had a manicure recently. His gaze lingered on her slender hands for a moment. On her ring finger was a cheap plastic ring purchased from a gumball machine a long time ago, back in their high-school days. He'd given it to her as a gag gift. He couldn't believe she'd kept it all these years. He was so touched. His eyes misted again. She loved him. He knew that now. How could he have been so blind?

The door clicked shut and both guards stayed in the room, flanking the door.

Lindsey smiled. "It's good to see you, Rob. How are you holding up?"

He forced his smile to stay in place. "I'm doing okay."

Lindsey folded her arms on the table and leaned toward him. "You're in jail, Rob. Don't lie for my sake. Tell me the truth."

He sighed. "I'm fucking miserable."

Rob's eyes flicked to the mean-spirited guard. The smug asshole was smirking.

Lindsey frowned. "Is there anything I can do?"

He shrugged. "Did you bring those books from my uncle?"

"Yeah. I had to surrender them when I came in. They said they'd get them to you."

The guard's smirk deepened.

Rob had a feeling he'd never see those books. Or if he did, some of the pages would be torn out. They'd done it before. Fucking assholes. One or two of the guards were okay and almost humane, but mostly they were sadistic little dictators, exercising power over the incarcerated just because they could. He doubted he could make Lindsey understand just how miserable prison life was. Or how unfair it was, in his case. He hadn't killed anybody. Julie had tortured and killed at least a dozen over the course of just a few days, but she got to sleep in her own bed every night. His uncle was helping out as best he could, but he just didn't have the deep pockets Julie's father had.

"Good. I'll look forward to reading them." He glanced at the guard. "Eventually. Thanks for bringing them."

She smiled again. "You're welcome." She sighed. "I hate that you're in here. You didn't do anything. Not really."

Rob's expression turned dour. "I know that. You know that. The problem is convincing a jury."

"What does your lawyer say?"

"He says there's no real evidence connecting me to any actual killings. Which makes sense, because I didn't actually kill anybody."

Lindsey's eyes flared as she leaned forward. "Hell, *you're* as much a victim as anybody. I can't stand that you're in here while that spoiled little princess plays at home. It's total bullshit."

Rob laughed softly. "Preaching to the choir here, sister."

"So . . . does this lack of evidence mean you'll probably get off?"

Rob shook his head. "He doesn't think I'll be convicted of murder, at least not first degree. But we're looking at some time for lesser charges."

"How much?"

"He says there'll probably be a plea deal and that I should accept it when it comes, which I guess I will. And he says it'll probably be a max of ten years, with a chance of parole in a few years."

Lindsey's eyes glimmered with fresh tears. "*Fuck.*" She wiped the moisture away with the heel of her right hand. "So unfair."

"Yeah."

Rob felt deflated. He'd so looked forward to the visit from Lindsey. He hated that he couldn't say anything that wouldn't upset her.

Or . . . wait.

Maybe there was something.

He smiled again. "I love you, Lin."

He saw the surprise in her eyes and was pleased by how happy she looked. She grinned. "Really? You mean that?"

He nodded. "Yeah. I guess I always have. I was just too stupid to ever do anything about it."

The hostile guard rolled his eyes. Rob wanted to flip him off, but the potential consequences made him think better of it.

Lindsey wiped away more tears. "I . . . love you . . . too. So much, Rob. You just don't know."

"I do, Lin. I really do. Trust me."

They talked the maximum amount of time allowed. Some of it was small talk. Things about family and friends. Things she might take care of for him while he was in jail. There were several more smiling professions of love. Then, all too soon, the time was up and she had to go.

She stood and the guard who'd come in with her led her to the door. "I'll be back as soon as I can, Rob. I love you. Never forget that."

His vision blurred as the tears fell. "I love you, too."

Then she was gone.

The other guard came over and jerked him to his feet. "That was so sweet. You keep that pretty face in mind when you're taking it up the ass in here."

He laughed as he steered Rob out of the room. It was the mean, leering laughter of a born sadist. He'd heard its like before.

But Rob didn't care.

As long as he had Lindsey's love, everything would be okay.

September 7

He had one last demon to face and that day of reckoning had come round at last. Chuck sat behind the wheel of his 2010 Porsche 911 Carrera, staring at the entrance to Big Sam's Bar & Grill.

The car was a gift from his father. A hundred-grand set of

wheels. A big gesture, even for his dad. The old man thought money was the answer to everything. Spend enough of it, make enough extravagant gestures, and eventually any pain you might feel should go away.

Dad was wrong.

His dad was like a god to him. It was a weird thing to know that even gods could be wrong. He'd learned a lot of hard lessons this year, many much harder than that. It was harder, for instance, to face your dead girlfriend's grieving parents and try to explain to them why you hadn't been able to save her. Why you were alive and she wasn't. And the real bitch of it was they didn't blame him. They even told him he needed to stop putting the blame on himself and lay it right where it belonged, on the killers. But Chuck couldn't help it. Zoe was gone and she was never coming back. He should have saved her. Somehow. He should have found a way. But he hadn't. He'd come up short, and the only girl he'd ever really loved was dead. A part of himself had died along with her. Sometimes he wondered if he'd ever be ready for any kind of intimate relationship again.

But today wasn't about Zoe. Nor was it about finding out whether there remained the potential for love in his heart. This was about Chuck Kirby being a man. This was about fighting back. And it was about regaining some small measure of pride. Zoe's killers were out of his reach. For now. But he could start smaller than that.

He got out of the Porsche and walked into Big Sam's. The joint wasn't exactly jumping. A few couples were dining at tables. Two old guys sat at the bar, nursing beers. Chuck approached the bar, pulled out a stool, and sat down. The barkeep today was a much younger man than the ones who'd attacked him. He looked to be in his midtwenties, not too much older than Chuck. He was tall and fit, with close-cropped brown hair. He was polishing a glass with a towel, but looked up as Chuck sat down. "What can I get you?"

"Bud draft."

"ID?"

Chuck almost smiled, remembering the high-quality fake he'd used last time he was here. It wasn't necessary anymore. He was legal these days, having turned twenty-one over the summer. He pulled out his wallet, extracted his license, and showed it to the barkeep, who nodded and began to fill a pint glass from a tap.

The barkeep looked at him as he set the glass down. "There ya go."

Chuck took a sip from the frosty mug. "Ah . . ."

"That's two-fifty. Or you can run a tab."

Chuck handed over his platinum card. "I'll run a tab."

"Cool."

"Maybe you can help me with something."

The barkeep arched an eyebrow. "Yeah? With what?"

Chuck took a longer sip of beer and set the glass down again. "I was in here a while back. Shit, almost six months ago, I guess. There was another guy working here. We really . . . hit if off. I'm wondering if he's still around."

"You remember his name?"

Chuck nodded. "Joe Bob. Kind of a big guy. Long hair in a ponytail. Receding hairline . . ." Chuck trailed off, noting how the guy's expression had darkened as he spoke. "Something wrong?"

The barkeep shrugged. "It's just weird, I guess. That long ago . . ." He scratched his chin and squinted as he thought. "Hell, you must have met him right before he died."

Chuck's hand was in the process of lifting the glass to his lips again. His hand froze for a moment. He set the glass back down. "Say that again?"

"Sorry, man. He's dead."

"Shit."

One of the old men signaled for another round. The barkeep put a fresh glass under the PBR tap and began to fill it.

"Yeah. It was pretty brutal, man. Joe Bob was the regular closer back then." He set the PBR pint in front of the old man and leaned against the bar again. "He got jumped out back one morning after closing. Somebody really did a number on him."

Chuck frowned. "What do you mean?"

The barkeep's expression turned grim. "Sorry to have to tell you this, since you guys hit it off, but whoever killed him cut holy hell out of him. He was tortured."

Chuck drained the rest of his beer in one pull and motioned for another. "Shit."

"Yeah. No kidding, right?" The barkeep poured him a fresh mug and set it down. "They found him handcuffed to the wheel of his own truck." He shook his head. "He was all fucked-up, man. Ears cut off. Eyes cut out. Cops figure it was a drug thing. Joe Bob was a distributor. The guess is he was moving in on somebody else's territory. And that somebody decided to set an example."

Chuck grunted. "Wow."

"Yeah."

Chuck knocked back the rest of his second beer. "I think I'm done here."

"Sorry to bum you out, dude."

Chuck shrugged. "Hell, I barely knew Joe Bob. It's too bad, but . . . what can you do?"

The barkeep swiped his card and handed it back with the receipt. "That's too true, bud. The lesson here? Stay out of the drug business."

Chuck signed the receipt and passed it back. "Yeah. No shit."

He walked out of the bar and got back behind the wheel of the Porsche. He started the car and drove around to the back of the building. There were two cars out back, a single small loading bay, and an overflowing blue Dumpster. A shiver crawled up his spine as he surveyed the back lot. Missy

Wallace had been here. He could feel her presence. He experienced a mixture of anger and deep confusion. Killing Joe Bob, he was certain, had not been a case of exacting revenge on his behalf. It made no sense. She hated him. There had to be some other motivation. He thought about it some more and came to the only conclusion that made any sense to him. Missy Wallace was a lot of things, nearly all of them bad, but she was smart. And cold. She knew what men were like. She would have known how likely it was he'd return here one day for his pound of flesh. So she'd decided to take his chance at that away from him, too.

Just as she'd taken Zoe.

You fucking bitch.

Chuck sat there a while longer and wondered what his next move should be. There were some immediate and obvious impulses. He could get blind drunk. Go back in the bar right now and just get started. He could spend the rest of his life getting hammered and stewing in his anger, lamenting his powerlessness.

Or he could just let it all go.

He could accept that things were the way they were and go back to just living his life. And moving on. He thought of something his father had said over and over during the summer. *It is what it is.* A stupid, overused phrase. It had always annoyed Chuck, but hearing his father utter those trite words so often had pushed him to the point of near insanity. But maybe Dad had been on to something there. Maybe there was some small bit of wisdom in those words.

And maybe, just maybe, it really was time to let it all go. His grief. His bitterness at Emily Sinclair's survival after playing dead. The deeper bitterness he felt every time he thought about Julie and Missy still being free. His regret and his self-loathing over his failure to save anybody.

Just . . . let it go.

He was pretty sure it was what Zoe would want.

And it would be the last thing Missy Wallace would ever expect.

For the first time in months, a genuine smile brightened Chuck's face. He put the car in gear and drove away from Big Sam's forever.

October 31

Early evening on Halloween, and the neighborhood was alive with a spooky vibe appropriate to the event. The leaves had turned and a strong wind was scattering brown piles of them across the streets and sidewalks. Adults and children wandered about in costume. One girl in a sexy nurse outfit staggered out of a house party and puked into the bushes as Lindsey drove by in her Pontiac Sunfire. An athletic-looking guy in a devil costume held her hair back as she heaved her guts out.

Lindsey had to chuckle.

Chivalry ain't dead yet.

She turned down another street, went down a block, and turned in at the parking lot outside the apartment complex where she lived. There were more drunken revelers milling about here. More parties and more people in wild costumes. She lived in the shadow of Vanderbilt University, in the Hillsboro Village neighborhood, and here Halloween was mostly a really good excuse to get stinking drunk. Lindsey was thinking she might crash one of the many parties happening later in the evening. She was in a mood to celebrate.

The prosecution had finally offered its plea deal and Rob's attorney had accepted on his behalf. And it was just like they'd been told. His sentence would be ten years, but he'd almost certainly be out earlier than that. When he got out, he'd still be a relatively young man in his late twenties. He would still have a shot at a productive life as a solid citizen. More importantly, as far as Lindsey was concerned, he would be forever in her debt. She smiled as she got out of the car and threw the door shut, barely resisting the urge to skip along as she walked down the sidewalk in front of her building and climbed the steps to her third-floor apartment. The apartment she was still essentially sharing with Rob. His uncle was covering Rob's portion of the rent for now, though lately he'd been making noises about helping her get a house. Lindsey was resisting, because she liked being in a place where she'd spent so much time with Rob. She liked to sleep in his bed and feel his presence. She could still smell him in the bedsheets and in the clothes that hung in his closet, especially in the collection of rock and roll and horror T-shirts he'd worn so often. That scent was there no matter how many times she washed them, and that comforted her. She slept in a different one every night, lying there in the dark as she stared up at the ceiling and thought about the future.

She entered the apartment and closed and locked the door behind her. After setting her purse on the dining-room table, she went into the kitchen and grabbed a cold beer from the refrigerator. She pried the cap off and took a deep swig. It was beyond refreshing. She carried the bottle out to the living room, curled up on the sofa, and turned on the TV. The local news was all over the story about Rob's plea deal, but on CNN and Fox, at least at the moment, it only rated a two-sentence ticker alert. Which figured. The cable outlets were way more interested in the girls. *Good.* Her hope was that Rob's story would continue to fade into the background over time. Then, when he got out, they could spend a relatively normal life together.

And again, it would be a life in which he could never forget or fully repay his debt to her. She would wait for him. She would see to his affairs. And she'd be loyal to him, with the small possible exception of the occasional one-night stand. Five years or whatever was a long time to go without getting laid, after all. Still, she wouldn't give her heart to anyone else during that time and would be there for him when he got out.

Her eyes grew wet.

She'd waited so long for this chance. He belonged to her now. She saw it in the desperate longing evident in his eyes every time she visited him. Heard it in his voice every time he told her how much he loved her. It filled her with an intoxicating sense of power. She had a strong hold on him now and she would never, ever relinquish it. In fact, she meant to exploit it to the fullest. Among other things, he'd never be allowed to forget what a mistake he'd made in ignoring her all those years.

She finished off the beer, stretched, and yawned. Maybe she should take a short nap before heading out to one of the parties. She returned to the kitchen and dumped the empty bottle in the trash can. The beer had made her feel a little tingly. Pleasantly so. Maybe she'd hook up with some guy later. It'd been more than a month since the last time.

She was smiling as she entered Rob's room.

That changed when she sensed the movement behind her and felt the hand at the small of her back.

She let out a yelp as she was shoved forward. The bedroom door slammed shut as she stumbled a few steps and dropped to her knees. Panic gripped her, made her heart race and her breath come fast. Someone had broken in while she was gone. She hoped she wasn't about to be raped.

She bounced back to her feet and turned around.

It was *her*.

"You."

Missy Wallace smiled. "Yes."

Lindsey moved backward, retreating until her back met the wall. She looked different from the last pictures that had circulated. The computer-enhanced ones that showed her with blonde, spiky hair. Her hair was longer now and black again. But there was no mistaking that face. Lindsey glanced at the bed and noticed a discarded ball cap and oversized black sunglasses. A very minimalist disguise, but apparently it worked.

"Please don't hurt me."

Missy laughed. "So you're Lindsey. Rob talked a lot about you."

Despite a terror level escalating by the second, Lindsey was interested. "He . . . did?"

Missy nodded. "He did. He said you guys were bestest pals and had been since you were kids. I thought he had to be fucking you, but he denied it. And I guess I believed him. Rob's a sincere motherfucker."

"He was telling the truth."

Missy smiled again as she moved a slow step closer. Her hands were clasped behind her back and Lindsey had to wonder what she was hiding. "But here's the sticky point. I knew you had to have some interest in him. And I guess I was right, huh? You see, I've been watching you a while. I know you visit him. I even found your blog online. So he says he's in love with you?"

She moved another step closer.

Lindsey scrunched up harder against the wall. There was nowhere to go. Nowhere to run without having to get around Missy. The room's lone window was on the opposite side of the room. Even if she could get to it and take a leap through it, she was three stories up. Her fingernails clawed at the wall as she took a step sideways. Her skin crawled as Missy's eyes roved over her body, frankly appraising her the way a man would. Scoping out the competition.

She whimpered. "Please don't hurt me."

"You already said that, you stupid bitch. Now answer my question. Is Rob in love with you?"

Hot tears streamed down Lindsey's cheeks. "He is."

Missy nodded and came another step closer. "Well, that's too bad. I have this thing. Personal quirk, I guess you could call it. I don't like to share. But it's okay. We'll get past it. I know he'll come back around in time. I guess I won't see him for a while, but that's okay, too. I've forgiven him for letting me down. I'm gonna give him a pass on that. But you, Lindsey?"

Her hands came away from her back.

One of them grasped a big knife with a serrated blade.

Lindsey sucked in air and opened her mouth to scream.

But Missy was too fast.

"You I'm gonna kill."

Bram Stoker Award–Winning Author

BRIAN KEENE

Brinkley Springs is a quiet little town. Some say the town is dying. They don't know how right they are. Five mysterious figures are about to pay a little visit to Brinkley Springs. They have existed for centuries, emerging from the shadows only to destroy, to kill. To feed. They bring with them terror and carnage, and leave death and blood in their wake. As the night wears on, Brinkley Springs will be quiet no longer. Screams will break the silence. But when the sun rises again, will there be anyone left to hear?

A GATHERING OF CROWS

ISBN 13: 978-0-8439-6092-1

Bram Stoker Award–Winning Author

JOHN EVERSON

Night after night, Evan walked along the desolate beach, grieving over the loss of his son, drowned in an accident more than a year before. Then one night he was drawn to the luminous sound of a beautiful, naked woman singing near the shore in the moonlight. He watched mesmerized as the mysterious woman disappeared into the sea. Driven by desire and temptation, Evan returned to the spot every night until he found her again. Now he has begun a bizarre, otherworldly affair. A deadly affair. For Evan will soon realize that his seductive lover is a being far more evil . . . and more terrifying . . . than he ever imagined. He will learn the danger of falling into the clutches of the . . .

Siren

"Superbly effective. Modern horror doesn't get much better than this!"
—Bryan Smith, Author of *The Killing Kind*

ISBN 13: 978-0-8439-6354-0

INTERACT WITH DORCHESTER ONLINE!

Want to learn more about your favorite books and authors?
Want to talk with other readers that like to read the same books as you?
Want to see up-to-the-minute Dorchester news?

VISIT DORCHESTER AT:
DorchesterPub.com
Twitter.com/DorchesterPub
Facebook.com (Search Pages)

DISCUSS DORCHESTER'S NOVELS AT:
Dorchester Forums at DorchesterPub.com
GoodReads.com
LibraryThing.com
Myspace.com/books
Shelfari.com
WeRead.com

☐ YES!

Sign me up for the Leisure Horror Book Club and send my FREE BOOKS! If I choose to stay in the club, I will pay only $8.50* each month, a savings of $7.48!

NAME: _____

ADDRESS: _____

TELEPHONE: _____

EMAIL: _____

☐ I want to pay by credit card.

☐ VISA ☐ MasterCard ☐ DISCOVER

ACCOUNT #: _____

EXPIRATION DATE: _____

SIGNATURE: _____

Mail this page along with $2.00 shipping and handling to:
Leisure Horror Book Club
PO Box 6640
Wayne, PA 19087

Or fax (must include credit card information) to:
610-995-9274

You can also sign up online at **www.dorchesterpub.com**.
*Plus $2.00 for shipping. Offer open to residents of the U.S. and Canada only. Canadian residents please call 1-800-481-9191 for pricing information. If under 18, a parent or guardian must sign. Terms, prices and conditions subject to change. Subscription subject to acceptance. Dorchester Publishing reserves the right to reject any order or cancel any subscription.